A CURIOUS INVASION

BY
MARIE ANDREAS

Vampires,
Aliens,
+ TER!

Marie Andreas

BOOKS BY MARIE ANDREAS

The Lost Ancients
Book One: The Glass Gargoyle
Book Two: The Obsidian Chimera
Book Three: The Emerald Dragon
Book Four: The Sapphire Manticore
Book Five: The Golden Basilisk
Book Six: The Diamond Sphinx

The Asarlaí Wars
Book One: Warrior Wench
Book Two: Victorious Dead
Book Three: Defiant Ruin

The Adventures of Smith and Jones
Book One: A Curious Invasion

CHAPTER ONE

Q UEEN VICTORIA WAS dead. Long live Queen Victoria.

The bells of Westminster sang out dolefully as Nettie Jones scurried from the morgue. Heavy drops of rain slammed against the glass casing of the nearby gas lamps. Gaston had called it down to the exact minute. At five minutes after midnight, January 5, 1848, Queen Victoria died at the hands of her own physicians, only to be brought back by the miracle of modern science.

Brought back by vampiric science, really.

The physicians surrounding the queen would steadfastly deny it, but Nettie wondered how many vampires had been drained this night to give England an immortal ruler.

Shivering with a cold not born of the midnight air, she walked faster. Rarely did she stay this late at work anymore; however, a pleasure dirigible had collided with an armored war zeppelin late in the afternoon. All told, thirty-five people had died that night. It had taken quite a while to document them all.

Nettie clutched her umbrella tighter and walked forlornly past the shuttered garage door. Gaston had made her promise she would never ride Lula Belle in the rain. She was a fine steamcycle, his newest invention, but he couldn't seem to make her navigate consistently in the rain. Of course, living in London, this deterrent meant Nettie was extremely limited in the days she could drive her.

Lost in her thoughts as she was, Nettie failed to notice the man until he grabbed her immediately outside her residence. He had one hand over her mouth, the other about her waist before she could turn or scream.

Her attacker was taller than her, an uncommon, and unwelcome, occurrence. He pulled her backward, briefly yanking her off her feet. She went limp, which forced him to stumble as her full weight suddenly fell upon him. With his misstep, she ripped his hand away from her mouth, forcing his arm upward until she heard a disturbingly satisfactory bone snap. Maybe even two; it was difficult to tell with the blood pounding in her ears. Slightly longer than average canines dropped into place inside her mouth. She spun out of his other arm, breaking it as well. The force of her movement, and probably shock, dropped him to the ground.

The man was clothed all in black, but the weave of his clothes was poor and ill-matched. With a snarl, Nettie moved into the flickering gaslight so he could see her teeth.

Already screaming in pain from his newly broken limbs, his tone changed to terror as he scrambled to his feet and fled.

Waiting a few moments to make sure none of her self-absorbed neighbors were going to come out and break tradition by questioning the screams, Nettie straightened her heavy dark blue dress and her favorite matching hat, picked up her reticule and umbrella, and made her way inside the boarding house.

She didn't need much light to see clearly; along with her above average strength, Nettie's unique condition granted her above average night vision. Her recent incident gave her enough pause to turn on all the lights in the sitting room. The somber and staid condition of the sitting room usually depressed her, but tonight it was comforting. The individual who had attacked her had more than met his match, but what if she had not been who and what she was? What poor woman might be lying ravaged and abandoned in the street somewhere?

Her hand tightened on the umbrella without her notice at the thought. She did notice when it popped and the frail metal pieces bit into her hand.

Drat, another one. Gaston often joked that she should buy umbrellas at a bulk discount with the way she went through them. Alas, they were frail, and she most certainly was not. Keeping the pieces together, she went into the kitchen and put them into the refuse box. The boarding house mistress, Mrs. Cruddle, would chastise her in the morning, that was a certainty. Nevertheless, it was not her landlady's money that was funding Nettie's one-woman umbrella destruction campaign.

After lighting a small fire in the well-used fireplace, Nettie allowed herself to flop into the overstuffed chair in front of the flames. There was no other way to sit comfortably in the beast, but since she was a boarder in this house she couldn't complain, nor normally would she sit in such a fashion.

The events of the afternoon and evening were eating at her. She was sure there was no connection between the secret transformation of the queen, the unfortunate collision of two flying machines, and a rude attack on her own doorstep. Unfortunately, the questing part of her cranium would not let the unexamined rest, even if it was well past the time she should be sleeping.

The collision of the airships was unfortunate, but not terribly surprising. The war ship had been lifting off, completely ignoring the passenger ship trying to land. The ships always fought for landing and lift off rights, with little rhyme or reason to guide them. The heavy war birds felt they deserved first position for landing or lifting off, regardless of how many other airships were in the flight area. Never mind that England's new war with the massive Indian Kingdom was thousands of miles from her coasts, and any ships in England now were older ones flying protection recon. They still felt they had the right to bully everyone about.

The situation with the queen was also not surprising, although Nettie was only one of a handful of souls outside of the palace who knew what those bells meant. The near death of her beloved husband had forced the queen into some slippery deals and plans. Her advisors called mystics from across the extended British Empire to find a way to keep Queen Victoria and her love alive and serving God and Country. What had started as a treatment suggestion for the disease that almost took the consort led to a way to make them both immortal.

Considering that the majority of the British population didn't believe vampires were real, no one would believe a transfusion treatment, begun once her own heart had been stopped, would give them a new kind of queen. And drain the lives of a dozen or more unwilling vampires, according to estimated calculations. Nettie had a feeling they might never know how many were really destroyed in the process.

Which left Nettie to deal with her attacker.

Most likely, he was nothing more than an opportunistic varlet trying to take advantage of a working girl returning home.

Luckily for Nettie, her half-vampire condition gave her strength far beyond her appearance. She was also graced with elongated canines that, while useless in the vampiric sense, did work to cause fear and terror.

There could have been more to the attack than what it appeared. For the past week, Gaston had fretted that someone had found the Society. Nettie believed any enemies of the SEU, the Society for the Exploration of the Unexplainable, would be far less clumsy and far better clothed.

The fire before her feet faded to embers, and she knew she must go seek her bed. Mrs. Cruddle would be up at dawn, smashing and crashing about in the kitchen. Often, her level of noise in the morning was directly proportional to how late Nettie had returned home the night before. And it was not only Nettie; if any of the other four boarders came in late, she delivered the same treatment swiftly and brutally.

Before she went upstairs, she jotted down a few brief lines concerning her attacker on a scrap of paper, and then set it outside under a large hollowed-out rock. Gaston's Runners would get it before dawn. Not that it merited any real perusal; however, they ought to examine anything extraordinary.

Feeling she had done what she could concerning the issue, she ascended the stairs and went to her room. The fatigue of the day finally caught her, and she had barely changed into her nightclothes when sleep overtook her.

THE NEXT MORNING, Mrs. Cruddle outdid herself with the sheer amount of noise she was able to create. How a skinny little harridan could raise that much noise was a mystery not to be solved during Nettie's lifetime, not even by the SEU.

Nettie took her leave immediately after breakfast, managing to avoid Mrs. Cruddle and the other boarders completely. Nettie held no grudges against them; but she knew she was not a pleasant person to be around the first thing in the morning. She found avoiding contact saved her many apologies later in the day.

Her shift in the coroners' department didn't begin for a few hours, and for once it was not raining. With a thrill of outlandish optimism, she went to the garage and freed Lula Belle from her confines.

The steamcycle was a marvel, all brass and copper with a few hammered steel highlights accented by thick leather trim. She was more of a show horse than the ponies down at the field.

Unfortunately, her power was in her appearance, not in her ability to function well.

Nettie felt surprisingly good today, in spite of the attempt on her sanity by Mrs. Cruddle in the wee hours. She gently un-pinned her hat, placing it on a small hook near the door of the tiny garage. Reaching up on a heavy shelf, she removed a pair of goggles and leather cap. She drew many stares when she rode, half for the bike itself and half—the more disapproving looks— for her apparel and being a woman on such a machine. She still had yet to find a way to ride with the long skirts that polite society dictated she must wear, so she had modified a pair of men's breeches into a pair of flowing skirt pants that she could wear under her regular skirts. They worked well, keeping her legs covered for the sake of propriety, and yet not impinging upon her safety while riding. She carefully rolled up her skirts and folded them into her reticule. There really was not an easy way to ride with it, but she could not be without her necessities.

The steam bike took surprisingly little effort to start. Nettie couldn't get the details out of Gaston as to how he built the engine, nor how he made it so tiny, and he'd threatened to take it away from her if she took it apart for her own investigation. A small, silver key started the tiny boiler and began the process. Once things were humming along, a few quick checks of the gauges to make sure the temperature was at acceptable levels and she was ready to ride.

Rolling the bike out onto the street, she secured the garage door and mounted her steed. It felt so liberating to sit upon her. Even though she had only ridden a few times, the events had stayed marked in her memory. There was something unearthly about riding freely without a horse under one. Like magic. She knew that one day; things like this wonderful steamcycle would replace horses and buggies completely. Hopefully, it would be while she was still young enough to enjoy them.

Almost as if drawn to return home, Lula Belle headed to the far end of Marsham Street and Gaston's mansion. Nettie shrugged and decided that was as good a place to go to as any. She was happy to be out and about, and perhaps Gaston had news to tell of yesterday's events.

Chateau Lyons sat high at the end of its own long drive, guarded by two stone lions carved to appear to stare at all visitors.

One thing about Lula Belle, she was not a stealth conveyance by any means. Gaston awaited her at the base of the stairs with a curious frown. Nettie disengaged the tiny steam engine and disembarked.

"I don't believe you have a reason to be cross. After all, it's not raining today," she said as she removed her cap and goggles. Being without a proper hat was not done in polite society, but it was difficult to travel with a hat. And it could be argued that Gaston was not polite society, even if one overlooked the fact he was French.

"That isn't it," he spoke and turned to ascend the stairs. "I am disturbed by your note."

Before she could answer, he turned and held one thick finger up to his equally thick mustache. "*Non*, we should not speak out here. It is not safe." His coal black eyes darted around his grounds as if enemies of the crown, or worse, enemies of the Society lurked under each leaf.

"Very well, but don't you think—"

"*Mon Dieu*! Nettie, you must keep it down. The dangers are everywhere." He cut her off then scurried back into his mansion.

She rolled her eyes and followed. Gaston was a good man, and as head of the London branch of the Society for the Exploration of the Unexplainable, he had a lot of weight on those stocky shoulders. Nevertheless, at times his paranoia could be frustrating.

He hadn't pulled back the thick drapes covering the front windows, and the massive entry room was dark and gloomy. Obviously, his housekeeper was off for the day.

"Come, we need to go into the dungeon," Gaston said as he turned down a narrow hallway off the main room.

Nettie unfastened her cloak and rolled her eyes again while

she followed him. Her attack had not been enjoyable, and could have ended far worse, but she was fine. It didn't warrant entering the dungeon.

The chamber was not truly a dungeon, but a small hidden room built long before even Gaston's grandparents had been born. It was disguised as part of a small hall, behind what looked like a linen closet. The walls were about three feet thick, the door made of heavy solid oak reinforced by steel bands. When that door shut, no one was getting in or out unless Gaston wanted them to.

"I do notice when you do that." Gaston pushed aside a stray invention so both of them could sit in front of the Mudger screen. "The rolling of the eyes, it is known to me."

"Sometimes, dear Gaston, you are worthy of eye rolling." She planted a sisterly kiss atop his balding head before taking the offered seat.

His "hrmph" was a classic response, which meant the issue was not forgotten. It was simply placed on a shelf in his vast mind for later discussion.

The Mudger screen was a bit of technological magic that could mean a new, and different, war if knowledge of it escaped the confines of the Society. It was named after a prominent eighteenth-century member of the Society, Thomas Mudge. Whilst known as a famous horologist to the rest of the world, he was far more than a watchmaker to the Society. He hadn't invented the Mudger, but his studies had led to its creation long after his death. With it, branches of the Society could speak to and see each other over long distances, although the images were grainy and glitches were common. Distance didn't appear to make a difference for this marvel—they could reach Cardiff as easily as the home office in Edinburgh.

It was a rare occurrence that Nettie was privy to its use. Had Gaston known she was coming? Or was it lucky happenstance on her part that she arrived at this time? Regardless, she felt fortunate when the screen sputtered to life within the confines of the heavy wood and copper casing. As a lowly field agent of the first tier, she was rarely allowed such a privilege.

"Agent Nettie Jones has joined us directly," Gaston spoke slowly into the cone-shaped device attached to the screen. His French accent came and went; while born in France, he had lived most of his life in Cardiff, Wales before relocating to London a dozen years ago. Therefore, his accent, while not pure French, did oft times cause discussion. The Mudger was fussy and could distort words. At least that was what the research she'd done on it said. Of course, that research had been limited to her brief time in the Society's secret library in Edinburgh.

The screen cleared and a black and white image of Agent Ramsey appeared. Nettie's excitement at being involved in the use of the Mudger increased at the sight of the second highest agent in the Society. Agent Ramsey was a classic Scot, large and bold, his voice and actions carrying on that same theme.

"Ach, welcome, Jones. Good to see you. Gave that rotter a run, did you?"

Obviously, Gaston had been quick to spread the word of her attack.

"Yes, sir. He was unprepared for my ability to defend myself." She tried not to sound smug, but she was quite pleased with her ability to dispatch the man.

"Show him a bit of the teeth?" The Mudger was grainy, but she could still see Agent Ramsey tapping on his canine. Time was, she'd be embarrassed to have someone call attention to her fangs, but since joining the Society, she was developing the same respect for them that others had.

"Just a little, sir. I broke both of his arms first."

The laugh that followed her proclamation rattled the Mudger receiver. Had they been in the same room with Agent Ramsey, she was certain it would have knocked them off their seats.

"That's m'girl! You showed him. Maybe he'll think twice before attacking another woman." His face sobered. "Now to it. Do you believe your attack was tied to The Event?"

Even though only the Society had access to Mudgers, they were still not secure. The changing of Queen Victoria into an undead was simply referred to as The Event in case their enemies had found a way to intercept transmissions. Nettie had never actually seen a list of these enemies, but Gaston assured her it was a long one.

"I honestly don't see how or why." She ignored Gaston's snort. Gaston saw spies in his breakfast pantry on a daily basis. "The attack appeared to be one of circumstance rather than planning. And he was dressed extremely shabbily." She cocked her head in thought. "I do not believe it was a disguise. The clothes smelled too well-worn for that." A bit of an understatement; along with increased night vision and strength, her condition brought the curse of an increased sense of smell.

"Aye, that could be telling," Ramsey said with a bit of sympathy tingeing his voice. "Then we shall assume there is no connection. Now, about the collision. Who survived?"

Nettie pulled back and spared a glance to Gaston. The air collision was horrific, but clearly an accident. "Sir? There were no survivors. The crew and passengers of both ships were killed."

If mountains could grumble in grief, that was the look she now faced. It took Ramsey a few moments to compose himself. "Agent McGrady was on the warship. He said he had information to bring to the home office that couldn't be trusted to the Mudgers. This is grievous and dangerous news."

Nettie didn't know Agent McGrady well; she'd only meet him at one occasion, her indoctrination into the Society. For the most part, agents of the Society stayed apart to avoid suspicion if their enemies were watching. Yet, the loss of a fellow agent, even one not well known to her, was saddening. And troubling. The dark look filling Gaston's face told her he had not previously heard of the news.

A thought struck Nettie as she watched the grief and anger impact both men. She had only met Agent McGrady the one time, but he was a handsome man. A man she would remember.

"Excuse me, sir, but I didn't see Agent McGrady's body. I would have noticed him."

Agent Ramsey's eyes narrowed. "What is it you do again, Agent Jones? Medical, right?"

"I'm a medical doctor, sir, but I work in the morgue. I saw all of the bodies that came in. There were eight from the warship and twenty-seven from the pleasure cruiser."

"There were nine people aboard the warship. I was able to obtain a copy of the manifest," Gaston said as he rustled through the papers invading his desk.

"Then where is Agent McGrady?"

CHAPTER TWO

"**C**OULD HE HAVE survived?" Gaston spoke the words that Nettie saw on Agent Ramsey's face.

She dreaded to ruin their hopes, but after seeing the remains of the victims, the idea that anyone had survived such horrors was faint to say the least. "I don't see how that could have happened. The victims were ill-used. Many were in pieces." Considering her chosen occupation, she was not one for squeamishness. Yet she had learned over the years that others were not always made of the same stuff.

Agent Ramsey clearly was not one of the delicate ones.

"Pieces you say?" His scowl deepened. "I could understand burnt. Clearly, a fire would have raged through the hydrogen, but pieces? Isn't that odd for such an accident?"

"I believe you are correct, sir. The injuries were more in keeping with close-range small explosives rather than an air collision. Unfortunately, the doctors I work under failed to agree with me." She perched forward on her seat. This same thought was why she was trying to create a formal order of medical death examiners. Many times, the dead could tell far more than the living could.

"Would there not be an explosion if two hydrogen powered airships smashed into each other?" Gaston asked.

"The contact between the two ships could have set off an

explosion, but the passengers shouldn't have been ripped to shreds." This was exciting. There was a mystery surrounding her cases from the day before. She was in no means glad that those poor people had been killed, but the fact that their deaths may have been planned gave her a new concern in the case.

"Ripped to shreds, eh? I thought you said a few of them were in pieces?"

Nettie was glad her red face would not show through the Mudger. "I didn't want to seem vulgar in my description. That now being a point of interest, I do believe I should be clear; most all of the bodies were in many pieces. More than a few of them could be said to be in shreds, or rather small pieces. There was extreme damage to their torsos in particular." She gave a small frown. "But their faces and heads were primarily intact."

"Which would not be in keeping with the type of collision." Agent Ramsey nodded in thought for a few moments. "Gaston, you need to investigate the collision further. Assume at this point that it was an aggressive act. See if you can find clues as to where Agent McGrady could have vanished. Perhaps someone saw him leaving the warship before it departed."

Nettie waited anxiously for Agent Ramsey's commands for her. When he continued to expand on the details he wanted Gaston to look into, she jumped in.

"What shall I be doing, sir?"

"I thought you could keep an eye on the bodies that come through your work..." Agent Ramsey's voice trailed off as her obvious disappointment must have shown on her face. She was a fairly new agent, yet to have to kill anyone in defense of her country, but she was more than ready to fulfill her duty. At least, she thought she was. There was a terror in her stomach at ever having to take another life.

Of course, it went without saying she would only kill those in need of it.

"I suppose we should give you a project as well, Agent Jones. I would ask that you keep an eye on any new bodies that come in and see if you can establish any connections. Be especially cautious of any that may have been involved in The Event."

That was a concern. Buckingham Palace was keeping the queen's treatment hush-hush, but it was not clear who was involved. Clearly, people who had been able to keep the details from the SEU—not an easy feat. If someone disposed of the drained vampires in a less than rigorous manner, questions might be asked. The smartest way would be to leave the bodies in the sun. Of course, this being London, and the month of January, sunlight was a rare and stealthy commodity.

"Aye sir." She let the unsaid *and* hang there. She didn't want to appear pushy, but she had already planned on keeping an eye out for any suspicious bodies.

"And I think you should be the one to greet our new agent." The look on Agent Ramsey's stout face told her he just thought that part up. Regardless, she was willing to take it.

"Are you certain? Isn't this agent an…American?" Gaston would grumble about the start of a new day, and often did. He also had a thing against Americans, but had yet to pass along the circumstances surrounding his bias. Nettie didn't know they were getting a new agent in London, let alone that it would be an American. She briefly hoped it was a woman. It would be nice to have a fellow agent of her gender close by.

"Gaston, none of that from you. Smith is highly recommended by the Yanks. He has a fair understanding of vampires that we simply lack, especially your branch." Agent Ramsey nodded toward Nettie. "No offense of course."

"None taken." She may have been half-vampire by birth, but her vampiric mother abandoned her when she was only six weeks old, and her father passed away by the time she turned two years old. She had been raised by a variety of distant and uncaring family and church members. None of whom knew the least bit of vampires. Nettie grew up thinking she was from unusually strong stock. She learned she was a vampire, or rather half, when Gaston invited her to join the Society.

"Smith will be there in one week. He was intended to be a replacement for McGrady as we were moving him to India. I had planned on bringing Smith up to speed slowly. With McGrady's disappearance though, I feel we must bring him to the task with the utmost haste." Agent Ramsey turned his look from Nettie to Gaston. "Oh, do stop scowling. I have no idea what your issue is with Americans and honestly, I don't need nor want to know. Besides, he is a compatriot of sorts. Originally hailed from someplace called New Orleans. They apparently have a vampire issue down there."

Gaston perked up at that, but the rest of the conversation was boring for Nettie, to say the least. The bureaucratic falderal that made up the underbelly of the Society had no interest for her. She wanted to get out there and investigate, wade into the mud, dig under rocks, find the—

"Don't you agree, Agent Jones?" Agent Ramsey's words pulled her back to the present. Unfortunately, she'd missed what he said previously.

"I think there was some static sir?" She ignored Gaston's rude snort behind her. He knew full well that she'd checked out momentarily. He wouldn't give her away though.

"I was pointing out that a young woman seen showing the sights to her cousin's brother-in-law would not cause untoward comments."

He had a point, and since she had moved around quite a bit as a small child, she could have family from anywhere. "Agreed, sir. Besides, if Gaston greets him, he'll take the first ocean liner back home."

Nettie politely gave a flash of fang to Gaston. She loved the old man like an uncle, but he was annoyingly steadfast in his opinions. A most bothersome habit, especially when those opinions were wrong.

"Americans. Rude, all of them. See that he behaves with you. One step out of line and I will take matters into my own hands." Gaston got up and poured a cup of tea. His expression was fierce as he handed it to her, and then turned to get one for himself.

Nettie refrained from pointing out that, as demonstrated to her unwelcome companion last night, she could very much take care of herself. He meant well. Gaston might be a short, round, cranky old man, but he was also probably one of the most dangerous people in all of London. Actually, since the Society's headquarters were in Edinburgh, he could be the most deadly person in England proper. Nettie believed in acknowledging Scotland as a separate entity from Mother England.

"I have great faith in Agent Jones. That being settled, I will let you get to your tea. Jones, the packet with Smith's particulars will be at your home by the time you get in this evening." With a quick nod to both of them, Agent Ramsey signed off, and the screen went blank.

"Hmph, I'm glad *he* has faith, I'm the one who will be stuck here if there are problems with *Monsieur* Smith."

Nettie knew Gaston's mutterings were meant for her, even though they were spoken to his steaming cup of tea. She chose to ignore him and instead drank a huge gulp of her still-warm tea to fortify herself.

"I should probably be going. I have some errands to run before my shift begins." She rose, picked up her belongings, and made her way out of the dungeon.

"How is she handling?" Gaston followed her out of the dungeon, pride clear in his voice.

"When I can ride her, Lula Belle is wonderful. It's all about the *when* issue." Thank goodness the sky didn't look ready to open up. She'd hate to have to take one of the carriages back. She started the boiler and checked the temperature settings as the steamcycle came to life.

"There's still work to be done, yes. But overall, she is a magnificent machine." He rocked back on his heels and looked pleased with his lot for the moment. "I do wish you'd refrain from calling her that name." He winced and the brief smile faded.

"She is mine, yes? Then I will call her what I want and her name is Lula Belle." Satisfied the levels were correct and the temperature of the small engine that powered the steamcycle was ready, Nettie put on her goggles and secured her cap and belongings. "But she is wonderful—I believe we made the best time ever today."

Gaston was stepping back into his doorway, but paused with a frown. "See that you watch your speed, young lady. It wouldn't do to have the constables pull you over."

With a negligent wave over her shoulder, Nettie mounted her steam-powered steed and ventured forth.

Truth was, she could have very well stayed and chatted more with Gaston. Quite likely, he had been expecting the same and was more cantankerous than usual at her leaving. Nevertheless, the fact remained that she rarely got a chance to ride this wonderful invention of his. She couldn't waste a single moment.

With little rhyme or reason, Nettie drifted throughout the streets, steering clear of anything too narrow. Not that her Lula Belle needed room, but she'd found horses really didn't like the machine and narrow streets caused problems for her and any horses they met.

She hadn't really been paying attention, her thoughts focused on what could have killed those people on the airships if they died before the collision, but she noticed she kept seeing the same man as she made her way through the streets. She'd go down two streets and he was there, cross three more over, there again. A nondescript man. He was covered head to toe in layers of brown clothing that looked like they actually started out life that murky color as opposed to simply being over-worn and filthy.

After the fifth time, Nettie knew she was being followed. He kept watching her, but had a brown cap that fell from fashion twenty years ago pulled low on his head. Even without seeing his eyes, she knew he watched her. She was about to stop Lula Belle and give him a talking to when he vanished. Clear as day, he was there one instant, gone the next. She slowed Lula Belle down, turning to coast back to where the man had stood.

Keeping an eye on the surrounding areas, she got off the steamcycle and marched over to where he had been.

Since joining the Society, she'd been exposed to many oddities, some within her own self. Yet, she'd never heard of a person being able to vanish.

The ground was covered in dirt and grime, and unfortunately, many footprints. She might have imagined it, but one set of prints seemed deeper than the rest, fresher. Grateful that she was wearing her wide trousers, she knelt down to get a closer look. She took off her gloves to see if touch could tell her what her eyes couldn't. Her reward when she pulled her fingers up was a faint green-grey dust that had settled upon the ground. Rather, on top of everything except for the two deeper footprints.

Rubbing the dust between her fingers didn't give her much clue as to what it was or why it was there. Unless her spying man in brown had dissolved into this, she wasn't sure that it would help her cause in the least.

Nonetheless, she would take a sample.

She had found it beneficial to carry small sample containers on her person at all times. To be honest, she'd carried them even prior to joining the Society, but now she had better reasons for doing so. Careful to leave the grime and mud behind, she collected as much as she could, gently shooing it onto a note from her pocket, then transferring it to her container. She could investigate this substance while at work. Sadly, the scientific equipment in the hospital was still trapped in the 1820s when compared to what the Society had. Yet it was better than nothing. She had a feeling this needed to be examined immediately, and she couldn't take the time to return to Gaston's and still make it to work in a timely fashion.

Closing the sample up tightly, she looked up suddenly to see if she could catch her mystery man. Unfortunately, he hadn't returned.

Her dallying had left her with little time before her work shift began. She could wander around and see if her vanishing friend reappeared, or get into work early and find out something about the dust. A further examination of those bodies not claimed by loved ones from the previous day's calamity might be in order as well.

She was about to board Lula Belle when a burlap bag snapped over her head.

CHAPTER THREE

FULLY AWARE OF the type of neighborhood she'd found herself in, her first fear was for Lula Belle. Not that most people would be able to figure out how to drive her, but they might take her because she looked valuable.

She kicked backward with her booted heel and was rewarded with a satisfactory *oomph* as she hit what felt like a shinbone. Hands seemed to be grabbing her all over. Clearly, there was more than one abductor. She continued swinging out with her fists and her feet. She needed to get the sack off of her head, but every time she tried to do so the hands moved in again. There seemed to be far too many for the amount of shuffling she heard around her.

She hated to resort to screaming—it gave the appearance that one was unable to defend oneself—but at that moment, she was unable to do that very thing.

The scream she let loose was fired by her anxiety at loosing Lula Belle and annoyance at being manhandled.

The hands stopped for a moment, then resumed with fervor. They weren't grabbing her per se, but rather pulling at her clothes. Too late she realized they were after her samples of the grey-green dust. She stopped trying to free herself from the burlap sack and concentrated on keeping the hands from her inner pockets. Alas, the varlets found the samples and pulled them from her jacket a moment before her hands got there.

With the hands no longer fighting her, she whipped off the sack only to find no one but a washerwoman watching her from adjacent alley. After checking to see that Lula Belle sat unmolested where she had left her, Nettie faced the old woman.

"Where did they go? The men who were here, did you see?"

The washerwoman tilted her head in that manner people often got when trying to ascertain the danger of an unknown situation. "Ain't seen nothin' but you, miss. No one else were around you."

"Come now, you didn't see them? There had to have been at least three or more." Nettie tucked her black hair under her leather cap. Luckily the expensive brass goggles had stayed in place and were undamaged.

"No, miss." She took a small step backward. Then, emboldened, took another. "I heards ye scream, but no one was around you." With a quick nod, she took a series of steps back that quickly switched into her turning around and fleeing.

Nettie couldn't imagine how the woman hadn't seen the attackers. Perhaps her eyes were bad. She thought to go after her, but most likely she would only scare her further.

After allowing herself a few moments of pity for losing her find, she turned around and ran back to the place where she'd found the dust. Obviously, even though she hadn't thought of obtaining more immediately, her attackers had. The ground was now stirred up so much she could no longer see the dust. There might still be some component of it, although separating it out from the grime would really be more of a job for the Society's best minds and gadgets in Edinburgh. Still, she had to try.

Bending down, she scooped up what mud she could find that looked less trampled, and put it into her last sample container. She kept her eyes sharp, jumping at every sound, until she was safely atop Lula Belle and on her way.

She arrived at her work with no further interruptions and gently secured Lula Belle in her garage.

The day shift, consisting of two wizened old men who never spoke to anyone except each other, was still in the front office. They seemed to be arguing over a session with the corpse of a round, older, gentleman. Judging by the clothing piled neatly to the side, he was a fisherman and most likely passed on while plying his trade.

Nettie left them to it and went to her office down the corridor. Granted, her office was small, and rather dark, but it suited her and allowed her to work on her detective medical work.

The police rarely called upon her, but in the last year she had assisted in solving no less than five crimes. Well, with the help of the bodies, that is. Death had much to tell the living. The problem was that the living usually wouldn't stop talking long enough to listen.

"Now ain't you a sight." Rebecca shook her head as she came down the hall opposite Nettie's tiny office. She held her favorite mug filled with her favorite India tea and looked quite pleased with herself.

Belatedly, Nettie looked down to see evidence of her accostment. Her clothes were ruffled and bits of grime lingered here and there.

"I believe I was mugged." She smiled at her friend as she held open her office door. Rebecca was full Welsh and looked the part. She was tiny and small boned with thick dark hair and startling blue eyes. She was also by far the smartest person Nettie knew outside of the members of the Society.

"Wouldn't you know if you had been mugged? Or wait, let me guess, you were too caught up in studying something and they mugged you before you became aware?" Rebecca fixed her skirts and perched in the chair across from Nettie's desk. "Oh, and you may wish to change."

Nettie followed Rebecca's pointed glance down to her trousers. While some parts of London were forward thinking enough not to be concerned by the sight of a woman in pants, this office was not one of those places. Especially with the two daytime doctors still in the building.

"I do wish certain people in this city would admit that women in trousers makes much more sense than skirts." Plucking up her reticule, she stepped behind a screen to change. The screen was a favorite of hers, the human body shown in intricate detail. In fact, the detail was so amazing she believed it had to have originated from someone in the Society. Gaston, of course, steadfastly denied it.

Nettie stepped back around and placed her pants into her bag. "I know I was mugged. I'm not sure what they wanted. That isn't even correct. I know they wanted my dust."

That got her. Rebecca choked on her tea. "Your what?"

Nettie regretted again, for about the hundredth time this month alone, that she couldn't tell others about the Society. Life would be so much more enjoyable if she could tell Rebecca about her discoveries. Sadly, she had to be censored in what she told

Rebecca. Hence, the younger woman oft times thought Nettie was crazy.

"Dust. I found some odd dust on Shallot Street. I wanted to examine it." That sounded daft even to her ears. But she couldn't take a chance and tell her about the mystery man in brown who had been following her. Not even to mention his disappearing, or that the persons who took her dust might or might not have been invisible.

"You found dust. And someone mugged you for it?"

Nettie could tell Rebecca was trying to make sense of it, but without all of the information, it wouldn't have made sense to her either, and she had a very open mind.

"Well, it was extremely odd dust." Nettie paced around her chair. "Perhaps it was from some illegal manufacturing plant and they realized I might find it."

"Yes, well too bad it's gone now." Clearly more than ready to dismiss the dust, Rebecca was moving on. "Are you going to take off your gloves and stay for a bit?"

Nettie laughed and pulled off her left glove. If Rebecca hadn't said anything, Nettie might have kept them on until a body came in. Her laughter stopped when she saw the faint sheen of dust sparkling on her fingertips. She had forgotten that since her gloves had been off while she was looking at the dust, her fingers still had some on them. She peered inside the glove; quite possibly there was some lingering on the inside as well.

"Nettie? What are you looking at?" Rebecca's query brought Nettie out of snooping into her glove.

"I think I may have found more dust," Nettie said. Holding out her hand for inspection, she angled it so the light glanced off of it. Interesting. Whatever it was made of had an almost iridescent sheen to it. Gradually, the glow seemed to be fading. She hoped it didn't disappear the way the brown man had.

"That is definitely dust. Yes, it certainly is." Extracting herself from her chair, Rebecca gathered her now empty teacup and took a step back. For some reason, she didn't always like to be around Nettie when she was working on her findings. She claimed it was the chemicals she used, but Nettie was not certain that was the complete answer.

"I'll leave you to your dust. The evil ones have me working on their daily write-ups."

Nettie looked up from her initial inspection of the dust. "You don't have to do that, you know. They really should be doing their own reports."

Rebecca waved her off. "I don't mind, and it helps break up the tedium. Oh, did I tell you about our visitor earlier?" She bustled forward again and resumed her chair.

Nettie carefully put her glove back on. Better to be cautious where evidence was concerned and it would be rude to kick her friend out. "No, you didn't. Who came by?"

Rebecca worked the middle shift, so she got in before Nettie did. Although she didn't have a full medical degree like Nettie and was considered only an assistant, she was far better at her job than any of the others. Aside from her tendency to gossip.

"It was none other than Lord Melbourne's secretary, himself." She nodded her head in case Nettie missed the importance of Queen Victoria's right hand man sending one of his personal staff over.

Nettie could think of reasons for it, but none of them were

situations Rebecca would be aware of.

"Truly? Whatever did he want?" She seriously doubted he was coming by to see if they knew about the queen's transformation. Perhaps he was coming by to see if they had some vampires the royal family could borrow. Nettie caught the giggle at the thought of such a thing occurring before it escaped. Or thought she did.

"What did you say?"

"Nothing, I choked on the…dust. Some of it flew up. Now what were you saying?"

Rebecca's suspicious half-scowl told Nettie that she was aware that something else had taken place. But being as she was used to Nettie's mysteries, and that Nettie often did things she didn't understand, she was not going to pursue it. Nettie knew the look well.

"As I was saying, Lord Melbourne's man was here asking about the airship collision."

Hmmm, perhaps more than the Society suspected it was not an accident. "What did he want then? I filed all the reports." She had been detailed on that, and those reports had taken some doing. There was a lot to detail in the deaths of that many people. Not to mention it technically fell under the day shift's coverage. But the two old gents fled the building as soon as the wagons came in with the bodies.

"Ha, that's the thing. He didn't want the reports, or so he said. He wanted the bodies." Her bright blue eyes grew wide. Rebecca usually was not one for a mystery, but when one of the top voices in the queen's ear came to claim thirty-five recently deceased persons, there was no way to avoid being drawn into the mystery.

Nettie pulled out a writing tablet, pen, and ink. "Now, he came and claimed the bodies? In the name of the Crown?"

She still couldn't believe Lord Melbourne would send his man down for such a job. Actually, she couldn't fathom why he would want the bodies.

"No, no. He was claiming them for sources he wouldn't say." She leaned forward. "He had official documents and went right to Dr. Wilson's office, but I saw them. Claimed all of the bodies. Took the last of them not more than an hour ago."

Her conversation with Agent Ramsey came burbling back up. The Society might need those bodies. Had someone else come to the same conclusion? Or had someone in the palace been involved with their deaths? Why would someone want the bodies? She didn't know, but she had a sinking suspicion it was tied to their missing agent.

Which meant someone suspected who he was, and that he hadn't been on the ship.

"You're gone again, I see. This ties into something, doesn't it?" That was the closest Rebecca had ever gotten to implying that Nettie had secrets of an important nature. The directness in her clear eyes chilled Nettie. Rebecca knew more about her hobbies than she'd thought. Nettie would have to count on her to continue being the soul of discretion she had been so far.

"They took the bodies an hour ago you say? Do you know where?"

"No, but I think we could find the original orders. I heard Dr. Fritz and Dr. Abernathy leave, and Dr. Wilson left a bit earlier."

Oh, her sneaky little friend. Rebecca was more than aware of

Nettie's situation, or at least that something was going on. "I don't want to get you in trouble…"

Rebecca rose to her feet with a negligent wave. "Don't be silly. I am simply discussing some paperwork issues we found."

Nettie followed her out and then pulled her sleeve. "Afterwards, we might wish to check the cold storage. Perhaps they left a clue that will provide more information."

"But to what?"

"I have no idea." She wished she could give her friend a better answer.

Rebecca nodded then continued down the hall.

The hallway was deserted. To be honest, Nettie wondered why the other doctors had been here as late as they had been. Usually, with enough timing, she could trust on them not being here when she got in. She counted on it, in fact.

Most likely, the reason had to do with the bodies. Even though they had managed to duck out of having to deal with them, after the hue and cry today once the story appeared in the paper, they most likely felt they had to get their involvement in as well.

Rebecca did the actual breaking into Dr. Wilson's office. Technically, as his assistant, it was not breaking in. Or so they told themselves. Not that this happened regularly, but it was handy being best friends with the department assistant.

They had found in the past that his small gas lamp in the corner let them see most of the contents of his desk without alerting others to the fact that someone was in a closed office.

Unlike the man himself, his desk was neat and spare. He usually spent a good hour at the end of the day making sure every item was back where it belonged.

The same could not be said for his own personal hygiene.

Waving her handkerchief in front of her nose, Nettie stood watch near the door while her companion broke into the desk. Little breaking was really involved; no one in the office aside from herself actually locked anything. Nettie had established that she was afraid of people reading her bad poetry that she wrote during down times, and therefore locked her desk. In fact, she had no interest in poetry, but had found that if she crafted notes to herself in iambic parameter, people would ignore them. And it gave her a great opportunity to secure any Society business that happened to be at hand.

"I believe the papers are here." Rebecca thrust a packet into Nettie's hands. She kept shifting her weight between her feet and peering down the hall.

Nettie tried glancing at the documents, but Rebecca's twitching distracted her. More than that, it worried her. Rebecca was a consummate gossip, but she was not a twitchy person.

"Whatever is the matter?" Nettie closed the papers back up. Clearly she would have to deal with whatever was disturbing Rebecca first.

"I don't know," she said. "I have an odd feeling...."

That got Nettie's attention right off. Some time ago, she had noticed that it appeared her best friend might be clairvoyant. She got physically ill a good two hours prior to the airship crash. Unfortunately, she couldn't narrow down where the dangers lay.

"What kind of feeling?" Nettie looked quickly around Dr. Wilson's office in case the dangers were lurking nearby. "When did it begin?"

Rebecca moved toward the door, rubbing her arms as if winter's deadly grip had taken hold. "It started when I reached into Dr. Wilson's desk. I can't explain the feeling." Her voice went up an octave and she began to furiously rub the space between her brows. "It's bad, whatever it is. I can't explain it…It's going to be bad."

A cold wind struck Nettie. She'd never been clairvoyant in her life, but something brushed her soul. And an odd smell trickled in. Not strong at first, but rapidly becoming so. It was nothing she had smelled before, but reminded her of the worst kind of burning rubbish. She turned to ask Rebecca if she smelled it as well, but was caught off guard when her friend started pulling frantically on her arm.

"This room, there is something wrong with this room." There would have been something amusing about tiny Rebecca trying to forcibly drag Nettie out of the office, except that her terror was contagious.

Nettie tried to stop when they got to the hall, but Rebecca continued to push her from behind. "No, we must get out, must keep moving. It was bad. It was bad."

Reaching back for Rebecca's hand and clutching the stolen papers in her other hand, Nettie used all of her half-vampire strength to drag Rebecca down the hall and fling both of them out of the building.

They landed in the snow an instant before the walls glowed red and then exploded in a blast of terrible beauty. Snow that hadn't been there moments before.

CHAPTER FOUR

B OTH WOMEN CURLED up into the tightest balls they could so they were smaller targets for the flaming embers flying into the sky. The snapping and popping of the newborn fire filled the early evening air. It wouldn't be long before London's crack firefighting team arrived. London had an entire force dedicated to fighting fires with high-powered steam equipment. They were far and above the rest of the nation, and the technology was something the Society would love to get their hands on.

There were rumors among those in the Society that it was not based in human technology.

Shaking herself out of her fanciful thoughts, Nettie pulled Rebecca into an upright position and watched as the flames began to lick higher. "You saved us."

The chittering that answered made her look over at her friend. It was not the cold that was rattling her, however; she looked more scared now than she did right before the explosion.

"What's wrong? You saved us. That should bring a smile to your face. I know it does to mine."

"I've never been that clear…Never, never…" Her voice was barely above a whisper and Nettie's medical training kicked in. Rebecca was rapidly slipping into shock.

"Rebecca? You need to look at me." Nettie pulled her around

so she had to face her instead of the flames. Why hadn't the fire team arrived yet? "It's okay. You saved us. We're out of the building."

Two tiny hands clutched Nettie's own. "But we didn't make it. We weren't supposed to make it. I saw our deaths, Nettie. In those last seconds, I saw our deaths." Tears were building in her eyes, and her voice was getting stronger. That was a better reaction than shock.

"You saw one path, Rebecca, one path. Clairvoyants see what *might* be. You were able to change the future."

"Clairewhats?" The word seemed to pull her out of her stupor a bit more. Nettie was going to have to tread carefully. What she knew of future seers came strictly from the Society. She'd need to make sure she stayed away from her source of knowledge.

"Clairvoyants, you know, in the novelty plays. All the rage in the West End. They see the future."

Rebecca pulled back, her fists tight. "Don't you mock me, Nettie Jones. I don't care if you have a Ph.D. or not."

Nettie laughed, although she found herself looking for the fire team. Surely the explosion had been felt? "I'm not mocking you. I think they are real. I believe some people can see the future. You happen to be one of those." She stopped as Rebecca began to shake. "What is it?"

Convulsions racked Rebecca's body and her eyes rolled back in her head. Flinging her head back, she began to make strange clicking sounds. An instant later, everything went black.

"NETTIE? WHAT HAPPENED?" Rebecca's voice was faint, but it was enough for Nettie to open her eyes.

And find herself clutching the pilfered documents from Dr. Wilson's desk, as she lay slumped against a wall back inside the offices. Rebecca was stirring slowly in front of her.

"I know this sounds extremely odd—"

"But we saw this place explode." Nettie finished for her.

Rebecca rose to her feet and started touching the walls. "They are real—solid and real. What just happened?"

A tendril of real fear crept down Nettie's spine. It was a rare visitor, her overwhelming curiosity usually managing to keep it at bay. She *felt* that explosion. The side of her face was still warm from the heat of the fire; her dress was damp where she'd sat in snow.

Except the building hadn't exploded and there was no snow outside. The ground was dingy and slightly damp from yet another rain—but there was no snow.

"Nettie, I know you know more of things than I do." Rebecca's round little face was pale with terror.

Nettie rose to her feet, dusting her skirts off as she did so. One thing was for certain, they shouldn't remain in Dr. Wilson's office. Luckily, even in her fear, Rebecca rose an instant after Nettie did.

"I don't know," Nettie said. "I must say I have never felt or heard of such a thing as just happened."

Rebecca quietly followed Nettie into her own small office and shut the door behind her. Technically, they should be the only ones in the office at this time of night. But it would not be unheard of for a late-night physician, bored with watching his own patients, to come down and poke around the dead.

"What did you feel right before it happened?" She steered Rebecca to the small extra chair and forced her to sit.

"Fear. All I felt was fear." Her eyes got wider. "Oh, and then we died. I didn't enjoy that at all. In fact…" She looked around and grabbed Nettie's small wastebasket. Then promptly threw up. With a delicate dab at the corners of her mouth, she took a deep breath. "Better."

"How do you know we died?" Not that she doubted Rebecca, but she needed as much information gathered as possible if she was to give a report of any sense to Gaston and the Society.

"Honestly, Nettie, sometimes I do wonder about you. I felt it. My heart stopped. Only for a moment, mind you, as if our leaving the building negated the effect. One minute we were in the office, then fleeing, then dead, then outside in the snow. Which isn't there."

Nettie hid her smile; Rebecca was clearly feeling better as her ability to natter on was back to full form.

"Nothing clearer than that?" Nettie was shooting in the dark, but she couldn't tell Agent Ramsey that her friend simply *felt* it. Defining the indefinable was a core goal of the Society.

Folded arms and a stern glare was her reward for poking. "How much clearer can I be than I felt myself die? You too. I felt you go an instant before I did."

There seemed to be a smug tone to that. Maybe Nettie was approaching it the wrong way. "Okay then, what about before the death? What did you feel when you became disturbed in Dr. Wilson's office?" She poured both of them some tea from the kettle, then sat down with her pen and quill.

"You are extremely difficult sometimes." Rebecca waved her hand to keep her from answering and took a sip of the tea and made a face. "The tea has gone bitter. Anyway, if you must be specific, I felt a chill. The room was frozen, with the focus of the chill lying in the center of Dr. Wilson's desk."

"Frozen. Okay, that's something. Have you ever felt that before?"

"No. Wait, yes. I did sort of yesterday, a few hours before the accident. The chill was from the outside though. I remember because I had to move away from the doors and windows."

Nettie wrote that bit down as well, and then drummed her fingers on her desk. If only she ranked high enough for a Mudger. She needed Gaston's opinion, but couldn't run halfway across town in the middle of her shift.

She would have to send for a Runner.

A thrill of excitement shimmied across her shoulders at the prospect. This would be the first time she had something interesting enough to warrant one of the mysterious Runners. A secret group within a secret group, the Runners did what their name implied—they ran. They could be counted on to carry important missives between Society members. They were also supposedly dispatched to the further reaches of the globe, even far outside the purview of the British Empire. They gathered intelligence far beyond normal agents, and made certain it got to the correct people.

Like all agents, Nettie was under the strictest guidance to only call upon them in times of extreme need. This was, in her opinion, an example of extreme need. A clairvoyant who managed to transmit not only herself but also a passenger into some other time? And managed to change that outcome even as it was occurring? Nettie had had her questions about Rebecca for over a year now. She had crossed from being a curiosity into being a full-fledged important interest. They may even recruit her into the Society.

"Nettie? Are you there? Did our adventure damage your brain?"

Nettie blinked, belatedly realizing that she had been woolgathering with her friend still in the room. Bad form on her part.

"No, no. I'm fine. I was thinking. About...these files." She grabbed the file packet they'd liberated from Dr. Wilson's office. Most likely, Rebecca saw through her rather feeble cover, but she couldn't tell her the truth. Not yet anyway. "You know, I should probably get looking through them, see what, if anything, I missed." Nettie let loose her most winsome smile.

Rebecca narrowed her eyes and folded her arms tighter. Clearly, she was having none of it.

Nettie was still smiling winsomely.

"You know, that smile and big innocent doe eyes would work better if I was a male." Rebecca blew at a straggling hair that had fallen into her face, and then shook her head. "I will take you at your word, Dr. Jones. As I too have work to do, and as I do not wish to have to stay here for all of your shift as well, I bid you goodnight." With a bow, she flounced to the door but then spun at the doorway. "Don't forget to replace those files exactly where I got them, and don't forget you wanted to look at your dust." With a pointed nod at Nettie's gloves, she slipped down the hallway.

Her dust! How could she have forgotten it? She carefully

pulled her right hand free of the fabric. The dust still glinted in the light. Thank goodness she'd had the foresight to replace her gloves prior to whatever had happened. Somehow, she doubted that the dust particles would have survived being stuck into the snow. Even snow that didn't currently exist.

Nettie was torn. She wanted to examine the dust, but news of what had befallen Rebecca and herself needed to be shared with Gaston and most likely the rest of the Society. Truth be told, she had never heard of a similar situation, and she had spent days pouring through as many of the Society's vast records as she could when first recruited.

She let out a sigh and slid her glove back on and secured both of them as tightly as she could. The incident with Rebecca was more important.

Reaching far into the back of her left desk drawer, Nettie pulled free a tiny envelope. The wax seal covered almost the entire side, the deep red mark of the Society almost making it look bloody.

A trickle of sweat made its way down the back of her neck. She had to admit, the prospect of summoning a Runner was almost as interesting as the anticipated Runner themselves.

Shaking her shoulders to settle herself, she gripped one corner of the envelope, and pulled.

Nothing happened.

Just as she pulled the defective summoning device to her eye, it began to fizz. She quickly held it away from her face. Not a moment too soon. The fizzing ended and an explosion of light and sound filed her office.

She shut her eyes as smoke billowed out of the small packet.

Had she gotten a bad summoner? Or were they supposed to do that? Seemed a bit off-putting to have a secret summoning device be so ostentatious and loud. Rebecca would be here any minute asking what had happened. Nettie could only hope that no one else had been close enough to the office to hear the sound.

Waving the last of the smoke aside, she cracked open her door.

No Rebecca. No hue and cry at the explosion she'd caused.

Nettie waited a few minutes to see if Rebecca would come in—perhaps the sound hadn't been as loud as she'd felt. She was settling down to compose her missive to Gaston when a rattling shook the small window behind her.

CHAPTER FIVE

NETTIE HAD TO admit she ducked. Rattling of a window shouldn't cause such fear, but with the recent events, she was taking no chances.

The rattling only lasted a moment. Then a person stood before her. Not a person small enough to have fit through that window, mind you. A full-sized, black-garbed man. At least, she assumed it was a man; the build was a bit broad in the shoulders for a woman. The clothing was tight, but gave the impression of shape, not of any distinguishing features. The fabric was unique so she couldn't determine at all what it was made of. Nettie's fingers twitched to touch it.

Somehow, she didn't think touching to see the weight of his clothing would be deemed proper.

"What is your need?" The voice was faint and deep all in the same breath. He may have had something covering his mouth, as all Nettie could make out was blackness from head to toe.

This had to be a Runner.

Nettie determined that a suggestion be made that new members of the Society be a bit more forewarned on both the summoning of a Runner and the Runners themselves. But then she supposed any member of the Society would be made of stern enough stuff to handle such a surprise.

"So you are a Runner? How is it? Do you travel a lot? Do you make it to Edinburgh often? Do you visit distant lands?"

The figure held perfectly still. He didn't cross his arms, or lean on one leg tapping his foot like many of her companions seemed to do with alarming frequency when she spoke. He simply went still. Like a giant black obelisk had been transported into her office and had no intention of leaving.

"What is your need?"

There might be a bit more inflection at the end of the sentence, but to be honest, the line sounded exactly like it had moments before. Clearly, getting anything useful out of this person was not going to happen.

"I need to get this information to Gaston. It is most urgent and can't—"

Before the word "wait" could leave her lips, the black shape picked the paper out of her hands and vanished in a cloud of smoke. The rattling of the window told her whatever way he got in, he was leaving the same way.

Now that did seem a bit rude. They both worked for the same organization, after all. The least he could do was wait to make sure there was nothing else she needed to tell him. It would serve him right if she had yet another document needing transportation and had to summon him again. She had no idea how he got in or what the smoke and window had to do with it, but she was fairly certain being called back would not please him. Fortunately for him, she'd used her only summoning envelope. Clearly, she would have to ask Gaston to requisition a few at a time for her.

Nettie allowed herself to stew for a few moments. She had long awaited her first encounter with the mysterious Runners, and the interaction had been extremely unsatisfactory.

After a few moments passed, she returned to other more important things. First, she needed to see if anything had been added or removed from her original reports on the bodies. The packet seemed fuller than she recalled when she handed it in last night, but she was extremely fatigued by the time she left. Not to mention more than a little distracted thinking of the untoward events taking place in the palace. She was all for a long, healthy reign for Queen Victoria and HRH Prince Albert, yet she didn't think anyone should be allowed to extend their lives forever. And at the cost of others, even vampires, was even more off-putting. Although she was half-vampire, she had no fondness nor affiliation for them. Yet, even they shouldn't have been killed for another. It also disturbed her that Gaston and the rest of the Society had no information about the change. She would feel a bit better if she knew responsible people were watching the situation as it occurred. The little she had heard about the change from human to vampire since joining the Society told her it was not a pleasant thing.

Sliding the pages out, she fussed to herself when she realized they must be backward. Turning them over brought a few light swear words to her lips. Not the type Gaston or Agent Ramsey would use, more like the soft-spoken ones used by fine ladies when they dropped a large book on their toe in an empty room. The pages were blank.

There were over fifty of them, looking for the entire world to be the selfsame documents she'd left the night before. With the notable exception that the areas where her practiced penmanship should lie were abandoned and blank.

Rebecca could be pulling a prank, but that would be out of keeping with her character. She could be flighty and was prone to a bit of gossip, but she would never play any type of prank with anything official.

Dr. Wilson would have looked at her report when he first got in this morning. Not thoroughly. She was not vain to think of her gifts in the forensics field to be such that he did not need to check her work. However, he would have glanced through out of simple curiosity.

He never sent for her, which he would have done had the pages been as they were now.

Or if a messenger had missed her, the good doctor himself would have been lying in wait for her to come in.

Which meant someone managed to sneak in after Dr. Wilson had left but prior to her arrival. During the earlier portions of the day it wouldn't be uncommon for any number of medical personnel to be crossing these offices.

Opening her door, she hoped that Rebecca hadn't left yet. Luckily, she was still at her desk. Her head was down, and she didn't even look up at her approach.

"Rebecca? I'm surprised you're still here. But I'm glad you are, as I have some questions." Nettie stepped forward to tap on her shoulder when she noticed a bloody knife thrust into Rebecca's back.

Nettie staggered backward, frantically spying for the assailant.

"Oh I am so sorry, Rebecca. This is my fault."

"What's your fault?"

The words came from behind her and almost made Nettie

split her skin.

"Rebecca, you're fine!" She spun to see her friend coming down from the file repository. Then she spun back to the desk. The image of Rebecca with the knife was gone.

"Of course I'm fine. I'm tired, but fine." She peered up as she passed Nettie and resumed her chair. "Whatever is wrong with you this evening, Nettie? You are acting far odder than your usual want."

Again, Nettie had to bite her lip. Even with the curious occurrence they'd shared earlier this evening, there was no fathomable way that she was going to tell her closest friend that she'd just seen her dead. Once in one night was enough for any sane person.

"I fear I am over-tired myself." Nettie held up the pages. She couldn't tell her about her vision, nor did she know what it meant, but she needed her help. "These are blank."

"Blank? Why ever did you turn in blank pages to Dr. Wilson? I am surprised he didn't run you to ground for that prank." She plucked the documents out of her hand and ruffled through them.

"I didn't turn them in that way. The problem is that they are that way now. Do you know when Dr. Wilson left, or who could have been in his office after he did so?"

"No, he was gone when I returned from my lunch break. I thought perhaps he had been called to the hospital." She handed me back the papers. "The only person near there would have been Lord Melbourne's man. He would have gone in to turn in the request for the bodies."

"At which time he replaced a full file with blank pages?

Doesn't that seem a bit odd?" She kept running things through her head, but none of them made sense. Of course, the other option was that someone broke in and wiped the information off the pages. That seemed too farfetched to share even with a close friend.

"Well, do you think little fairies came in and replaced it while we were out in that explosion? The one that apparently never happened?"

The fold of her arms and look on her face told Nettie she was being facetious. Although, perhaps she had a valid thought. They didn't have the slightest idea who or what caused that explosion or the vision of it, as it seemed was the case. That both she and Rebecca had visions was also cause for concern. Could there be a connection?

"Oh, come now. I was not serious." Rebecca poked her shoulder.

"What? I hadn't said anything."

"You were thinking it; I can tell. You get that look as if you're seeing India in the distance. It never bodes well when you do that." She pulled out her seat but continued watching Nettie as if she was about to sprout wings.

"No, I was simply thinking that since we have no knowledge of what really happened, or how it happened, then it's not too farfetched to entertain the idea that the two items might be related."

Rebecca rolled her eyes and stuffed her belongings into her reticule. "Next you'll be saying that horrific accident last night was deliberate."

Luckily for Nettie, Rebecca was not watching her face at the time. Nettie had a feeling she wouldn't have liked what she saw. There were too many things pointing toward the collision being anything but an accident. There was a good chance that it was not only planned, but involved an agent of the Society who might or might not have gone over to the other side.

Not being able to tell Rebecca about the Society meant Nettie certainly couldn't tell her about the handsome Agent McGrady or his questionable disappearance and possible involvement with the collision.

Life would be much easier if Gaston and Agent Ramsey agreed with her request to bring Rebecca into the Society. Nettie hoped Rebecca agreed with her as well. People who were invited to the Society had limited options if they declined. Most opted for a memory removal. She certainly hoped that she had judged her friend correctly.

"You have the look again." Rebecca had finished packing her belongings and spoke as she passed Nettie. Perhaps she was right—Nettie hadn't even noticed her standing. Fine agent of the Society she was.

"I simply have many things on my mind." She shooed Rebecca toward the door. "And I think one of the first things will be to try and recreate the files which have vanished. So be gone," she said as she marched to her office. "I shall see you on the next day."

Rebecca's laugh carried down the hall as Nettie shut the door to her sanctuary.

She was graced with an extremely formidable memory, but she was afraid that even for one such as hers, reconstructing the autopsies of thirty-five persons would be problematic to say the least. Not to mention that while she might have overseen all of them, she hadn't performed them all. Therefore, she was only going to be able to focus on the vaguest of impressions for the ones others had worked on.

Luckily, this was a quiet night, and she managed to get in a good few hours work before the outside bell rang.

She placed the documents she'd been able to recreate into her desk drawer and locked it prior to going to the front. Nettie was all for hard work; she prided herself on her diligence. But replicating documents for a third time was a bit much to expect of anyone. The doors were kept locked at night, but if needed, anyone could sound the bell.

Two men could be seen through the small side window, but neither looked toward the door. They seemed to be holding a third person upright, but the shape was difficult to make out.

They rang the bell again without bothering to see if anyone was coming.

"Do be patient," Nettie yelled through the thick door. Mostly likely they couldn't hear her but that never stopped her from responding. Given the recent series of events, she did pause before opening the door. She would have to count on her SEC training and half-vampire strength should something go awry.

"Now see here, do stop ringing that bell." The last word vanished into the cold night air as she opened the door to find one still form lying on the stoop, but no sign of the men who moments before had been so insistently ringing the bell.

"Hello? Is anyone there?" She reached back into the morgue and grabbed a long, stout pole they kept there. She'd never had to use it on a living being but there was always a first for even the most horrific of events. "Good evening? Anyone about?" She stepped toward the body gingerly. It appeared dead to her, but there was some movement near it. Would rats have attacked so soon?

She heard the crunch of distant footsteps start running, two sets if her hearing was true. It could have been anyone, but she believed it was the two who brought her this poor person. Body dumps weren't terribly common, but not unheard of. Poor people who couldn't afford a burial and didn't want questions asked sometimes left people behind.

She tilted her head, listening as the footsteps went out of even her hearing range. Deciding they had left the area, she turned him over. Now how could they have thought a single person could move someone this large? Had she not been of her unique constitution, she would have been hard pressed to bring this poor body inside.

Alas, even turning him upright gave her no indication as to his appearance. It was male, and she thought under all of the clothing she could still detect a heartbeat, although it didn't sound right. Beyond that, she would be unable to tell more until she got him inside. Granted, the coroner's office was not designed for the living, but she certainly was not going to drag this poor soul around to the hospital entrance. Not to mention, they'd been closing their doors at night as of late.

Taking another look around to make sure there were no watchers, she grabbed the thick legs and tugged the man into the building. She apologized silently to the bundled man as his head thumped over the doorframe, but he didn't respond. Once she got him in, she shut the door and pulled him in front of one of the tables.

A cold feeling washed over her as she'd moved him. There was something *other* about him. She couldn't see much of him, not with all of the clothes wrapped around him, nor honestly could she smell him. That stopped her.

She could smell extremely well. In fact, she had trained herself to block out the everyday smell of most people. It was a habit borne after years of dealing with assaults on her nose.

Nevertheless, she smelled nothing. The clothes were shabby, but shockingly clean, almost sterilized clean. She grabbed one trailing sleeve and held it close to her face. A faint antiseptic odor trickled out. Plague rags.

Not the real ones. The clothing found on the victims of the Glouster Plague had been burned along with the bodies themselves. But these were the clothes of people on the edge of the plague—meaning the rest of humanity. It had been fashionable to get rid of all of the clothing one owned when the plague had struck. Poor houses took the clothing after the hospitals, backed in secret by the Society, had sterilized the fabric. The fear in the Society was that the rich were using the cast-off clothing to destroy the undesirables in London. The plague had hit fifty years ago, so why did this poor man's clothes look as if they had been discarded only months ago?

Dropping the sleeve, she looked again at the shape on her floor. Man shaped, but extremely bulky, with the mass of his weight in a broad upper torso. There was nothing to be done for it but to see who or what he was.

She first made certain the outer door was locked. It wouldn't do to have some badly timed passerby see her lift a man three times her size. Satisfied she was alone, she quickly lifted him onto an examination table. It groaned when she settled the weight on it, but the table held firm.

Her first instinct was that he was dead, regardless of what she thought she'd heard in his chest. The first patch of skin she uncovered was paler than the moon, thin and waxy, and thick veins glimmered in the lights. Yet she heard a heartbeat, but it was faint. She unwrapped more, freezing when she got to his neck. Two sets of clear puncture wounds sat there gaping on the pale white skin.

Her hands clenched on the wads of fabric. Was he a vampire victim? But the skin was like no living thing that she knew. Could a vampire be a vampire victim? Aside from the way in which most were reported to be made? Nettie appeared to be unique in her half-vampire status, but while she'd never met one, she had heard the morality plays of the curse of the vampires. Not to mention the more scientific version of them from the Society. Although they had yet to capture a full vampire, it was believed that vampirism was a disease spread from extreme contact with the blood.

A thrill went through her; might he have been involved in the turning of the queen? The limited information they'd received said that the vampires used in that grim process were drained completely. Maybe one had escaped?

There was nothing to be done for it except to continue the examination of the form before her. She would take careful notes to make sure to give Gaston enough information.

He was about fifty years old and clearly had lived a hard life. Looking at the broad hands she thought of the fisherman the other doctors had been working on when she came on shift. The man before her had hands of a fisherman.

Now, if the two had come in together, she might have believed it to be a ship gone down. But she hadn't heard of any lost ships. This one looked like he had been dead for a few years, odd heartbeat or no. His nails were long, cracked, and darkened—like ones belonging to a body that had been in the ground.

That answered the question: he was a vampire. But one who'd stayed in the ground for a few years? That was not in keeping with the Society's hypothesis of them.

It wouldn't be prudent to be negligent about all of the Society's views on the topic. Nettie knew for a fact that she was stronger than most people. Therefore, it would stand to reason that a full vampire, even one who had spent more time than usually required underground, would probably be much stronger than even herself. Trying to keep an eye on him, she looked about until she found two long strands of good chain.

Nettie took the chains and secured her new visitor. It wouldn't do to have him get up while she was trying to investigate him, after all.

The fact that he didn't even move during the chaining process was not a good sign. Or maybe it was—she was not sure she wanted to him to wake up. "Now see here, Mr. Vampire, if that's what you are, I have taken you in when your friends abandoned you. So do not think to bite me." After she tested the chains for steadfastness, she continued unwinding clothing from him. His torso was malformed, clearly an affliction from when he was alive, a disease perhaps.

The bones seemed to be at such an odd angle movement

would have been horrific for him. It was as if he had laid in a box somewhere and not fit in it properly.

Twisted body aside, and ignoring the gaping holes on his neck, he appeared to be perfectly fine.

"You have a message."

Nettie thought at first the body had spoken and so felt justified in leaping a foot back. Only to collide with the real speaker, another of the mysterious Runners. Or maybe the same one; she had no idea how to tell them apart. Perhaps there was only one and he magically flew across the world.

"You know, you would gain more friends if you didn't sneak up on them." Nettie grabbed the paper he held out then took another step backward. Fear was not common to her, but these Runners disturbed her.

"The message said to wait for a response."

If he had felt chastised by her response, he didn't show it. Perhaps that was why they bothered her so. They sounded human, but didn't interact properly.

With a scowl at the black-garbed figure, she ripped open the paper. Gaston's tiny, neat handwriting was clear as usual. He would present her idea to Ramsey, but he thought there was something else wrong. One of the other agents had been found murdered in Bath and he wanted to make sure she hadn't seen anything suspicious.

Nettie raised an eyebrow and looked at the odd, nearly dead vampire on the table in front of her. She had to admit, he was distinctly suspicious to say the least. There was not much else to the note beyond his arrival. Supposedly Gaston wanted her to send back information of any further events out of the ordinary she had discovered. As if being flung into a real or imagined future was not enough.

With a sigh at her mentor being more difficult than usual, she summed up the rest of the evening's events, and then also added a single line about the men who had vanished after leaving their vampire friend for her. She knew she would have to meet with Gaston tomorrow concerning all of this, but he clearly wanted something to tide him over until then. If it weren't that he absolutely hated leaving his mansion, he most like would have come out to interrogate her himself. Once he knew she had a vampire, he might find a way to do it anyway.

"This should be it. Now if you would be so kind as to use the door?" She unlocked the door, pulling it open only to find the black-clad shape had vanished again.

That was most disturbing. Clearly, she was going to have find out more about these so-called Runners, and someone, most likely her, was going to have to teach them a thing or two about manners. Mysterious was all well and good, but bad manners were completely uncalled for.

With a sigh, she shut and re-locked the door and turned back to her patient. Interesting. Coroners rarely had patients, but a dying, undead being would be probably the best one for one such as her.

He still hadn't moved, but his pulse was getting weaker. Pulling away the last of his clothing, she saw another thing distorting his body: a long thin ash wood stake pressed into his chest, but flattened by the tight wrap of clothing. Whoever tried to kill him clearly had hideous aim, or didn't believe the stories about vampires and a stake through the heart. The stake was a good five inches south of where his heart would be.

Now she was faced with a true dilemma. Should she pull out the stake, and maybe bring this vampire back to life? Or let it stay and let him go out on his own? She may be half-vampire herself, but she found from the Society tales she had read that she had little, if any, vested interest in her mother's people. For the most part, vampire-kind had little interaction with humans. They mostly stayed out of large cities and were little more than reclusive animals. Or so the works Nettie had read declared.

Now, if she saved him, Gaston, Ramsey, and perhaps even the highest rank of the Society, known only as Agent Zero, would be pleased. They had wanted a vampire to study, but there really didn't seem to be many in London, and they could never catch the few that were here. The ones that supposedly were brought in for the queen were captured from a small village in Transylvania. Of course, since no one in the palace was admitting the actions of the queen to anyone, there could be no confirmation.

The man before her had value to the Society. That was one point for taking the stake out; he also might be able to give her real-life answers to some of her questions. Would she ever succumb to blood lust? The idea of drinking another person's blood was positively vile, but what if as she grew older she had to do it? At twenty-five, she was still young, at least from what she had read of vampires. Was she immortal? Another tic in the column for taking the stake out. Nevertheless, if she did, he could attack her. She had no real understanding of the strength of a full-fledged vampire. The chains she had wrapped around him might be completely useless. Not to mention, she might not really want the answers to those questions. They might prove to be unsavory. Once she knew them, she couldn't go back to her blissful state of ignorance concerning her half-vampire nature.

She tapped her booted foot for a few moments, then reached forward and yanked the stake out. Curiously was going to be the death of her one day.

Hopefully, it wouldn't be today.

The tiny trickle of blood that pooled to the surface was disappointing. Not that she had expected or really wanted a gusher to form, but the trickle was anti-climactic to say the least. Not to mention she had also secretly thought that perhaps he would jump to his feet, or try to, once the stake killing him was withdrawn. Alas, he still looked exactly the same.

"Hello?" She pressed on his shoulder. Maybe it took vampires a few minutes to wake up. "It's okay. You can wake up now." She tried to make her voice sound as friendly as possible; there was no reason to tell him about the chains until she had to.

Absolutely nothing.

A few more pokes gave nothing in return aside from bruising where blood gathered under the skin. After debating the pros and cons of pulling the stake out, this outcome was certainly not what she would have expected.

"One would really think you'd recover faster." She felt his neck, avoiding the holes, and felt his pulse was faster. Still slow, but better. In the tales, giving blood would restore the vampire. While she was willing to remove the stake, that was as far as she went.

Which left her with a half-dead undead in the middle of her examination room.

Unchaining him from the heavier fixtures in the room, she

rolled him, table and all, into the cold storage. An invention from the Society, the coroners now had a freezing cold room in which to hold their bodies. The Society had secretly donated the technology involved through a number of inventors, but the outcome was wonderful.

And particularly useful in this case. Freezing wouldn't be good had her patient actually been alive, but being undead, he should be fine. And rendered harmless for the time being in case he did recover. The cold room was huge, easily holding the missing thirty-five missing bodies. It positively made the one she was wheeling in seem like a child.

"Now, do be a good vampire, and stay still. No getting up and wreaking havoc. I'm sure someone will be along for you shortly." Nettie didn't know whether the Runners would carry more than a missive. To be honest, considering the large size of the vampire before her, she couldn't imagine how a single person could carry him a block let alone all the way across town to Gaston's mansion.

Locking the cold room, she returned to replicating what she could of the previous night's files. To cover anything that would be of notice from her undead visitor, and keeping him off of the daily log, she said that two men had brought a body in, then came back and stole it before she could begin an autopsy.

A completely ridiculous story, but there was nothing to be done for it. She had too many things going on at the moment to think of a better one. There was no way to be certain that no one saw them come to her door.

She was halfway through them when for the third time that night a black-clad shape stood beside her. This time, there was no window rattling, but still no clear way of entrance either.

"Now see here, I asked you to use the …" Her voice dropped as she saw there were four Runners this time, carrying some sort of cot-like sling.

"The vampire." Not a question, not a request, just a simple statement.

Nettie folded her arms, narrowed her eyes, and sent forth her best scowl. They were not intimidating her, and she was tired of their boorish behavior. Alas, if they were cowed by her stance, they gave no indication.

"This is not over, you know." With a whirl of her skirts, the only thing the dratted things were good for, she marched over to the locked cold room door. She toyed with telling them she had forgotten the combination, but aside from resolving some of her pique at their behavior, it would really accomplish nothing.

"He is all yours. I do need the chain back." Although the chain had never been used that she had seen, tomorrow would probably be the day it was needed if they absconded with it.

The four silent figures flowed around her, lifting the vampire up as if he was nothing, and sliding him into their sling. They turned and paused in front of her.

"What, you can't slide through closed windows and doors with a passenger?"

When their only response was to continue standing there silently, she held the doors open for them. One of them carefully piled the chain exactly where it normally lay near the door. That a Runner knew where a never-used chain normally lay was more than a bit disturbing.

They vanished a moment later, not unlike the mysterious

person in brown from earlier that day. Perhaps he was a Runner in disguise? Letting those thoughts wander about in her head, she went back to her office.

The rest of the night went quickly, with the next shift coming in just as she finished two copies of the reports, and had secured the one back into Dr. Wilson's desk.

It was not until she was putting on her coat to leave that she realized her gloves were still on. Drat. There would be no way she could wait until she could visit Gaston in the morning to remove her gloves, yet she was loath to lose the little bit of dust she had managed to save.

She was simply going to have to roust Gaston from his bed and have him take the dust off her hands.

CHAPTER SIX

THE STARS WERE going her way. It was an unseasonably dry evening; the clouds of earlier had wandered off. She would be able to ride Lula Belle. Scurrying into the small garage, she quickly changed into her trousers and donned her riding apparel. No doubt, some drunks lying about on the streets would spread tales of a speeding demon—it seemed late-night rides never were treated as normal—but there was nothing to be done for it.

Securing her brass goggles, she kicked Lula Belle into gear and ventured into the night. The air carried a biting cold that even she could feel. She would be relieved to get to Gaston's warm mansion.

There were few people about, and the majority of those were huddled near the bases of buildings, trying to stay warm.

The mansion was dark, which was not too surprising, although she did often wonder if Gaston ever slept. Evidence indicating that he did was a bit disappointing.

Once she entered the gates, Nettie dismounted from Lula Belle, but she continued to roll her up as far as she could. There really was not anyone out and about in this part of town who would try to harm the steamcycle, but the motto of the Society was: be prepared for the most improbable of situations at all times.

The mansion carried an air of foreboding in the dark night, and even though she knew Gaston would never hurt her, she couldn't help but shiver. Rising her hand to knock, she bit back a scream as the door opened before her.

"You took long enough, you did." Gaston might have been sleeping mere moments before. He was dressed in bedclothes, but the look on his face was anything but sleepy. "Get inside before I catch a chill. We don't all have your physical temperament."

"You don't have to be so disagreeable. I have had a trying evening." Nettie allowed her pique to show as she stomped through the open door. Gaston was often curmudgeonly, but she was not in the mood to coddle him. "And why are the Runners so wretchedly rude?"

Gaston shut the door. "You are an odd one, Nettie Jones, of that you can be sure." He walked past her and led the way into the study. Of course, the one time she felt the dungeon might be called for and he chose the study instead. She let loose an audible sigh and followed him.

"Whatever are you sighing about? If you have something to say, be out with it." Gaston had a small fire going, one he had managed to block from view of the outside, and two cups of tea steaming in front of it. In the beginning of her association with the Society, his foreseeing had bothered her. Then she realized he was not really seeing the future; he simply had a powerful understanding of behavior.

"To begin with, don't you think the night's events warrant the dungeon?" She stayed standing. There was no reason to get seated if he was planning on picking up and moving underground. Of course, he was bad about not taking her suggestions, so most likely they would be staying in the study.

"I am far more comfortable here. The tea is here, the biscuits are here, and the fire is here." With that, he resumed his tea, picked up a biscuit, and watched the fire.

Nettie thought to retort, but held back when the reason for his mood struck her. He was not behaving at all like his normal self. His missive had mentioned that an agent had been murdered in Bath. She had been too wrapped up in her own issues to let it sink in at the time.

"I'm sorry; did you know the agent who was killed?" She removed her outerwear and took her seat before the fire.

"Not close, no. But I knew of him. We consulted on events together." He shook his head, still starring at the yellow and orange flames dancing before him. "But with McGrady missing and presumed dead, this is two in as many days. *Mon dieu*, I don't like it."

"Do you think they are related?" Nettie had intended to get the dust off her hands and head for her own bed as soon as possible, but it was unusual for Gaston to express his concerns.

"I don't know. This thing with the queen is nerve wracking, then the collision, the murders, and your series of events," he said while waving her missive to him. "I've an ill feeling that things are stirring that shouldn't be moving."

When he didn't add any more, Nettie decided he was done sharing. "I wanted to come tonight because of the dust."

He pulled his stare free of the fire. "Dust?" He shook his head trying to refocus; clearly he was extremely concerned and had forgotten her mention of the vanishing man and his dust.

"The man in brown who followed me left some dust, which

he and friends seemed to have come back and taken, but I have found more."

Gaston held her note up to his eyes, squinted, and then popped his spectacles on. "I don't see any mention about dust, or a vanishing man in brown. 'I was followed on the way to work.' That is the extent of it."

Nettie bit her lip, she had meant to have more information than that, but to be honest, there had been a lot of things happening. As quickly as she could, and with sufficient detail to appease her mentor, she filled him in on the events of the afternoon. "So that was when I found I still had a small sampling on the dust on my fingers," she finished, waving her gloved hands at him.

"I see." Gaston had been suspiciously quiet while she told her tale, very unlike him. It normally would take forever for her to tell him anything of interest since he questioned everything.

"Don't you think that's a bit odd? Shouldn't we investigate the dust?"

"Yes, on both counts. But it is more than odd. It is dangerously disturbing." Gaston rolled out of his chair and shuffled to his writing desk. He came back with a pile of papers.

"The agent who died this night sent me these over the last few weeks." He thrust the papers at her, and then resumed his seat and his analysis of the dancing flames.

Frowning, Nettie peeled off the first one. It was dated almost two months ago, and although the handwriting was difficult to read, she eventually pried out the words. "A mysterious man in brown has been seen around the station. He seems to be following me, but vanishes before I can approach him." Scanning the rest of the papers she saw repeats of this comment interspersed with information on a variety of topics and ongoing investigations.

"So he had been visited by the same man." She was not going to say it didn't disturb her, but at the same time, this was the reason she joined the Society, to solve mysteries and stop the evil doers. She never had one after her before. The chill of excitement was replaced by a trickle of fear.

"Nettie, he was being stalked. We didn't realize it at the time, but he was." Gaston leaned forward and stabbed one thick finger on the pile of papers. "I know that man in brown had something to do with his death."

"How did he die?" Part of her really didn't want to know, but she knew she needed to know.

"He was flattened. The other agents in Bath are trying to get as much information as they can from his body, but he was smashed like a gourd. As if he was dropped from a dirigible."

"In the middle of the night in Bath?"

"Exactly. There were no airships up tonight in Bath. Yet, he appeared in the middle of town, smashed beyond recognition."

Nettie stopped in mid sip of her tea. "Then how do they know it is him? It could be anyone."

Gaston didn't answer at first, but he did reach over, take a small flask from his side of the table, and pour a generous dollop into his teacup.

"I really was not going to tell you this yet. We usually don't inform agents until their fifth year, but there's nothing to be done for it." He took another long pull of his tea, and then set the cup down. "We have a way of identifying any agent, or other person of interest, no matter what condition the body."

She leaned forward; he certainly had her attention, although at the rate he had obviously been drinking it was hard to say she completely believed him.

"We have certain technologies that we've obtained and invented over the centuries. One of which plants a tiny tube in a person, under their skin. If we scan for particles, we can tell who that person is. All of our agents have them."

"What? How can such a thing exist? Not to mention I think that I would know if such a thing were done to me." She folded her arms and sat back in her seat. Something told her she was not going to like his answer.

"All agents go through a screening interview."

Nettie frowned. Why was he telling her things she knew? It had only been two years since she was recruited, after all. She fully recalled the week of screening up in Edinburgh.

"Now, what you don't know was that there was a second screening." His face fell and Nettie couldn't recall ever seeing him look so worried and at the same time sad. "During the time in Edinburgh, you, like all agents, were subjected to rigorous testing. Some of it was done while you were unconscious."

It was only the cold foreboding that something nasty was about to leave his lips that kept her from dropping her teacup. She had been raised better that that, but her hands still shook as she set the delicate cup on the table. "Go on."

"This isn't easy. No agent aside from a few high placed operatives, and the staff in Edinburgh, know this. But I think the time has come that you have more information." He pulled himself up and held her stare. "We test everyone for any type of Trojan horses. We have enemies that are far beyond anything you have heard of so far, enemies that aren't human." He raised a hand when she started to speak. "I can't add more to that yet. I simply can't. The risk is too great, but let it be said, we do not do it from unwarranted paranoia. Part of the process while the agent candidate is unconscious is to plant this small, alien device." He fussed around in a small box for a few moments, and then held up a narrow tube. Not more than half an inch long, it was no wider than the tip of a fine writing quill. Miniscule gears somehow seemed to be functioning inside.

Nettie's heart was in her throat as she reached for it. She had led a life of vagrancy, sent from home to church to commune to home her entire life. Settling in London had been her first adult idea made with no outside influence. Joining the Society had been her second. She had looked at Gaston as a father, one she never had. How could he have betrayed her like this?

The tube was heavier than it looked. Cold and hard, it sat in the palm of her hand. Her disappointment at Gaston and his actions warred with her curiosity. Curiosity, as usual, won. She spied one of Gaston's magnifying glasses and held the tube up. The tiny machine, for that was what it truly was, was fascinating. Gears no bigger that the tip of her fingernail whirled and clicked in their own tiny, perfect world.

"What does it do?"

"It does nothing harmful, I assure you. It allows us to track our agents to some extent, and identify their remains if need be. To be honest, they don't function well until the agent is deceased. But it is vital that any lost agents be found, since they could have been killed with important information on them. Being able to find them in a morgue of unnamed dead is vital."

"Or identifying one that no longer even looks human," Nettie added as she fingered the thin tube. The idea that the group she now devoted her life to had kept such secrets of what had been done to her—nay, to all agents—would have to be addressed later. Right now she was not sure how to deal with it. A thought sparked. "If you can find us, then why can't you find McGrady?" Handing him back the tube, she stopped short of asking him where it had been planted in her skin. She would guess her back, back of arms, back of legs, something not usually seen by her.

After Gaston put the tube in a small case, he set it in a shelf under the mantel of his fireplace. "It's not that simple if the agent is still alive. We do have technology in Edinburgh, Cardiff, and here that can pick up an agent's unique signature, but it isn't always clear. Not to mention when the agent is alive, his or her own life force interferes with tracking. And there is a good chance that McGrady was aware of the device and removed it."

"How could you know if he did? How would he have found out?"

"The device appears to remain operational and, as far as we can tell, is still in his possession. However, the readings we are receiving are from the bottom of the Atlantic Ocean."

CHAPTER SEVEN

NETTIE DECIDED IT had been safe to venture for some more tea, but Gaston's last comment made her regret that. She didn't choke, but swallowed hard. "You are saying there is an agent alive in the bottom of the ocean?"

"That can't be said with certainty. The system may be having problems, or there may be a third party involved whose impact we're only seeing the edge of, or, well, I suppose it could be an agent living at the bottom of the ocean. Although the signal isn't really at the bottom, but deep enough that he shouldn't be alive."

"Didn't the Americans come up with some submersibles? I read that their Society branch had made some excellent progress."

Gaston shook his head. "They have, but not enough for someone to stay under there any true time. Oh, I suppose for short periods, but this signal has been down there for over thirty-six hours. We didn't pick it up until the Bath lead activated the system to scan the dead agent."

Nettie rubbed her forehead with her fingertips. She usually was not one in need of large amounts of sleep, but the recent events had simply worn her down. "I think all of this will have to be dealt with later. I need some sleep." She set her teacup down, and then rose to get her outerwear.

"The dust?" Gaston's annoyance in those two words sounded more like his usual self.

"What? Oh, there I go again. I believe this should be done in the dungeon. I've no clue as to what it is made of, but it is quite fine."

Gaston nodded, then followed her to the heavy door and went through the elaborate procedure of unlocking the mechanism. His back blocked Nettie's ability to see all of the steps, which appeared to involve the moving of many levers and cables.

"Why are you keeping it locked when you're right outside in the next room?"

"Recent events indicate that there's a storm coming. I'm not sure if we've even seen the headwinds yet." With a jangle of keys, he unlocked a small lock in the center of the door and pushed the door open. Somehow, that final step was anticlimactic.

Nettie took the same seat she had yesterday, but waited until Gaston pulled out some equipment and a foot-long mirror.

"Very well," he said positioning the mirror in front of her on the desk. "Remove your glove over the glass and I will contain it."

Gently peeling back the glove, Nettie's heart leapt into her throat when at first it looked like there was nothing on her hand. An instant later she relaxed. It was all down near her fingertips. Obviously the riding around and other events of the evening had caused some settling.

"When I first found it on my hand, it was iridescent." Nettie gently tapped her fingers, one at a time, on the mirror. The dust was still a soft grey-green, but it didn't shimmer at all in the bright lights of the dungeon.

"It appears to be dormant now." Gaston seemed to be talking

more to himself than her as he carefully slid the contents of the mirror into a small sample container.

"Dormant as in it was alive? Have you seen this before?"

"No, no, I spoke wrongly," his accent came out heavier as he sealed the container. "I don't know if it was alive, and no, I have never seen it before. I simply meant whatever it was doing before, it is not doing now. But since we do know that it was previously glowing for some reason, I will take precautions until I can study it in the morning." Holding the container by the tips of his fingers, he opened one of the small, lead-lined safes in the room and sealed the dust inside.

Turning, he brought out one of the Society's machines, a thin wand, and waved it over Nettie, focusing on her hands.

"There now, no radiation. Whatever it was doing, it was not doing that."

Radiation had been discovered by the scientists in Edinburgh. They weren't ready to let the rest of the world in on the knowledge of it, since explaining how they discovered it would be problematic. But Nettie knew enough as a member of the Society to know she was grateful she hadn't been exposed to it.

A wave of fatigue washed over her and she almost slumped forward in her chair. "I had better be off. I can't seem to keep my eyes open."

Gaston leaned forward to catch her as her attempt to stand was met with failure.

"Easy, lass. Sit back down for a bit." His brown eyes were pinched with worry as he studied her face. "You don't look well at all."

He carefully checked her eyes, her glands, her forehead. "No fever, but your pulse is far too slow. That vampire didn't attack you, did it?"

"No, he never even woke up. The Runners came and got him, but he stayed asleep."

Gaston poured a glass of water and forced her to drink. "Can you pull back your scarf for me?"

"Gaston, I think I would have noticed if someone bit my throat." Nettie rolled her eyes, but she did what he asked. To be honest, she was a bit concerned at her condition as well.

"Nothing. There are no marks." He continued studying her, trying to find clues he might have missed. "There's nothing else that happened when he arrived, nothing beyond what you told me?"

"No, everything was as I said. I secured him with the chain—"

"You touched him?"

"Of course I did, how else could I have examined him? Or pulled out the stake?" Really, sometimes Gaston said the oddest things.

"You didn't tell me about a stake, nor about pulling it out." He moved closer, pulling the top of her collar away from her neck, checking for anything he missed.

"Whatever are you nattering on about? I am certain I told you about the stake and the examination. The stake was not in the heart, but a few inches below it. He was dying, again, very slowly because of the ash wood. But he didn't even respond when I pulled it out. I ended up putting him in cold storage."

"He got you somewhere," Gaston muttered as he poked around. "Take off your other glove and pull back both sleeves, please."

"This is absurd. Can a half-vampire even be attacked by a vampire?" She fumed but removed her glove. The buttons on the left sleeve were mis-buttoned, skipping the last two entirely. How odd.

"Oh dear." She didn't pass out, or scream, but there, marking her flesh, were two quickly healing puncture marks. Within hours, they probably wouldn't even be visible.

"What does this mean?" Nettie forced her voice not to shake as she stared at the marks. One comforting thought was that even damage done by a full vampire healed with her normal swiftness.

"It means we have a powerful vampire playing games with us." Gaston pulled her sleeve back in place, gently buttoning the long sleeve. "I'd say he got a kick of energy from your blood."

"How could I not have known?" She still was not able to disassociate herself from it. She prided herself on her ability to notice things. And she admitted she believed she would have immunity to the mythological powers of a full vampire. Clearly, she was deluding herself.

"Now, don't you get that look. We all thought you might be immune to their powers, and you might still be to a younger vampire. I'd say you were set up." His eyes grew round. "How long ago did the Runners appear at your work?"

"About three hours ago now. You don't think that he could have taken them? Four fully trained Runners?" That was almost more disturbing than the fact she had obviously been helpless while an unknown vampire hypnotized her and took blood. A shiver went through her. Since joining the Society, she'd felt safe—between her skills and her heritage, little could touch her. Her lack of prior contact with a full vampire had shown how misplaced that confidence was. She took a deep breath to steady her nerves, and then shoved the fact that he could have killed her, had he wished, far back in her mind.

"I don't know, but had someone asked me an hour ago could you be fully hypnotized by a vampire, I would have said no. The Runners wouldn't have been expecting him to move."

He went to the Mudger and got the gears in back moving. They seemed impossibly slow. Finally, the brown and white screen showed an image.

A small, mousy man appeared on the screen. If he was surprised at being called at such an unnatural hour of the evening, he gave no sign. "Agent Gaston Bessette, to what do I owe this call?"

"Clarkson, do you have intelligence on the Runners that were dispatched to Agent Jones' work?"

Gaston's agitation was affecting Nettie; her fatigue was wearing off as concern and fear took over. Had she consigned those Runners to their deaths by giving them a foe they were unprepared for?

The small man moved out of the view of the screen, coming back a few tense minutes later. "Not yet. They haven't checked in, nor has the vampire been documented. But they were taking him to the base in Cardiff. Considering their mode of travel, they should still be en route."

"Damn it, they may be in trouble." He raised a hand to hold off Clarkson's comment. "Yes, *they* may be in trouble. The vampire they have isn't injured and dormant. He might have been injured originally, but he feasted on Agent Jones, and who knows what half-vampire blood would have done to him?"

"Oh. Oh, dear." Clarkson pushed his thick spectacles further up his nose even though Nettie couldn't see that they had slipped down at all. "That's not good." He looked at a screen or board beyond the view of the Mudger. "The only thing out there that might help would be the support squad A-12. Although having them find Runners might be difficult."

"We don't have a choice. And I'd wake Agent Ramsey and Agent Scot. This could be ugly indeed if it was deliberately planned."

Nettie's heart sank. Planned? As in someone knew she was part of the Society and that she would call Runners? Her value as an agent held only as long as she was unknown. What would happen to her if she no longer operated in secret? Would she have to move to a distant land? Or even worse, become a subject of study because of her unique condition? Locked away in a dungeon in Edinburgh, never seeing the light of day?

"You're letting it get away from you again aren't you?"

Gaston's words were so close to where her mind was that Nettie almost fell off her chair. Someday, she really was going to find out if Gaston was clairvoyant or not.

"I'm sure I don't know what you're talking about." She tried to give him a haughty sniff but failed.

"Yes you do. You're playing worst case again. Didn't we break you of that in training?"

Nettie looked down at the table, and then finally met his eyes. "Yes, you did. But you have to admit this is unique."

He didn't even have to say anything, simply arched one brow.

"Okay, so that could be said of everything the Society deals with and if I can't handle this, I shouldn't have joined in the first place. But if I'm compromised, what good am I to the Society?"

Gaston pulled back a step. "You're having an internal tug of war because you are afraid you'd be kicked out of the Society?" The booming laugh that followed was almost terrifying in its rarity. "That is a new one. Trust me, plenty hope to leave, but it's not easy. Nor does it happen against an agent's will."

"But what if they know who I am?"

His laughter, while annoying, was reassuring as well. He certainly wouldn't be giving a rare laughter display if things were as she feared they might be.

"Then you'd best make sure we find out who they are and make sure they can't use that information against you." The laughter had fled and the cold killer that lurked inside the round man showed. He slid a small gun across the table. Nettie honestly hadn't seen many guns, aside from her training and testing up in Edinburgh. But this one seemed to have small gears on its side and top.

"You scored well on your markswoman tests and I believe it's time you have a dissembler of your own. Don't let it out of your control, and never let anyone outside of the Society get their hands on it. This is not like the military guns you trained on."

Nettie pulled it closer. The tiny brass gears made a soft almost soothing sound. She was not any more squeamish about firearms than she was about dead, and should be dead, bodies. It was just that no one in London aside from the military, a few hunters, and Society members even had them.

"Is there a place I can practice with it?"

"You are in luck. One floor below this one is a firing range. You never needed to see it so you never did." He answered her question before she voiced it. "But while I think you are looking better, I believe you will avail yourself of one of the guest chambers here tonight."

It was not even a suggestion, but a command. Not that Nettie thought it was a bad idea, but she did so hate giving in on things. Even when they made sense.

"But what will Mrs. Cruddle think?"

Gaston was already herding her up the stairs and down the hall. "You actually have been in your bed for the last two hours. Mrs. Cruddle heard you come in. You even stubbed a toe and let out a very unladylike swear word. Which Mrs. Cruddle was not surprised to hear since she does believe you are a bit odd."

"How…" Nettie found herself standing in the doorway of a spacious guest room.

"You think I haven't been doing this a long time? I knew something was wrong and feared we might have to keep you out. I sent another undercover agent over as soon as you arrived." He turned and started to go down the hall. "Now go to sleep."

Nettie contemplated following him and demanding that she be allowed to go home. But to be honest, she was so tired she could barely keep from tumbling fully clothed into the grand four-poster bed. Her options were fighting with Gaston for argument's sake, a fight she knew he would win anyway, or getting some much-needed sleep. As usual for her, logic overruled emotion.

She found a pleasant surprise when she opened the antique wardrobe: an assortment of brand new sleeping garments of assorted sizes. Clearly, Gaston used this room for his agents on a regular basis.

After changing, she found some paper and a pen and crawled into bed. She really should write down exactly what that vampire looked like. He was one tab she would be paying.

She had only two lines down when her eyes won the battle and sleep overtook her.

GASTON WAITED UNTIL he felt Nettie would have certainly fallen asleep—it wouldn't do to have her up and running about with what he needed to do next. She was easily one of his best up-and-coming agents, but there were some things none of the agents knew. Like the real nature of the Runners.

The Society had been in place since the late 1500s, always hidden from the cultures around it, but always working to keep them safe from things far beyond their ken. The Runners had come along some time in the early 1600s. At first, they had been an element to be investigated, and they managed to elude capture or even significant information gathering for a good twenty years. It had been Agent Zero, the current one, who had finally caught one. Agent Zero's true nature and real age was a secret guarded even deeper than the Runners.

What the agents knew as the Runners were, in fact, not from any land known to man. Not even a planet known to man. They were the surviving crew of an ether-faring ship that had crashed in the Atlantic. Eons before, they had made contact with the citizens of the now-lost world of Atlantis. When that world had been lost, they sent forth a ship to reestablish communications.

The world from whence the ether-faring ship had come had

begun to decline, hence their looking toward their distant friends, the Atlantians, for help. The ship made it to Earth, but only as far as the middle of the Atlantic. Failing to find both the land and the people they were counting on, the ship crashed into the ocean. Out of the four hundred who had made the trip, less than seventy-five survived.

The survivors stayed on the edges of society, trying to find clues as to what had happened to the far-advanced Atlantians, and the only technology that might get them back home.

Slowly over the years, the Society gathered enough information about the ethermen to build an interest. Once the information was relayed to Agent Zero, he convinced the Runners to come work with the Society. They were perfect at moving through ether, unlike anything human. Or anything alive. The Runners were mechanical men, functioning at a level so far beyond even the Society, that they had no way of getting home. They had lost their primary conductor in the crash, so their functioning was simplistic even as they themselves were far beyond anything known even today.

The fact that four of them might have been overwhelmed by a vampire was a truly terrifying thought.

Gaston made his way back into the dungeon and cranked the gears on the Mudger again. Agent Zero would be rousted by now, and there was much for them to plan.

CHAPTER EIGHT

E VEN CRUMPLED OVER a dry pen and paper, Nettie woke feeling surprisingly refreshed. Until she happened upon the almost completely healed bite marks marring her pale wrist. The pen snapped in her hand as she glared at her arm.

Damn it. She counted on her abilities and skills to be an asset to the Society, not a hindrance to be watched over. She would find that vampire and shove that stake back in. Properly this time, with no room for mistake. She had a photographic memory; she would remember what he looked like for a long time.

Quickly disposing of the evidence of her mangled writings, she pulled out new pen, paper, and ink and made a second attempt. The details were vividly clear, but she wished she had taken better notice of the men who dropped him off. There was little chance they weren't involved in this caper to some extent.

Satisfied that the sketches were sufficient, she did three, looking at the vampire from above and two angles as if he were an example in an anatomy book. She added what new details she could recall and gathered her papers. With any luck, he *would* be nothing more than an example in a book before the year was over.

Donning her clothing from the night before—at least she

should have time to run to the boarding house and change before she was needed anywhere—she went into the hall.

She had been in Gaston's home many times since she had joined the Society, although, the private rooms were new to her. This wing alone looked to have at least six more rooms on this floor. If all were as large and expansive as the one she spent the night in, there was clearly a huge amount of space here. And this was only one wing.

She allowed herself to wander slowly down the hallway that led toward the parlor. The décor was luscious, with pieces from centuries past intermingled with some of the recent Egyptian finds. Far older and far newer than the rest. It must be amazing to live in such a place. Like living in a museum every day.

With a sigh, she came into the empty parlor.

She hadn't expected much, but Gaston probably didn't have guests that often. He could at least be there waiting. Even as the thought hit, she brushed it off. Most likely, Gaston stayed up the entire night, doing things far beyond her knowledge in trying to find the missing Runners.

A pang of guilt hit her. She had been awake for almost an hour and hadn't spent one thought for those poor, lost Runners. Granted, they were rude beyond belief, but they didn't deserve to be slaughtered by a vampire that she had been responsible for bringing back. She allowed the sorrow and guilt to swarm her for a full sixty seconds, and then shook it off. One thing her scattered raising had taught her, feeling sorry for oneself or feeling guilty didn't help anyone or anything. Her efforts would best be spent on finding the Runners and tracking the vicious beast responsible for it all.

The teapot in the sitting room was still quite warm under its cozy, so she helped herself to some tea.

She was finishing her tea, thinking it must be time to head for home, when a ruckus took place outside the front door. At least it sounded like the front door; it could have been anywhere in the park-like front grounds.

A large steam car was winding its way slowly up the narrow path toward the door. The path was spacious for a coach and four, but grossly overwhelmed by the rounded machine waddling down its path.

The vehicle was like Lula Belle in that it was clearly running purely on steam, but unlike her beloved bike, it obviously had the ability to run in the rain since the normal London drizzle didn't appear to be slowing it down. It squatted on eight wheels, sets of two at each corner. Short, round, but at the same time powerful, it reminded her of nothing less than Gaston in mechanical form. The giggle she let escape caused Gaston himself to pop out from where he was hidden as he directed the lumbering monstrosity up the path.

"There you are. Excellent timing. Your things are here," he tossed over his shoulder then went back to encouraging the madcap driver to creep even closer up the narrowing path. Nettie predicted only a few feet further and the bricks guarding the roses would be in serious jeopardy.

"My things are here.... What things?" Certainly, she would have remembered had he said anything about supplies coming in for her? Not to mention she didn't recall requesting any supplies.

"Your belongings. Arrangements have been made. Mrs. Cruddle is quite happy with a new tenant who keeps normal hours and is paid up in advance for the next six months." He finally motioned the vehicle to stop. It was a truck of sorts, and a nondescript driver bounced out and flipped open a back gate.

Nettie looked down at her clothing. Yes, she still wore what she had on the night before. No days had been lost where plans could have been made that she would have forgotten.

"I have no idea what you are talking about, Gaston. My lease with Mrs. Cruddle was unbreakable…" Her words dropped off as the nondescript man brought out her luggage and began stacking it on the porch. Those were her bags, there was no question of that. But whoever packed them?

"As I stated, Mrs. Cruddle is quite as happy right now as she has ever been. She never did approve of you. Right now, she thinks her new boarder is the saint she always wished for. And will continue to do so for six months."

"What happens then? Or don't I want to know?" Nettie desperately wanted another cup of tea, but couldn't be so rude as to leave while they were out in the rain moving her belongings. Even if she still had no idea why they were moving her belongings. Or where. Clearly, they were coming here for now, but where were they going to end up? Had Gaston decided she had been too far compromised and was moving her on? A knot of uncertainty built in her stomach. Being part of the Society, particularly the London branch, meant the world to her.

"In six months, her perfect boarder moves out of town suddenly. But she will have forgotten you by then, which is worth paying six months board for. Now, are you going to help move these in, or do you really prefer soggy belongings?" As if listening to him, the rain went from drizzle to drops, and increasingly heavy drops at that.

Realizing the futility of getting to the bottom of the situation at the moment, Nettie marched over and began bringing in her worldly belongings. The full rainstorm was nice enough to wait until everything was in and the lumbering steam truck sent down the path before completely opening up.

Nestled in the sitting room, tea in hand, and surrounded by everything she owned in the world, Nettie tried again. "So where am I to live then?"

"Here, of course. I told you that." Gaston frowned, then an eyebrow quirked up. "I did, didn't I? Tell you that you would be living here?"

"No. I went to bed last night living in Mrs. Cruddle's boarding house down on Francis Street." She lifted her own eyebrow to accent her words as she sipped more tea.

"Oh, I do apologize, *ma chère*. Many things happened last night, one of which is that I am now running a boarding house."

Nettie barely contained her tea. Gaston was not a complete curmudgeon, but he certainly was not someone who should be running a house of boarding tenants. Not that Mrs. Cruddle had been a good candidate for that either, come to think of it. But she did it for the money, and the last thing Gaston needed was money.

"I should clarify—I am running a boarding house for agents. We have decided that the time for keeping most agents separate from each other is past. Within the larger cities, we will be creating boarding houses or places of common employment to keep our agents together. There is safety in numbers, and we need to combine resources."

He bounced to his feet and topped off her tea. "You are my first boarder. If you liked it, you may have the room you stayed in last night. Or any of the others in the wing. Although right now you are the only one, that will be the women's wing."

His round face grew pensive as he returned to his seat. "I will have to hire at least an assistant or two for Cook, as he will not be pleased with the change. Finding vetted cooks is not an easy task."

Nettie shook her head with a laugh. "I had been wondering what it must be like to live in such a place. Apparently, the universe has interesting ways of answering questions."

"Pah, the universe had nothing to do with it. It was all me. You were the easiest agent to get out, and to be honest, the one we most needed to move right now. I will be officially telling people that increased costs have forced me to take in boarders. Agent Lisselle Wilding will be moving in within a few days to avoid talk. You recall her, don't you?"

An older agent, thin and tiny with short, steel grey hair and an intense, ice blue stare, popped into mind. She was like a fox, tiny but fierce, and diligent. "Yes, I do. She will make an excellent housemate."

"We'll see about that," Gaston said with a queer look. There was something there he was not going to share. "But she'll be a help with the situation, and having another woman, especially one of a certain age, will keep tongues from wagging."

Nettie knew Gaston well enough to know he didn't care about impropriety; the rest of London could fall off the face of the Earth for all he cared. Lisselle was coming down from York for other reasons.

Reasons she knew she wouldn't get out of him any time soon. But there were other, more urgent issues to which she did need answers.

"Have they found the Runners?"

Gaston's face sobered. "Not yet. The Cardiff office tracked back to Bath and found nothing. They would have gone through Bath on their travels, but the Bath office never picked them up."

"Can we go after them? I have drawings now that can be handed out."

Gaston was shaking his head even as he took the pages. "Alas, no. You need to stay away from him for now. Cardiff has quite a large Society contingent without your help. I will show them these via the Mudger."

"You don't trust me around the vampire." Nettie stated it as fact. She knew, no matter how much she protested that the vampire wouldn't hold sway over her, Gaston wouldn't believe it. To be honest, neither would she. The fact she had been glamoured once was a cold thing, lying hard in her stomach.

"*Non*, and by the look on your face, neither do you. It's not a bad thing, nor speaking ill of your strength. *Ma chere*, we've no idea which vampire attacked you, and until that time arises, you are to stay clear of the search for him and the missing Runners."

Nettie slumped back in her chair. Even though those were the exact thoughts she herself had ventured, she still didn't like having to stay out of things.

"I do have some interesting information about that dust of yours."

She perked back up. She would gladly trade the vampire issue for her mysterious green dust. Or rather, the person or persons who left it.

"Well, what did you find?" she finally prompted when he didn't answer soon enough for her.

"Easy there, *mon petit chou*." He got to his feet, taking his cup and the teapot with him. "I thought perhaps it might be better for you to see it with me. This is now your place of study as well."

She hadn't thought of that. "The entire dungeon?"

"Not yet," he said. "I've created a small laboratory for you to call your own. It uses some of the items from the dungeon, but I can't allow unfettered access. For your own safety, after all."

She sighed, but smiled anyway. Too much to hope for after only two years in the Society, but worth a try.

Her own laboratory sounded promising. She tried to use the one at work, but it was so primitive that she usually ended up coming to Gaston anyway. Having her own equipment would allow her some freedom in her exploration.

Gaston led her down the hallway to the dungeon, but a small wooden door stood open to the right of the huge dungeon door. At first, she pulled back. Had he just created this door? She couldn't recall any other doors in the stone hallway, yet there were three others now besides this one. She knew Gaston had resources far beyond what she saw, but creating rooms?

She folded her arms and stared down at the additional doors. When she mentally pushed hard, she realized they had always been there, but they hadn't been noticed.

"You put a glamour machine on doors?" She still hadn't budged and Gaston had to come back into the hallway to address her question.

"That makes it sound so trivial. There was a reason, I assure you."

Nettie didn't move, just tilted her head in prompt for the answer.

"Okay, if you really must know, it was originally done by the previous owner. She thought the dungeon looked more imposing without the extra doors."

"Wait, so this house was owned by a Society member before you?"

"It was built by a Society member in 1708. It will always be owned by a member of the Society, or it will be destroyed." He turned to go back into the small room and this time Nettie followed. She wanted to ask how it would be destroyed, but decided that sometimes her curiosity needed to not be indulged.

It was not a huge room, but well appointed. State-of-the-art examining equipment sat awaiting her use on one long wall. A fully equipped desk stocked with parchment and ink lined the other.

Most of the machines were clearly designed, their purpose easy to grasp.

One was definitely unlike anything she had ever seen before. Approximately one meter tall, it looked sort of like a microscope, except that on the top a series of gears and levers whirled silently. In the front, a slide had already been placed. A slide with a familiar looking dust trapped between the glass pieces.

"What is this and what have you found about my dust?" She rushed forward, barely stopping herself from pressing every button and lever.

"Ah, you're showing commendable restraint. I had feared you might take it apart in front of me."

Nettie scowled. When she had been in the testing session before she was offered a position in the Society, she had taken apart three of the testing machines. But it was hardly her fault that they left her alone with unknown machines for almost a full hour. And she did put them back together once she understood what they did.

"As I recall, they all worked better once I put them back together."

"Yes, and you gave our engineers nightmares for weeks. But I wouldn't recommend taking this one apart. It's a Spectra Graph Analytic Computator. As for what it does, it breaks down anything you put into it into the smallest components known to the Society." He leaned forward and tapped the side. "And it has come out with some interesting analysis of your dust."

Nettie looked where he had tapped and saw that a typed sheet had been spit out. The analysis was mostly chemical; luckily she still recalled her chemistry from university. Common dirt seemed to be the majority of what was there, along with oil from her fingers, and the components of the fabric of her gloves. Then the sheet started printing an entire different language.

"I don't know what this is." She frowned and handed the sheet to Gaston. Clearly he had already seen it.

"Ah, neither do we." His grin was larger than the grins found in an opium den.

"I don't know why you're so happy. If we don't know what it is...?"

"Then it is something outside of this world," he finished for her. Although that hadn't been how she would have ended the sentence. Nor would she have sounded so jovial about it.

"Something not of this world? I assure you, I saw someone very real." Maybe the machine did need to be taken apart and recalibrated.

"Oh, I've no doubt of that. There are things that aren't terrestrial in origin. Things far beyond our small world."

Nettie tested the chair placed in front of the SGAC machine with a thud. Gaston's smile was still disturbingly wide, but he was not kidding. He believed in people, or things, from other worlds.

"Isn't it a bit of a step to attribute an unidentified molecule or two to something from another world?" Her voice sounded distant even to her own ears.

"Yes, very good. You should question it all. And you would be right; simply stating that anything that was unidentifiable belongs to another world would be unconscionable. There is this." He pulled out another slide marked example AZ, and replaced the dust slide with it under the contraption's lens. "This is from our files, something I was not going to share with you yet, but with this find of yours I think we must."

The slide bore no similarity to hers. At least it didn't at first glance.

Carefully, Nettie adjusted the power of examination, then after a false selection or two, requested a data output.

Silently, she held the two reports up to each other. There was one element, one of the unknown ones, that was the same in both slides. "What is this? And if we already had it on file, why are you insisting it's from another planet?"

"Ah, my dear, hold on to your underskirts, because your world is going to get a lot larger." Gaston pulled her around to face him, and then kept his hands on the arms of her chair. "That element, that unknown bit of mystery, is what we have code named Star Stuff. Not a great code name, mind you, but far better than its real name. We know that first slide came from beings not of this world."

"But how—"

"There are many things beyond your knowledge at this point, and this was to be one of them. Those beings we call Runners? They aren't human, nor technically living. They are mechanical men from a world far from here."

Nettie's mind shut down. Her greatest ally, the one thing that had never let her down no matter what the situation, and it deserted her in her time of need. Finally, after a hard shake of her head, thoughts began to burble back to the surface.

"I was actually in the presence of mechanical men? Mechanical men from another world? How exciting." She knew something had been disturbing about those Runners. They hadn't seemed human for a good reason; they weren't. The thought made her forgive them immediately for their perceived rude behavior.

"How long have they been here? The Runners have been part of the Society for decades, have they always been these machine men? What do they look like? Do you think the man following me was one of them? Maybe a Runner gone rogue?" She thought about her encounter with the being in brown. "They can't disappear into thin air can they? They appeared to do that, and so did the man following me."

Gaston's rumbling laughter was infectious. "I knew you'd be able to handle this, Jones. I can leave the history of the Runners in your room for tonight's reading, but I don't think the person who left this dust is a Runner. The Runners aren't biological. As I said, they are strictly machine. More advanced than anything our species will likely ever see, but machine. However, there was a biological component to the Star Stuff molecule."

Nettie looked closely at the two sheets again. She hadn't noticed it. It was subtle, but there it was. A marker of biological life, similar to her own, but unmistakably different.

"We have found living beings from a different planet." The implication was enormous, yet Nettie couldn't think of what else to say.

"Aye, *chère*, we have. Now we need to know why they are here."

CHAPTER NINE

B Y THE TIME Nettie left for work it was dry enough for Lula
Belle.

After getting her gear on, she decided to take the long way to
work, the long way involving the pattern she'd followed the
previous day. Alas, the brown clad man didn't follow her. She did
see the old washerwoman, watching her again with narrowed
eyes. She would have seen the attackers taking the vial of dust.
But the woman clearly thought Nettie was crazy and stayed far
enough away that she couldn't ask any questions.

The daytime doctors were gone by the time she got to work.
In fact, no one was around but Rebecca.

"Dr. Wilson was not surprised when he saw the files were
there, so we know he didn't take them. It must have been Lord
Melbourne's man." Rebecca flitted up as soon as Nettie came in.

For the briefest of moments, Nettie couldn't recall what her
friend was talking about. Then she remembered the missing
bodies and the vanishing reports.

Nettie had joined the Society to help her country, to get to
explore new frontiers, and because she loved being right in the
middle of things. But the last few days were proving to be
adventuresome, a little more so than she would like, in some
cases. She'd checked the fang marks on her wrist this morning,

but they were clear and healed. Unfortunately, she couldn't say the same about her mind.

"Ah yes, the bodies." Nettie walked into her office with Rebecca trailing behind. "Have we found out anything more?" That was another thing she would hold that vampire responsible for. She had intended to take home and study the copies of the files she had made. Obviously, the thought had fled her mind during whatever glamour the man had used on her.

"Nettie? Are you okay?" Rebecca's hand on her shoulder brought her back.

"I'm fine. Why ever do you ask?" Looking down at another shattered pen, she had her answer. "Drat."

"You do go through a lot of those, don't you?"

"Nervous habit." She released the crumbled bits into the waste receptacle. "I'm a bit out of sorts. Made a move today." She hadn't planned on telling Rebecca about her move yet, but as her best friend, she really should know. Not to mention she needed something to distract her. She couldn't very well tell Rebecca that thoughts of a vampire attack, here in their workplace, had led to the early demise of the writing implement.

"Old Crumble let you out of your agreement?" Rebecca poured tea for both of them, and then settled in the chair across from the desk.

"Yes, she did. I was able to find another boarder. I found this amazing house up on Marsham Street. It was a wonderful opportunity, and I won't have to deal with that witch anymore."

"Oh, Nettie, that is wonderful. I may even come pay a visit on you." Rebecca used to visit her at her old place, but six months ago, when she had to take the room at Crumble's boarding house,

Rebecca had drawn the line. She got as far as the steps, saw Mrs. Crumble in the front room, shuddered, and left. She claimed a sudden cold had struck, but she was fine the next day. And she never went back to the boarding house.

Hmmm, Nettie made a note to see if Gaston had researched Crumble. It was appearing more and more that Rebecca was indeed a clairvoyant. If so, perhaps she had picked up on something from Crumble on a subconscious level.

"I would love to have you over." Nettie looked around the empty offices to make sure they were truly empty. "Have we found anything else about the bodies?" She didn't think so. Gaston had been unhappy about that, but the Society had no information on them either. But the suspicion was that Melbourne might be acting on his own. Or someone in his house was.

"No. There was not much I could do," Rebecca said. "I can't walk up to the House and ask his lordship directly." An unusual frown crossed her face.

Nettie studied her friend, noticing for the first time since she came in that faint lines worried the edges of her eyes and mouth, and the skin under her eyes was a dusky color.

"Are you all right?"

"Of course I am." But the snappish retort proved otherwise. Even Rebecca realized that and gave a small laugh. "I am sorry," she said and rubbed her eyes. "I didn't sleep well last night. Kept thinking of that odd vision I had, missing bodies, and most disturbing of all, someone was following me in the dark."

The vision, which Nettie knew of had been far too real to be a mere vision, and the missing bodies, she could understand. The man following her disturbed her.

"A man? Do you recall anything of him?" A chill had run up her back at her friend's words. Two men had accosted her recently—had they also been after her friend? She hadn't tied in her attacker of the two nights before with anything, believing him to have been an opportunistic failure. But had she been too hasty in that assessment? Had it been more of a master plan that was now drawing her friend in?

Rebecca seemed to calm as she sipped the tea, but still shook her head. "No. Just that he terrified me. He was all in black. I couldn't see anything, not his face, nothing. He didn't do anything, but he kept following. Watching me." She fluttered one hand dismissively. "It's foolish. After all, the man was not doing anything to me."

"But he scared you." It was not a question; the truth of it was clear on Rebecca's face.

"Yes. Yes, he did." She stared into her teacup for a few moments. "I forgot to tell you, I also got an odd invitation. A group of teachers is forming a brain trust of working women in the intellectual fields. They invited me to interview with them."

Nettie smiled, as would be expected by such news, but she knew what it really meant. The Society was considering Rebecca. Yesterday, Nettie had wanted nothing more. Having her best friend be able to know of her exploits and abilities was something she truly wanted. Now, it seemed like a selfish wish.

"That's wonderful, but you don't have to go, you know."

"What? Of course I will go, this is a marvelous opportunity." Her face stilled. "They didn't call on you as well? I would have thought..." Her voice trailed off.

"No, alas, I must not have been top grade for them." Her friend was so excited, and who was she to stand in her way? She would have seriously damaged anyone who tried to stop her from joining the Society, once she knew what it was.

They chatted on for a bit about local gossip. Rebecca was clearly excited about her upcoming interview, but at the same time felt bad relishing it in front of the perceived slight to Nettie. Finally, she gathered her things and left for the evening, leaving Nettie to prowl the rooms, looking for any signs of the recent misdeeds.

Bodies missing, aliens following her, vampires overpowering her. Hopefully, the Runners would be found soon. Simply because they were not biological beings didn't mean they didn't deserve concern.

The night passed slowly, and for once, Nettie regretted spending it at work. It seemed as if there were so many other more important things outside of her small office.

COMING HOME THAT evening proved to be as uneventful as the shift at work had been, even if the excitement of actually being able to ride Lula Belle home did perk things up a bit.

She knew she shouldn't detour, being well past time for proper ladies to be out, but she couldn't help but want to drive by Buckingham Palace. Besides, she'd never thought about being proper before.

In all of the events of the last few days, she'd almost forgotten about the current status of the queen. Although he hadn't said anything, she knew Gaston and the Society would not have been so careless in thought. There was an extremely good chance that the ruler of the most powerful empire in the world was now a walking undead.

The palace looked disappointingly normal. Torches at all the usual spots, guards standing at attention. She didn't know what she had expected, but she thought if the Queen of England had been turned into a vampire, something should show evidence of that.

She coasted her bike down a dark alley, peering out enough to see the front of the palace.

A rustling behind her, almost quieter than a mouse, caught her attention. She froze, letting the assailant think she was unaware. The smell hit her now, stale and unwashed, like a body left rotting in a field for a day or two in the height of summer.

She ducked her left shoulder down and spun as the man's hand reached toward her.

He stumbled back at her move, his red eyes glowing, but unfocused. He had the motor skills of a nine-month-old child. Only the unnatural silence of his kind kept him from making more noise.

A newly made undead.

He watched her carefully as a starving man would a mirage dinner. Her heart went out briefly to whoever he had been before he was turned, and then she punched him hard enough to snap his neck had he been alive. He folded to the ground, out for the moment at least.

Clearly, her expedition to the palace had not been without some reward. Gaston had wanted to pull in another vampire to see what he or she knew. Of course as new as this one was, he probably wouldn't know much. But she couldn't leave him here to attack some innocent passerby.

She pulled the fragrant man across her bike, securing him as best she could, then trundled her way back to her new home.

Luckily, Gaston's mansion wasn't a long trip; she almost lost her unconscious passenger three different times. She was about ready to leave the vampire by the side of the road by the time she turned the corner onto Gaston's lane.

Unlike most of her trips to his home this late, all of the lights and outside torches were merrily blazing away.

She was trying to maneuver her vampire off the bike near the front door when the wide doors swung open and a slender, dark haired man of no more than twenty years scurried out.

"Good eve, Dr. Jones. Please allow me to get that for you." His accent was clipped, and Nettie couldn't quite place the dialect. She was about to wave him off—clearly a human of his size wouldn't be able to bring in a full-grown vampire—when a series of whirls and clicks started behind him. He stepped aside and a rolling bed came purring out the front door. Brass and copper gears and wheels filled the bottom, far too complicated for her to figure out from a distance.

But, however they worked, the bed moved at the man's slightest pressure.

"There you go. Master Gaston and guest are awaiting your arrival. I shall secure this."

He was exceedingly gracious, but Nettie had the distinct feeling she'd been dismissed.

"I do hate to be impolite, but I don't believe I've met you

before." She flashed her broadest smile and held out her hand.

"Ah, yes." He smiled briefly, shook her hand briefly, then went back to directing the floating bed next to her vampire. "I am the master's new manservant. You may call me Damon."

Manservant? Gaston had mentioned that he would need more help, but surely he couldn't have found vetted housemen and cooks in a single day?

Still pondering the new mystery, Nettie almost walked right past the parlor.

"I say, won't you even greet an old friend?" The female voice was low and throaty, as if the wielder would always know something no one else did.

"Lisselle?!" Nettie took a step backward into the door of the parlor and saw the slight, grey-haired woman relaxing before the fire. That was another surprising item. Gaston had said the lady agent would be moving in, but she had no idea quite so soon.

The tiny woman flung herself into Nettie's arms, grabbing her in a tight hug. Then she pulled back and clear, piercing blue eyes studied her gravely. "You look okay. How do you feel?"

Nettie sighed and followed her friend into the parlor. Lisselle was someone you instantly became friends with. Or most likely, she killed you. Not that Nettie thought her friend would kill people for not liking her, but it would be so hard to not like her, that anyone who didn't must be an enemy of the Society.

"I suppose I'm fine, but things are changing far too quickly for even me to follow."

Damon happened to pass by with the filthy vampire loaded on his floating bed.

"That, for instance. We haven't seen vampires in London for

years. Now, I've been attacked twice by them." She paused; it almost felt like cheating to give information away before Gaston had been informed. But he'd brought Lisselle here for a good reason. Therefore, she had as much right as any to know first. Plus, she, being of the gentler sex, would be a welcome confidant for the more emotional ramifications of the recent events. Not that Gaston didn't care, but any emotions other than anger seem to make him extremely uncomfortable.

"That one I brought in is a baby. He couldn't have been made more than a day ago. Or two judging by the smell of his clothes."

"Hmm. I'll have to look in once Gaston has had a peek at him." Lisselle began pacing tightly. "Where did he attack you?"

Nettie stalled by pouring herself some of the herbal tea Lisselle had been drinking. A light flower blend from India, it was known to soothe the nerves. "Outside of Buckingham. I was in an alley."

Lisselle burst out with a roaring laugh. "Waiting to see if she'd be running about the towers biting her guards?" The twinkle in her eye told Nettie no harm was meant.

"No, not at all," Nettie said with a sniff. Then she amended, "Yes. I mean, I truly did not expect her to be flying around grabbing guards. I did expect something to have happened."

Lisselle settled in across from her. As usual, the tiny spy was wearing modified men's trousers. In black. Nettie couldn't think of a time she hadn't seen Lisselle in black. "Well, the royal enclave is quite good at keeping their lives under wraps when need be." She leaned forward and lowered her voice, even though there was no one else around. "Don't you want to know why I'm here?"

"Gaston said he was trying to build a stronger base. And that it wouldn't look proper, me living here without…" Nettie let her words trickle off. She had no idea how old Lisselle really was. She would guess, mostly by references rather than how she looked or acted, that the woman was in her late thirties to early forties. Not ancient, but far older than her own twenty-seven.

Lisselle burst forth a bold laugh and rocked back into her seat. 'I've no trouble with my age, young one. I'll be fifty-two next May. And since when has Gaston given two figs about propriety?" Her grin grew wider, but less innocent. "I'm here to see the queen."

Before Nettie could respond, Damon came racing into the parlor. His face was pale and the sleeve on his jacket was torn down from shoulder to elbow. "I believe master Gaston needs some assistance." With that, he ran back toward the dungeon. Good sign. At least the new manservant was going to be able to deal with the dangers of living with the Society.

Lisselle reached behind her and pulled out a long gun, not unlike the smaller gear gun Gaston had shown her the night before. "Come along. I'd venture to say that gift you brought in is proving more interesting than expected."

Nettie didn't have a gun, but she grabbed a stake she'd sharpened and stored in her reticule. She'd started it two nights ago, but didn't think she'd be using it so soon. "But I thought bullets wouldn't stop them?"

"Oh, this won't stop him. But it'll distract him long enough for you to get in there and take him down."

Nettie almost stumbled.

"Me?" She took a deep breath as her voice froze. "I mean, I

thought you would take care of things. You are the senior agent."

Lisselle kicked in the dungeon door with her booted foot, then turned and flashed a quick smile. "Sometimes agents need to be made in fire." She spun and pushed Nettie forward. "This one is yours."

After shoving Nettie toward the enraged vampire, Lisselle started firing off shots. Gaston had been unable to reach any weapons, and he and Damon were trying to stay out of the vampire's reach as well.

Nettie studied the situation.

Her first instinct was to run. Perfectly natural, but not something that would be appropriate or helpful in this situation.

Which meant she had one option. Take the vampire down.

Luckily for her, the vampire was extremely new and disoriented by the other three. He also wasn't holding his blood very well. The holes Lisselle had shot into him should have healed almost immediately. Instead, he was leaking about the dungeon like a cracked teapot.

Wishing she had her trousers on instead of these messy skirts, Nettie dove at the vampire's legs. He crashed to the floor and thrashed about, twisting to reach her. But she held firm. Slowly, she climbed up his legs and sat on him.

It wasn't that she was heavier than he was, it was leverage. She sat in such a way that he simply couldn't get enough leverage to get up.

"I do hope you have a tranquilizer dart down here, Gaston." Her back was turned to the others, and she didn't dare move in case the slowly struggling vampire made another break.

A muffled sound from behind her almost made her turn

regardless. Finally, she realized it was laughter.

"I thought perhaps you would incapacitate him." Lisselle's laughter echoed in the room.

"After all the work I went through to bring him in for Gaston?" Nettie folded her arms and scrunched down on her prey. "I think not."

She couldn't see the others, but if Gaston was laughing as well, so help her…

"There, there, *ma petite*. I appreciate it." Gaston came into view with a smaller gear gun. He kneeled next to the writhing vampire and shot him twice in the head at point blank range.

"Gaston!" Nettie leapt to her feet. Even though the vampire she brought in was a fully changed one, as compared to her own half-bred status, she knew she'd been in complete control of him. "There was no reason to kill him. I had him under control."

"Those were my special vampire tranquilizers; I couldn't get to my gun until you distracted him. He's not dead," Gaston said. He prodded the vampire with a toe. "Although that may not last. He's losing too much blood. Even a new vampire should have healed by now."

Lisselle knelt down as well. Without asking Gaston for permission, she pried open the vampire's mouth. Not satisfied, she started moving his head back and forth.

"Something isn't right. There is a disturbance in his makeup. Something on a cellular level is interfering with the vampire virus. He's not fully made, but he's not human anymore either." She jumped back, falling flat on her behind as the vampire convulsed, then started to burble.

"That's not right at all." Nettie looked down at the twitching body. Green oozing foam poured out of his mouth and nose. Within seconds there was nothing left but clothing and green foam.

"Lock this room down now!" Lisselle leapt to her feet and ran past Gaston and Damon. Knowing exactly where to go, she slammed a hidden button.

Nettie spun as the dungeon doors slammed shut behind her and bolted into place.

CHAPTER TEN

"**D**AMN IT, LISSELLE, this *is* my mansion," Gaston grumbled, but Nettie noticed that he made no move to undo whatever his field agent had set into place.

"There is a chemical danger here, Gaston. Don't make me pull rank on you." Lisselle marched over to Gaston's table, took a clean, thick workman's glove, then went back and sopped up some of the green goo.

Rank? But Gaston was the ranking agent. How could Lisselle outrank him? Nettie thought Lisselle was coming down as part of the current investigations. Or had she been sent to replace Gaston?

Her confusion must have shown on her face.

"Easy there. Gaston is still in charge. Except when it comes into one of my domains." Lisselle folded her arms and stood fast, mere inches away from Gaston. "And you know chemical attacks are one of mine."

"A chemical attack?" Nettie jumped in before Gaston could speak. But to be honest, the round man didn't look like he had anything he wanted to say. "It was a vampire."

"Aye. One who didn't behave like a vampire and who disintegrated before our eyes. Turning, if you will, into a puddle of some sort of *chemical*." Lisselle took the glove, wiped part of the slime off on a slide, and slid it into Gaston's microscope without so much as a by your leave. "Exhibit A, a chemical attack."

Gaston looked annoyed, but he didn't argue. This was interesting. So, obviously, certain agents had specialties. Perhaps she too would have a domain area one day. Nettie had let her thoughts wander when Gaston pulled her back.

"I said, what's that on his shirt?" Following Lisselle's cue, Gaston didn't touch the vampire remains directly. But he had taken a long rod and was lifting up a piece of shirt. He'd managed to pull it free before it became completely covered in the green foam.

"What? It's a shirt, Gaston." Nettie shook her head.

"On the shirt," Gaston said. He held the rod and shirt up but not too high. The splatter factor of the unknown green foam would be far if something fell. "The dust." He finally pointed out to her.

"Dust? My dust?" Nettie charged forward, only stopping when her boots were inches away from the form on the floor. "Not my dust. But you're saying you think it's like my dust?"

It was all she could do not to grab the fabric with her bare hands. Maybe since she was half-vampire, the green goo was wouldn't hurt her.

"I know what you're thinking, and don't think it." Gaston narrowed his eyes and stared her down. "Lisselle, can you get containment on the dust particles on this fabric? It looks similar to the dust Agent Jones found."

That did it. Using her title reminded her she needed to act like an agent. With a sigh, Nettie rocked back and stayed out of the way.

Lisselle bustled forward, secured a scraping of the dust, then retreated to the microscopes and scanners in the far corner.

"Can I help?" Nettie held back. She didn't want to interfere with Lisselle, but at the same time, it was her dust. And her vampire.

"Of course." Lisselle held up a pair of thin, metallic-looking gloves. "Just put these on first." She slid on her own pair and flexed her fingers as the fabric tightened to her small hands.

Nettie gingerly took the gloves, but to be honest, she wanted to examine them almost as much as the dust. They felt far lighter in her hand than they looked and were quite cool when they settled in over her fingers.

"Fascinating. Whatever are they made of? Do they conduct heat?" Nettie held up her hand trying to figure out what they were made of.

"I know you need to know everything about everything," Gaston said as he interrupted her analysis of the gloves, "but perhaps examination of the dust should take precedence?"

Nettie felt her face grow hot. That had always been a problem, wanting to know everything about everything. She had hoped that the Society would work that out of her. So far, all it did was give her more things to be curious about.

"Sorry." With a bright smile, she took a slide and made a sample of the dust. It was difficult, as the green foam had already covered most of it, but she managed to get enough on the slide for one clear look.

"What is this dust, Gaston? Could the vampire have gotten it off of Nettie?" Lisselle asked while she continued her own examination of the foam.

Gaston worked on getting the foam contained, then swept it into a small bucket. Nettie was startled to see a full-grown male end up in a litter container.

"Nettie can fill you in. It's her own find, after all. But no, there wasn't enough left for it to have been transferred from her to the unfortunate before us. Unless there are multiple sources of this mysterious contaminant, which of course is possible, I believe we have to speculate that he got it from the same beings Nettie got it from."

Lisselle swore. "I do hate when you're cryptic *and* long-winded, Gaston. In this case, waiting might be prudent. I'm not having any luck with this foam." She pushed back from the microscope, and then slid the slide into the spectrograph. "This won't be ready until tomorrow, but maybe it will tell us something."

Nettie peered at her own slide. The particles looked identical to the sample she'd gotten from the mysterious, disappearing brown man of two days ago, but there must be more to the substance than they originally thought. After all, she'd had the dust on her hands for almost eight hours and she hadn't dissolved into green goo.

But the more she looked, the more they looked the same. Then she made a second slide with the goo and the dust together. The introduction of the goo caused the dust to vanish, but she couldn't tell if it had absorbed it or changed it.

"Not much here either." Nettie sighed and filled the other two in on her findings, or lack of them.

Lisselle set up another slide for the Spectra Graph Analytic Computator. "Well, it does look like the bulk of tonight's mystery will have to wait until I get some answers from our little friends here." She fondly patted the bulky, whirling machine.

"Lisselle, we are not staying down here until tomorrow." Gaston had been watching Lisselle with narrowing eyes, and now frowned openly.

Lisselle turned toward him with equally narrowed eyes and folded her arms tightly. Nettie didn't like the way this was going. She didn't want to risk contamination if there was something contagious in the vampire's remains. She also didn't want to spend the night on one of the examination tables down here.

Finally, Lisselle wrinkled her nose and laughed. "Think I'd want to be trapped down here with the likes of you? I don't think that there's a chance of contamination. Nor do I think this was a deliberate attack against us. So you can open the doors, Gaston."

"Excellent. We need to prepare for Agent Smith's arrival." Gaston and his new manservant bustled toward the door, but he turned right before they passed through. "Oh, and don't forget that Agent Ramsey wanted you to pick up Agent Smith. He comes in on the nine a.m. train from Liverpool."

"But, Gaston—" Nettie started to speak.

"Oh, and don't take too long down here. I also need to find out some background on your friend, Rebecca." He vanished before she could point out what she really wanted to do was curl up and get some sleep.

"He'll do that to you every time." Lisselle peeled off her silvery gloves and dropped them into an incinerator. She motioned for Nettie to do the same. "Gaston will keep pushing you until you tell him to stop."

"It's that obvious?" Nettie wiggled her fingers at the tingling sensation the gloves left on her hands.

"Child, you look ready to sleep for a week. He knows that as well. The difference is, he'll ignore it to get what he wants. I would be sending you to bed. Sleepy agents make errors. Gaston feels that working through exhaustion builds stronger agents." She led the way out of the dungeon. "Just one of our differences. Moving in here should be quite the experience."

THE NEXT MORNING, Nettie found herself waiting in the classical London fog for Agent Smith. She blew on her hands to try and warm them before shoving them back into the opposing sleeves of her coat. Gaston still had her good gloves from the examination of the green dust. She would need to remember to get them back. Winter was settling in and it wouldn't do to have her fingers fall off.

"Why did he have to come in so blasted early, anyway?" she muttered to herself. Stretching on her toes, she tried to catch a glimpse of anyone matching Agent Smith's description. Of course, everyone had to get off the train in one solid mass. It didn't help that she was in a foul mood. Gaston had been up all night and wanted to pick her brain for most of it. Then she still had to come pick up the American agent, get him settled, and then put in a full day of work.

She was not in a good mood.

The crowd folded around her, brushing close, but leaving her standing like an island. As much as she stretched, she couldn't see anyone matching Smith. She'd gotten a physical description, but the photograph had been grainy and useless. Tall, Gaston said he was six two, with sandy blond hair and brown eyes. And she expected him to look American. She was not sure what that meant, but it would be helpful if he wore one of those western hats from some of the cowboy mystery novels she read as a child.

The crowd had dispersed, and still no Caden Smith.

Stomping her feet to get some feeling back into them, Nettie turned to make her way out when a shape sitting on the chairs caught her eye. Long legs stretched out, a black, western-looking hat pulled down over his brows.

She had been looking for him for fifteen minutes in the mass of humanity, and he was sitting there relaxing.

Clearly, American agents didn't hold themselves to the same serious guidelines of Mother England.

Muttering words of vengeance under her breath, Nettie stomped over to his side of the station. Considering there was hardly anyone left, the least thing he could do would be to look up. But he stayed still.

She was going to make him pay for this. All of her annoyance in the recent situation came out as she stopped in front of him.

"I do not know how your people behave, but this is not how it's done in England. You'd best get used to our ways quickly. Or you can be replaced." She felt foolish as she added the last bit. Not to mention she had no power to replace him, but he didn't need to know.

He didn't move.

She felt much needed warmth flood her ears and her face. If she could focus her anger enough to warm her toes and fingers, she would stay mad all winter.

"I said, Mr. Smith, this is highly—" She reached forward to yank off his hat and found the man matched the description for Mr. Smith. He was an ashy white color, and judging by the dried blood in his hair, he had been hit in the head. The hat looked a bit too large for him, but had dried blood on it as well. His long face was decidedly bookish and his fingers were smoother than hers. He also had an odd, musty smell of mothballs and pipe tobacco.

She had to touch his neck to see if he even lived.

"This is not good." Looking around, she tried to see if any help was nearby. He was exceedingly thin, and while she knew she could lift someone his size with ease, she knew she shouldn't be able to. Causing people to ask questions with an injured secret agent on hand would simply not do.

"Can I be of assistance?" The voice was low, rich, and extremely masculine. The type of voice that belonged to an exceptionally handsome man. And one who knew he was.

Nettie disliked him before she even turned around. She readjusted Agent Smith's hat slowly as a cover story came to mind.

"No, thank you." Nettie had to force her voice to be civil, although the man oozed looks and charm. Tall and slender, his deep brown eyes matched his hair perfectly. He even had a dimple in his chin. His accent marked him from somewhere uptown, very upper crust.

"My husband has decided to take a nap." She folded her arms waiting for him to leave.

When he stood there grinning at her, she waved him on. "I'm fine. Thank you for your offer, but we're fine."

He opened that perfect mouth, but she cut him off before he

could say anything.

"Fine. Good day, sir." She whirled back to Agent Smith, fussing with his jacket until she heard the footsteps vanish.

Carefully, she studied the area looking for her Good Samaritan and relaxed when she didn't see him.

Nettie looked around the station once more, but few people were left about. Unusual, considering another train would be in within a half hour, but welcome. She reached for a packet to summon a Runner then shook her head. Until the missing four were found, none of them were being used. There was no way to tell if any compromising of the four could have affected the others. Communication from Edinburgh indicated the lead Runner believed that could be a risk. It was he who had pulled the rest from active duty for now.

Which severely limited her options. She didn't want the gentleman from before coming back.

Patting down Agent Smith, she found an unopened bottle of whisky. It was vile stuff, but it could work. Working quickly and as stealthily as possible, Nettie poured the whisky liberally on Agent Smith's clothing. Stuffing the bottle and remaining sloshing liquid back into his pocket, she raised her voice. She wanted an audience. She also pulled her scarf tighter around her face; her words would still get out, but hopefully few would remember what she looked like.

"Damn you! You're drunk again. I have told you not to come back from your trips drunk. I've a mind to leave you here." She leaned forward as if listening to him.

"Don't you take that tone with me! You're lucky I need you back home." She let her accent take on a rougher tone.

Whirling on a steward lingering nearby, she added a pleading tone to her voice. "Please sir, might I borrow a wheeled chair? My husband is too...ill...to make it to our carriage out front." She let the emphasis linger on ill in case he hadn't been paying full attention to her one-way argument.

The small man scowled, but snatched up the coins she held out. He grunted something that sounded like an agreement, then left.

Moments later, he came with a battered and ill-used wheeled chair. Patrons sometimes needed assistance leaving the train. Handing him more coins, Nettie shooed him off when he almost appeared to want to help.

"No, no. It will serve him right to have a few more bumps from weak little me having to move him around. Thank you so much though."

The man shrugged and scurried off.

She knew she only had a few minutes before the next rush of passengers. The hat on Smith's head was big enough to cover the damage, but blood was noticeable at the back of his jacket.

Making sure no one watched, she pulled him into the chair while trying to look like she was struggling.

There was no way she would be able to keep his head upright while wheeling him out. She would have to make it look good. Raising her voice to the appropriate screeching tone, she rattled the chair a bit.

"Don't you pass out on me. Damn you, I told you not to pass out on me. You're the worst excuse for a husband the world has ever seen." An older lady passed by, nodding encouragingly. Nettie aimed a kick at his leg, but pulled the movement back under her skirts so she didn't actually hit him. She stuffed the ratty blanket she'd found in the chair around him. With a nod toward the woman, Nettie wheeled him outside.

She pushed the chair forward, moving as fast as she felt wise. She needed to get him to Gaston's, but whoever did this to him could still be lingering to finish the job.

Getting him to the carriage worked and she took back her complaint that morning about having to use the regular, non-steam powered carriage for this. This would get them to the mansion unobserved and with less jostling. Securing her passenger in the carriage, and checking his pulse again to make sure he still lived, she made her way quickly to the mansion.

CHAPTER ELEVEN

N O ONE WAS about, so she rang the bells and pounded on the doors. It was faster than trying to dig Gaston out of where ever he was lurking.

"Damn it, girl, you don't need to make such a ruckus." Gaston had actually been asleep, and at first Nettie felt bad about waking him. But that only lasted until she recalled who it was who kept her up all night. Since Lisselle hadn't been right on his heels, she must have already taken off for her recon trip. She was planning to prowl around the area surrounding Buckingham Palace to see what the locals noticed.

"Smith has been attacked. I found him slumped on a bench in the train station. I think he is still alive, but he needs help."

"Aren't you a doctor? Is he alive or not?" Gaston threw on a few coats over his nightclothes then jammed on his boots.

"He was alive before I came in here. If you want him to stay that way, I need him on an operating table right now." She could understand him being grumpy, but there was no call to go after her medical skills. She may not get live patients often, but she still had been one of the top in her class.

Gaston's new manservant appeared out of thin air. "Excuse me, miss."

She stepped aside allowing him to pick up Smith and carry

him inside. The voice was low, but as before she couldn't tell what exactly the accent was. One thing, he was extremely strong. He lifted Smith as if he were a child. Interesting that he hadn't tried that with last night's vampire.

"I gotta say you take good care of your villains here," the voice from the station came out from the back of the carriage. Although the upper British crust accent had vanished and a rough American tone had taken its place. "But what about us heroes?" The sleek, handsome man from the station tumbled out from where he'd been clinging to the back of the conveyance. Nettie started to raise her voice to yell for help when he collapsed, face first, right in front of her. Blood leaked out of a wound in his shoulder, covering the back of his jacket. Not a fatal wound, judging by the amount of blood, but he looked like he'd gotten stabbed a while ago. It had taken a while to seep through his clothing.

"Who is that?" Gaston motioned for Damon to put down Smith and go secure the injured attacker.

"He's an idiot who wouldn't leave Agent Smith and me alone. I was afraid he may be working for our enemies." She dropped her voice for the last bit. The tall man was twitching as Damon bent to pick him up. Most likely, the fiend wasn't truly unconscious. She'd think he was faking the injury as well, but that was real blood. And more importantly, his pale and drawn face showed the results of real blood loss.

"He followed you from the station?" Gaston frowned as he followed Damon inside. Agent Smith was propped up in a wheeled chair, not unlike the one she had borrowed from the train. Gaston rolled the agent forward in the wake of Damon.

"Did he say anything that gave away his plans?"

Nettie frowned. "No. But he has an unwholesome look about him."

"Well, I do encourage my agents to follow their intuition, I suppose. We will keep him under guard once you have operated on him and Agent Smith. I can staunch his bleeding until you get Smith's head wound addressed."

Gaston lead the way deep into the dungeon, pushing back one of the screens in the back to reveal an operating room. This room was far more advanced than the place they'd taken the vampire to the night before. It also didn't look like a prison.

"Shouldn't that one be in the room from last night? He might be dangerous." Nettie pointed to the man who had collapsed at her feet.

"No, I think we can secure him here. Besides, I want to see both survive and we have the best equipment in here." As he spoke, Gaston pulled back another screen. High-end medical equipment, unlike anything Nettie had even seen, lined the entire wall.

Nettie raised an eyebrow and gave her best, 'we will be talking about this later', but was too focused on saving Smith's life to question providence. The unnamed handsome varlet would be dealt with later. Hopefully, Gaston would be none too gentle in his treatment. Imagine him following them like a common sneak thief! What could he have been thinking? He had to have realized he was bleeding to death.

The gossip in the Society was that Caden Smith was a heart-breaking womanizer, using his spy status to play fast and loose with hearts as quickly as he killed his enemies.

That may be true under normal circumstances, but there was nothing attractive about him now. Maybe he looked better when he wasn't injured. Nevertheless, he was too skinny for her tastes, and his face had a tight, bookish cast to it. Dark blood matted his light hair, clumping it into unattractive spikes. His face was pale and drawn; to be honest, he looked far worse than that vampire they'd dragged in.

"Ach, whoever did this knew what they were doing. There's a lot of blood, but the damage isn't severe. Whoever attacked him wanted him down, but not dead." Nettie quickly cleaned the wound, using tight tiny sutures to close it.

Then she pointed to the other injured man. "This one must have fought with Smith. Smith stabbed him, but he managed to get in a good blow before I arrived. We really shouldn't let him remain uncaged."

"Now you're going beyond your intuition into speculation." Gaston helped her clean up and don new gloves. He looked down at the second man with a scowl. "I need this man able to answer questions. I did what I could, but there seems to be something more wrong with him. His pulse is fading."

"What?" She rushed to the man's side. "There must be something else," she finally said, "He has lost too much blood, but his wound doesn't look that deep. It shouldn't have caused that kind of loss." Nettie carefully peeled back the man's shirt to see the damage done to his shoulder. Gaston brought a bowl of warm water and rag.

"I need him stripped to the waist." She pulled forward a small tray with scalpels and knives. "There must be more damage than just that shoulder wound."

Gaston nodded to Damon, who quickly dispatched with the mystery man's clothing.

A low grunt of surprise from Damon grabbed her attention. As he peeled off the man's clothing, it was clear what his layers of clothing and heavy jacket had hidden. A ragged stab wound inches above his right kidney, and a wound that looked redder than the almost black blood dried around it. Frantically, Nettie wiped away the blood. The unhealthy redness explained his near death situation. Obviously, he had been mobile not too long ago, indicating that he hadn't been stabbed on the train or the station. Or he had and had a very high tolerance for pain. Nettie concluded that the blade that had stabbed him must have been coated in poison. Standard infection wouldn't have had time to settle in.

"I need alcohol, the purest you have, and a lot of it."

"He has been poisoned?" Gaston had held back.

At Nettie's nod, he sent Damon to go get whisky. "How can you treat it if you don't know what with?"

"I don't know. But I have to do something. The thing is, it looks like infection, but this wound is no more than a few hours old. It makes no sense." Once the wound had been cleaned, she could see it didn't look like any blade wound she had ever seen. More than two inches long and viciously jagged, it would have hurt far worse coming out that going in.

Damon was silent as he held up the whisky. Without looking to Gaston for approval, she opened the bottle and liberally poured a good fourth of it into the wound.

The man's torso seemed to ripple as the liquid hit. It was a good thing he was already unconscious, as the pain would have probably knocked him out.

"I can clean it and hope we get it all, and I can sew both injuries back up, but I can't be sure if it will be enough. I don't think the knife hit anything vital or he would be dead by now. They missed all of his organs, but it almost seems deliberate." She looked up at Gaston. "Whoever attacked him could have easily killed him immediately, so why didn't they?"

"I don't know. You don't believe this happened in the station?" Gaston looked older than he had moments before, and it was more than just not enough sleep.

"The injury on his back was done a while ago, while he was wearing both his jacket and shirt." She held up the remains of his shirt. "This one was done while he had his shirt on, but slipped in under the jacket. The blood is barely dried. I'd say he was stabbed once on the train or not long after. Then attacked again before he grabbed on to my carriage."

She poured another liberal dash of whisky into his wound. "The weapon was poisoned with something, and the blade unlike anything I've ever seen."

Gaston frowned and looked up from his scribbling. "I've got an extensive collection in the study. Do you think you might recognize it if you saw an example?"

Nettie looked at the wound again. "I suppose so. It's going to be difficult with only this to go by, but I can try." She shook her head, trying to get into the attack itself. This second man was a fighter; his lean build and tight muscles told her that. He wouldn't have been easy to get the jump on, and even harder to stab, even when injured. She looked at his hands again.

"I think he didn't go down completely, even when stabbed."

She looked closer at his hands. "There are no defensive wounds, but these look like offensive ones. He attacked whoever went after him." She studied the wounded man before her with new appreciation.

"That sounds like Caden." Gaston turned from one injured man to the other. "Similar of height and coloring. How did you know that man was Agent Smith?" He pointed to the one with the head wound.

"Why I…" Nettie studied both men, the frown deepening on her face. "I made an assumption. I came across *that* Agent Smith first. He fit the description, and I thought it was him. This one's hair is too dark besides." She felt awful. What if the second man was the real Agent Smith? He must have been injured when she spoke to him in the station. What if she had rescued his attacker and left him to die?

"Now, don't you go second guessing yourself. There was no way for you to know." Gaston dropped behind a small curtain and came back with a small whirling stick. "But there is for me. The Americans use a different type of tracker than we do, but this will still find which of these is our new agent. If either of them are."

He waved the wand over second man. As soon as he got to the left shoulder, the gears inside began clicking.

The location was about an inch down from where the smaller knife wound was.

"They'd been trying to remove his tracker?" Nettie was aghast that whoever the attackers were, they had such knowledge of the Society, and at herself for almost leaving the wrong Agent Smith behind to die. "I'm so sorry, Gaston. I didn't—"

"You didn't know. How could you? We were told he was a light-haired man, and they are of similar build with their clothing on. I think the scene is as you played out, only our attacker has the head wound. He clearly was trying to replace the real Agent Smith." He shook his head as he removed the manacles from Agent Smith. "But why didn't Smith identify himself to you? He didn't give the code?" He continued talking as he ducked behind the curtain again. She didn't know what he was looking for, but it involved a lot of noise.

"No. Not the one you told me to ask for. I didn't give mine either. I thought I had the right man already."

"Because I didn't know if you'd been compromised." The voice was so unlike his former smooth, seductive tone, Nettie almost didn't recognize it came from Agent Smith. Like outside, his accent had slipped into an American twang.

"You shouldn't be talking." The doctor part of her took over from the agent mindset and she scurried over to poke at him. "To be honest, you shouldn't even be conscious. How are you doing that?"

"You don't have to sound so accusatory. I'm the one who got stabbed." He did not look good, but he was trying to sit up of all things. "Repeatedly."

"Gaston? We need those manacles back." She gently pushed the stubborn Agent Smith down. "And you need to stay still. You were almost dead, you know. I will be annoyed with you if you undo all of my hard work."

"My hard work as well." The new voice came from her other formerly unconscious patient, who was now conscious, had gotten free of his manacles, and was holding a small gear pistol that happened to be aimed not at her, but at Agent Smith.

"He's the false agent. That one stole my tracker. Then knocked me out." The first injured man's accent was softer, but still noticeably American.

"Oh dear," Nettie looked from one to the other. She knew that as a trained agent, she should do something. But to be honest, she wasn't quite sure to whom she should be doing something. A movement next to her pulled her eyes away from the head wounded Agent Smith.

Only to find that the stabbed and poisoned Agent Smith was likewise holding a small gear pistol. She really was going to have to make sure to keep one of the small things on her person if there was going to be this much of a call for them.

The stabbed and poisoned Smith gasped out in pain as he pulled on the lovely needlework she'd done on his wounds. The head wound Smith almost tumbled to the floor as disorientation tipped him forward.

"Now, this will not do. I am not going to stand around while you two idiots destroy my handiwork." A mere moment before, she'd been a bit intimidated by the guns, but now she was vexed.

"I will not," she whipped the gun free of the head wound Smith's hand, "have you two damage yourselves on my watch." Tapping into her vampiric speed she disarmed the second Smith an instant later. She gave each a hard punch where they weren't injured for causing her more stress.

Just in time for Gaston to come back into the operating area.

"I say, sorry. What did I miss?" He peered at both men who were both looking extremely annoyed. And in pain.

"I had to hit them. They are both far more conscious than

they should be, considering their wounds. And they pulled these on each other." She dropped both guns in Gaston's startled hand. "I thought about crushing them, but thought you might need them for evidence."

"I see." Gaston carefully approached both men. With a sigh, he reattached the head wound agent's manacles, and then brought a new pair for the poisoned agent. "Well, it does appear that you got to his poison before he died. I'd say it was supposed to look like a regular infection. I'd also say both of you will be guarded under lock and key until we gather the truth of this situation."

"Call in McGrady." The toll of trying to sit up had finally taken down the stabbed and poisoned agent. His face was about three shades paler than his sheet. "McGrady knows who I am."

The head wound agent didn't try to remove his manacles again, but he did try to sit up. "That sets it. He doesn't even know McGrady is dead. The man died in the Zeppelin explosion. Any agent would know that."

Nettie met Gaston's eyes. Actually any agent might not know that at all. A select few, including any that Edinburgh assigned here specifically, would know that McGrady wasn't on that Zeppelin.

Gaston nodded to Damon, who carefully began patting down the head wound agent for weapons. Two more guns, a garrote, and a wicked-looking knife came out of various hiding places.

"What are you doing? You can't believe him! I'm Caden Smith." He tried to pull free, but Damon secured him easily with a few more sets of manacles.

The real Caden leaned back with a sigh. "Took you all long

enough." He waved off Nettie's look. "Not that I'm not grateful, mind you. I am. But it was touch and go there for a bit. I take it you can't debrief me until we get him secured?" He nodded toward the imposter, and winced when his movement pulled at his wounds.

Nettie ignored him. "I'd say this was the weapon used on Agent Smith." She held up the nasty-looking dagger. The teeth on it were small and twisted. "I can't say I've ever seen anything like it though."

"You can't do this! You can't—" The imposter continued yelling until, at a nod from Gaston, Damon injected him with a sleeping solution. Nettie was a bit disappointed. For all the trouble he'd put her through, she wanted to put him out the old-fashioned way. Come to think of it, she wanted to put out Agent Smith that way as well. Most likely, Gaston wouldn't let her do that either.

"Thank you, Damon, that is much nicer." Gaston pulled up a chair next to Caden's bed. "Now, boy, why don't you share with us how some skinny, bookish villain got the jump on the great Caden Smith?"

"Eh, it's not a pretty tale." He looked up at Nettie. "But should your secretary be here? I mean, I know she works for the organization and everything. But still..." He had the decency to trail off as Nettie folded her arms and glared at him.

"She's not a secretary, is she?" Agent Smith rubbed his forehead and slid back down into his bed.

"No. I am a fully trained agent of the *Society*. My name is either Agent Jones or Dr. Jones, and you may choose what to call me of those two."

"*Mon dieu, mon garcon.* Rule one, never annoy your doctor. Especially when that doctor could snap you in half." Gaston leaned back in his seat looking smug about something. Nettie didn't like him looking smug. It usually never boded well for others. Usually her.

"Snap me in half?" Agent Smith let loose a laugh. "I'm wiry, but strong. No matter what special British skills you are teaching your agents, I assure you that little lady couldn't snap me."

Nettie was in the process of pulling forward another chair. She still had some time before she had to go into work and decided to stick around and hear Agent Smith's tale. His smugness was even worse than Gaston's. His uncultured American voice oozed with it.

"I don't need special training, Agent Smith." Faster than the eye could see, she leapt to his side, her fangs bared inches above his neck. His breath completely stopped. Holding his wide-eyed look for a few seconds, she let go then returned to pulling her chair forward.

"Oh." Caden reached up and rubbed the side of his neck even though she had done nothing but breathe on it. "You're *that* Agent Jones. Please accept my apologies for any unintended insult given. I had no idea you'd be so...normal looking." He winced as the words came out. Nettie could tell he clearly never gave a thought to what he was about to say until he'd already said it. Most likely the reason he tended to get into a lot of fights.

A look from Gaston told he realized the same thing, but to let it pass. With a nod, she turned back to Caden.

"Go on, boy, before she decides to see if those fangs are now real."

Caden clearly wanted to follow that line of questions, but after a quick look from one face before him to the next, he swallowed his questions. Nettie knew when the full debriefing came, Gaston would fill Caden in on her new status. So far, she hadn't noticed any changes. They weren't even sure if the vampire had tried to feed her his blood to turn her. But if he was going to live here and work with them, he needed to be apprised. She couldn't help the brief thought that ran through her brain. If she did fall prey to the vampire who attacked her, she really hoped Caden was her only victim.

"Very well. That one followed me up from Liverpool. His accent is good, but I don't think he's American. He chatted me up in the bar of the train, and then put something in my drink. I woke up to find him trying to remove my tracker." A shiver went through his bare shoulders. "He knew exactly where it was. I didn't even know where it was." He gave his head a shake. "As I said, I woke up. Whatever he put in my beer either didn't work or was one of the poisons I've built up a tolerance for."

"Why didn't he kill you?" Nettie smiled as she said it, but she wasn't giving him one of her nice smiles.

"He couldn't, not if he wanted Agent Smith's tracker to stay active. Most likely, you would have had an accident off the train afterwards," Gaston added.

Caden nodded before continuing. "We fought; he got me with that damn knife. And yes, lady Doctor, it was poisoned. Would have killed me too, but it's one I've got a tolerance for."

Nettie fumed at his term for her. "Perhaps you could give us a list of those?"

His laugh bounced around the room. "Not likely. I'd like to

not hand you a shopping list."

"Am I going to have to separate you two?" Gaston leveled his best Napoleonic glare at both of them and Nettie wiped the smirk from her face.

"Not at all," Nettie said. "I do believe, however, that I should get ready for work." She rose, dusted her skirts off, even though there was nothing discernable on them, then made her way to the door. "Some of us do have jobs outside of the Society, you know." Caden's deep brown eyes lit up, but she exited the dungeon before the snide comment could tumble from his lips.

As much as she wanted to stay and find out the truth behind the attacker and the vile Agent Smith, Nettie knew she'd be hard pressed to hold her tongue in his presence.

Besides, getting in to work a bit early would give her a chance to see if Dr. Wilson knew anything about the missing bodies or the missing report. She'd have to proceed carefully, since he thought the bodies had been taken legitimately, and he had no idea the report in his file was a copy.

Pondering how exactly she was going to find out what he may know, Nettie wandered into her room to change. The room still caught her breath every time she walked in. The ceilings were twice again as tall as she was, and the molding along the walls was of such detail it made her wish she could fly up to view it better.

To be honest, if she had realized that one of these rooms could be hers, she would have badgered Gaston long ago.

She had changed, and was about to open the door, when she heard voices coming down the hall. At least three or four women, voices demurely low, were coming down from further in the wing.

Gaston was planning on bringing in more agents, but she didn't think he was planning to do so this quickly. Nettie waited until the voices had passed her door, then cracked it open and peeked through.

Lisselle, two matronly looking taller women, and a smaller one in the front were walking down the hall. Nettie almost gasped aloud when she realized the smaller woman was Rebecca. Luckily, her memory caught up to her before she gave herself away.

The meeting with the 'teaching group' had been today. But Nettie had thought Lisselle had been spying on the queen. Not to mention she was more than a little surprised that they'd brought Rebecca to Gaston's mansion on her first meeting. Nettie hadn't seen his home until her final round of interviews.

The ladies all stopped at the end of the hallway and chatted pleasantries. Which left Nettie frustrated in many ways. She couldn't leave until they did. Obviously, she couldn't be living here if she wasn't affiliated with the 'teaching group' such as she had implied to Rebecca the day before.

But even more frustrating was that she couldn't hear what they were saying. She focused on the backs of the women, willing them to raise their voices a bit.

Before she could hear anything though, Damon appeared in front of the women. He seemed to glance at Nettie's nearly shut door—she swore he looked her right in the eye—and he pitched his voice a bit louder than the women. Loud enough for Nettie to hear him clearly.

"I am sorry. The master has been called away by an urgent matter. He requests that the rest of testing be rescheduled."

Rebecca looked down, clearly noticing for the first time that she was late for work. Even though Nettie couldn't hear her, the mannerisms were clear.

Within a few minutes, the farewells had been said, and Rebecca left the mansion.

"Oh, do come out, Nettie. I can hear your curiosity from here." Lisselle was blocked by the two far taller female agents.

"How did you know?" she asked as she gathered her things and made her way into the hallway.

"I heard you go into your room before we entered the hall. Then you were still as a mouse. It wasn't hard to make the connection." Lisselle smiled as Nettie came into view.

"Greta and Mary, this is Dr. Nettie Jones, one of our best agents."

Nettie pulled herself up straighter as the two tall women turned around. She had seen a few of the other London agents, but she didn't recognize either. Both were dressed like Quakers, which would have made them extremely noticeable had they been Londoners. Not to mention Lisselle's comment of "one of our best" implied they weren't from here.

"Very nice to meet you both." She smiled, but neither woman smiled back. Neither took her extended hand either.

"You are the vampire, yes?" Greta, judging by her accent, didn't seem to make it a question.

"Half vampire." Nettie hadn't had that many run-ins with other agents, but most had been more than accepting of her vampire status. This was the first time she felt like she was being judged.

Lisselle frowned, and took a step closer to her. "Is there a problem, ladies?" Her hands twitched a bit.

"You did not tell us we were going to be in her presence," the other, whom Nettie assumed was Mary, said with a sniff.

Obviously, both of these were older agents, and for an instant Nettie felt ashamed of her vampire half. Then she saw Lisselle's face. Her friend didn't have a problem with it, and neither did Gaston.

"I did not think it would be an issue." Lisselle stepped forward, clearly itching to start a fight of some sort.

"I believe it is. After all, who knows what she will do?" Mary was doing more of the talking, but Greta's face was becoming lined with anger.

Even Lisselle looked furious.

"That is enough, Agent Smith. Call back your experiment. You have demonstrated the effect." Gaston's voice came from behind the door next to the hall entrance. A small box-like object with tiny wheels came out from behind one of the tables and disappeared down the hall. An instant later, a noticeable pressure fled the area and all three women shook themselves.

"What was that, Gaston? Damn you, you can't run experiments on me." Lisselle was still mad, but now it was more rational and aimed appropriately.

Nettie felt her own temper raise as Caden Smith appeared behind Gaston. He leaned heavily on a table and his face was lined and pale.

"It was my fault, Agent Wilding," he said in his most charming manner with a slight bow. "I told Agent Bessette about a device I invented, the Ameligalating Agitator. He doubted its ability to work on strong minds."

"But why did it not work on Agent Jones?" The warm smile Mary flashed Nettie showed the earlier ill will was because of the machine, not true personal feelings on her behalf.

"You didn't feel anything at all?" Agent Smith's voice wasn't strong. Plus, he was starting to tremble a bit and shouldn't be up at all.

Nettie refrained from rushing forward and making him sit down. The man was going to be one of *those* types of patients.

"Nothing beyond concern at the feelings of my fellow agents." She shared a smile with Mary and Greta to make sure they knew there were no hard feelings. "I'd say it may have to do with the vampire nature of my mother."

"Not at all." Agent Smith looked agitated as he leaned forward. Gaston grabbed one shoulder before he could completely tip over. "You don't understand. That has worked on full vampires. We caught two of them in New Jersey. As a test, the machine was used on them. They killed each other before we could get in there and shut it off."

Gaston let go of Smith's shoulder, causing the injured man to fall to the side. "You let me test that thing without knowing it had led to two vampires' deaths?"

Smith picked himself up and used the wall to pull himself to his feet. "We changed it after that. It wouldn't have made them mad enough to kill, but it should have been strong enough for Agent Jones to have been affected."

Gaston still looked ready to damage his newest agent more than he already was, and Lisselle didn't look too far behind. Nettie almost felt willing to defend Agent Smith, but not quite. Unlike his other actions and foibles, this one she could understand. He had an invention that he felt would work and didn't want to be stopped in testing it. But she was still annoyed with him.

"I do believe I am needed at work. If you all will excuse me?" Stepping around Agent Smith, she nodded to the three women. "I take it Rebecca has passed the test?" She had no idea how it went, but it would be nagging at her all night if she didn't ask.

"She has potential." Lisselle pushed her toward the door. "And that is more than you need to know until the interviews are over and a decision has been made. Have a nice evening at work, Agent Jones." The last was said through the door.

Nettie shrugged. She didn't think she'd get anything out of them so soon, even if they were already bringing her to Gaston's home. But it was worth a shot. That hope, along with the secret glee at Agent Smith's fumble, had her whistling as she mounted her steamcycle and trundled off to work.

CHAPTER TWELVE

S HE HADN'T GOTTEN far when she noticed she was being followed again. Like the other day, it was a single person, garbed in brown. Unlike the other day, this time Nettie knew it was no citizen of Earth who followed her, but an alien.

Determined to get something more than only a pinchful of dust this time, Nettie slowed her steamcycle and wandered down back roads.

The man, or alien, she corrected herself, stayed with her. She noticed he'd begun following her moments after she had turned off Gaston's street. Thinking logically, that told her a few things. He—or it, since she had no idea if it was an alien female or male—was obviously aware of the area she frequented. But were they interested in her, or her steamcycle? She couldn't imagine why they would want the bike. While the technology was relatively new to London, it wouldn't be to a race who could travel between stars.

Which told her that, for whatever reason, the alien was interested in her. Yet when it had her a few days ago, all it did was reclaim the samples she'd taken of it.

Did they know she'd had more? Suddenly, her little game of slow-moving tag with the alien didn't seem so intriguing. Gaston may be cavalier about beings from other worlds, yet she wasn't sure how she felt about it.

Riding her steamcycle further into the less crowded areas of London in hopes of meeting up with her alien pursuer was sounding less and less like a good idea. The problem was that she'd managed to get herself properly lost.

She hadn't seen the man in brown for at least three minutes, so perhaps he had gotten lost as well. Or at the very least, decided not to continue following her.

Feeling better about her decision to give up trying to track the man in brown, Nettie drifted down a few wrong turns, but eventually found herself on a smaller street that led to the main road that went by her work.

And almost ran over the man in brown.

It wasn't her fault she'd almost run him over. Although she was distracted, no one would blame her for failing to see the lump of tattered brown fabric in the middle of the lane. Lula Belle squealed horribly when she slammed on her airbrakes.

"Oh dear." She turned off Lula's steam engine, and then slowly stepped off the bike. No one else was around; even the local businesses looked shuttered. A bit early for closing, but it might be for the best. Nettie had no idea what the Society rules were for civilians seeing injured or dead aliens, but she thought it probably was frowned upon.

Unfortunately, that also meant that she was the only one who could deal with it.

Taking another pair of the thin gloves Lisselle had given her in the mansion, Nettie slipped them on and approached the still form.

He seemed far less substantial than he had when following

her. Or perhaps her ill ease at being followed by a person from another planet made him appear larger. Taking a deep breath, she rolled him over.

As she pulled back the brown tattered fabric, all of existence blinked out.

REALITY BLINKED BACK an instant later, but the connection with her previous reality was tenuous indeed.

Nettie had been bending down, her hand clutching the brown fabric, when things blinked out. She was still crouching, her hand extended, but there was nothing in it. Nor was there a prone alien in front of her. Nor a street.

Nor, for that matter, London.

She straightened up slowly, wondering if she hadn't hit her head. Perhaps she had, in fact, hit the alien and was lying unconscious in a hospital somewhere. The room she was in was small and metal. Entirely metal and the sides slightly bowed as if she was in the bottom of a sailing vessel. There was no door, and the light seemed to illuminate from a seam along the top edges of the walls. She made a tight circle of the chamber, tapping the walls in case there was a secret passageway. There had to be something. Who would make a room without a door? Not to mention, how did she get here without coming through a door?

She'd returned to the center of the room, when the seam at the far end split open. Within a second, a slender door popped into existence. Nettie started to run for it—anywhere was probably better than here—when a brown-clad being came through.

She didn't think it was the same alien. While he was wearing brown, it wasn't the dusty London cast-off brown of the one who had been following her. But he did have far less covering him than the one or ones who had been following her. This afforded her a chance to get a real glimpse of her first alien.

The being before her was almost her height, but impossibly thin. His arms and legs were no wider than her own wrist bones and showed no muscle bulking. His skin, what she could see of it, was a luminescent green-gray, similar to her mysterious powder. His face was smooth and round. His nose bridge was almost completely nonexistent and his nostrils were little more than flat slits. A tiny part of her screamed that she really should run and do so immediately. However, she wasn't sure where she could run. And the other part of her brain wanted to catalogue the being. Examine him and find out what he was under those robes. He, if it was in fact male, seemed to be having the same mental impasse as he continued to simply stand and stare.

Or he was thinking of the best way to kill her. That face was so blank there was simply no way to gauge what he was thinking.

"Hello? I don't think we've met…" Nettie held out her hand and pasted on her widest smile as she took a step toward the creature.

His immobile face took on a new mobility as it scrunched up like he'd heard a horrific sound. He shook his head and scratched the sides of his head. Two small ear slits briefly flapped open, and then shut quickly.

She took a step backward when he blinked. His eyes were far rounder than a human's but she still was startled that his eyelids were vertical instead of horizontal. Right after he blinked, a faint membrane lingered. Double eyelids.

She almost stepped forward again, but then he starting talking. Or at least, she thought it was talking. The sounds were clicks that were far too foreign to even take a guess at. She could possibly mimic, but considering she had no idea what each click meant, she'd probably insult the creature.

She couldn't understand him and by his reactions to her speech earlier, she had to assume he couldn't understand her, either. Slowly he began taking steps backward. When she went to follow, he raised a silvery gun she hadn't seen before. She may not know what it did, but there was no doubt it wouldn't be something she'd like.

Nettie was not stupid. She was unarmed, and as much as she wanted to learn more about this alien and why his people were popping all over London, she knew this wouldn't be the time.

An instant later, the being and the room flashed and Nettie found herself back in the alley she'd left. She had enough time to think of how excited Lisselle and Gaston would be to hear about her adventure when vertigo slammed into her and she tumbled to the ground, unconscious.

"YOU KNOW, IF you wanted to spend some time with me, you could have come for a visit."

Nettie fought her way out of a fog and heard the snide American voice before she opened her eyes.

Taking advantage of her shut eyelids, she quickly tried to figure out where she was and why that insufferable Agent Smith was talking to her.

The alien. She'd seen a real alien and what could only have been his ship. She still had difficulties accepting the other fact that creatures lived on a different planet and the ship she'd been on had been flying through ether, but if she was to stay in the Society, her provincial outlook needed to change.

Other issues popped into mind, far more mundane ones. But she still didn't feel up to opening her eyes.

"I say, what time is it?" She tried to put on her most unassuming voice as she spoke.

"You don't have to try and sweet-talk me. I still can't get out of bed." His insufferable tone told Nettie that there was simply no way to deal with him. "And it's been about five hours since Gaston brought you in. As for the actual time, I've no idea. My watch was destroyed when I fell off your carriage."

"Five hours?" Her eyes flew open only to cause a whimper of pain and a quick shutting of lids. The room was too loud. Too bright, the colors too loud, too busy. It hurt behind her eyelids.

How could she have been laying here for five hours? "Do you know how long I was missing before they brought me in?" She had only been in that metal ship for a few minutes at the most. Her eyes may be pounding, but she remembered that.

"What's wrong with your eyes?"

"How long?" Nettie couldn't answer him about her eyes; she had no idea.

"Fine, don't tell me." He huffed, and she thought he had stopped talking to her, but then launched into a coughing fit. The medical training in her almost slammed her eyes back open to go help him. Luckily, the fit passed. If there was anyone on this planet she could do with not having to save, it would be Caden

Smith.

Fighting against the pain, Nettie squinted her eyes open enough to see the clock behind the hospital beds. Well, that did it. She would be in far greater trouble than mere alien abduction. She'd missed her entire shift of work. It was now half past eight in the morning.

"Try this." Lisselle's voice came from over her shoulder along with a small scrap of fabric. "Your eyes have been exposed to something odd, so they may need time to adjust."

Nettie sat up and tied the fabric around her head. She opened her eyes slowly, but she was able to open them. The thin gauze of the fabric cut the room glare down to manageable levels.

"Now, Gaston has gone off to make sure everything is settled with your employers," Lisselle added as she pulled up one of the heavy wooden chairs next to Nettie's bedside. "Why don't you fill me in on where you were before the constables picked you up for being passed out drunk in the poor quarter?"

"What?" Nettie almost leapt out of her bed. They couldn't think that she…

"That is rich." Caden was still lying down—he'd rolled to his side when she'd refused to answer him earlier—but he clearly was still listening.

Nettie had hoped that his earlier stunt would have lent him some caution. Apparently, it had not.

"I can assure you, I was not drinking." She aimed her words at Caden, but she kept her eyes on Lisselle. After all, it was Lisselle's opinion that mattered. Not the blustery American's. "I was abducted."

"A likely story told by a proper British lady caught doing

something she shouldn't." He still didn't roll over, so Nettie couldn't glare at him.

"Is there somewhere else we can speak? I assure you I am fine. Very fine."

Lisselle let her eyes dance between Nettie and Caden, but didn't let the smile in her eyes move any further. "I see. Well, then yes. We wouldn't want to tire out Agent Smith, now would we?" Lisselle rose from her chair, hedging forward in case Nettie needed balance.

"I don't want you little ladies to leave on account of me." Caden started to roll over.

"Let's go, Lisselle." Nettie refused to even meet Caden's eye. There was something more than a rough American attitude with him. It was as if he was trying to provoke her. She would look into his files herself.

LISSELLE LED HER to the parlor and immediately set in to brew some tea. It wasn't her light India one this time, but a full-bodied, black English tea. Clearly, she felt one of them might need fortification.

"Biscuits?" Lisselle looked very domesticated as she puttered around the small cupboards in the parlor. Gaston might have been born French, but his love of tea was extremely British. He kept a well-stocked supply of teas and accessories in a number of rooms in his mansion.

"Probably a good idea. I think I'm starting to feel a bit peckish." As she spoke, her stomach made a most unladylike noise. "Actually, I am apparently dreadfully peckish."

Lisselle laughed and brought over a heaping plate of assorted biscuits. "Let me also send for Damon to have Cook make something for you. You've missed a few meals on your adventure. And I do want to hear all of it before you pass out from hunger."

Before she'd even reached for the bell, Damon appeared in the doorway with a covered cart. He briefly looked up, flashed a smile, then silently set up a huge repast in front of them. Then, just as wordlessly, he started to leave.

"Why thank you, Damon, but how did you know?" Lisselle said.

He bobbed his head, and then shyly smiled. "The master told me to watch for Lady Nettie to come out. He said when she did, I was to feed her. A lot." He blushed a bit. "And he feels both of you are too skinny." He wheeled his cart away before either could speak.

Nettie laughed and bent forward to load her plate. "Well, I'm far more substantial than you. I think Gaston has a new project."

Lisselle twitched her nose. "He has been trying to fatten me up since we met. He refuses to believe I simply have a fast metabolism. Now, whoever abducted you?"

IT TOOK ALMOST two hours, and almost the entire contents of the food platters before them, for Nettie to tell her tale. Like Gaston, Lisselle felt the need to go over these types of events repeatedly. In the most minute detail possible.

"This is important," Lisselle said for easily the tenth time that morning, although Nettie had lost count so it could have been far more. "There was so much time lost between when you say you were taken up, and when the constables found you. I wish there was a way to know how long you were in their ship."

"I wish I knew as well. But as I said, it did only feel like the shortest of moments." Nettie paused. "I do wonder what they did to my eyes. And if something about them or their ship affects their eyes down here as well. Both times I have seen these beings in London, their faces have been covered." Nettie had been able to remove the protective cloth within an hour of coming into the parlor, but her eyes still felt sensitive.

Lisselle bounced to her feet for at least the thirtieth time since they'd begin talking. Nettie knew the older agent was active, but she'd come to realize that she honestly didn't think Lisselle could stay still for more than a few minutes.

"That has bearing as well." She spun on her low heel and dug through a cluttered cabinet toward the back of the parlor. "Do you think you could render a proper drawing of the alien? It might help us sort things out."

Nettie gave a slight frown, but took the offered pencils and papers. "I can try."

"You can try what?" Gaston's gruff voice broke in. "I say, Lisselle, you better not have debriefed my agent without my attendance." He shoved his cloak onto a waiting hook, changed into his house slippers, and stomped into the parlor.

Nettie glanced to see if Lisselle would look contrite about debriefing her, but the tiny agent smiled and poured another cup of tea.

"There was no debriefing." Lisselle waited until Gaston was settled, then added, "It was simply two dear friends discussing adventures. Well, her adventures. We hadn't gotten to mine yet."

Gaston let a few French words fly. Nettie really didn't know much French, but she knew the words Gaston used most often. Almost all of them were swear words.

"I couldn't let the poor girl sit there with all of that information inside. She would have burst by now," Lisselle said in her sweetest tone. "Besides, I did think you would get home long before now."

"Don't get me started!" Gaston snarled then took a long sip of tea, and the tension fled from his shoulders. "I have never seen such a wretched pair of professionals in my life." He turned toward Nettie. "I almost told them you quit."

That got her attention. Nettie had been mid-sip at his comment but she managed to finish the swallow before answering. "You didn't, did you?" She didn't love her job like she did her involvement in the Society, but she had worked far too hard to leave it now. Besides, she still believed that coroners could make a difference in solving crimes and the mysteries of murder.

"No, but it was close. Those two *bâtards*, Fritz and Abernathy, caused me more than enough grief about your illness. I explained you were my boarder and unable to leave your bed. They all but accused me with having absconded with you."

"Oh dear. But wait, when did you go in? Dr. Fritz and Dr. Abernathy shouldn't be there now. Dr. Wilson should be." That would explain the other two doctors being more annoying than usual.

"That is precisely what they said. They said he had not come in for work for the last two days, and now neither had you, and how were they supposed to get any work done?" He shook his head and violently stirred more milk into his tea. "I had to call on friends in the hospital itself to get them to back down."

"Gaston, something has gone wrong." Nettie found herself uncommonly sluggish as she tried to leap to her feet. "Dr. Wilson being missing would be akin to you going missing. It simply doesn't happen."

"Now, now, easy there." Lisselle pushed Nettie back into her seat then turned to scowl at Gaston. "Don't you dare get her riled up again. I got her calmed down. She's had an experience none of us can even imagine and now you come in scaring her."

Nettie waved Lisselle off, but stayed seated. Clearly, traveling to an ethership and back was extremely draining. "No, I'm not overwrought. But the fact remains, if Dr. Wilson is missing then something is wrong. He's never missed a single day. And something I didn't tell you—someone stole the words off the report I'd given him on the air crash." She knew she'd turned in a full report.

Lisselle continued to refill her teacup as quickly as she drank it down. At this point, she'd be awake for weeks.

"Stole the words? Lisselle, what are you putting in her tea?"

Nettie fluttered her hand at him. "They took a full report I had turned in and replaced it with blank pages." Another long draw of tea brought her feeling more like herself. "It was right after Lord Melbourne's man took the bodies."

Now it was Lisselle's turn to look upset. A look that was echoed by Gaston. With a start, Nettie realized that with everything that had been going on, she had neglected to inform them of the previous events.

"I mentioned it in my report…" She let her words drift off at the look on their faces. She may have mentioned it, but not to the extent she should have. "I do apologize. I seemed to have pushed it out with the other events."

Gaston had gone from upset to thoughtful. "Or someone wanted you to forget to tell us. Think back. Was this the day of the vampire attack?"

Nettie felt the blood drain from her face. "Yes it was." So the attack had been to make her forget Melbourne's man and the missing documents? That didn't make her feel much better about the attack, and more concerned for the people working in the morgue.

Like Rebecca.

She jumped to her feet. The tea had given her a false sense of recovery; alas, her legs didn't echo it and she tumbled back to her chair. "Rebecca may be in danger."

"I'm sure she's fine, my dear." Gaston patted her hands. "Unlike you, she is not part of the Society." He glanced to Lisselle, but she gave nothing away. "Yet, at any rate."

"No, but what if they know she's being considered? She was the one who signed Melbourne's man in. And I showed her the blank documents." Something poked about the back of her memories. "But you say the attack made me forget. I know Rebecca and I discussed the fact that Dr. Wilson didn't react to the replacement file I'd placed in his desk. This would imply we remembered it then."

"Do you know why you wouldn't have told us?" Lisselle pushed aside the hand Nettie had over her teacup and filled it to the top again. She even added two sugar cubes for good measure.

"Maybe I forgot?"

Gaston gave a huge guffaw at that one, startling Damon, who happened to be walking past. "Not bloody likely. I don't think you've forgotten a single event since you were born. Which asks the question of what is going on?" He turned pointedly to Lisselle. "You're the vampire expert, so you tell me, could he have diffused her memories when he bit her?"

"Yes. It isn't something normal vampires can do. But we've tracked a group of extremely abnormal vampires to Bath. We've had no luck finding their lair. But we've not tracked them outside of Bath either." She bounced to her tiny feet and started circling the room. "As for Nettie being able to recall it when with Rebecca, that could be proximity. She and Rebecca shared the event the vampire was blocking. If they come together, it must undo some of what he did." She circled to a stop in front of Gaston. "We have to find that vampire. Immediately. And I think we need to secure Rebecca. Nettie is right; she could be in danger as well."

"Finding the vampire isn't going to be that easy. He did manage to abscond with four Runners. We have been looking."

Nettie looked at her timepiece. They'd been discussing and debating for over two hours. Rebecca would be showing up at work soon.

"I've been tampered with, Dr. Wilson is missing, the bodies are missing, the Runners are missing, and Rebecca will be showing up at work soon. Shouldn't someone do something?" She knew she couldn't go warn her friend or she'd risk undoing the hard work of Gaston in covering her absence. But if neither of them were going to act, she *would* go down there herself.

"Of course." Lisselle came and laid her hand on Nettie's arm. Almost immediately, a calm feeling flowed over her. "I will go and get her myself." She gave Gaston a pointed look. "You'll need to secure a room. And neither of you can speak to her when I bring her in. She'll be in a trance. She's not been cleared yet, so we can't let her know what is really going on."

They were going to drug her friend? "What do you mean, trance?" Nettie mentally ran through any drugs that could lead to a trance and none of them made her happy.

"Easy there. You'd best explain it quickly, Lisselle. She's ready to see if she can best you," Gaston said.

"I would not be so rude, Gaston, and you know it. I have a good knowledge of medicines—"

"Fear not. This won't harm Rebecca in the least." Lisselle slipped on her long black coat. "But it is important that no one speak to her when I bring her in." She started to turn to go out, and then swung back. "Oh, and you may wish to introduce Agent Smith to the politeness of not eavesdropping. He has been right outside the door for the last five minutes."

"Four minutes and I couldn't hear anything." Caden hobbled into view. He really shouldn't be up yet. He appeared to healing far faster that Nettie expected, but he was still pale and shaky.

"I know." Lisselle gave him an enigmatic grin, patted his cheek, and marched out the door.

"Well, she has left me with two invalids," Gaston said and fixed a pointed look at Nettie. "Yes, you as well. We've no idea what being on that ship in ether has done to you. I've convinced your wretched co-workers that you will not be in today either. You are to go to bed and only get up to work on your report. I want you to start with the alien, and then work on any other unusual happenings that you may or may not have already reported."

"Thank you, I will do that." Recording everything would soothe her. Right now, she needed to get her balance back. She surprised him with a peck on the cheek, carefully ignored Caden leaning against the doorway, and went to her room.

CHAPTER THIRTEEN

Nettie had feared that with all of the tea Lisselle had been forcing down her, she wouldn't be able to sleep for days. But the moment she'd gotten into her room, exhaustion overwhelmed her. Clearly, Lisselle had put something other than sugar in her tea.

She had intended to work on the reports for Gaston. Whether he needed them or not wasn't germane; the fact was she needed to do them. After her nap, that was. Well, it couldn't really be called a nap when she'd slept for eight solid hours she supposed.

It took her a little while to sort herself and get started on the reports, but she'd gotten a good stream of information flowing when a light rap on her door broke into her thoughts.

"Oh good, you're awake." Lisselle bounded in, then carefully surveyed Nettie's nightdress. "That won't do. You'll need to get dressed if you're to join me." She opened the wardrobe and dragged out some clothes.

"Join you?" Nettie thought she recovered from her adventure aboard the mystery ship, but she certainly was at a loss right now.

"Yes." Lisselle poked her head out of the closet, squinted toward the window at the dreary sky, and added another jacket. "I need to go shopping and you need some fresh air. Besides, all the best shops are near the palace." She gave Nettie a wink, then stepped outside to let her change.

Shopping seemed a bit frivolous what with all of the recent events, but since Lisselle never did anything without a reason, Nettie put away her writing implements and changed.

A FEW HOURS later, Nettie had two new dresses, a pair of women's trousers, and a new hat. Lisselle had twice that much. While the tiny, gray-haired agent had been watching the palace carefully as they made their way down the shops, she'd also been far more serious about shopping than Nettie had expected.

Nettie had made it in the door of Gaston's mansion when Lisselle stopped dead in front of her, directly in front of the parlor door.

"What is *he* doing here?" Lisselle swore and dropped her packages on the floor. Nettie almost stepped on them and Lisselle herself. Luckily, seeing over the tiny woman was not hard.

The object of the venom in Lisselle's cultured voice was studying them a heavy chair near the fire.

He was a bear-like man, stroking a great iron-colored beard, which obscured half of his face, echoed by a thick thatch of hair the same color that was long enough to hit his collar. Clad mostly in a dark assortment of well-worn brown leathers, he puffed on a foreign-smelling cigar as he held her gaze. Although of an age to be a contemporary of Lisselle's, he clearly was not one for lurking out secrets in the height of society—at least not dressed like he was. His boots dripped mud from where he had propped his feet in front of the fire.

"Excellent to see you too, Lisselle." His accent was light; clearly he had lived in Britain for a long time, but buried in there was a faint American twang.

"Homer. I thought you'd been butchered by pygmies years ago." Lisselle hadn't budged. Her shoulders even lowered as if to make her less mobile.

"Ah, not yet. ' Twas the headhunters that almost got me. But they decided my mug was too ugly to collect. What's made you crawl out of your hole in York? Visiting old stomping grounds?"

"Investigating the recent airship collisions. Your work?"

Nettie rocked back. Lisselle was accusing someone who clearly knew Gaston of working for the enemy? She kept her face immobile, but let the small knife she now carried concealed in her right sleeve to drop down into her waiting palm. The man was huge, but it would be a disservice to think that there was not a fair amount of muscle under that mass.

"Hardly. Heard there was a vampire incident in the palace. Your work?" He took a long drag of his cigar through clenched teeth.

Nettie could see Lisselle practically shaking with the attempt to keep from charging him.

"I don't do vampires, *pirate.*"

"Now that's a harsh thing to be saying. I have never been caught."

Nettie reassessed. He didn't have a look of the sea to him, but the term, 'pirate,' fit. His leathers didn't match, as if they'd come from assorted collections.

"You old airship pirate."

"Witch."

The tension in the room grew, and then exploded as Homer rose from his chair and he and Lisselle rushed toward each other with murder in their eyes.

Nettie let the knife in her left sleeve drop into her palm. Gaston had given her these toys two nights ago, but she didn't think she'd need them so soon.

An airship pirate? Now that fit, unfortunately. She never expected to be attacked in Gaston's home, so all she had were her two knives. They would have to do. Lisselle had shown herself to be a fierce fighter, but the pirate was at least a foot taller and more than a few stone heavier.

Lisselle launched herself toward the pirate with a speed Nettie had never seen before.

An instant later the leather-clad man swung Lisselle up in the air and caught her.

In a hug.

Nettie let out a sigh of relief as the two obvious friends held on to each other.

"Damn you, girl. You need to eat more. Naught but skin and bones."

Lisselle laughed and freed an arm to poke the leather-clad belly. "And you need to stop eating so much. Your damn ships won't be able to get off the ground." She wriggled out of his arms to drop to the ground.

"I do fine. You forget, this is all muscle," he said then let out an "oof" as Lisselle punched him in the gut.

"Not all of it. Not by a long shot." She pounded his back, at least as high as she could reach. "Where the hell have you been? We could have used you when the queen turned."

"Places not to be spoken of lightly, I'm afraid." His grey eyes darkened. "There is unrest in more than just our island home. I can't find the start of it, but I fear the full brunt of it will travel quickly." His sober turn was shaken off as he looked to Nettie with a smile. "And who might this lovely young one be?"

"Someone who was ready to gut you should the need arise." Gaston's voice came from the hallway behind her. Nettie had no idea how long he had been there. She pressed the mechanisms that reloaded her knives back into their sheaths and smiled at the airship pirate.

"Captain Homer Tremain, I'd like to present Agent Jones, Dr. Nettie Jones." Gaston brushed Nettie's arm as he went by, hinting she should follow him in. Now that Homer's loyalty was established and her knives put away, she had no issue following.

"Dr. Jones, eh? Not many lady docs running around and it's good to have one our team." He stuck out a plate-sized hand and pumped her own enthusiastically. "And I'm retired. You can call me Homer."

Lisselle smacked his arm then went to pour herself a drink. "Since when have you retired, you old air rat?"

"Officially, I no longer work for Melbourne. Therefore, since my only official title was as a royal Air Force Zeppelin Captain, and I have left that, I am retired. Technically, I've tried to retire from my other obligations as well. Certain people wouldn't let me."

Gaston reclaimed the chair Homer had vacated. "You said it yourself, something worldwide is going down. We'll be needing you and your ships before the year is out, I fear."

"Are you really a pirate?" Nettie was fascinated. She had

never met a pirate of any sort, but an airship pirate seemed extremely dashing.

"Don't encourage him, *ma chère*," Gaston said. "He fancies himself the scourge of the skies."

"Ignore our rotund friend, Dr. Jones. I have from time to time engaged in unofficial airship activities in the name of the Society." Homer held his hands out wide. "I do what needs to be done."

"Please call me Nettie," she said. "I mostly practice my medical skills on those who are too far gone to notice."

Homer smacked himself in the head. "*That* Agent Jones. You're the one who's part vampire, yes? I should have known you'd be here in tight with Lisselle."

Nettie was becoming a bit more comfortable with people knowing her secret, but it was still disturbing that people she didn't know knew of her. "I'm not sure what you mean." Lisselle had been a great teacher and confidant, but they'd not spoken of Nettie's condition beyond that one night.

"You haven't told her?"

"I was waiting for the right moment." Lisselle flashed her old friend a dirty look; clearly she would be talking to him about this later.

"Told me what?" Nettie looked at all three faces carefully, but clues weren't there.

"I *am* a witch. Homer was not calling me that as a term of endearment." Lisselle ran her fingers through her short hair leaving it spiked up. "I use spells, magic, whatever you want to call it. I'm not that strong—" A choking sound from Gaston cut her off.

"I am not. That was an odd coincidence." Lisselle folded her arms tightly around herself and glared at both men.

Nettie held up her hand to her head. "A witch? They don't exist. How can they exist? Science leaves no room for magic." It was all very fine if she did small parlor tricks and the like, but as a scientist, Nettie knew magic simply could never exist.

"Oh, it does, and our tiny grey dervish is a strong practitioner. Damn near blew up the dock in Cardiff a few years ago." Gaston nodded.

"But...magic?" Nettie wiggled her fingers in the air, pantomiming spell casting. In her time in the Society, she had seen more than her share of odd things, but they were always explainable through science.

"Ah, child, I knew this would hit someone like you hard. Which is why I wanted to wait to tell you." Lisselle hugged Nettie while she glared at the two men. "You yourself are an example of an ancient spell. Vampires came into the world long ago through a bereaved witch who lost her loved one. Through a spell gone wrong, he came back as a mindless undead and killed her, but he carried the spell like a disease and it spread. Now vampires, while rare, are found everywhere in the world."

"Magic can't exist." Her scientific brain fought what Lisselle was saying.

Lisselle chucked her under her chin. "You keep telling yourself that, lass, if it makes you feel better. Just ignore anything odd I do."

"But no, you can't...do something for me?" Nettie was having a hard time with the concept. Science was her soul, but at the same time, an unhealthy curiosity often took control of logic.

"Spells aren't like a steam engine. It's not as if I can turn a faucet. And my reserves are limited." Lisselle studied Nettie for a few seconds, both men watching as well but saying nothing.

"Okay, how about this one? I can't lift much beyond my own weight, nor for long, but here it goes." A series of arcane words flowed smoothly out of her lips, ending with a blessing. Shutting her eyes and lifting her arms up, Lisselle slowly rose off the floor.

Nettie looked for wires and strings, but found none as her friend rose until her feet were even with the top of Nettie's head.

Lisselle opened her bright blue eyes and flashed a smile. "This magical enough for you, Nettie?" A slight movement of her arms swung her over to the middle of the room. It was as if she had become lighter than air.

"How is that possible?" Nettie's scientific mind searched for any machine or item to could create what she saw. The rest of her wondered if it was something she herself could learn.

"It's an ancient spell, not used much anymore. As you saw, it took too long for me to become airborne. And not being able to lift much besides my own weight reduces the applications even further. But still, sometimes it comes in handy." As she spoke, Lisselle lowered her arms and slowly began her descent. "Sometimes you can hear things others don't want you to when you can listen outside three-story windows."

"Pah, and almost become a human pin cushion." Homer held out a hand to steady her as she landed. "That is why magic isn't strongly used in the Society, Nettie. It causes as many problems as it solves. Give me good steam power and a sword any day."

"Pin cushion?"

"He always brings that up. Yes, I needed help. It was not as dark as it should have been and I was spotted three stories up. I couldn't drop down, and I couldn't move away quickly. They were drawing up archers when Homer and his ship, *The Drunken Harlot*, came and saved me." She punched Homer. "I did get the information though."

"Aye, that you did." He looked ready to say more but held back, clearly this argument had been going on for a long time.

Nettie got herself some tea, then sat down then shook her head. "So magic is real. Really real. People can fly. Aliens come down from other worlds. Oh my." Setting her teacup down, she buried her face in her hands.

"I knew we should have waited to tell her. Now look what your bullying has done." Lisselle dropped to her knees in front of Nettie.

"*Ma chere*, are you alright? Don't cry, things aren't all...." Gaston let the rest of his words drop as Nettie raised her head.

She was crying, but they were tears of laughter. "This is marvelous! I could never have thought all of this up in my wildest dreams." She jumped to her feet and planted a kiss on Gaston's cheek. "I can't thank you enough for recruiting me, Gaston."

CHAPTER FOURTEEN

A FEW HOURS later, Nettie found herself pacing in agitation as she fretted whether her best friend would have the same feelings once she was brought into the Society.

Most likely due to the recent events, and the danger and importance of them, Rebecca was being brought onboard at an expedited rate. Lisselle had retrieved her earlier out of safety, leaving her in a slight spell-induced trance in one of the guest rooms. Then, an hour ago Agent Ramsey had called down on the Mudger and announced the official decision to bring Rebecca into the Society with haste. She wasn't even being sent up to Edinburgh until the current troubles had been settled. Agent Ramsey said that between Gaston, Lisselle, and even Homer there was enough Society intelligence there to vet the girl for the time being.

Nettie hoped she hadn't been wrong in her assessment of her friend's character. She felt that Rebecca would be an excellent agent, and she believed that she'd be excited about being invited to join.

Even as she was reminding herself of this, a small part of her mind suggested that Rebecca hadn't reacted that well to the vision she'd had. She had gotten quite ill there for a bit. To be fair to Rebecca's strength of personality, there may have been a physiological reaction to that entire event that Nettie had not been privy to. Nettie had been along for the ride, however it had been Rebecca's gifts that dragged her along. Having seen fatigue on Lisselle's face after her short burst of magic demonstration, Nettie realized that these gifts came with a cost.

What if using her gifts would be too taxing for Rebecca? What if she was frightened by the things Nettie relished? Worst of all, what if she treated Nettie differently because of her vampiric status?

All of those thoughts and more flew around Nettie's mind as she walked a nice deep rut into the parlor rug.

"You know, you're leaving a groove in the wood below the rug with your stomping."

As usual it seemed, Nettie heard Caden before she saw him. The man either enjoyed warning people he was coming by speaking in advance of his arrival, or else he was too impatient to wait until he was seen.

"Ladies do not stomp, they pace. And I'm sure you are not so rude as to imply that I am large enough that my pacing would damage two-hundred-year-old wood." Nettie spared a glare through the doorway where Caden now lingered, but didn't stop her pacing.

Her choice to pace out here in the public portion of the mansion was partially fueled by the desire to have someone ease her out of her fears. Caden definitely would not have been her choice for that task.

"Ladies also invite injured gentlemen into their stomping grounds so they don't have to linger in the hallway." He leaned heavily against the doorframe. "I could pull out a stitch while standing here."

He didn't look near as weak as he was implying. His rich brown eyes were quite dangerous, and his thick hair had enough muss to it to appear rakish.

Nettie shook those thoughts of his attractiveness free of her head as soon as she realized they'd entered. There was no denying Caden Smith was an extremely handsome version of maleness. He was also difficult, problematic, and extremely aware of his effect on women.

"This is a public portion of the mansion, you know. You may sit, lean, or collapse wherever you wish." She paused and studied him as he slowly came into the parlor. "I do think we may have sent the wrong Agent Smith to the Edinburgh prison. I had heard that Agent Caden Smith was far hardier than you seem to be. You have been languishing about for more than a few days."

The fact was, any other man should have been laid up for at least a few weeks for the amount of poison that had entered into his bloodstream. His recovery had been uncommonly swift. Aside from his determination to keep to his sick bed in the dungeon, and his affected slowness when up and about, Nettie would say he was fine to return to duty.

"I assure you, I am the right Caden. Besides, I'm better looking than he was and didn't the reports say I was a ladies' man? He wasn't dashing enough for that moniker." The self-mockery that filled his face as he sat was quick to vanish.

Nettie stopped pacing and took a seat. This was interesting; perhaps there was more to the dashing American than appeared. He clearly knew who people said he was, and he wasn't happy with it. Yet he obviously didn't try to change his ways either. She would have to contemplate this change.

"Were you close to Agent McGrady?" There was no way she would find out who he really was if they continued to only communicate in barbs flung back and forth like school children. Besides, she did want to know more about his relationship with the missing agent.

"Right to the point eh? Aren't you Brits supposed to offer a man tea first?"

He was clearly trying to annoy her. He'd walked right past the tea service as he entered the room. That was another interesting tidbit to store away. The interaction between them hadn't been friendly since they first met. Nettie had assumed that it was simply a conflict of personalities. Now she suspected something more. Perhaps Smith had a reason for keeping them at odds?

"Would you like some tea, Caden?" Nettie softened her manner and her voice. If he wanted them at odds, then she wanted to make that as difficult as possible. Without waiting for his response, she pulled the teacart forward and poured two cups. "Would you desire some sugar or milk?"

If he was annoyed at her change in tactics, Caden didn't let it show. Well, outside from a slight narrowing of his eyes. But a moment later, he flashed a too wide smile. "Sugar would be fine. I'm afraid I can't get used to the thought of milk in my tea. I'm too American it seems."

"Ah well. You know, perhaps you Americans have the right of it. I'm not always in agreement with milk in my tea either." Even though she usually put at least a dab in, Nettie made sure both teas were clear and milk-free when she served.

"Biscuits?" She made the word a question, but had already

placed two on a small saucer and laid it down in front of him.

The eyes stayed narrow for a bit longer this time.

"Thank you." He took an appreciative sip of the tea, and then leaned back in his seat. "One thing you Brits have down is tea."

"Why, thank you, Agent Smith, that is so gracious of you to say. So you and Agent McGrady were close?" Nettie settled back in her chair and nibbled demurely on a digestive biscuit.

"Please, do call me Caden." Now the same sugary sweetness in her voice was echoed in his. Clearly, he'd caught onto her plan to put him off guard. "I actually never said how well we knew each other, but yes, I counted him as a friend. We only worked one case together. He was stationed in New York for a few months a few years ago. I was assigned as his partner during a rather gruesome case involving rabid vampires. I had been looking forward to working with him again."

Nettie digested the information as she swallowed the last of her biscuit. "I see. I didn't know him well at all. Only met him on a few occasions here in the mansion." She leaned forward. "So do you believe he had something to do with the collision?"

A real grin made a brief foray onto his face. Nettie was surprised at how much younger he looked. A moment later, his set charming smile replaced it.

"The man I worked with wouldn't have been involved in any way except to stop it if he could. Yet, it has been a number of years. He may not be the same man at all."

Nettie had to give him credit for his answer. Very well put and nothing there to cause suspicions should McGrady prove to have gone to the other side. Whichever side that was. They still had no idea who had been behind the collision. The papers were still claiming it was an accident on behalf of the passenger ship. They even backed it up with a false report generated from the Society.

"I see." She sipped her tea and tried to think of other things that might catch him off guard. Perhaps an inquiry into the real reason he wouldn't leave his sick bed? It wasn't as if the dungeon was particularly attractive after all, and the sick quarter was positively dreary.

She didn't bother to hide her frown when she figured out what he was up to.

"So how long have you been working on your project, and was Gaston made aware of it?"

That worked. He actually gave a slight choke as the biscuit he'd bitten into went down the wrong pipe.

"I assure you I don't have anything I'm working on. I have been ill, after all. Confined to the dungeon as it were. Lost from human interaction—"

"Left alone all night with equipment that could take apart anything?" Nettie leapt to her feet. "I ask you again, sir, is this work with the approval of Gaston or not?" She didn't bother to drop her small blades into her hands. He was still weak enough that she could take him by bare hands if need be. She made certain her stance showed she'd be willing to do just that if he was working without Gaston's knowledge.

Lisselle appeared at that moment, leading a sleepwalking Rebecca back into the house. Lisselle had some tests she needed to run on Rebecca outside and had kept her in the trance state.

Nettie bit her lip. The cause for Rebecca's numb state no longer existed since she was to go through the full agent induction, but Lisselle wouldn't know that yet. They'd been out in the garden testing when Agent Ramsey had called. Since she had no idea what Lisselle had done to her friend, she didn't know what would happen if she startled her out of it.

Lisselle nodded her thanks when both Caden and Nettie dropped their conversation.

Unfortunately, Gaston broke the silence coming up from the dungeon. "Damn it, Smith, where are you? I asked you to finish up your..." He froze as he saw Lisselle, but it was too late. Rebecca gave a shake, and then tumbled to the ground.

"*Merde.* I knew I should have gone outside and warned you. She doesn't need to be in a trance now; Ramsey has approved her agent status." Gaston let a few more French swear words fly as he raced to Rebecca's side.

"What difference would that have made?" Lisselle was upset, but not frantic; obviously, whatever the breaking of the spell did to Rebecca wasn't dire. She pushed Gaston aside as if he were a child and brought out smelling salts.

Unfortunately, Rebecca's dark head stayed unmoved.

"Oh, bother. Gaston, can you carry her to her room? I am afraid she'll likely take a few hours to sleep this off. I had to go far deeper than I normally would to put her under."

"I would be honored to carry the lovely lady in." Caden spoke before Gaston and rose effortlessly from his chair. "She is the newest agent, yes?"

The ease with which he scooped Rebecca up annoyed Nettie fiercely. So did the way he was effectively getting out of her line of questions. She was about to charge forward and demand answers when Lisselle started to crumble.

"Oh dear," was all she said before she fell into the chair in front of her. She raised a shaking hand to the side of her suddenly pale face. "I'm afraid putting her under took far more out of me than expected."

Gaston waved Caden on, but Nettie noticed the look the two shared indicated they'd have words later.

"You need to watch that, Lisselle. You won't do anyone any good if you collapse somewhere out in the field." He covered his concern with gruff words and a gruff voice, but Nettie saw it linger in his eyes.

Nettie was torn between following Caden and Rebecca, and taking care of Lisselle. Clearly, Lisselle needed her more. And even if there were something odd about Caden, he wouldn't hurt Rebecca here in Gaston's household.

"Take some tea, Lisselle." Nettie gently pushed Gaston aside and forced a steaming cup into her friend's shaking hands.

"You don't happen to have something a bit stronger, do you?" Lisselle's laugh was weak, but she sipped the tea as ordered.

"It's a bit early for drinking, young lady." Gaston couldn't be much older than Lisselle, but that didn't stop him from awkwardly patting her head.

Nettie watched him for a moment. It was disturbing that she had such a bad reaction to whatever she had done to Rebecca, but fatigue shouldn't be that worrisome. Unless there was something else behind it.

Nettie stood up once she was certain Lisselle intended to drink the entire cup of tea. She motioned for Gaston to follow her out of the parlor.

"As the closest thing to a fully trained physician we have in here, it is vital that you tell me what is disturbing you. It's more than her simply being fatigued, isn't it?"

He shook his head and took a few more steps away from the parlor doorway. "Ah, *chere*, you would have made a fine physician. Far too observant for your own good sometimes though. Yes, I am concerned. I have seen Lisselle use her powers for days without so much as a winding. Yet, here twice in as many days a simple task has tired her. I've never seen her like she is in there." His face was tight. "It is more than a little worrisome. What is worse is that if something is seriously wrong, she will not tell me."

Nettie nodded. "Meaning, she might tell me? I can try to engage her confidence. I am her doctor at the moment, after all. But I cannot promise anything. If Lisselle has always only shared that which she wants to, she may not be forthcoming with me either."

"That's the truth. But try. I need to contact Edinburgh concerning this and a few other things. Will you see that she's comfortable before you leave for work?"

At her distracted nod, he turned to go down the corridor toward the dungeon. Nettie shook herself out of her thoughts. She needed to ask about Caden.

"Wait, I did have a question about Caden. Why is he still in the dungeon? He's well enough to go into a room."

Gaston rocked back on his heels and a sheepish look crossed his face. "You caught that, did you? I feared you might. Caden has been working on a special project for me." He raised a hand before she'd done more than draw a breath. "No, *chere*, I can't speak of it now. It's too dangerous for any other than he and I to know of it now. Lisselle and Homer are unaware as well, so don't wave that look at me."

Nettie folded her arms. "I still don't think he should be down there all the time." But she knew she sounded sulky.

"Now, see? I thought you two were getting along better today. I didn't even hear any shouting."

"You were spying on us? Gaston, we are not children."

"Then stop acting like them." He softened his words with a smile. "I need you two to get along then. You are to be a team on this current rash of troubles."

Nettie did not know whether to scream or cry. "A team? But I thought Lisselle and I would be working together?" It had taken all she could do not to strangle the dolt in the parlor. If she had to work in close quarters with him, she may give into her desires.

"*Non, chere,* I need Lisselle to be doing something else. You do need to be with an experienced agent, so you will be working with Caden. He'll be the senior agent on your tasks."

Nettie felt that Lisselle had had the right idea about something stronger to drink. She certainly could use it now. She knew she wouldn't be the senior agent, but she had hoped to work with someone she could stand. It would be bad form if she were forced to attack her senior agent if he annoyed her too much while on a mission.

"But really, I don't—"

"He's an American, so he will be difficult. But you could still learn from the boy." Gaston smiled again and started walking back down the corridor. "So glad you two are finally getting along. Don't forget to see to Lisselle before you go to work." With that, he vanished around the corner, leaving Nettie to stew in silence.

"He's done that to me too." Lisselle's voice came from inches behind her. She'd obviously gotten up at some point but said nothing. "He did that to Homer and me when we were both young agents. I think he thinks it's funny. Although he'll claim he does it because it makes for stronger agents."

Nettie turned and was ready to catch Lisselle, but the tiny agent waved her off. "I'm fine. It's simple spell fatigue. Gaston is an old mother hen. He's seen me get tired before. He has selective memory when it comes to more things to worry about." She turned and went back to her seat.

"Do you think Rebecca is the cause? Could there be something wrong with her?"

"No, she's fine, and I'm sure she'll tell you herself when she wakes up. However, her own unique set of skills could have actually been what hit me. I've never tried to put a clairvoyant under before." She gave a shrug. "It may have been a cross between our two abilities. But for whatever reason, it put more of a strain on my spell than I was expecting. Trust me, we'll both be fine." With another final drink of tea, Lisselle rose to her feet and reclaimed her jacket.

"You can't go out now. You need to rest."

"Nettie, you are a fine doctor. But I know my body. Now that the strain of the spell has worn off, I'm fine. I have a meeting tonight that I can't miss. And you need to report to work if you don't want to lose that job of yours, so don't even think of following me."

"I wasn't—"

"Ah, my dear girl, you may be strong, and will someday make

a great agent. But you are an awful liar. Not to mention you project everything you are thinking." She reached up and patted Nettie's cheek. "You'll be fine, Rebecca's fine, and I'm fine. Go to work."

Nettie put on her own coat and held the door open. "Can I at least ask who you're meeting?"

Lisselle looked around for any extra listeners. "Melbourne. I need to talk to him about the queen. And some bodies."

Before Nettie could respond, Lisselle had climbed aboard the carriage and engaged the horses.

"But, Lisselle, isn't that dangerous? You should take Homer with you."

"Pah, that old reprobate has his own tasks. And Melbourne and I are friends." She winked at Nettie as she got the horses down the lane. "Of a sort."

Nettie wanted to go after her, but the fact was, she was late for work. While this job wasn't the meaning of her life, she did take her responsibilities seriously. And having missed two days under mysterious circumstances did not bode well in her book.

The day was dry enough to risk Lula Belle, and she was late enough to take her. As much as the temptation to try and find that alley she'd been in prior to being taken aboard that ether-faring ship pulled at her, she knew she needed to get to work.

Doctors Fritz and Abernathy were both there, but they had no bodies on the tables with them. Both looked ready to yell at her, but then, as a single person, backed down.

Now that was peculiar. Even though they were not her superiors, they'd often felt the need to take her to task for her shortcomings. She'd gotten so used to politely ignoring them that not having to do so was actually disturbing.

"I see Rebecca has already left?" She thought it best not to let them know that she was fully aware of Rebecca's location. Besides, if they were behind any of the troubles of late, they might let something slip.

"She has taken ill," Dr. Fritz answered with a scowl. "Perhaps she caught the same illness as you. A tall doctor lady came and took her."

Nettie gave a start. Tall? She could see Lisselle passing herself off as a doctor, but no one could consider her tall.

"The lady wasn't tall, she was short and round. You can't even see with your eyes open." Dr. Abernathy hit his companion.

As the two dissolved into an argument over what Lisselle actually looked like, Nettie smiled. Clearly, Lisselle's magic was good for far more than simple things. If no one could remember what you looked like, it would be far easier to go about Society business unnoticed.

"Well, thank you very much. I don't suppose that Doctor Wilson has left word?" Gaston hadn't been able to find out anything about her supervisor's disappearance. He'd been headed home two days before and vanished. Gaston had kept a lookout posted near Dr. Wilson's apartment in case he returned.

"As if you weren't privy to it." Dr. Fritz broke off his argument to snarl. "A bit suspicious, you both vanishing at the same time and both coming back on the same day."

"That's not our business." Dr. Abernathy looked to Nettie with what could be fear in his eyes. Since she'd never done anything to him to warrant such a look, she had to assume it was whatever Gaston had said or done while here.

"I assure you, I have been—"

"Yes yes, quite ill. We shall be off now." Dr. Abernathy practically grabbed Dr. Fritz by the collar and hauled him outside.

Nettie didn't watch them go, but made her way back to the larger offices. How could Gaston's man have missed Dr. Wilson's return? Unless he came here after vanishing before going home? How peculiar.

The door to Dr. Wilson's office was shut and that in and of itself was odd. While he wasn't a cheery man, he was always open to serious discussion, and therefore felt the need to always be available to his staff.

Leaving her reticule and coat in her own little office, Nettie went to his door and knocked.

"Yes? Please enter." It was his voice but far more stiff than he normally sounded. It also sounded as if he wasn't sure of the correct thing to say.

Nettie opened the door slowly, prepared for anything to be on the other side at this point.

She was almost disappointed when only Dr. Wilson's unsmiling face greeted her.

"Ah, Dr. Nettie Jones. Please, do come in." He rose, but his movements were as stiff as his speech. Had he been in some sort of accident?

"Dr. Wilson, I am pleased you have returned. We were concerned for you, sir." She stepped into the room, but didn't sit. There was something wrong here, and it was making the loose hairs at the back of her neck rise in agitation.

"I had…a family emergency." As he turned his face to meet her, she realized what disturbed her so. There was nothing in his eyes. His clear blue orbs were completely lifeless.

"I see, sir. Are you certain you're feeling all right? You are looking a bit tired." There was something wrong here. He was now clutching his desk in pain. Or what looked like pain. It could have been anger. The most disturbing aspect was the effect his fingers were having on the desk.

It was crumbling under his white-knuckled grip, and unfortunately familiar green foam was beginning to spread between his fingers.

CHAPTER FIFTEEN

NETTIE REACHED FOR the doorknob behind her and forced her terror-frozen legs to flee the room. Ducking into her office, she grabbed her things as well. There was no noise from Dr. Wilson's office, but whatever was in there was no longer her superior. She automatically reached into her reticule for one of the Runners' summoning envelopes, then stopped and let loose some unladylike swearing.

Edinburgh had the Runners locked down since the missing four were still at large. She would need to notify Gaston of Dr. Wilson's issues directly.

But she didn't want to risk Dr. Wilson getting out, or some poor unsuspecting soul getting in. She could barricade the door, but not with herself on the outside.

The window in her office had been big enough to let the Runner in and out. Actually, she still wasn't sure how he did it, but she was smaller in width than the mechanical man. First, she took the chain by the main doors and twisted it around the handles of the main door in such a way that anyone except for a full-blooded vampire would be hard pressed to remove it. Then, she grabbed the long security pole from the door area and ran for her office. The window was bigger than she'd noticed, but she would still be working hard to fit through it. Mostly due to the vile skirts she wore. She debated removing them and leaving them behind, but riding through London at night in her little clothes was a bit much, even for her.

She settled for removing the offending skirts, tossing them and the pole out the window, then forcing herself through. She secured the window as best she could, but whatever Dr. Wilson was, there was no way he could get thin enough to get through it.

Donning her skirts, she twisted the pole through the front handles for the main doors. With the chains on the inside, and this twisted pole on the outside, anyone would be hard pressed to get inside. With a quill and a scrap of paper in her reticule, she left a note on the door of a dangerous chemical spill and that no one should enter.

The ride back to the mansion seemed far longer than it should have, but she was certain it was simply her nerves. She'd never been close to Dr. Wilson, but still it was sad to think the man she'd worked with all these years was most likely reduced to a puddle of green ooze by now.

The thing was, he hadn't been himself at all, even before the foam made its appearance. Which brought forth the question, were these people who were dissolving actually people? Lisselle had been running studies on the foam, but as far as Nettie knew, nothing had been discovered.

Gaston was nowhere to be found when she finally got to the mansion. Considering he usually seemed to be lurking around the dungeon as of late, she made her way down there. She left her coat on and reticule at hand since they would most likely be having to run out to the hospital immediately.

The door was closed, but not locked, so she let herself in. She didn't mean to spy; she was naturally quiet. By the time she realized the two people in the dungeon hadn't heard her, she was caught up in what they were saying.

"I know, Gaston, but this will work. I'm telling you, it worked on the vampires back home." Caden's voice was far stronger than it had been, yet another example that he was nowhere near as ill as he pretended.

Gaston's was as strident. "Smith, we can't go around aiming that thing at vampires across the city. The point is to find out why there are more and what their mission is. Not annoy them so they start ripping apart innocent bystanders." He paused. "Ha, you hadn't even thought of that, had you? Even if we were able to find a way to make this monstrosity of yours work over a wider range, we'd have no control over what the vampires would do once they were affected by it. I do not see how this will help. Not to mention we have no idea how it would affect the queen. Vampire or not, she is still England's sovereign, regardless of her current indiscretion."

"I'm aware of that, but I still think it can be adapted…." Caden's voice dropped as Nettie came into the room.

So that was what he had been working on down here all this time. That annoying machine that made people get angry for no reason.

"I know I wasn't asked, but I fail to see how you would think it would control full vampires when it didn't affect me in the slightest." She folded her arms. "Or were you planning on experimenting on me until it did?"

"Nettie, good to see you," Gaston said. "Although shouldn't you be at work?"

Nettie pulled her glare off of the now-silent Caden. "Actually there seems to be a slight problem with my employer."

"He's come back? My people didn't inform me. Where has he been?" Perhaps picking up on the fact that Nettie still had her outerwear on, Gaston started marching them toward the entry and his own coat and gloves. He waved off Caden as he began to follow. "No, no. You stay here, Smith. Disassemble that toy of yours for now. I don't want it accidentally going off."

"Dr. Wilson was dissolving into green foam when I left." Nettie thought she kept her voice neutral, but Gaston still stopped and turned to her with a start.

"He came back and dissolved?"

"Well, his hands were starting to. But he hadn't been at all right prior to that. Very stiff and ill at ease. As if he wasn't sure of the appropriate response or behavior." She shook her head as a thought struck her. "There was something familiar about his mannerisms. He moved like the men in brown, the aliens."

Gaston swore, and then rang for Damon. He appeared before the bell finished. "We will be back soon. Please do not let Agent Smith leave the premises. If Lisselle or Homer return, keep them in as well. I assume Rebecca is still sleeping?" At Damon's nod—the man had already learned to not try to talk when Gaston was in a rush—Gaston continued. "Excellent. Oh, if Lisselle does make it back before we do, have her set up a safe area in the dungeon. We may have another chemical issue to address." At Damon's efficient nod, Gaston spun and dragged Nettie out the front door.

Luckily, her legs were significantly longer than his, so she regained her steps after a foot or so.

"Shouldn't we have more backup? Or at least something to safely bring him back in?"

She didn't mention a bucket would probably be the best solution, but the fact was, she didn't think there'd be much more than that to bring back. Either the green foam was making people dissolve or it was what the people had become. Either way, there usually wasn't much left.

"I've got it all taken care of. The Rambler has a full chemical kit on board. Come, *chere*, let's go retrieve what is left of your employer."

Nettie had no idea what the Rambler was until Gaston lead her to the garage with the large steam truck inside. "Rambler?"

The engine was much larger than her steamcycle, but he had the boiler running with amazing speed. "Well, er, yes. I decided if you could name your steamcycle, I could name my truck. The name fits and is not unduly ridiculous." He didn't say it, but that was clearly what he thought of the name Lula Belle.

Nettie shrugged. "As long as you are happy with it, Gaston." Lifting her skirts, she climbed into the monster. It was a good thing it was dark out. There were more and more steam-powered vehicles appearing on the streets, but Gaston's Rambler was far too filled with gears and weapons to be anything normal. The fewer people who saw it the better.

Gaston said nothing, but quietly hummed to himself as he engaged the engine.

The streets were nearly empty, so they made good time. Still, Nettie had been holding her breath during the final block as she waited to see if the door had been forced open.

She let it out when she saw her pole still held.

"I say, whatever is that? How are we going to get in?" Gaston guided the Rambler to a side alley and turned off the engines. The gears on the inner set of wheels whirled to a stop after everything else.

"I had to do something, you know. I wasn't certain that Dr. Wilson was going to completely dissolve, we've no idea if the foam disease is contagious, and I thought it best no one chance upon him in his current condition." She left her coat and reticule in the truck, and then started to untwist the bars.

"You shouldn't be able to do that," Gaston said quietly from behind her.

"Of course I can do this. I've always been strong." Nettie kept her voice confident, but his statement raised a sliver of doubt. That pole had been solid steel and was a wide as her wrist in diameter. She'd never bent something that size before. Of course, to be honest, she'd never tried.

"Not this strong." Gaston's frown bespoke far more than concern about the condition of Dr. Wilson. "We will need to have Lisselle run some more tests on you when we get back."

"You think I'm going to turn into a full vampire, don't you?" The fear that had been lurking in her mind crept out.

"No. I'm not sure what he's done to you. Not to mention we've no idea what being up in the darkness of ether might have done. Perhaps that's the culprit."

Nettie didn't like the way he was being so nice and patting her arm, but now wasn't the time for confrontation.

"I'll need to go around and slip in through my window. Then I can let you in. I put a chain inside the door, and while I may be able to open it from out here, it would destroy the door."

"I understand. I'll wait until you open from the inside." He put a hand on her shoulder briefly. "But be careful, *ma petite*. We don't know if all of them dissolve." He wordlessly handed her one of the dissemblers. "It's time you carried one regularly." The one he had shown her before was still in her room.

This was obviously a newer one and the gears gleamed prettily in the glow of gas lamps.

"Thank you," Nettie said. "I suppose I will need something to carry it in besides my reticule." She turned to the alley. The dissembler was a bit nerve wracking, but she was becoming quite tired of being caught unawares.

The window was no larger than it had been on the way out. Even worse, she'd forgotten the slight drop she had when she'd gotten out would now cause difficulty getting back in. She had formidable upper body strength, but she wasn't sure how easily she could pull her body up that high.

Looking around the abandoned piles of refuse, she managed to find a wooden dowel that had contained rope at some distant time. Standing on its end, she was able to climb into the window.

Her office looked the same. She wanted to see if Dr. Wilson had completely fallen to foam, but knew Gaston would be most vexed if she went in without him.

After adjusting her skirts to make sure they were straight, she ran to the front door and removed the chain.

"About time," Gaston said. "I'd been ready to go around looking for you." He pushed his way inside, then led the way to the office at the end of the corridor—Dr. Wilson's.

Nettie didn't ask how he knew where to go. The one time he'd been here, Dr. Wilson had already been gone. But Gaston seemed to know many things that he should have no knowledge of.

Nettie pulled out her dissembler as Gaston slowly opened the door. She wasn't certain what they would see, but the sight before her would not have been anything she'd expect.

Dr. Wilson was at his desk. Sitting at his desk, eyes wide open. He made no move when they opened the door and she couldn't tell from this distance whether he was breathing or not.

He certainly wasn't blinking. He also looked relatively solid and the only sign of green foam was some drying around his hands where they still clutched the wood.

"That is about where I left him." Nettie would have moved forward to investigate, but Gaston kept himself planted solidly in front of her. "Don't you think we should at least move closer?"

"I'm trying to determine if he is human or not." Gaston kept his voice low, but had taken out a small triangle-shaped metal box. He seemed to be scowling at it, turning knobs randomly, and keeping an eye on Dr. Wilson all at the same time.

"What is that and why are we whispering?" Nettie didn't raise her voice although she really saw no reason not to do so. The fact was either Dr. Wilson was alive and human, in which case he was in a trance, or he was dead and possibly not human. In which case it also didn't matter if they spoke at a normal level.

"Because he might...Oh, very well." Gaston resumed his normal speaking voice. "As for this little beauty—" He held out the item to her, but it still looked like a small, metal pyramid with knobs on it. "—it's the latest invention from Edinburgh. Sent down by Air Zeppelin this morning for our current situation. It's an alien scanner. Or rather, a non-human scanner. Since we don't know what the aliens are made from, we can't program for that. But we can program for anything that isn't us."

Nettie waited a few more minutes, then gave Gaston a nudge. "Well? It doesn't seem to be doing anything. Can we go into the room and see if he's alive?"

Gaston hit the sides a few more times, and then finally slipped his new toy back into one of his dozen or so pockets. "*Oui*, very well. Either he is too odd for the machine to read him, he is dead, or it doesn't work."

Nettie noticed he had his own dissembler in his hand. As he went further into the room, he picked up a large black umbrella that Dr. Wilson always kept by the door. Although she wanted to march up and see what was wrong with her employer, she stayed behind Gaston and his slow walking.

Finally Gaston got close enough and could poke Dr. Wilson with the umbrella.

At first, it looked like he wasn't going to move. Then the tip of the umbrella sank into his arm.

Nettie wasn't sure what he was, or what had been done to him, but no normal human would have arms that squishy.

After another few seconds, Dr. Wilson fell over. His arm took the umbrella with him, yanking it right out of Gaston's grasp.

"Back!" Gaston pushed her against the far wall, but not out the door.

"I don't think anything is going to happen," Nettie finally said after a few minutes. She couldn't see much more than the top part of the umbrella sticking up over the top of the desk.

"I believe you're right." Gaston crept forward and peered over the desk. "That cannot be good."

Nettie went around the desk for a better look.

Dr. Wilson still had his eyes open, and there was a bit more in the way of green foam. But what was most disturbing was where the tip of the umbrella had punctured his skin. Wires and gears could be seen underneath.

Nettie yanked out the umbrella, her dissembler ready in case it stirred the thing on the floor to action. When it made no move, she stepped back so she could turn to Gaston but not take her eyes off the body on the floor.

"Is that what the Runners look like underneath their black covering?"

"I had the same thought. But not exactly. They are more advanced. At least, that is what I have heard. Only Agent Zero has seen the inner workings, but his descriptions were far different than this." He took the umbrella back from her and studied the tip.

"How many different ways are there to make mechanical men?" Nettie truly never thought she'd be asking that question in her lifetime.

"That is a good question, my dear. And one which we may want to ask the Runners when they get back on track so to speak. But for now, let's use that extreme strength of yours and get whatever this is to the mansion." He paused and laid a hand on her arm. "I am sorry, but I believe we can assume Dr. Wilson is deceased."

Nettie looked at the odd mix of metal and flesh before her and nodded. "Thank you, I think you are correct. I may not have to worry about leaving my job—it seems to be leaving me." She and Gaston wrapped the form in heavy canvas that had been folded in the back of the Rambler. With a frighteningly little amount of effort, she scooped up the stiff form of her former boss, and carried him out to the Rambler.

Gaston stood outside a minute longer before turning toward the hospital. "I shall go warn the night administrator that there has been an accident. I will say Scotland Yard is coming to investigate and for no one to enter the morgue until they've cleared it."

"When are they coming? Might I speak to them? I have a few questions concerning some of their cases," Nettie said. Even though she was now a member of an organization far more mysterious that Scotland Yard, they had always fascinated her.

"That's what I'm telling the hospital, *chere*. The Yard clearly can't be called in on this. We have a few agents who carry Yard credentials, and they will be here tomorrow. Actually, you have met one of them, Mary, who was interviewing Rebecca. She carries a full inspector identification." With that, he trundled off to the hospital night entrance.

Nettie carefully ignored his emphasis on inspector identification as opposed to that she was a Scotland Yard inspector. Some things might be better left unknown.

She adjusted the Dr. Wilson copy, or whatever he was, a few times. To be honest, she wasn't quite sure where he should go. It seemed off a bit to put a human in the back storage area, yet she didn't feel comfortable in the slightest with him in the cabin of the vehicle.

By the time Gaston had come back and gotten into the vehicle she had moved him back and forth five times.

"Where is Dr. Wilson?"

"In the storage trunk. I couldn't have him up here. I also secured the trunk with the chain from the morgue. You never can tell. He may not be completely dead, or not functioning, or whatever would happen to a mechanical man."

Gaston reached across the truck and patted her arm. "You're handling this like a seasoned pro."

There were a few bumps coming from the storage trunk on the way back to the mansion, but there had been a lot of noises on the way out as well. The Rambler might be an example of modern steam ingenuity, but it was not stealthy or silent.

When they stopped as close to the front door as Gaston could get without taking down some of the yard, Nettie got out and lifted Dr. Wilson out of the trunk. Damon had been waiting and reappeared at the front door with the moving table.

Gaston gave him some sort of instructions for after he secured Dr. Wilson in the dungeon, and he vanished down another hall. All before Nettie had completely removed her outerwear.

Gaston waited for her at the entrance to the dungeon, but she could tell he was trying to be polite. Most likely, he would be doing any investigation into what this Dr. Wilson was made of, regardless of the fact that she was the trained coroner.

Gaston had his lab coat and gloves on before she'd even cleared the doorway.

"Now, I assume whatever was making him talk and look alive has ceased to function. Let's take no chances. Can you secure him to those posts?" He didn't even look up, and went about assembling his collection of instruments. Some were what she would have used, others were items used to repair machinery. Considering what they would be taking apart, she agreed with his choices.

As Nettie secured their prisoner with chains, it was easier to think of him as that than the man she knew. She realized that he really didn't look like Dr. Wilson. The face was a bit too narrow, the shoulders not as broad.

"It looks like a Runner," she said. It was meant to be to herself but came out aloud.

"No, no. We established that. This looks far cruder than the drawings I've seen of the mechanics...Oh." Gaston had turned and noticed she wasn't looking at the wiring poking out of the arm.

"How would you know what a Runner's face looks like? To be honest, I don't think they really have them. Not like we would know them, anyway."

Nettie stepped back to let Gaston and his tools through. "Not like that. His build, the proportions of his face, torso, arms and legs are off. They are more regular. All of the Runners have exactly the same proportions. I should have noticed it when I saw all of them together. This thing has the same proportions."

Gaston nodded slowly. "I've never doubted your uncanny powers of acute observation, my dear, so I won't stop now. But I must say I've never noticed the proportions of the Runners, although they do all seem to be the same."

"Da Vinci."

Gaston had been ready to cut into the chest area when she blurted the name. "Excuse me?"

"Da Vinci's Vitruvian Man. That's what they used. The Runners are the same."

"You are serious. You are saying that you can tell if the proportions are exactly the same as in Da Vinci's fifteenth century drawing of ideal human proportions?" Gaston may have claimed not to doubt her observational ability, but his face said otherwise at this moment.

Nettie felt her face blush, an uncommon and unwelcome occurrence. "I spent a lot of time working on those proportions in medical school. A lot of time, sadly. I can assure you that if you were to measure exactly, you would see this being has those proportions." She had a difficult time with the more artistic end of medical school. One of the requirements had been to render bodies in all positions using the Vitruvian Man as the guide.

Gaston looked ready to ask more questions, but her obvious discomfort led him to refrain.

"Again, I will take your word. It is something that we should bring up to Agent Ramsey. The collective in Edinburgh may not have made that connection."

He'd started peeling back the flap of skin-like material covering the chest when the front door chimes rang.

Gaston looked up from his operation and nodded toward the dungeon door. "Damon is running some tasks for me. Could you be so good as to answer that?" He didn't even seem perturbed that someone was ringing his door well after midnight. Then again, if standing there taking apart a part-human, part-alien machine man wasn't enough to throw him off his game, a late-night caller certainly wasn't.

Nettie thought about asking where Homer had gotten to, but the man seemed to come and go as he pleased.

And she was too happy that Caden wasn't here to wonder where he'd gone off to.

The person at the door was quite impatient for a caller at this time of night and pressed the bell twice more before she could get to the front.

"Oh, do be still," she muttered as she opened the door.

The man before her was slim and young; he had the emblem of the telegraph office on his sleeve, yet didn't look like someone who would work there. Ah, Gaston had mentioned a lower tier of agents that would be pulled in to help carry information until the Runner problems was resolved. They basically spied for the Society without leaving their day jobs.

This one obviously knew at least one of the agents well.

He waved about an envelope. "You must come quickly for I believe something has happened to Agent Wilding. She sent this message, but has yet to return. And there appears to be blood on it."

CHAPTER SIXTEEN

NETTIE RAN DOWN into the dungeon. She desperately wanted to open the message, but it was addressed to Gaston and the agent who had dropped it off had said only he should open it. Actually, he had practically yelled it as he fled down the steps. Either Gaston had a more terrifying reputation than she thought, or the messenger had more errands to run.

"Something has happened to Lisselle," she said as soon as she could get into the dungeon. "A boy at the door left this." Nettie froze as she saw what Gaston had done in the few minutes she was away. Bits and pieces of the former Dr. Wilson were all over the room.

"Ah yes." Gaston waved his gloved hands at her. "As you can see, we've had some adventures down here. It seems he wasn't securely put together." He looked at her expectantly. "Well? Do open the missive if you would. I can't stop now, can I?" As he spoke, he placed one foot on a long coil of cable that rolled out of the mannequin's chest.

With a shrug, she slit open the envelope and read aloud. "'Gaston, if this comes to you, then I have missed my rendezvous. The Event did not go unnoticed. Couldn't get into home base, but there are other eyes watching it. The seabird is alone.'" Nettie read it again under her breath, but it still made no sense to her.

Nor did it contain anything that indicated it was from Lisselle.

"This is worrisome, yes. But not to fret, Lisselle and Homer have gotten out of worse, I assure you." With a patriarchal smile he went back to his work.

"But how do you know what it means? It makes no sense, nor does it mention either agent." Nettie waved the paper under his nose. "Besides, there is blood on it."

"Hmm," he said. Taking his wrist he pushed up under her hand to steady it and see the document better. "Gravy. Homer must have been carrying the paper before they separated and Lisselle wrote her note."

"How do you—"

"Have I not told you when going into a dangerous area or situation to leave a last comment note? This was Lisselle's. That is what she meant about missing her rendezvous. She didn't use a more stress-filled wording, so she wasn't too worried if she didn't get back before the letter was delivered, but she did want us to know. You know what The Event is; others are aware of the queen's change and are watching the palace. Even though she thought she had a way in, she was unable to do so. Which—" he raised one gory hand to accent his words, "—indicates that they are aware they are being watched as well. And the seabird flying alone means she and Homer were together, but have since separated. He most likely got the gravy on the paper as Lisselle is a fastidious eater."

Nettie took another look at the note. It made sense now. What bothered her was that she wouldn't have recognized it without his help.

It must have shown on her face.

"Ach, don't worry. Most of that you hadn't been taught yet. And the rest comes with experience. Now, what I need is for you to go to bed. Tomorrow will be a busy day for both you and Rebecca."

Nettie winced—she'd almost forgotten her friend. How would she explain Dr. Wilson to her? Neither of them were that fond of him, but Rebecca was closer to him than she was.

"Now don't you worry. I have a cover story on the morgue for the next week at least. Our Scotland Yard friends will be looking into some missing bodies and a missing Dr. Wilson. They will find that whoever stole the bodies unfortunately killed Dr. Wilson and buried him outside London."

"I hadn't even thought of that. Although I'm so glad you did. No, I was wondering how I'd be explaining that—" She pointed at the scattered body before them. "—to Rebecca. She will notice he is missing."

"Good point, and good luck with that. Tomorrow, I will need you to bring your friend up on things as much as you can. Don't shock her unnecessarily, but do get her up to speed. I'd also like you both to go out at some point tomorrow afternoon and see what news is about." With that, Gaston turned back to his investigation, clearly dismissing her.

The checking for news was something she often did on her days off. She would wander different areas of London, stopping in at various pubs and markets to chat up the common folk. Oftentimes, the best leads came from some baker who knew someone who knew someone who saw something odd. At least it should be a relatively easy day for Rebecca. Once the shock of everything wore off, at any rate.

Nettie had to admit living in the mansion was exposing her to far more of the Society, and life as an agent, than she'd seen in the two years previously. It seemed to be longer than a few days since she lived in the boarding house. Living around Gaston was more difficult than only working with him.

With a shake of her head, she left him to his mayhem and went to bed. She was still worried about Lisselle, but she would need to take her cues from Gaston on this. If he wasn't calling out the dogs, so to speak, then neither would she. Not to mention she was extremely exhausted.

THE NEXT MORNING, Gaston was not around. Neither was Damon, which left Nettie with a bit of a situation. Cook didn't like anyone ordering food except Gaston or Damon. As he also didn't want people going into his domain to fix their own food, she was stuck without a proper breakfast until someone came along.

She was about to see how many biscuits were in the tea pantry of the parlor when Gaston finally came into view.

"It's about time you got up. You know Cook won't talk to anyone except you and Damon, and he's missing too."

"Up? I haven't gone to bed yet." He stomped over and took a long pull of whisky. "There was a bit of an accident last night. One I think was anything but, in actuality." His clothing was almost as wrinkled as his face. Most likely, he'd fallen asleep down in the dungeon at some point. "The doctor, or whatever he was, finally dissolved into green foam. I saved my notes and the photos I was able to take, but he disintegrated before my eyes."

Nettie agreed that was more than a bit suspicious. "But why did it take this one so long? The others were gone within a few minutes of discovery."

Gaston began pacing, but there wasn't much heart in it. "I've given that some thought. It appears that our alien friends have taken at least one of the Runners. Whether they or the vampires are behind the missing four is not yet answered. But they got one, and tried to make one of their own to slip into our Society." He surrendered his pacing and threw himself into his chair by the fire. "I'd say the others weren't mechanical in origin, so they turned to goo faster. It does force the question of whether it was our actions that caused the change, or if he would have done this on his own."

Nettie went back to nibbling on her biscuits. "He had already exhibited some foaming when I saw him. And if they had been trying to pass him off in society, they would have been hard pressed. He wasn't moving anymore at all."

"True." Gaston seemed to finally notice the way in which she was rapidly consuming all of the pantry's holdings and rang the bell. "I'll call Cook for some breakfast, but we should be aware that they may have ways of telling when one of their spies has fallen under our control. We can't leave out that the foaming, while seeming harmless, may not be."

Cook appeared with a short bow and a tilt of his head. The huge man was from some distant island—no one seemed to feel the need to clarify it more than that—and spoke little. He was an amazing cook.

The chance to have him make all of her meals was almost as

exciting for Nettie as her new chambers and study place in the dungeon. Most proper women in London dreamed of finding a man, raising a family, and being good housewives. Nettie wanted excitement and a place to study. Gaston had warned her that she really needed to watch what she wished for on more than one occasion.

"Breakfast, my good man, and lots of it. Coffee too, if you will. I have a need for something stronger than tea." Gaston may eschew Americans, but he did enjoy many of their culinary contributions to society, coffee being one of them.

Cook nodded, and then left. Nettie put down the remains of her biscuits and dusted off her hands.

"I forgot to look last night, but was there any dust?" The cookie crumbs made her think of it. She hoped the false Scotland Yard people would be on the lookout for any while they were taking apart the morgue.

Gaston's face closed up. "No, and that does worry me. We had speculated a connection between the dust and the foam, but I found none. I did mean to ask yesterday if you had seen any on the ship."

"No." Now it was her turn to frown. This mystery was difficult enough, even when they were slowly putting the pieces together. If the dust was unrelated to the foam, it would throw them back a few steps. "The ship was as I said in my report, spotless. Yet, I did only see that one room. It could have been a clean room of some sort? The alien who faced me did not appear to have any dust on him."

"Perhaps the dust is a byproduct of their physiographic nature and something on Earth. The former Dr. Wilson wouldn't have any since he wasn't human, or alien for that matter. It may not affect mechanicals." He stopped as Damon appeared in the doorway. "Ah there you are, my good man. Everything taken care of?"

Damon looked neat as usual, but there was a slight bagging under his eyes that bespoke a lack of sleep. "Yes, everything is as you asked. Scotland Yard has arrived at the morgue."

"Very good, very good. I have one more task, then off to food and bed with you. We can survive the day without your services." Gaston was holding himself up, clearly trying not to appear as tired as he was, but Nettie doubted Damon was fooled any more than she was. "Please see that Agent Rebecca is awakened and led into the dining room. We will all be taking breakfast there. And by all, I do mean you as well."

While it was common for most servants to dine in the kitchens of the great mansions, Gaston hated that. However, he had yet to break Damon of that habit. Clearly, today would be the day he won.

Damon looked ready to disagree, but Gaston verbally stepped over him. "You are exhausted. You have completed a task far above and beyond that of a normal manservant. Therefore, you do not have to abide by those horrific standards of class found in the most backward of proper homes. Besides, it will make things easier for Cook to have us all in one place." His tone said he would brook no argument and Damon wisely simply nodded in agreement.

"I will go make sure Agent Rebecca is up." With one of his signature short bows, he left the room.

"Thank goodness. I thought I would never break him of the

kitchen dining habit." Gaston rose to his feet and held out his arm. "May I walk you in, Dr. Jones?"

"That would be lovely, Gaston." She took his arm and realized he may have needed it more than she. For a moment there, he looked faint.

"Are you certain you are all right?"

He looked up with a scowl. "I'm fine. Can't an old man get tired without being on death's door?"

Nettie had enough medical training to know the difference between exhaustion and something else. He was exhausted, there was no denying of that, but there was something else at play as well. It could be a cold; there had been an influx of viruses about lately, but she would watch him all the same.

"Fine, but I expect to see you sleeping right after breakfast. You'll not do any of us any good if you collapse." They'd arrived in the dining room and she was surprised to see only four places had been set. "Are the others not back yet?" She knew she had been encouraging Agent Smith to get out and about, but she'd hoped he had enough intelligence to not stay out all day and night right after his recovery. Clearly, she had given his intelligence too much credit.

Gaston seemed to notice the place settings for the first time. "It would appear so. I had believed that if Lisselle or the others were going to be later in returning, they would have had sent word. Lisselle would have had a second non-rendezvous note established and she must have met that one or it would have been delivered." He broke off when he heard voices down the hall coming from the women's wing.

"I dare say, this place is far larger than I thought. And you say

I am to live here?"

Nettie smiled at the tone in Rebecca's voice. It held a mixture of wonder and flirtation. Clearly, the slender Damon had caught her friend's eye.

The look on Rebecca's heart-shaped face as she and Damon entered the dining room verified that impression. There was a gleam there that Nettie had seen many times when a new doctor would come down to the morgue.

Rebecca wasn't hunting for a husband per se, but she did enjoy men far more than her job, unlike Nettie.

"Nettie! You are part of this as well? Why ever didn't you tell me?" Rebecca charged forward and settled next to her.

"As Gaston said, I couldn't tell you." She grabbed her friend's hands as she sat. "But I am so glad that you are part of this now. You are happy as well?" She looked into her friend's face for any sign of strain or nerves. Nettie let out a sigh when she saw none.

"This is amazing, Nettie. Although…" Rebecca's face started to redden slightly. "Is it too bold to ask about your teeth? Master Gaston informed me of your unusual situation."

Gaston looked over from his low volume conversation with Damon. "I told you, you may simply call me Gaston. Everyone does except this one." He pointed to Damon. "But I am hopeful of breaking him of it soon."

Nettie let her fangs drop into place, and then smiled coyly at her friend. She was gladdened that she wasn't going to have to be the one to inform Rebecca about her vampire status, however she felt a big smile might be too much. Even if one was informed.

"Oh my!" Rebecca's eyes grew round, but she didn't seem in the least upset. "So you've had those your entire life? Fascinating!"

Nettie had a feeling her friend was going to ask to touch them, but luckily Cook came out bearing a bountiful repast and interrupted the dental examination.

"So, Damon was telling me that I am to move in here? Do I get to stay in that lovely room I was in last night?" Rebecca frowned a bit. "Although I have to admit, I don't recall coming in there, or this mansion for that matter, last night."

Nettie shot Gaston a quick look—obviously he wasn't telling Rebecca everything yet. A slight shake of his head told her there was something he didn't want her told at this time.

"I believe you were extremely exhausted. The fumes that had invaded the morgue had far overcome you." He smiled as he spoke, then dove back into his meal like a starving man.

"Ah, that might explain it. Were you overcome as well, Nettie?"

Nettie wasn't quite sure what Gaston had told Rebecca, but figured if she got too far off track he would nudge her. "No, actually. I was stopped before I got down there. It's a good thing they got you out when they did." She got a few bites of food in, and then added, "And yes, you get to live here. We shall live in the same wing and be housemates. Right now, there is only one other woman agent in our wing, Lisselle."

A frown crept across Rebecca's face at the name. "That name sounds familiar. Have I met her?"

Nettie caught Gaston's eye, but he was already dabbing his mouth with his napkin. "You did last night. She was the one who came to get you before Scotland Yard could arrive. We were aware of the problem, but knew we couldn't wait until the Yard got there to get you out." Always keep your lies as close to the truth as possible, that was one of Gaston's favorite sayings.

"I see, but she isn't here now?" Rebecca was eating the slowest of all of them, mostly because she seemed to be trying to get answers for everything at once.

"No, in fact I think you and Nettie will spend the day soaking up news and finding our missing agents." He raised his hand, palm out, as panic filed Rebecca's face. "Never worry, they may be missing, but that is fairly common in our line of work. Sometimes, you simply can't get away from your task to report in. Alas, since we will all now be in each other's pockets as it were, we will be far more aware of comings and goings than we normally would."

"Do we know where they were heading?" Nettie picked at the rest of her breakfast but the truth was, she'd eaten too many biscuits. She downed some more tea instead.

"Aye, general ideas. I'll fill you in when you leave."

"Do we know if Dr. Wilson had come back? I saw him briefly yesterday…" Rebecca's voice trailed off as she searched her memory. "At least I think I did. I don't recall him saying where he had been though. Then he left again before I did." The tone of her voice said she was fighting to regain those memories.

Nettie realized they needed to find Lisselle first. If Dr. Wilson had been there when Lisselle had gone to get Rebecca, she might be able to answer some questions.

"I'm not sure, since I didn't go into work." Nettie had been about to say she hadn't seen him, then realized she'd earlier said she hadn't made it in at all. Gaston told her to fill Rebecca in, but not to shock her. Finding out that your boss had been replaced by something alien was going to be a shock.

"Well, then if you have both finished your breakfast, I will leave you to go about your day." Gaston rose and handed Nettie a note. "This is where I assume our missing agents were. I presume that I will see both of you this afternoon for tea?"

Nettie almost jumped to her feet to help him as he tottered a bit, but a quick look from him stuck her to her seat.

"We shall be back by then."

After Gaston left, she opened the note. Caden was in the stews, and hopefully they wouldn't need to find him. Homer and Lisselle had been around Buckingham Palace. The note added that if Homer had been on his own, he most likely would have gone to the airship landing dock. There was also an added memo to not take the note with her, and by all means keep any mention of the morgue or aliens out of her conversations with Rebecca for the day.

It was a trifle off putting to have him feel the need to remind her not to take the document with her, but at least he gave her information on her limits with Rebecca.

"Do we need to change? I'm not sure what spies wear when out and about." Rebecca was bouncing in her shoes as they went down the hall. Perhaps all of Nettie's worries about her friend not being suited for this life after all were wrong.

"No, we're fine as we are. We'll need a proper coat, of course, but these dresses are more than suitable." Nettie slipped into her long coat and pulled on her gloves. Truth was, as a half-vampire, she didn't feel the cold as others did. Nevertheless, it was crucial to keep up appearances. Especially now.

"And we aren't spies. We're agents of the Society. And that is something we never mention outside these doors."

Rebecca twisted into her coat. "What?"

"We don't mention the Society or agents. If you see an agent that you are supposed to know, such as one of the ones living here in this boarding house, then you may call them by the appropriate name. But do try not to use the term, agent." Nettie rolled her eyes.

"Oh, that looks like a good tale. What did you do?"

It had been a mortifying moment, but it had also happened two years ago and might help Rebecca feel more at ease about any impending mistakes.

"I was so excited about being an agent, that I called out to Agent Gaston one Sunday in the market. In front of many people. Luckily, Gaston is an expert at dissembling, so he was able to start babbling in French and acting like a crazy man. My slip was ignored at his behavior, but I was red for days, I assure you."

Nettie looked up and down the street for any of their alien friends. Not that she was certain she would be able to spot them if they were aware she knew of them, but she needed to try. She needed to be subtle. For reasons of his own, Gaston didn't want Rebecca knowing of the aliens at this time.

"What are you looking for?"

Darn it all. Nettie had wanted to be subtle. "Vampires." At least it was okay for Rebecca to know about those.

"It's ten o'clock in the morning. Would they be out?"

Obviously, the late night had taken its toll on Nettie's wits. "I'm out, aren't I?" She gave a quick flash of fang. "We have no idea if there are any others like me. Besides, the rumors are they can take humans to do their daytime bidding. So we should watch for any suspicious people." There were no such rumors, but she needed to say something. She really had hoped that she wouldn't have to lie to her friend anymore.

They spent most of the day wandering around listening for news. The only consistent gossip involved creatures floating around the night sky, then vanishing before anyone could call for help. Nettie made a mental note of it, but didn't think it would amount to much. Last time there had been strange monsters roaming the night skies, it ended up being a group of lads who had stolen an airship as a prank.

They made their way back in time for afternoon tea with Rebecca as full of knowledge about the Society and current events as she safely could be. Nettie had a close moment when they'd seen a strange, brown-garbed man trailing them. Unable to explain the situation to Rebecca, Nettie had been ready to abandon her friend and track the alien on her own. Luckily, before she could act, the brown man pulled off his hat and revealed a human face. Mistaking a ragman for an alien would not have gone well with Gaston.

Both Homer and Caden had been back to the mansion, then both gone out again. They still hadn't seen or heard from Lisselle.

"I should be back out there, Gaston," Nettie said. She had been saying it all through tea and he had yet to give in. He supposedly rested all day, but there were still bags under his eyes. Alas, it didn't slow down his will any.

"I need you to stay here and help Rebecca get settled. Damon brought all of her belongings from her flat and she'll need assistance sorting it all in." He beamed at Rebecca. "Won't you, my dear?"

"Actually, sir, it does sound to be more important that we find that lady agent. She has been missing for twenty-four hours now, and it must be a concern with all of the vampire problems." She gave him her most innocent smile, which told Nettie she was fully aware of what he was trying to do, and she was not supporting it in the least.

Nettie had a direct approach most times: charge over people until they gave in. Tiny Rebecca had one better fitting her size and demeanor. She was extremely proper as she politely herded you the way she wanted you to go. She was sort of like a Corgi in human form.

Nettie stifled a giggle at the thought.

"Did you want to add something, Agent Jones?"

The use of her title usually indicated Gaston's level of annoyance. "Nothing. However, I do agree with Agent Rhys. I think it is high time a concentrated search for Lisselle was launched. I know," she continued, as Gaston looked ready to argue, "that under normal circumstances her absence wouldn't be cause for alarm. But with the recent activities and The Event, I believe we can no longer wait."

"It's all right, Jones. I told Rebecca about the queen." Gaston took a deep sigh; one that left him even more fatigued looking. "There is no way I can convince you both to stay in?" The tone in his voice said his question was nothing more than a formality.

"And let the boys have all the fun? Never! Besides, Rebecca must get her feet wet sometime." Nettie bounced to her feet and made to head for the entry and the waiting coats.

"Do be careful, Nettie. I feel we are only seeing the tip of the disaster."

Rebecca gave a quick bow to Gaston then grabbed her coat as well.

"So will we see real vampires? I mean not that you aren't real, but you know what I mean."

Nettie laughed to show she held no hard feelings. "I understand. And considering how they've been behaving as of late, I think it would be best if we didn't see them. Or rather, if we see them, they don't see us." She was certain that Gaston would not have informed Rebecca about the attack on Nettie, or the unknown consequences.

Twilight had come and gone and the night lamps were flickering brightly by the time they stepped out of doors.

Nettie had already decided on her plan in terms of the search. Their finding Homer could increase their chances tenfold. He had told Gaston he was keeping an eye out for Lisselle, but he was also following a lead on the airship collision. As a long time pilot of the massive ships, he didn't believe for one moment that it had been an accident.

"Where are we going?" Rebecca didn't seem to care, but her innate curiosity would make her question everything.

"I want to find Homer. He has connections to the airship fields, so I believe that is where we shall start. He was also the last agent to see Lisselle, therefore, he may have a clue about where she is."

"But wouldn't he have told someone?" Rebecca skipped sideways to avoid a raggedy man splayed across the sidewalk.

"Ah, but sometimes people have clues that they didn't know of. We should start there, then work our way toward the palace."

Rebecca nodded, but within a few moments of walking, and nothing happening, she was back to questions.

"So, the Agent Smith you have deliberately not spoken of, is he handsome?"

Nettie stumbled forward as her foot caught on an uneven pavement. "What? Why ever would you say such a thing? I am not deliberately not speaking of him."

"Nettie, I have known you for over three years now. I have known you longer than anyone else in London, I'd warrant. You have had some sort of issue with the young American agent and find yourself inexplicably drawn to him at the same time. Therefore, you are trying very hard to ignore his existence." The smugness in her tone struck hard, but not as hard as the truth of it.

Which was still a truth Nettie was willing to shove into some dark pantry somewhere and let sit. "He is handsome. He is, however, also extremely aware of it. I've not spoken of him because there is simply nothing to say. Please don't mention your speculations to Homer."

Rebecca said nothing further, but the look in her eyes did not bode well for further conversations on the subject.

The fact was, Caden Smith was handsome, far too clever for his own good, and probably one of the best agents from America, at least per the records Nettie was able to find. He was also bullheaded, stubborn, and extremely difficult. Not at all the sort of man Nettie wanted to spend time on. Besides, she was not in the market for male companionship. If she were, it would be with a calm, agreeable, and bookish sort. The type who would wait patiently for her to come back from her adventures, and not question her on every turn. But for now, her love was the Society and it was her job to become the best agent she could.

"Nettie lass, what are you doing about this evening?" Homer's voice came out of the shadows an instant before he did. The fact that Nettie had been too distracted thinking about Caden to notice him there was yet another point for ignoring Caden.

"Lisselle still hasn't returned. I thought I'd find out more from you as to where you left her." Nettie shook her head and stepped back. "But I was rude. I should have introduced you both immediately. Rebecca Rhys, meet Homer Tremain."

"Nice to meet you, Rebecca Rhys. Please call me Homer." Homer's huge hand swallowed Rebecca's as he pumped it up and down.

Rebecca smiled, but her eyes kept darting to the stationed airships. "Are you a captain of one of those? I would dearly love to go up one day."

The look on his face told Nettie that Rebecca had won him over.

"Aye, lass, I'm officially retired from the royal air fleet, but I do have my own ship. She's not here, but in a private yard in Chelsea." He finally stopped shaking Rebecca's hand. "That's worrisome news about Lisselle. Gaston filled me in when I went back briefly, but I thought for certain she would be back before now. Well, we must go rescue fair damsel, it seems." He turned and started out of the airfield.

Nettie had nothing against Homer. Quite the contrary, she liked the large man a lot. But she didn't know if all of them sticking together would be the best way to find Lisselle. Although she did have to admit that this way she'd be less worried about someone attacking Rebecca.

"Fine. Now what was she last doing?"

"Lass, she was doing what she was supposed to, trying to get into the palace." He shook his head. "But things have changed there. The people she knew a few months ago are gone. Very worrisome. They were people who had been in their positions for years. Any rate, she couldn't get in the normal channels, so she tried some of her own secret ones. Then she left me, saying that her friends wouldn't like someone like me lumbering about. That's the last I know."

Nettie pondered the lack of information given. It wasn't that Homer was deliberately leaving things out, just that he was less observant than some agents. "Do you think—"

"Thief! Stop!"

An instant after the yell cut Nettie off, a man in brown came barreling through them. Nettie got to the side, but Homer and Rebecca weren't so lucky. Rebecca tumbled to the ground at his impact.

The thief was small and covered in brown rags, perhaps the same one whom she had seen in the market that day?

Unfortunately for the thief, while he'd be able to easily push Rebecca out of the way, Homer was another question entirely.

The thief bounced back after meeting Homer's fist and landed on the ground next to Rebecca.

Rebecca looked confused and concerned, but still kept enough of her wits about her to scramble to her feet and move away from the raggedy man.

The man clutched something to his chest that looked suspiciously like a gun.

"Get back. He's armed." The same voice who had yelled for the thief to stop ran into view.

Caden Smith.

"He stole my weapon when I was trying to see if he was hurt." Caden was not looking well. He clearly had been exerting himself far too much during the last twenty-four hours.

"Now see here, little man," Homer said as he loomed over the man on the ground, "you can't go about taking things that aren't yours."

Nettie was an advocate of being brave, but standing right over him if the man had a loaded weapon wasn't brave—it was fool hardy.

The man's face was covered in rags and a chill went up Nettie's spine. It was dark enough that he shouldn't be able to see with that fabric across his face.

"Back up, all of you." She grabbed Rebecca's arm and pulled her closer.

"Now see here, Jones, I'm not letting some sneak thief make off with my best firearm." Caden caught a glimpse of Rebecca and flashed a huge smile. "Ma'am."

Nettie shot him a glare. "That's not a normal thief, Caden." She'd hoped the emphasis on his name would get him to pay attention, but he kept smiling at Rebecca.

"Homer, I wouldn't recommend getting close. Unless you want a much further trip than you expected." Hopefully Homer would be more in tune with what she was saying. Although why she was trying to hide the alien from Rebecca, she had no clue. Unless he ran out of here on two feet, she was going to notice he wasn't normal.

Homer nodded and stepped back. "I'd do as she says, lad."

Caden looked ready to argue, then finally got a good look at their faces. He scrambled back faster than Mrs. Cruddle seeing a spider.

And not a moment too soon. An instant later, the image in brown vanished and Rebecca fainted.

CHAPTER SEVENTEEN

"OH DEAR, GASTON is not going to like this. He didn't think she should know about them yet." Nettie ran to her fallen friend and lifted her head up. Her eyelids fluttered, but she wasn't moving yet. "That was bad form of you to chase him into us, Agent Smith."

"I didn't really have a choice, Agent Jones. Besides, it wasn't as if I knew where you were. Or that you'd have the new agent with you. Or that the thief I was chasing was one of *them*." Caden glared sullenly at the patch of ground the alien had vanished from as if he could see his lost pistol if he looked hard enough.

"I'd say they are moving their studies up to our weapons," Homer said. "Did it make any noises when you were fighting with it?"

"Fighting? Who was fighting? I bent down to help some poor man and he grabs my pistol out of its holster and takes off running."

"Didn't you notice its face was completely covered? Wouldn't that seem an odd thing to do when it's dark out?" Nettie continued to pat Rebecca's hand and she was slowly stirring.

"I didn't have time to really think about it," Caden said sullenly.

Before he could continue defending himself, Homer stepped

in between them. "Now, children, no use pointing fingers. If you can't play nice, I'll send you both to bed without your supper. Fact is, that alien was moving fast, and I believe we were all caught off guard. See here, she's coming around."

Nettie helped Rebecca to her feet. She was at a loss for how to explain the vanishing. She understood Gaston's reasons for not exposing Rebecca to too much at once, but it was more difficult when the matter landed right in front of them.

"Are you feeling better? I know that was quite a start." Nettie had briefly toyed with trying to pretend it didn't happen. She knew Rebecca was far too sharp for that.

"Oh, I'm fine, my skirts slowed my decent. But it wasn't the vanishing that did me in, it was the feeling." Rebecca shuddered as she dusted off her clothing. Then she met and held Nettie's eyes. "I felt like I did right before the explosion. I think my premonitions might be tied to your vanishing friend, whoever he is."

Nettie looked over Rebecca's head to catch both sets of male eyes watching them. She wasn't supposed to tell Rebecca about the aliens, yet if they were involved in her premonitions...

"But I thought you have had visions for years. You told me about them when we first met." Nettie reached down and picked up Rebecca's reticule.

Homer and Caden hadn't said anything yet, and Nettie hoped they took her hint and stayed quiet. Rebecca seemed calm, but she didn't want to startle her into another collapse.

"Oh, I've had them off and on since I was a girl. Well, actually it started when we moved to Cardiff." Rebecca shook her head at her own memory. "Regardless, I've had them for a long time. But recently they've been far more vivid. Not as vivid as that one you and I had in the morgue, mind you. That was positively the worst. But they've been getting to feel like a real waking moment."

"How long?" Nettie should have known Caden's couldn't keep his mouth shut.

Rebecca tipped her head, but kept looking at Nettie. "I'd say the last month, maybe two?"

Did that mean the aliens had been spying on London for two months? And worst of all, the Society had been unaware? This would be grievous news for Gaston. A thought struck her.

"Have you ever caused others to have visions? I mean beyond the one we shared?" Nettie could tell that both Homer and Caden were dying to inquire about the visions. She hadn't known if Gaston had told anyone outside of Edinburgh, but the look on the men's faces said they weren't aware of it.

"Not that I've noticed. And you would think someone would say something if they had an odd vision around me, wouldn't they? It's not like it would be common."

They had all started walking toward the palace and Lisselle's earlier rendezvous. Homer and Caden stayed behind the ladies, but they were so close, listening, that they'd be on them in an instant if the ladies stopped.

"Oh dear." Rebecca stopped her prattling as she caught a look at Nettie's face. "You had one. Of my visions, I mean. Whyever didn't you tell me?"

Nettie shot a look over her shoulder to convince the men to back off a few steps. She fancied she could feel Caden's breath down her neck.

"First of all, you have just joined the Society as of today. I couldn't very well have told you prior. Secondly, it really wasn't a good vision." She knew Rebecca had felt the two of them die during their shared vision, but she thought her reaction might be different at her being killed.

"Well?" Rebecca stopped and planted her feet.

So much for trying to save her feelings.

"You were at your desk, stabbed in the back." She couldn't look her friend in the eye. The vision was so real she had smelled the blood.

"Stabbed in my…Was this the night of our vision?" At Nettie's glum nod, Rebecca continued. "I thought something was amiss. I was feeling awful after our vision. But I didn't want you to be concerned. And my back was hurting like the dickens from the explosion. That wasn't really an explosion, but still left a pain in my back. I may have been projecting, and you caught the vision." She scurried over to a street light and pulled out a paper and pencil. "I need to write this down. It could be important."

Nettie shook her head. Here she thought her friend would be upset at dying in a vision, yet she wanted to record the event for posterity.

"I've written down what I felt when we went through that. Actually, I already gave Gaston a report, but I may have left some details out. It has been an exhausting few days, hasn't it? Anyway, now about your vision. What exactly did you see?" She looked up at Nettie expectantly.

Nettie shook her head. She'd always thought she was the more thorough one between the two of them. Clearly, she'd underestimated her friend's dedication to detail. "You were hunched over your desk and there was a large knife between your shoulder blades, buried in about half way to the hilt. I would say the blade was a good six inches long." She wracked her brain, but alas, the shock of seeing her friend in such shape had blocked out some of the details. Except one. "And I could smell the blood."

Rebecca nodded and continued writing. "Well, we did smell things in our adventure, did we not? Perhaps that makes sense." She turned toward the men who had been silently standing by. "I will need one of you to take this to Gaston."

Nettie held her gloved hand to her mouth. She didn't want any of them to see her smile but Rebecca was quite the sight. Her entire world turned upside down in less than twenty-four hours, and she was giving orders to superior agents. She might work out fine.

"Not Homer. We need him to take us to where Lisselle last was spotted." Nettie beamed at Caden, but she wasn't sure if he could see her well enough in the shadows. She had put enough false cheer into her voice she was certain he couldn't miss it.

"I can't. I need to follow my lead—"

"Actually, lad, you should. You had recent contact with…one of them. You need to tell Gaston what happened and how you lost your pistol." Homer nodded to Rebecca and her stretched-out hand. "And it would be polite to take the lady's note in as well."

Caden scowled, but being as Homer was the most senior agent of the four, he didn't have a choice. "As always, there is wisdom to your words." Caden gave a florid bow and removed the note from Rebecca's hand. "I shall see you all back at the mansion." With that, he stalked off into the night.

"Thank goodness we've gotten him out of the way. Now, shall we?" Homer held out both arms, one for each lady. "I think we have a little minx to find."

IT HAD TAKEN an hour to search all of Lisselle's regular haunts. Nettie had to admit she had a hard time seeing her friend in some of them. Such as the gentlemen's gambling club. She and Rebecca drew some unhealthy stares, but one nod from Homer and everyone backed down. How would Lisselle fit in there?

They were about to see if any of Homer's sources had heard anything when a scream shattered the evening quiet.

"This way!" Nettie lifted her skirts and ran toward the sound with Homer and Rebecca not far behind. She was grateful for Homer holding back. She knew she could out run both of the others but didn't want to leave Rebecca untended.

The origin of the scream quickly became clear as an old washerwoman stumbled in front of Nettie.

"Them's gone, animals gots them. Them's GONE. We're all done for." Without waiting for Nettie's response, the woman grabbed her shabby cloak around her and vanished down an alley. The scent of her terror filled the night.

But so did the scent of blood.

CHAPTER EIGHTEEN

NETTIE WAITED UNTIL Homer and Rebecca joined her before walking the last bit down the alley. She knew she was strong and could handle herself, but they were all up against some powerful and unpredictable foes.

"I assume you heard her?"

Rebecca nodded, but was clearly out of breath. They'd have to work on her stamina, that was for certain.

"Aye, lass." Homer shook his head and lit a small lantern. "It's not going to be pleasant in there, whatever it is. I don't supposed you'd consider me going in first?"

"Do you really think that I'm that frail?" Rebecca got out before Nettie could do more than frown. "I *have* assisted in taking apart entire bodies before."

Nettie folded her arms tightly and tilted her head. "You may go in first if it will make you happier. But we shall be immediately behind you."

Homer shook his head. "I figured as much. Come on then. Who knows who else heard that scream?"

The bodies before them were the remains of at least three royal guards. All of them were shredded, but had distinctive bite marks on their arms and necks. They had been brutally attacked and it wasn't to make them vampire kind.

"Why would the vampires do this? And why drag them this far from the palace?"

"The only explanation is that they know. The vampires know what happened to the queen." Homer looked down at the carnage beneath his thick black boots. "And I'd say they aren't pleased."

"Why are they taking it out on the guards?" There was more than a little fear in Rebecca's voice. Her excitement at their investigation had dimmed the moment they came upon the bodies. She was right, she did work at a morgue and had seen bodies in disrepair. Seeing this level of carnage outside of the morgue was an entirely different manner.

Tonight was supposed to be something to introduce her slowly into the Society. Nettie watched her friend closely.

"I'm not sure." Homer looked to Nettie, but she gave a slight shake of her head. She didn't feel any vampires nearby. Of course, the other time may have been a fluke, or a new addition to her changing abilities.

"I think Rebecca and I should go back to the mansion and get Gaston and Caden. There's no way we can continue our search for Lisselle at this moment." Nettie hated to leave her friend, but she knew that Lisselle could more than handle herself.

Homer studied the body closet to him, but didn't touch anything. Finally, he looked up. "I agree. And when you get to Gaston, warn him they know about us." He scowled, then nudged the body he was near onto its back. A bloody note lay in the shattered hand, as if the person had grabbed it as he fought to survive. Most of it wasn't legible, the only few words were the Society and vampires.

"But how could they…" A freezing chill that had nothing to do with the damp air went down Nettie's back.

"I don't know, lass, I don't know. But if I had to guess, I'd say they know about us, and they are blaming us for the vampires the royal household took. I will stay here until Gaston sends people. Then I will find Lisselle." Homer's face didn't bode well for anyone, vampire or not, who got between him and Lisselle. As much as Nettie wanted to stay and hunt for her friend, she knew he was right. Getting the bodies out of here would protect against public hysteria, but might also give some clues as to what the vampires were doing.

Homer's dark words swarmed around Nettie the entire way back to the mansion. She felt responsible for Lisselle's disappearance. Lisselle had gone deep undercover to find the vampire who attacked Nettie—she was sure of it.

"Nettie. Nettie, someone is following us."

From the tone in her voice, Rebecca may have said her name a few times and had gone unheard. Nettie shook herself. This was no time for wool gathering. Slowing her steps minutely, she kept her ears out for any noises.

Rebecca was right. There was a slight rasping sound behind them and to the left. She felt no vampiric presence, but she may have been over-counting on that new skill. It could be one of the aliens except that Gaston's theory meant they couldn't come back down to Earth yet. Unless they had more than one of those ships. They had no idea how many aliens and ships there were. If one were planning on invading a planet, it would make sense to have more than one ship.

"What is it?" Rebecca's voice was small, but she didn't sound scared. She sounded almost excited.

"I've no idea. But I think we need to wait for it." Nettie pulled Rebecca off to the side. They'd been passing through a wide alley that was relatively free of debris, but a large wooden crate lingered against one wall. Both women quickly darted behind it.

"Now you must stay here. If I am overpowered, you must not try to help me. It is vital that you get back to Gaston." Nettie had put her most dangerous voice on, but Rebecca still looked ready to argue. "Rebecca, this information could save many others. My one life is not worth the risk. Whatever happens, you must run."

"But I—"

"Will do what I say."

"Fine." Rebecca's hand came out of her dress pocket. Clearly, she'd carried one of the small dissemblers on her person.

"And don't use that whatever you do," Nettie added as she listened for the rasping.

"Why? Is it top secret?"

"To some extent. Yet you haven't been trained, and this is not anything like the guns your parents had in Wales." Nettie leapt forward. While she and Rebecca had been bantering, the rasping had grown closer. Hopefully, they would think they'd gone undetected.

Throwing back her coat, she leapt on the tall shape as he drew near.

Only to be thrown over his shoulder. The man followed through on his throw, but she rolled out of the way. With lightning fast reflexes, she grabbed his right arm and was twisting it to break when she recognized his scent. Her heart pounded hard when she realized what she'd almost done and how easily she'd almost done it.

"Caden?" She flung him away so the movement she'd already started on his arm wouldn't actually break it.

"Ow, dang it, first them, now you." He tumbled to one knee then got back up. As she moved into the dim light of the alley, Nettie could now see that his clothing was torn and filthy. Blood marked some of it, but she wasn't sure if it was his or someone else's.

"You were supposed to have gone back to Gaston." She hid her concern beneath a gruff voice. But even more concerning was the speed at which she dispatched him. She could have not only broken his arm, but ripped it off with ease.

The feeling made her more than a little sick.

"I did. Then I left again and came back out to look for Lisselle. A gang attacked me." He looked up and cocked his head. "Not really a gang, more like three thugs. But they got the jump on me one street over from the palace, that street where you said you found that contaminated vampire."

Rebecca slowly came out from her hiding area. "How did you fight them off?"

Caden held himself up proudly, then winced when an injury pulled him back down. "As much as I'd like to say I beat them off, the fact is, they had me to rights. McGrady got a stick of wood and that was all I remembered until I woke up and started following you two."

Nettie had been looking for injuries—most of the blood did in fact appear to belong to someone else—when his words hit her. "McGrady?" Gaston had assumed the agent was dead. No one could have lived under the water as long as his signal had been down there. And removing the tracker would have sent a different signal.

Caden smacked his forehead then winced again. "I think they may have scrambled my head a bit. One of the attackers *was* McGrady. He didn't look too good, sort of rabid if you ask me, but it was him." He paused. "He didn't seem to recognize me though."

Nettie was torn. She wanted to find McGrady. If he'd survived the crash and drowning, there was something the Society needed to know about. And now that Caden was here, Rebecca would make it safely back to Gaston.

"Don't even think about it, Jones." Caden continued walking the way they'd been headed. "I outrank you on this caper, remember? Gaston needs us back. All of us."

"I hadn't said anything." Nettie fumed. She knew he would throw his higher rank at her again. A day didn't go by without him flaunting it.

"And you didn't need to." He stared at her closely. "I've been watching you, Jones. I know how your mind works. As soon as I said McGrady, your thoughts were immediately to finding him."

"Not all of us need to go back to Gaston. Lisselle is still missing. Three royal guards were slaughtered—"

"And you almost ripped off my arm without so much as trying." He dropped his voice as he said the words and studied her face before continuing. "I noticed you pull back at the last second. And I saw your face when you realized how easily you almost did it." There was gentleness in his voice that she'd never heard before.

"I'm fine." Even as she said it Nettie knew she was lying. Both to him and herself. Her heart was in her throat as the reality of her abilities hit her. That she seemed to have little control over them made things even worse.

He leaned close, his voice even lower. "No, you're not."

Nettie felt her face go warm under his concern. He was really quite handsome when he wasn't being an absolute beast. "You are right. I need to talk to Gaston. And so do you and Rebecca."

Caden was still close to Nettie's face so she couldn't see around him. When her friend gave no response, she shoved him aside.

Rebecca was gone.

CHAPTER NINETEEN

"WHAT HAVE YOU done? Where is she? Rebecca!" Nettie yelled her friend's name, but nothing answered her. How could someone have taken her with them right there? Because she had been too busy noticing how nice Caden could be, that's why.

Nettie made to run down the alley, but Caden blocked her.

"She's not here. If she'd gone off on her own, she would have responded, so someone took her. We need to get to Gaston immediately."

"No. I'm not leaving without her." Nettie pulled her arm free and flashed her fangs. If she didn't want to go back, there was no way Caden could make her. To be honest, at the rate she was changing, she doubted any agent could bring her down at this point. She shoved the fear that accompanied that thought far away.

Caden had been watching her face closely and slowly held out one hand. "You know I can't stop you, don't you? Think about it, Nettie, who could have taken her without our noticing? Without *you* noticing?" His voice was low and soothing, the type you'd use on a rabid dog that was blocking your path.

His words cut through Nettie's rage and anger. He had a valid point. Her sense of smell had always been keen, and it had become a serious nuisance since her abilities had begun changing. She would have noticed had anything human, or vampire, been in the alley with them.

"The aliens." Even as she said it, she knew she was right.

"Them or the missing Runners. They could have been reprogrammed by now. And they might have taken Lisselle as well." He shook his head. "I don't know why we didn't think of that before."

"It makes sense they were behind Rebecca's capture." Nettie was pleased that her heart rate was slowing and her voice was calm. Maybe she could control this condition. She wasn't going to admit that Caden had been successful in calming her down. "But why would you make the assumption that Lisselle was captured by them as well? She was on the trail of vampires. It makes more sense they took her."

"Not really." Caden started to take her arm to start walking, then thought better of it. "She was on the trail of something, but she didn't say who. Homer said she wouldn't even tell him. I think we all assumed she'd found the vampire nest since that's what she's good at. But think of where she was heading. Who could have easily gotten her out?"

Nettie let an unladylike swear word slip out. "The aliens who can somehow send themselves down here without a fuss. But they are growing bold if they took Lisselle and Rebecca right in front of us. Well, Rebecca at any rate. We can't be sure when Lisselle was taken."

"Not only bold. This means they are improving their ability to come down to our world faster. If they find a way to bring their ship down…"

Nettie didn't fill in the rest of his thought. She didn't need to. Both of them knew what that would mean for London. And the entire world. An invasion the world couldn't defend against.

They stayed silent all the way back to the mansion. Gaston hurried them down into the dungeon and instructed Damon to make sure all the windows and doors were locked.

With things secure, and Nettie and Caden both seated and with hot tea, Gaston got to business. "Where was Homer heading?" Gaston stood in front of his map of London, a map no one outside of the Society would ever see. It was color coded with locations of holdings only known to Society members as well as known areas of vampire infestation. Previously, it had only had red circles for the known vampire activities. Now green circles had joined to show where the aliens had appeared.

Nettie stepped forward and indicated it on the map. "He was here. He was going to hide the bodies until you could get a crew out to them, and then go this way."

"Quite good. And, Caden, where were you attacked?"

Nettie frowned as his finger intersected the line of Homer's path.

"Here. And I know I couldn't have fought them off. I was going down when I was knocked unconscious." Caden said without any embarrassment or self-conscious reaction. He might be cocky, but at least he admitted defeat. Sometimes.

"And we were here when Rebecca was taken," Nettie said and pointed in the middle of Gaston's collections of marks.

"Which means we have unknown assailants attacking our agents, someone who was able to fight them off, vanishing aliens, and Homer, all in a one-block radius."

Nettie nodded. "We have to go after him."

"Normally, I'd agree with you. But we have beings out there with unknown technology snatching our agents off the streets." Gaston turned and frowned. "Homer is on his own for now. I'm sending you two into the belly of the beast. If there is a chance they were the ones behind Rebecca's kidnapping. We must get you up there soon."

"But we don't know where their nest is," Caden said. "That's what the problem is."

"He's not talking about the vampires, Caden. He's talking about the aliens," Nettie said. "Aren't you?"

"You have always been my best girl." Gaston had listened to her full disclosure of her increasing abilities and alarming results once they had filled them in on the evening's events. Then patted her on the head, and said he still trusted her with his life. That was enough to reassure Nettie.

"How are we going to get up there though? I went up by accident." She wasn't afraid of going up, especially if they had taken Rebecca. But even the Society had nothing that could breach ether.

"Wait a minute. You want us to go up there?" Caden pointed his finger toward the ceiling. "Impossible."

"It's not impossible. I did it before. We somehow have to find one of those strange men in brown and tag along when he goes back up." Nettie nodded as she thought about it. Use their own technology against them.

"Nope, up is not going to work for me. Sorry." Caden looked distinctly uncomfortable as he hunkered down in his chair and folded his arms. "If you must know, I'm terrified of heights."

"What? Don't be daft, man." Gaston had a flash of concern at Caden's pronouncement. "You won't know you're up there. I doubt they have windows. Did they have windows, Nettie?"

Nettie had taken ink and paper and was making her own map of the best possible locations to find one of the aliens. "Not that I saw. I don't think you can have windows in ether."

Caden gave a violent shiver. "I'll know."

"Are you saying you'd rather Agent Jones went alone?" Gaston was appealing to the male pride that lurked close to the surface in Caden.

"No, never." Caden looked from Nettie to Gaston, then back. "You're right; I can't let a woman go up alone."

"Ach, boy, you never learn, do you? I was saying you'd not want to let a fellow agent go in alone." Gaston's comment had been voiced at a low level, but Nettie heard it regardless.

"Never mind, Gaston. I can certainly handle them on my own." She picked up her things.

"You're as bad as he is. Neither of you are going without the other. Male, female, vampire, human, I don't care. Are you forgetting those aliens brought you back unconscious? Not to mention it is three in the morning. I'm sure the aliens don't use time the way we do, but the fact is even you need some sleep. And Caden and I are just poor humans. Exhaustion creates mistakes."

Nettie turned on her short boss. She was ready to fight him on the sleep issue, but a part of her admitted he was right. But there were other issues she didn't agree on. "Are we certain they could do it now? I've changed since then."

Gaston folded his arms and glared. "Do you know what they

did to you?" When Nettie bit her lip he continued. "I thought not. No agent goes out alone. Says me. Go sleep, and then get ready, whatever you need to do. In six hours, we send the two of you to the aliens."

"Oh, great." Caden's voice was not a happy sound as he turned down the hall of the men's wing.

Nettie didn't say anything, but nodded in agreement, then continued to her room.

PART OF NETTIE was too tense to sleep, and it wasn't the part worried about her missing friends. She had been extremely disturbed at telling Gaston, and Caden since there had been no way to get him out of the room without a fuss, about her increasing abilities. She was surprised at how much tension had been released from her shoulders when he had taken the information, yet not shown any sign of worrying about her.

Even though she'd been there almost a week, her new room took her breath away each time she came in. It was easily as large as many of the entire flats she'd lived in growing up.

Taking a deep breath to pull in the relaxing grandeur of the chamber, she went to her writing desk.

She agreed that she needed rest. Yet, she also needed to find her friends. One thing she had always been good at had been recognizing patterns. She could often remember odd bits and images long after their relevance had ended simply because she recalled their pattern.

She quickly sketched out recent events in a childish version of

Gaston's larger map. It would have been better with the actual map, but then she would have to fight Gaston about the entire sleep issue. She would sleep after she made some headway.

The locations all seemed to have something in common. At least the locations of the alien sightings, vanishings, and reappearances.

Tapping the end of her pen against her teeth, she pulled out of one of books she'd started storing in her room. The mansion had a huge library on the first floor and Gaston had told her to avail herself of the resources.

She cocked her head. There was something there, something she was forgetting. With an impatient shake at her sluggish memory, she pulled out a book about the Romans. Although Bath was more noticeable in its Roman heritage, London—or Londinium, as it had been called at the time—had also a wealth of Roman artifacts, tombs, and statues. The current modern city was built on the bones on that ancient past.

That was it.

Every place where there had been a sighting of the aliens was also a location of Roman ruins or artifacts. In the case of that night, Rebecca had been standing no more than five meters from a bit of Roman bricks.

The Runners had been taken on the road to Cardiff, but never made it past Bath.

What if it hadn't been the vampires who took the Runners, but the aliens? Since they weren't sure what the aliens were ultimately up to, it was difficult to say which was the bigger threat: furious vampires coming to avenge their own, or aliens bent on who knew what but somehow connected to the ruins of an empire that collapsed hundreds of years ago.

Making a few more quick notes—nothing she found tonight would change Gaston's mind about rest—she changed and tumbled into a dreamless slumber.

"I STILL THINK we should wait until Homer comes back. He could go with her. It makes more sense if I try to track the vampires—" Caden cut himself off as Nettie came into the dining room.

"I will repeat what I said last night," Nettie said as she pulled up a seat next to Gaston. Of all the things Caden Smith had struck her as, a coward wasn't one of them. She was honestly more than a little surprised at his fear. "I can go by myself. Besides, he'd be more of a hindrance if he was too terrified to move."

"I am not terrified. Granted, I might be if you were to throw me up in one of those unnatural airships. Man is meant to stay on the ground, damn it. There is no way that flying can be safe." Caden took a sip of his tea, but from the look on his face, he wished for something stronger. He satisfied himself by adding another lump of sugar. "But the fact is, I know my skills. They're going to be wasted on some metal cabin up in the air."

"Homer is checking out some other leads on the vampires that attacked those guards. He may have a lead on McGrady as well. He came back after you'd both gone to bed. Just left again about an hour ago." Gaston ignored Caden's obvious nerves. "The fact is I have two agents with me right now, and I need two agents to get into that alien ship."

Taking pity on Caden—why, she wasn't sure—Nettie spoke. "While I don't agree with Caden's assessment, I do think we have a problem. How are we supposed to get up there? You pointed out before that I have no idea how they got me up or back previously. It's all well and good to say we need to go up to find Lisselle and Rebecca, but I'm at a loss as to how." Damon laid a huge breakfast in front of her so she began eating while Gaston gathered his thoughts.

"Exactly. How are we going to get up there? A large catapult? We don't even know where they are." There was a bit of relief in Caden's voice, but also some embarrassment. Nettie would venture to say no one in his home country knew of his fear of heights. Most likely, they believed his façade of fearless charm.

"Now you are being hysterical. Of course none of those options will work. We will simply have to have the aliens grab you both. Of course, you'll be prepared for it this time, Nettie." Gaston looked smugly over his cup as if he'd resolved everything.

Caden said nothing but sputtered out some tea.

"I find myself siding with Agent Smith, I'm afraid, in his disbelief of this working." Nettie dabbed the corners of her mouth in surprise as she looked at her plate. She'd finished off a breakfast big enough for two men in less than a few minutes. That must be another side effect of whatever change her body was going through. She supposed she should be grateful her increased metabolism wanted more food…and not something more liquid.

"I was unconscious when they took me up. Do you expect Agent Smith and I to lie about various places in London waiting for them to stumble upon us?" Her eyes went wide as she suddenly recalled her findings of the previous night.

"What is it? Are you choking?" Gaston leaned over to pat her on the back.

Nettie waved him off. "No, not at all. I'm sorry. I meant to tell you of this when I first came down. I think I've found a connection of some sort between where the aliens come down. I'm not sure how helpful it will be in our current circumstances, but it may be the only lead we have. I think they are somehow drawn to the sites of Roman ruins."

Gaston said nothing. Caden let out a snort.

Nettie pulled out her map. "Here are the locations of their appearances, at least the ones we know of. Each one had a Roman finding or site nearby. I have no idea why, but for some reason, they are drawn to the Roman ruins. Of course, for most of London, any remains are deep under the city."

"Let me see that." Gaston leaned forward and Nettie pulled the small book on local Roman finds out of her pocket and held it up as well.

"See here? Where Rebecca was taken there are noted Roman ruins. The current building even incorporated some of the original Roman wall. Not much, granted, but enough to be documented, and enough to lend evidence to my hypothesis."

"Now she'll be waving that advanced degree about as well." Caden shook his head. "What possible connection could there be between beings from some other world—which I'm still not sure I believe in completely, by the way—and ancient ruins? You're looking for connections that aren't there and backing them with a constructed hypothesis."

Nettie leveled her best glare at Caden, but directed her comments to Gaston. "As you can see, the events have been correlated far too often to be a coincidence. Would you prefer I use smaller words, Agent Smith?"

"You may be on to something here." Gaston pondered as he glanced between the map and the book. "This is far more than mere coincidence, Caden. Yes, yes, this does help. Although we don't know why, at least we have a good clue as to how to narrow down the places they would come down to take you." He looked up with a grin. "I have been building my own theories and I believe we can make the two of you extremely interesting to the aliens."

Caden slumped in his chair, but stayed silent.

"You see, I believe they are also after examples of our technology. They followed Nettie when she left here that first day." He rose to his feet and paced in the dining room as he spoke. Damon wisely dodged out of his way. "This mansion is a bastion of technology, but they haven't gotten in. As far as we know, they have yet to appear inside any building and may not be able to. But they tracked Nettie leaving here on her steamcycle. I think they were just following you that first time, but when you gathered some of their dust, they took action to get it back. They took Lisselle, or so we believe, and she was carrying one of our newest gadgets with her—a vampire sensor that came down from Edinburgh. Rebecca likewise had one, although much smaller." At Nettie's surprised look, he reddened. "Yes, I didn't tell you I'd given it to her. I wanted to see if you could sense a vampire before it could, but I didn't want you to be biased by knowing there was a machine in place."

"But if that's so, then why did they take Nettie up that first time? And if your theory holds about the Roman ruins, where were you?" Caden had clearly gotten over his huff and was now starting to function like a trained agent.

Nettie pushed the map over toward his side of the table. "Yes, right here. Not much but a few coins were found ten years ago when the restaurant owner decided to dig a trench behind his business." She turned toward Gaston. "His other question is valid, and I think I was a mistake. I believe something happened to the alien I had been following, and when I went to check on him, they brought me in as well. Even though you claim I was gone for a few hours, it truly felt like only moments in the ship."

"Then I'd say we have our plan. I'm loading both of you with useless mockups of recent technology. Basically gizmos that have a lot of gears but do nothing but perhaps shoot sparks. I'm also having you take some regular pistols, no dissembler gear guns. If they are able to track the technology, they would take those gear weapons, but a pistol might miss their notice." He waved his hand as Caden looked ready to speak. "But a warning against using these things. We have no idea what a gun would do on an ether-faring ship. We have to assume it would be akin to shooting out the bottom of a sailing ship. So do not do it unless you have no recourse at all."

CHAPTER TWENTY

C ADEN HAD LISTENED to the rest of the plans in silence, but it looked to Nettie as if he was finally coming to terms with the need to go. To be honest, even with their plans and theories, she really didn't have much faith in getting the aliens to come get them.

Until Gaston walked them out back for his secret weapon.

He beamed like a schoolboy as he had Damon remove a sheet from a tower sitting in the back lawn. Luckily, neighbors in this part of town made it a practice to ignore the comings and goings of those around them. Nettie was certain the six-foot-high collection of gears and brass cables would attract attention anywhere else in London, even in the private back yard of a house.

"What does it do?" Nettie leaned forward as two-foot-wide wheels started spinning slowly. There were smaller wheels within the larger ones and they also began to move. But aside from a bit of steam coming from the back, she couldn't see what its possible purpose was.

"Absolutely nothing. Isn't it grand?" Gaston walked around the structure, flicking one of the wheels that hadn't started spinning yet. "And more important, it's made out of technology obtained from the Runners. While it won't do anything to anyone, it should attract our friends. When one of them comes down to investigate, they grab you and you both go back up to their ship with them."

"What makes you think they'll take both of us up?" Caden walked around it shaking his head. "I will admit this is an interesting thing you've made."

"Now, there isn't much we can do to get aboard a ship in the sky. The best thing we can do is have them want to take you two aboard. If we have the two of you out here, loaded with technology and fussing with this monolith, I believe they will want to visit. If they don't seem to take you right away, both of you grab the alien when he appears. Whatever you do, do not let go." He patted his invention then motioned for Damon to follow him back to the house. "We will be watching from the house to gather information, but we will not interfere. Good luck."

Caden watched her but made no move toward the tower.

"I think we should pretend that we are working on this. We've no idea what draws them down here." Nettie took a small wrench that Gaston had left in a pile of tools by the base and started poking at one of the gears.

"Do you really think that they can tell if we're working on something? I don't see how this will work. I mean it's great that this mansion is on a Roman ruin and has technology they seem to follow, but if there are two of us, won't they be afraid to send a single alien down? I think only one of us should be here. If they send too many, we could be in a bad spot."

Nettie let out a sigh. "I have had it with your not wanting to go up there—"

"That's not it. You shouldn't be out here." He pulled her

away from the structure. "What if people aren't supposed to go back and forth the way these aliens travel? It could do something to you."

Nettie had enough time to blink stupidly at him before a soft whoosh of air behind her ended the discussion.

"Don't move, Nettie. He's right behind you." Caden kept still, but she saw one hand reach into his jacket.

"Don't you dare pull out that pistol."

Another whoosh followed. This time a small brown figure stood behind Caden. This one wasn't looking at them, but seemed fixated on the structure Gaston had built.

"There's one behind both of us...."

As if they shared the same thought, both Nettie and Caden spun at the same moment and grabbed a hold of the distracted aliens.

Nettie really hoped that Gaston was paying close attention and took notes of what happened. The second she touched the alien, her entire world went black.

"I DON'T SUPPOSE you've come to yet? Perhaps just sitting there, gathering your British calm?" Caden's voice was low and right next to her.

"Funny, I don't even recall falling asleep, yet I'm having nightmares." Nettie spoke before she rolled over and looked up. Caden was far too close to her. Clearly, they'd been dumped in here, wherever here was, after grabbing the aliens.

"It seems that Gaston's plan has worked. Now we have to

figure out how to find our friends and get out of here." Nettie rolled to her feet without assistance and dusted off her skirts. Never mind that there wasn't a speck of dirt on the smooth, metal floor. One always felt better composed after dusting off one's clothes.

"That and they took my gun." Caden had silently assumed his feet as well and was already feeling along the walls for a way out.

Nettie patted her pockets. The fake gadgets that Gaston had made were gone. But her inner pocket still held her small mundane pistol. Which raised the question of why they would have left it.

She frowned at Caden's back. "Did you perchance still have the gun in your hand when you attacked the alien? Even without technology, they might have gathered it was a weapon of a sort if you had it out."

Caden turned with a scowl, which was the only answer she needed.

"Well, I still have mine." She went to another part of the wall and started poking. "The last time I was up here, they came through this end. Or one like it. I'm not completely sure it's the same chamber. It appears to be a bit smaller."

Nettie tapped the smooth walls, but there was no spot that sounded different, indicating a doorway or false wall. She knew from her visit before that there were seams of a sort. Unfortunately, she hadn't seen the seam until it opened.

Caden continued his pounding but was coming closer to her side.

"No! Stay across from me," Nettie said. She didn't turn around but could all but feel Caden's eyes boring into her.

"You can't stand to even be near me now? That's taking it a bit far, don't you think?"

Nettie stopped taping to whirl around. "That could be true, but that's not why. When I was trapped up here before, the aliens opened a seam across from me. The wall had looked like these, no marks. Then all of a sudden they had opened something. If we are on opposite sides, we stand a better chance of grabbing one of them when they come in. I didn't get to see any of the ship last time as they shot me with some ridiculous little pistol and sent me back to London."

"Good point, Agent Jones." Caden gave her an approving nod, and then went back the way he came as he tapped the wall.

Nettie paused for a moment in surprise. That was possibly the first time in their short acquaintance that he agreed with her immediately. Perhaps it was something in the alien air.

Air.

"Now that is another thing odd," Nettie said. "These people from another world breathe the same as we? Or is it that they don't and know we do and have this room filled with air for us? Perhaps the rest of the ship would kill us?"

Caden let out a sigh. "I'm glad you are so intelligent that you figure these new things out to worry about, but do you think you could keep them to yourself? I've got enough concerns at the moment thank you...." His last word faded off as a whoosh of air came from his side of the room.

Nettie turned to see him fall through a sudden seam then vanish.

"Oh no you don't! You don't take him and not me!" Lifting her skirts, she ran to where Caden had been standing and started pounding as hard as she could on the metal skin. "Do you hear me? You cannot take him without me!"

She stopped pounding for a moment and put her ear to the cool metal. She thought she could make out a low-level hum, but nothing beyond that. No yelling and screaming indicating that Caden was succumbing to some horrible thing out there. Or he could already be dead.

She wasn't quite sure how she felt about that for a moment. Then she resumed pounding and yelling at the wall. How she felt was annoyed.

Finally, she pulled out her small pistol. Logic dictated that the aliens didn't have her in here for no reason. Most likely, even if they couldn't understand what she said, they would have a basic understanding of her actions.

She hoped that they had figured out what Caden's gun could do.

"If you don't let me out to see my friends, I'll have to shoot." She slowly held up the gun and, with over exaggerated motions, made to shoot the floor. She had absolutely no intention of doing any such thing. By her own mental calculations, Gaston's comparison with a wooden sailing ship wasn't quite right. She believed it would be worse. Probably more explosive, like a large balloon being punctured. But she hoped that if they understood it was a projectile weapon, and her movements, they would act.

It only took a few moments after the appearance of the gun before the seam reappeared. Unlike when Caden had been grabbed, it opened slowly. And wide enough to show Caden with one of the alien's guns pointed at his temple.

Clearly they understood what a projectile weapon could do to their ship.

"I think you got through to them," Caden said. He kept his head perfectly still and seemed a bit worse for wear. "Good thing you did too. I'm not sure, but I felt like a laboratory rat. They were taking me into a room with a long table. Had what looked like hand and foot cuffs on it too."

Nettie raised her gun to the alien next to Caden. "That's not good. It also does not bode well for what has happened to our friends, if they took them. You didn't happen to see either of them, did you?" It felt a bit odd, to say the least, having a calm conversation with her partner while on a ship in ether while an alien held a weapon to his head. But she believed that rash action or tone right now would do none of them any good.

"No, unfortunately they surrounded me the moment they pulled me out of here. They have some sort of camera in here that takes moving images of you. They started getting excited when you waved the gun about." He gave a half smile. "On the plus side, I have demonstrated that they breathe air similar to ours, even if it smells funny."

Nettie had noticed that as well. The air that came in when the doors were opened was different from what had been in with her. But since she and Caden were still able to breathe, the difference must be minimal.

"I'm afraid I'm at a loss right now. I must admit I've yet to face a hostage situation in my career, let alone one in ether with aliens." Nettie kept her pistol up and aimed but her arm was beginning to tingle. "Any suggestions you might be willing to send forth would be appreciated."

Caden caught himself before he laughed out loud, but it

showed on his face. "I am glad to hear you admit to something unknown to you, Agent Jones. My suggestion might seem rash, but I don't think we have much choice. We have to assume the aliens are not looking out for our well-being. Therefore, our goal must be to get free, find our friends, and escape. Agreed?"

Nettie nodded and shifted her weight more equally between her feet. She was prone to rash actions, but somehow, taking one directed by someone else wasn't as reassuring.

"First, how good of a shot are you with that?" Caden shifted his shoulder slightly forward.

"I scored the highest marks in the last five years in Edinburgh." Nettie followed Caden's eyes and retrained her pistol on the alien next to the one with the gun.

"That should be good enough. Aim for flesh. You hit something else and we all die." He dropped his left shoulder another tiny amount. "We need a distraction. Can you sing?"

Nettie frowned at him. "Badly. Trust me it is not something I am proud of, to say the least. But I don't think this is the time or place to discuss that."

"That's perfect. Listening to their speech has given me an idea. When I blink my eyes, sing anything as high and screechy as you can. And loud, very loud."

The blink came an instant later and Nettie launched into England's national anthem at full volume. The aliens cringed immediately.

Even though she expected something like it, Caden moved so fast she almost missed her chance. In one blur of speed he ducked down while at the same time reaching up and ripping the alien gun out of the alien's hand.

Still singing, she fired her gun at the middle of the alien's leg. She didn't want to kill it, and its legs seemed to have the same heavy fleshing in the thighs that humans did. At least she hoped they did under all the fabric.

The one she shot collapsed immediately. Caden kept his newfound weapon trained on both of them, but didn't fire. The injured one clutched his leg and a thin green ooze trickled out. Luckily, the bullet must have stayed in his leg.

"Excellent shooting, Agent Jones, but you can stop singing now. It could be considered cruel and unusual punishment."

Nettie shook herself and lowered her weapon. "I was actually singing worse than my normal ability, you know. I'm not that bad naturally."

"One would really hope not," Caden said. He waved the weapon at the non-injured alien then pointed to himself and Nettie. "Our friends, the ones like us. Take us there."

At first the alien simply blinked. If Caden was taken aback by the vertical lids, he gave no show of it.

When he repeated himself three more times, carefully pointing at he and Nettie, the alien finally nodded.

"I guess we follow him. Keep your pistol on him though. I don't want any of his friends to find us and ambush us along the way." Caden started to follow him when Nettie called out.

"Take that gun from the other one's robe first. It's what they used to send me back down, I'm sure of it." At first, she had thought they'd used one of their weapons on her and somehow sent her down separately. But somehow she knew that thing they'd shot her with had sent her back. "Don't ask me to explain, but that gun had something to do with me getting back."

Caden took it quickly while Nettie kept her pistol trained on the aliens, but he didn't look happy as he tucked it into his pocket.

"That sounds a bit farfetched. A gun can't get you sent somewhere. Most likely, it knocked you out for their experiments." He nudged the uninjured alien and they started moving.

"Then why didn't they use it on you? Or me when I was standing there? I think it has another purpose, but even if it won't get us back, we need to bring it to Gaston."

Caden shrugged. "Agreed."

"Now how do we get him or it to take us to our friends?"

"Don't you have a plan? You seem to have an idea about everything else."

Nettie lowered her eyelids and folded her arms. The fact was she did have a plan, but she knew she'd look silly. For some odd reason she was bothered by looking silly in front of Agent Smith.

But she had people she cared about depending on her. Besides, how people saw her had never bothered her before.

"I think I can communicate with them." She gave a wince. "I've always been exceedingly good at charades."

Caden had been moving toward the alien but stopped short. "You're going to try and use a parlor game to find out where our missing agents are?"

She couldn't tell whether he was fighting not to laugh or yell. "It's not only a game; it's a valued way to communicate with people who don't speak your language. Since their language doesn't sound like anything I've heard before—and I am fluent in five languages, you know—I think it is our only option. The clicks and whistles they make are their words. I'm hoping some gestures will translate."

Ignoring Caden, Nettie took a place directly in front of the alien and began pantomiming. First, she acted out her and Caden as people, not aliens. Then she held up two fingers, and then pointed to herself. Acting out that she knew the aliens took them took a bit more doing. But after some pulling around on the uninjured alien, he seemed to understand. At least the clicks he made sounded like he was agreeing with what she said. He agreed even faster when she used her gun to nudge him.

"I can't believe you did that." Caden held back, but his voice sounded surprised. "Although I'll be more impressed when we get the other agents back."

Nettie noticed that her alien wouldn't move too far from his injured comrade. "Smile and show that his friend is okay."

Caden stepped back with a nod. "Agreed, but we need him to hurry. There have to be more than two aliens up here."

Nettie waited until the one she held the gun on nodded after seeing his friend, then nudged him to lead on. With a few clicks he started leading them down a corridor.

"That raises a good question. How many of them are there? I think we can presume this is not a peaceful visit?" Nettie kept close on her alien's trail, but the fact was she also needed answers. She wasn't sure why she felt that Caden would have them, but the ship was so foreign perhaps she needed to hear another human voice.

"Wait a minute." Caden had been a few steps behind them when he called out. It took a few moments for the alien to understand she needed him to stop.

"Keep him there. I want to check something." Caden started

to dart into a side corridor which agitated the alien. "Keep him back. He doesn't want us to see what's back here, which means we need to."

Nettie raised her gun and forced the alien back a few steps. "No, no."

Caden stuck his head back out and looked around. "Who are you speaking to?"

"Him. Or her. I'm afraid I don't know if they have genders. I'm hoping to teach him some words. He knows I stopped him, and by saying no, he should attach that word to stopping an action." Nettie nodded at the alien.

Caden started to say something then shut his mouth and turned back into his corridor. Nettie waited to see if the alien would give her another teaching experience, but he hunched down into himself and stayed still.

"That's not good," Caden said as he came back. "There are maps of what I can only assume is the entire world seen in sections from up here. A few larger dots, such as one that looks to be exactly where London is, have pins like this on them." He held out a pin that looked like a small disk with engines and waved it at the alien.

"This is a ship, isn't it?"

When the alien pulled back at Caden's yelling, Nettie took the pin.

"This," she pointed to the pin, "is the same as this." She pointed to the ship and repeated the moves a few times. Finally the alien made some clicks and gave a nod.

"He understood! Nodding for yes." Nettie beamed and turned to Caden.

His scowl wasn't a pretty sight. "Which means if you are right, then there are about eighty of these ships all over the globe. At least half of them are over England."

Nettie pushed in closer to the alien waving her pistol in his face. "Is that true? You have ships all over? Is that true?"

The alien's eyes blinked rapidly and his skin started to pale.

"I seriously doubt he knows what you said but I think you're scaring him," Caden said.

Nettie glared down at the alien for a few more seconds, and then nudged him to continue walking down the corridor. "Good. How dare he come to our world with a bunch of ships, planning to do who knows what. And taking our people too." She jabbed the alien in the back to emphasis her annoyance. "That is rude. You don't see humans flittering off to other lands and taking over places."

Caden had moved to walk alongside her so she heard his snort. "No, it's nothing like the British empire trying to take over the entire planet."

"What? Of course it's not the same…Not really. Well… No, not the same at all." Nettie shook her head, but she knew she didn't believe it either. As much as she loved Mother England, the fact was her history wasn't as nice as it could be. "That is beside the point. The point is, they don't belong on our planet. Or above our planet."

The alien stopped in front of a small door and didn't move until Nettie nudged him again. "I will shoot you if I have to. Don't think that I won't." She gave him her best grimace, letting her fangs slide down for good measure.

The change to the alien's mostly immobile face was amazing.

Instead of reacting with fear, he started popping his head and pointing to her teeth.

"You them. No tell we." The words were English, but coming out of a non-human, they lost some tonality.

"You can speak English?" Nettie rocked back on her heels in surprise. And the alien seemed to be smiling. Or at least its version of a smile.

"Lish yes noise. We give bait you. But have only one, not two." He bobbed his head and quickly put a palm on a small box next to the door. "Here bait, you leave with."

As he spoke the door slid up and Rebecca sat before them. She was propped in a chair and didn't look harmed. She also wasn't conscious.

With a cry, Nettie ran forward to check her friend's pulse.

"You need to warn me before you do that," Caden said from behind her. Once she was sure Rebecca was breathing she noticed that Caden had hold of the alien's arm. "Your friend was trying to leave."

"No," Nettie said as she picked up Rebecca.

"Others come." The alien pointed to his own teeth. They were small and flat, but she had no trouble understanding what he was pantomiming at.

"Vampires. The aliens are working with the vampires."

CHAPTER TWENTY-ONE

"WHAT?" CADEN TOOK his eyes off the alien but not his hand. The alien twitched then stopped trying to pull away. "How can you possibly have gotten that from his mangled speech?"

"He reacted when I slid down my fangs. He doesn't see us the same way he did before. How else did he learn English? It makes sense the two enemies are working together." She marched out holding Rebecca in her arms. "Since I can communicate with him better, you'll need to take her." She smiled at little as Caden sagged a bit under the sudden weight, but then he adjusted quickly.

There was a window not two feet from where they stood and she pointed at it. Caden carefully took a step backward and refused to look directly over at it.

"Now, you…" She flashed her fangs again, this time trying to put more vampire into it. She didn't have the nerve to turn and ask Caden if her eyes had gone red though. To be honest, she didn't really want to know. "We need to go down." She tapped the window for emphasis as she motioned down.

The alien clicked and gave another human-like nod. "There, use there. That there." He pointed at the alien gun sticking out of Caden's pocket and a small round disk in the middle of the floor.

"Show." The alien walked over to disk, then pulled out a second gun and shot himself. He vanished an instant later.

"That's not a good thing. First off, I swear he only had the one gun on him." Caden swore as he looked around for a place to put Rebecca down. "Secondly, he could have gone to get reinforcements."

Nettie stood in the panel. "No, he thinks I'm one of the vampires they are working with. He was showing us how to get back to where we came from. Come stand here. I'll try to shoot all of us at once."

Caden started to back away, but Nettie's superior hearing picked up an unwelcome sound. They may have convinced the first alien she was one of their allies, but she couldn't take the chance she could do it to more of them. She reached out and dragged Caden and Rebecca onto the panel. Then, using her strength to keep them together, she held the alien gun in between them all and fired.

To say the experience was odd would be akin to saying the Tower of London was dreary. Nettie wasn't even certain they had returned to Earth for a full two minutes after the whirling in her head stopped.

"Are you okay? Nettie? Speak to me?"

Caden's voice was near, but dancing black spots continued to block him from her view. She was aware enough to realize that he called her by her given name. And that his voice actually sounded concerned.

Something must be wrong.

Shaking her head, she forced the black dots to vanish. It was worse than she feared.

Caden was lying beneath her.

"Oh my!" She scrambled to her feet quickly. "Where is Rebecca?" She brushed off her skirt and tried not to think where her head had been. How had they landed like that?

Caden rose and blushed.

"She's fine. I set her down over there, but you were still out and I was worried, so I tried to move you…"

"See here, I do not weigh that much. Are you implying you are so weak you couldn't move me?"

"Now don't get testy. It was my fault. My head was swimming after your stunt up there, Jones. But I shouldn't have moved anyone until I was more stable."

Nettie took a good look at him. He was in bad shape, but he looked almost embarrassed at having been concerned for her. Her ire died a quick death. When he wasn't being cocky, he was a charming man. She shook off the thought that branched out from that and took a good look at their surroundings. They were behind the British Museum. If she knew her museum well—and she was proud to say she did—she would bet they were behind the section where the Roman pieces were kept.

"Oh! Quick, did you see any of their little disk-shaped things when we got here?" She didn't know if they would be in the landing place, and she didn't recall seeing them before. But they might not be permanent.

"You have an interesting mind, Jones. But no, I didn't see anything." He looked around the darkening sky. "Now, since we've no idea how long we were up there, and your friend is still unconscious, what say we find our way to a cab and get back to the mansion?"

Nettie poked at the building before answering. She wanted to stay here and look for clues. But the fact was the aliens were planning an attack of some kind and it was up to her to stop it. "Very well. Keep an eye out though. Lisselle wasn't up there. That alien distinctly implied only one person. We may have been hasty in assuming they took Lisselle as well."

I T TOOK A bit of time to hail a horse cab, and even longer to make their way to the mansion, but Gaston agreed with all of Nettie's assessments.

"This is not good." He paced the small, clear space in the dungeon. He'd been down there when they had arrived, talking to Agent Ramsey. There had been a rumor that afternoon that someone had actually seen Queen Victoria out of the palace. It had not been confirmed and the odds of the Queen of England, even a vampiric one, traveling about unattended were extremely long. "We are being stalked by the aliens. If what you said of their map is true, then they are in place but waiting."

"But why wouldn't they attack?" Rebecca asked from her reclining position on one of the medical tables. Nettie was doing a quick check, but Rebecca seemed to have come out no worse for wear.

"Strategy," Caden said. "They are waiting to see how strong we are."

Gaston shook his head. "I don't think so. Their technology is far beyond anything England has and we are the most powerful nation on Earth. They wait for something else. Damn, I wish we had access to the Runners. They might have an idea as to what the aliens are waiting for."

"Isn't the main Runner in Edinburgh still active? Couldn't Agent Ramsey ask him?" Nettie asked. She then patted Rebecca on the knee and helped her sit up.

Gaston shook his head. "No, unfortunately whoever took the missing four has found a way into their interconnected brain. The main Runner could tell what was happening and shut himself and the remaining ones down. He couldn't reach the other missing Runners."

"Then it is up to us. Why would they not attack when they can easily overpower us?"

Caden, Gaston, and Nettie all began debating why they felt the invasion hadn't started yet.

"They can't." Rebecca froze as all three turned to look at her. "I mean what if they can't? Maybe they have problems down here?"

"Good thinking, girl." Gaston nodded then turned to Caden and Nettie. "Now you said the air was breathable, but different? Could you have stayed up there long?"

Nettie started to nod, then saw Caden slowly shaking his head. "No. At least I couldn't. Agent Jones probably didn't notice it because of her unique situation, but there was something...thin...about that air. I think that was what kept Rebecca unconscious. I'd hate to admit it, but I couldn't have functioned up there for more than another hour."

"He's right. I did wake up at one point, but I couldn't seem to stay awake," Rebecca said. "It was like there wasn't enough air to breathe."

"But shouldn't I have noticed it? I do need air, you know." Nettie couldn't help but feel a bit defensive. This changing business was starting to make her feel like a freak in one of those traveling carnivals.

"Of course you do, but the fact is, vampires don't. It would make sense you'd need less than others." Gaston spun toward the Mudger. "I think we need to be ready—"

His words were cut off by the Mudger suddenly sputtering to life. "Gaston...come in...."

It sounded like Agent Ramsey, but the picture was nothing but wavy lines and white spots.

Gaston rushed to the monitor and twisted two sets of knobs. The picture didn't come in any better, but Agent Ramsey's voice was clearer.

"Gaston here, damn it, man, what's happened? The picture is gone."

"Bad news. Three more agents have been found dead. One in Warwickshire, one in York, and one a few miles from Edinburgh." The rustling sound took some of his words. "—think all died the same. Worst of all, The Event has moved north."

Nettie watched Gaston's face, but he looked as confused as she felt for a moment then he closed his eyes. "Holyrood. They've left London?"

"Yes, we are not sure when they traveled or how. But the queen is in Edinburgh." The Mudger chose that moment to go out completely and no amount of swearing in English, French, or Welsh on Gaston's part brought it back.

"What did you mean, Holyrood?" Caden had stood back while Gaston fought with the Mudger but finally stepped up.

"The queen has taken residence in Holyrood Palace. She hasn't for a time, and the dead of winter would never be when she'd go. Most concerning are the dead bodies that followed her travel." Gaston sat down heavily and dropped his head into his hands. Although a Frenchman, he respected Queen Victoria greatly.

"The dead agents followed the path from London to Edinburgh. It was clear that they were drained by a vampire," Nettie said it softly, more so for Caden's sake than Rebecca's. The look in her friend's eyes stated she understood the ramifications already. And Gaston had clearly made the connection immediately.

"*Non*, she would not betray us." Gaston kept his head down but his voice was clear. "No matter what they did to her, Victoria is a good person."

Nettie walked over and patted his shoulder. She wasn't good at providing comfort, but he clearly needed some. She had no words of comfort though. The logical explanation was that Queen Victoria's personality turned when she did, and not for the better. Nettie had a bad feeling that there would be more agents found dead along their trail. The queen or her new companions were removing the threats along the way.

"So we follow your queen and the vampires there," Caden walked over to a large wall map and stuck small nails in each town where a body was found. "We work our way up and track them down. It's not like she's going to be hard to find."

Gaston took a deep breath, then shook his head and looked up. "Yes, we will send agents along their route. I will have Homer check for airship travel, and Gerveay and Anderson take teams on the train and roadways. We could really use the Runners now." He fortified himself with a swig from his flask. "But you three need to stay here. We are facing menaces on multiple fronts and we cannot let the queen's actions distract us from the alien peril. First, we save the land. Then, we save the ruler."

Nettie saw that Caden was set to argue, so she stepped forward and spoke before he could start. "I'll agree that others might be better to travel given our unique experience with the aliens. But we have to do something. And Lisselle is still missing." She shook her head. "I do not believe that the aliens took her."

Gaston smacked himself on the side of his head and shook off the remaining broodiness that hung around him. "I am sorry. With the tales of your adventures, then the other things...I completely forgot to tell you." He rustled about the desk behind him then finally waved a light brown and extremely wrinkled piece of paper. "I received a *communiqué* from Lisselle while you were up there." He pointed toward the roof. "She found out something about the vampires who took the Runners."

Nettie stepped forward and snatched the note out of his hands and read the short missive quickly. Lisselle found the lair of what she presumed was the vampire who attacked Nettie, and she found evidence of the Runners.

"She says she's been unable to get into the palace, but that rumor was the queen would be retiring to Bath." She looked up at the others. "Well, she got the movement part right, not the direction."

Gaston frowned and took back the note. "Yes, and it is quite disturbing that Lisselle's network of informants had the location so horrifically wrong. But I still think that's where I need two of you to go, Bath. We need to find Lisselle and we need to retrieve those Runners. Without them, we are sorely restricted on many fronts."

"Which is probably why they took them," Caden said from his corner. He'd been so silent Nettie had almost forgotten he was there.

"I don't see how they would know what it would do. There's simply no way anyone outside of the Society would know the way in which the Runners are interconnected." Nettie shot a look at Gaston. "I'd venture to guess that the majority of the agents in the Society are unaware of that as well."

"But what about McGrady?" Caden asked. He unconsciously rubbed the side of his head as he spoke.

Gaston looked thoughtful for a moment before he spoke. Nettie could tell he was almost as unhappy about McGrady turning as he was the queen.

"Yes, he would know. It is possible that he knew exactly what we would do if the Runners were compromised. Any agent with enough inner information would guess they would shut them all down if they were taken."

"But who was he working for?" Rebecca asked then promptly turned and smiled at Damon who had come down to serve tea.

"That's a good question. Either the aliens or the vampires could have bribed him," Caden said. He took his tea without thinking, clearly adapting to the British way quickly.

"Why couldn't some of them be working together?" Damon was often around for their conversations and meetings, but this was the first time he spoke.

"What would the two groups have in common?" Caden returned to studying the map.

"I think Damon may have a good idea," Gaston said. "Why couldn't they be working together in some manner? Do you really think that the universe is that perverse to have two such outlandish groups appear at the same time?"

"We're in the Society. As such, I expect odd and outlandish things to happen all the time." Caden looked toward Damon. "Not saying that's not a good idea, but I'd want to see some sort of evidence before I'd agree."

"What about that vampire with the green dust? The one who dissolved before Agent Smith joined us?" Nettie said. "The dust has only been traced to the aliens, yet it was in his system." She wasn't sure if the two groups were working together to be completely honest, but she didn't like Caden's abrupt dismissal of the idea.

"That is an excellent point." Gaston rolled out a huge piece of paper which he had filled with scribbles of all types. "I shall add it to the file, and you both shall have to pay extra attention for any green dust. Take sample containers with you. I had some put in your lab area, Nettie." He stayed engrossed in what he was doing so he didn't see the looks all four of the others shared.

"Gaston? Just what is…that?" Nettie looked over his shoulder, but the circles and lines and diagrams made little sense to her. It certainly would be no sane person's version of a file.

"My file for our current case." He leaned back and smiled proudly. "It has all of our data in one easy-to-read spot. All of the connections will be found here, mark my word."

"How can you find anything? It looks like a mad man wrote it." Caden stepped back as Gaston's proud smile turned feral at his words.

"A mad man? I know you Americans are provincial about things, but this is the way of the future. No bits of paper to get lost and disorganized. Everything in one giant sheet, easy to find, easy to make the connections."

Nettie leaned over at a particularly obtuse bout of gibberish. "But what good is it if only you understand it? What if something happens and you're not around to translate it?"

Gaston had looked down where she was trying to read. "It's not all that bad. You're exaggerating. I assure you…" He stopped as he looked up to find all four people nodding at him.

"Really? It makes perfect sense to me." He scowled a few seconds more, then shrugged. "Then I suppose all of you should to keep me alive then, eh?"

He went back to scribbling on his massive sheet of paper for a moment, then looked up. "You two should be preparing for your trip to Bath since you'll be on the first train in the morning, you should be preparing food, and you should be reading." He pointed to Nettie, Caden, Damon, and Rebecca in order as he spoke. His attention lingered on Rebecca.

"I know you are being rushed into this agent position, my dear, but it is important we keep your training on par. Your little adventure set us back a bit. I expect a full report about the history of the Society by tomorrow at tea time." He waved at them all then returned to his paperwork.

Rebecca frowned and looked to Nettie for guidance.

"Oh, don't look to your chum, believe me, she went through this as well. Move along, ladies and gentlemen. There are vampires and aliens who need us to stop them."

Rebecca stayed close to Damon on the way out, making some comment about needing a bit of a snack as she followed him to the kitchen.

Nettie found herself walking out with Caden. She felt she should say something; she wasn't sure what.

"I know you don't like me, but we do have to find a way to work together." He said the words that she was thinking.

"Now, I wouldn't say I dislike you." She studied the wallpaper as they passed. "It's simply that we have extremely different styles of approaching our jobs. Plus, I believe we got off on the wrong foot when we met."

"You mean when you ignored me, saved my attacker, and then tried to kill me?"

Nettie had been walking slowly down the hall but froze at his last comment. "I never tried to kill you! I saved you, if you will recall."

"Ah, so no one has ever told you of your driving? I was in more danger on the back of your carriage than I was from the man who attacked me." He leaned back against an antique cabinet and smiled.

"You enjoy stirring people up." It wasn't a question. "That, Agent Smith, is why you and I will never get along. I take my job seriously, and you are constantly poking around looking for a fight. For fun." She marched down toward the women's wing. "Since we will be leaving at first light, I assume you will go spend time getting ready."

"I am still the senior agent." He didn't even try to keep the laughter out of his voice. But Nettie refused to turn around.

"I'm sure the aliens will be quite glad to hear that. However, we will have to leave exceptionally early to assure we can get a decent seat on the train. I will be leaving, with or without you, no later than six a.m."

THE PREPARATION FOR the trip was quick and, luckily, could be done without dealing with Caden. Still, Nettie kept mulling around her interactions with him. Part of it was as she said. He deliberately provoked people, her especially, simply to get a reaction. From her studies of human behavior, she knew he partially did that to keep people off balance. It was easier to dismiss someone who was a braggart and a fool.

But she'd read his folio thoroughly before his arrival. He was an expert marksman, and considered one of the top agents in America. The only negative comments were his tendency to annoy people.

But she'd been around annoying people before, so why did he get under her skin like no one else? She truly feared if they were standing on a train platform and one happened to come by, she might simply push him onto the tracks.

Her musing was cut short by a light rap at her door. It was still only four-thirty, certainly that lag-about wouldn't be ready yet.

She cracked open the door a slice. She was decent, her sturdy robe covered her completely, but she didn't wish to face Caden in her bathrobe.

"Nettie, I was hoping we could talk before you left." Rebecca stood before her.

"Of course. Come in," Nettie said. As she stepped back to let her friend in the room, she noticed there was an odd smell about her. She took another step further back.

She'd known Rebecca for a number of years and subconsciously knew the way her friend moved. Not only was there a peculiar chemical smell, not unlike something left on a burner too long, she moved in a jerky fashion.

"What is it, Rebecca? Please have a seat while I finish getting ready." Nettie motioned to the chair furthest from her. It was also the most comfortable and should have been Rebecca's choice. Her friend stepped sideways to a hard wooden chair by the writing table instead.

She kept facing Nettie the entire time.

"Nettie, dear friend, I am scared of you leaving. Won't you comfort me?" Her voice was as stilted as her footsteps had been. And the tone and words were not ones she'd ever heard come out of her friend's mouth.

Nettie put down the skirt she had been folding and carefully moved so that the bed stood between her and her friend. Something was extremely wrong. She wasn't afraid Rebecca could hurt her, but she was afraid that if Rebecca attacked her, Nettie would hurt *her*.

"What is wrong with you? Why won't you come closer?" Rebecca rose from her chair. She kept her left hand down tight against her side.

Nettie realized with a start that there was something in Rebecca's hand and that she'd been moving to keep it hidden. They thought they had rescued Rebecca before the aliens had done anything to her. Had they been wrong?

"You look a bit faint. Why don't you sit?" Nettie moved slowly to confront her friend. She no longer had the luxury of not confronting her. If the aliens had gotten to her, perhaps done what they had done to Dr. Wilson, she needed to contain Rebecca immediately.

Rebecca looked uncertain, as if she was fighting something inside her. Finally, she looked down and collapsed with a soft sigh.

Nettie ran to her friend and rolled her over. Her heart dropped. The thing in her hand was a knife from the kitchen. She pried it out of Rebecca's hand and threw it across the room. Someone had done something to Rebecca, there was no way her friend would have tried to kill her on her own. She brushed back a stray hair from her friend's face.

She took a deep breath. Whatever had compromised her friend, she needed to secure Rebecca in case she woke up. The only thing at hand was the long tie to her robe, so she quickly removed it and bound her friend's wrists. Now that she was restrained, Nettie looked for any signs of the alien dust. Dr. Wilson had actually had it coming out of his pores right before he fell apart, but Nettie couldn't see any evidence of it on her friend.

There was, however, evidence of vampires.

CHAPTER TWENTY-TWO

T HERE, RIGHT ABOVE Rebecca's left collarbone, were two tiny puncture wounds. If she had to guess, Nettie would estimate that they were less than 24 hours old.

She rocked back on her heels and racked her mind for any clues the alien had given them.

He'd called Rebecca bait. She hadn't thought much of it at the time. Getting into any type of communication with the alien, that had been her focus. But he had clearly said bait. Most likely, the alien obtained the term from someone who spoke English, such as a vampire ally.

Hopefully, this futile attempt at an attack had been the only planted command they'd had time to give Rebecca.

Scooping her friend up, Nettie opened the door and went in search of Gaston.

For the first time since she'd known him, Gaston was asleep. To be honest, she had wondered if he actually ever did sleep. At least now she had evidence.

He didn't answer the first round of knocks on his bedroom door. She decided to give him one more round when the door swung open and a gear rifle was aimed at her head.

"Do put that away, Gaston. It's not my fault you didn't wake up to send us off. Rebecca's been attacked." Nettie shoved the rifle out of her way and marched into his bedchambers.

The room was not at all what she expected. Instead of the largest chamber in the mansion, decorated in the manner fitting a high-ranking spy, he had a tiny chamber. No doubt this room had probably originally been meant for a chambermaid.

A chambermaid with exceedingly bad taste, that was. The bed was a single and shoved up against the far wall. Tattered beige curtains covered the small window and part of a closet. The rug was clean, but threadbare in more than a few places.

Clearly, her assessment of Gaston not spending time sleeping was correct. No one would want to spend much time in a room like this.

"Please do come in," Gaston said. He looked down the hall for any others, then shut the door and motioned to a small chair. "You might as well put her down while I dress." He sat the rifle on the bed before ducking behind a screen.

"Might I ask why you are bursting into my room in the dead of night carrying your friend over your shoulder?"

"Firstly, it is not the dead of night; it is well after five a.m. Secondly, she's been attacked by a vampire. I'd have to say—I'm not an expert at time and bite marks—but my guess would be that it happened while she was on the alien ship." Nettie adjusted her friend in the chair so she looked more comfortable. "She collapsed when she tried to attack me."

"You didn't hit her?" Gaston came out from behind the screen fully dressed and adjusting his suspenders.

"Of course not. I will admit I would have, had she actually approached me with the knife and I had no other options, but she stood there for a bit, then sighed and collapsed. She had been trying to get me to come close prior to collapsing. But it was an awkward and unrealistic attempt."

"Bring her down to the dungeon. I want her fully restrained. And you need to finish getting ready."

"But I can't leave now. What if something has been done to her?" Nettie had picked up Rebecca, but paused as they entered the hall.

"Something has been done. Now we need to control it. The best way to take charge of this situation is to get back our vampire expert."

Nettie adjusted Rebecca over her shoulder and followed him. She realized that over the shoulder possibly wasn't the most comfortable way to carry someone, for her or the someone in question. However, this way she could have a hand free in case something went wrong. She didn't even second-think her caution. So far, no alien or evil vampire had been able to get inside the mansion, but it would be foolish to think that situation would hold. The fact was, the Society was facing far more powerful enemies than it ever had. Whether it was up to the task was still open for debate in Nettie's mind. Her faith in the powers of the Society had been unshakeable, but recent events indicated there were things even beyond their knowledge.

"Lay her here. I'll get a pillow." Gaston pointed to the smaller cot. He came back a moment later with two pillows and a pile of blankets. "I'm not sure how cold she'll be, so tuck these in around her."

Nettie put her friend down and surrounded her with the blankets and pillows. She'd been forcing herself not to think of what would happen to Rebecca. The Society had books on vampires' bites, and it was believed that the victim could fight off a single bite. There had been cases of the victims going mad and spending the rest of their days in a sanatorium.

"You will look after her while I'm gone, won't you? When we are able to reconnect with Edinburgh, see if you can get one of their experts to come down. And make sure—"

Gaston reached over and took her hand. "She'll be fine, Nettie. I'll do some blood draws and search for anything abnormal, but she'll be fine." He gave her a mock stern look. "And last time I checked, I was the head agent down here."

He pulled a small lever and a full metal cage slowly arose around Rebecca and the cot.

Nettie took a deep breath, then forced a smile. "I… I feel like this is all my fault. If I hadn't told the Society about her and her abilities, she wouldn't be like this."

"She may still have been attacked and left without the resources behind the Society. You can't second-guess your actions in our business, Nettie. I thought I'd broken you of that."

She looked back toward her friend. Rebecca looked so peaceful, it was easy to imagine she was sleeping and not in some vampire-induced stupor. And he was right. He was also right about not second-guessing. She'd gotten better, but it was difficult when one felt responsible for the problem.

"You're right." She flashed him a grin. "I know that. I suppose I should go finish packing and get dressed. It really wouldn't do to have Agent Smith ready and waiting on me." She stopped when she reached the door. "We'll check in with the Bath office. You'll notify them if there are any changes?"

"I promise. Now go. You're right about Caden, and he'll

never let you live it down if you're late." At her look he added, "I heard you two in the hall. We'll deal with those issues when things have settled down."

Nettie had time to change and finish her packing when a loud pounding rattled the wooden doorframe. How she could have thought Rebecca's delicate knock from before could be Caden, she had no idea. Picking up her bag, she flung open the door.

"Darn, I was hoping you were still asleep." His smile was sincere enough and his normally sarcastic tone removed enough that she knew he'd already spoken to Gaston.

At least it saved her telling the whole tale over again. It was one thing to know logically that something wasn't your fault, but it was another thing to get through to the heart. If she could avoid speaking about it during the trip, she might be able to get by.

"Yes, well, you didn't catch me off guard, Agent Smith." She softened her tone with a quick smile. She wasn't up to sparring for the next few days. "Shall we find Lisselle and perhaps end this vampire menace?"

His laugh was genuine as he stepped aside. "I like your way of thinking. Let's us be off, Agent Jones."

The friendly status stayed until the train was five minutes from the Bath station.

"I don't think it's right for women to be airship pilots. I'm sorry, you can call me a provincial American, call me old fashioned, but I don't think it's a good idea."

The debate had started friendly enough, with both sides stating their views on women's suffrage. England was far ahead of America in terms of women's rights, so Nettie had been pleasantly surprised to find that Caden was in favor of all rights for women. Except one. Piloting airships. Women were still not allowed to pilot airships. They could serve on the crew, but not pilot.

"There is no logical reason in the world for your view, Caden. Women are as apt in the air as men are. You don't feel the same about women and ships, do you?"

Caden actually smiled. "I like it when you use my first name. You only do it when you're distracted, did you know that?"

"That has nothing to do with our discussion, Mr. Smith." She felt the blush creep up even as she fought it. One would really think that being half-vampire and then some, she'd be free of blushes.

"I know, but I thought I'd point it out to be helpful." He slid out another charming grin that failed to falter at Nettie's responding scowl. "But as for our disagreement, no, I don't think women should pilot sea ships either. Now, before you think about using those fangs on me, hear me out. There is a field that is looking into the differences between male and female brains. The fact is, women simply don't have the same spatial reasoning men do." He nodded. "On average. I'm sure someone with your special situation and skills might buck that prognosis."

"There is no proof of that, as women haven't been given a chance. When you can show me empirical data for tests and trails that women do not have the spatial reasoning to pilot a ship, then I will believe you."

Caden looked ready to continue the argument, but Nettie raised her hand as the train conductor announced their destination. "Since the leader of the Bath office might be meeting us at the station, might I suggest we table this discussion?"

"Agreed. But don't think this is over, Agent Jones." He took her bag as well as his, and made his way out.

Nettie was right behind him. "I can carry my own bags, you know. I could probably carry both bags and you." Part of her was flattered that he took her bag, but she still felt the need to defend her own abilities.

"And unless you want to look like something you don't want regular people to notice, I wouldn't suggest it." Caden stepped out of the way of the rest of the people as they exited the train. "Nettie, I know you are far stronger and faster than me, and you always will be. But unless you really want people asking what you are, you need to tone it down some."

Nettie shook her head. She was usually conscious about making sure regular people weren't ever aware of her condition. It went back to Caden simply getting on her nerves and throwing her off. Even when he supposedly trying to do the opposite.

"Fine." She was tall, but the crowd was still too close for her to see anyone waiting for them at the station. To be honest, she didn't think they would send anyone. The Bath office was fairly small and mostly acted as an in-between for the London and Cardiff offices that seemed to be more hotbeds of activity. Rising up on her toes didn't clarify things. At least, until she spied a familiar brown-clad shape.

"They're here." She dropped back on her heels and clutched Caden's arm. "The...foreign visitors...are here." The crowd was too close for her to mention the word aliens.

Caden was brighter than he looked. "Don't point, just tell me which direction."

Nettie ignored the condescending remark. Of course she wouldn't point. "He's right under the far sign in the left corner. He seems to be looking for someone, but I'd say it's not us. He spotted me the moment I saw him and hasn't reacted at all."

Caden looked down as if he was adjusting his bags. When he looked up again he was facing the direction Nettie had given. "How can you tell? He looks like a vagrant ragman."

"Because unlike you, I have been accosted by them repeatedly. If you notice, his clothing is almost uniformly brown. And try to get a look at his face."

Caden coughed then looked again. He started swearing under his breath after a few seconds. "I can't seem to. It doesn't look like anything is there, but if you actually try to see his face, it's blocked by something. Damn it."

"What do we do now?"

"Exactly. There isn't much we can do. The crowd is thinning, and if whoever he is waiting for doesn't show soon, we'll be suspicious."

"We could wait and follow him." Nettie was determined to get one of the aliens into her lab. That this was Bath and not London was an inconvenience.

Caden seemed to weigh it for a bit. "No. I don't like it. You're right, it looked right at us then pretended it didn't know who we are. But I think after our little sojourn on their vessel, we have to assume they know who we are." He readjusted the bags and started moving away from the alien. "And I think that with all of the attention they have been paying to you, we can definitely assume they know who you are. This has trap written all over it, and we're not the ones springing it."

Nettie gave another secretive glance at the alien, then finally turned and followed Caden. She didn't want to admit it out loud, but he might be right. The alien had again held her glance. Or at least, he'd kept his face aimed carefully in her direction.

Caden marched through the crowd, but Nettie noticed his back was tight and he held himself carefully. Obviously, he didn't feel that the threat was limited to the alien in brown.

Caution aside, they made it out of the train station and were halfway to the guesthouse they would be rooming at when Nettie hissed for Caden to stop.

"These bags aren't as light as they look. I'd like to get in and settled…" His voice dropped as he turned to face her. Across the street and a few houses down stood another sentinel in brown. "Damn it, this isn't a coincidence."

"Now it's not. But how did they know we were coming here? The Mudgers were still out so Gaston couldn't have told anyone."

Another being in brown appeared down a side street. He walked forward a few steps to make sure they clearly saw him, and then stopped.

"What if Rebecca told them?"

Nettie took her eyes off the brown-clad aliens and spun on Caden. "Aside from her not being the enemy, just how do you think she told them? We didn't decide to come here until after we rescued her, if you'll recall."

"Now, don't get upset. I'm not questioning your friend's loyalty. But we know vampires can implant commands into their victims, right?" At her nod he continued. "Then how do we know that the aliens can't do something as well? Only instead of giving her commands, she sends them information?"

"Caden, she didn't have anything on her which could send information. I gave her a thorough checkup when we got her back."

"And yet you somehow missed those fang marks." It wasn't a question and his voice was gentle.

Nettie had to look away. She'd been asking herself that since she saw them. She had been extremely thorough when she checked Rebecca. There is no way she could have missed the fang marks. On the same issue was the age of those marks; they weren't new by a long shot.

So, how did she miss them?

"I know it upsets you, but we really should—"

"Hold a moment, I'm following a thought." Nettie waved at him as she cut him off. "Fact one, the marks were too old to have been done in the mansion. Therefore they had to have occurred on the ship. Fact two, I know I saw her neck when we got her back and I saw no marks." She paced around on the street, ignoring curious stares and Caden's attempts at getting her attention. There was an answer in her head, but it was farfetched, and wasn't going to make anyone happy.

"You've figured it out. Either that or your breakfast didn't agree with you." Caden pulled her out of the way of a horse and carriage. "Perhaps you should limit your pacing."

"Get the bags. We should get ourselves checked in, then go to the Bath home office immediately." Nettie didn't wait to see if he followed her orders. Her mind was busy trying to dredge up anything she'd read about master vampires.

The guesthouse was small, and most likely held no more than six or seven rooms for rent. Gaston had called ahead and booked two rooms for his employees, Mr. Whittle and Miss Albright. The owner had them sign the guest book, then hooked a thumb over her shoulder to the stairs.

"Now, nothing funny. Never seen a man and woman traveling together what wasn't married. Make sure you're all on the up and up. I don't run a brothel."

Nettie stopped with one foot on the stair. "I assure you, ma'am, that would be the furthest thing from either of our minds. Moreover, I will have you know I am a researcher of the highest caliber. I do not appreciate being treated in such a manner." The haughty attitude brought the owner down a few pegs, as Nettie knew it would.

"Aye, miss. You have m' apologies." She bobbed her head and flashed a small smile.

Nettie gave her a stern nod, then led the way up to their rooms.

"You certainly played that part well." Caden put down her small bag outside her door.

Nettie picked it up and marched in her room. "Who said I was playing? Now put away your belongings and meet me back here. We must get to the Bath office as soon as possible." She had turned to her door when she heard a laugh from across the hall. "Is something funny, Mr. Whittle?" She was proud she used his undercover name. This was her first undercover assignment and she'd been afraid she would call him Agent Smith out of habit. Or worse, Caden.

"I was wondering again who the senior employee was. I will meet you back here, Miss Albright."

He was gone before she could chastise him. It wasn't her fault that she was smarter than him. Each person had their own skills. She was quite sure he could tie up a cow, or whatever it was those Americans did, far better than she could. Should she ever find the need to tie up a cow, that was. She doubted that would ever be the case.

She continued to ponder how best to warn Gaston about this newest development. He was not going to take it well.

When she had first joined the Society, and began reading up on vampires, she'd come across some less than scientific entries. Gaston had tried to get her to not read them and the scientist part of her felt the same. But there was something fascinating about the vampire lore that had been passed down through generations by word of mouth.

Many of their myths were nothing but that. But a few were more than a little intriguing. Enough so that she had requested a chance to go study the myths in Transylvania. Gaston had denied her request, saying it would be the same as if she made them up herself. She didn't speak to him for a full day after that.

But one of the myths was speaking to her now. The myth of a master vampire. The idea was simple: When vampires created others of their kind, they had a level of control over them. The more fellow vampires they created, the more control they could exert. In theory, there could be a level of vampire that had control over so many others; it had become something more than a normal vampire. The myth of the master vampire gave them a wide variety of strengths, including transformation and mind control. There was another: mind projection through their victims.

Gaston had stuck by the research done in Cardiff and Edinburgh years ago by Society scientists, that vampirism was a blood-borne disease and no one controlled the vampires except themselves.

Nettie had to figure out a way to convince Gaston to test her theory that they were dealing with a master vampire, one who had infiltrated the mansion through his biting of Rebecca. And she had to do so in a way that would make him believe her.

She didn't think Gaston was in danger. Unless they'd turned Rebecca, she wouldn't be strong enough to get out of the straps in the dungeon. But they clearly had a problem if the master vampire had been able to warn the aliens that she and Caden were coming to Bath.

All three of the mysterious aliens in brown had vanished while they were navigating their way. She had little doubt they would see them again though.

"Now, were you going to tell me what you were thinking so much about that you almost got run over by a buggy?" He let her lead down the stairs.

"I'd rather wait. If the…communications are back up, I'd like to tell our boss and I don't want to have to repeat myself." Luckily, she caught herself before saying Mudger.

"Fine, but I'm not going to warn you if you step in front of a buggy again." Caden moved forward and held open the door.

It only took a few minutes to get to the small cottage that was the Bath base of operations. Actually, the owner called it a small cottage—Nettie would have called it a shed. But, be that as it may, the tiny woman in charge seemed quite happy with it.

"Come in, come in. Set yourselves wherever you please." She waved toward an interesting collection of mismatched furniture then went toward the back where a kettle was whistling. "We don't sit on propriety here, not like you London folks."

She reappeared an instant latter with a full tea tray. Nettie had barely taken her seat and Caden jumped forward to help.

"Let me get that for you, Mrs. Allsmythe." He flashed his most roguish smile as he guided the tray to the teacart.

"Ah, you are American! How delightful. I thought you might be, but one never does know, does one? Please sit, sit. I'm sure you could use some fortification after your long trip."

She served the tea then peered expectantly at both of them. "Well then? Has it started? The invasion?"

Nettie almost choked on her tea. Truly, it was only years of training around Gaston that kept it in check.

"Invasion?" Mrs. Allsmythe was the mostly retired leader of the small Bath group of operatives, but Nettie didn't know who was aware of the beings in brown. She'd gathered that Gaston and Edinburgh might be it.

"Oh yes, yes. Gaston and his secrets. I know, you see. He never believes me. But I know." She tapped the side of her graying head. "I'm a clairvoyant. Like your friend. Only I see specific people and their lives. Gaston hates it that he is one of those people. I see the events around him."

Caden hooked a finger at a faded poster near the front door. "So that is you? Allsmythe the Magnificent?"

The image looked nothing like the tiny round lady before them. Bright colors were echoed by a garish outfit worn by the red-haired young lady sitting at a gypsy table.

"Oh yes, that was my cover once. Years ago. Do ask Gaston about it." She tapped her lips in thought, and then added, "When he is in a good mood." Her grey eyes lost their focus and a light milky film took over. "Which, I hate to say, he is not right now. One of those dratted airships is annoying him. Or its pilot is. Tsk, he is dreadfully annoyed."

"I was wondering if I could contact him? I know there were problems with the Mudgers yesterday...."

Mrs. Allsmythe cocked her head. "Mine was fine. Chatted with Murphy up in Chelsea for a good two hours. But it could be interference from the invasion. Which, I dare say from the reactions of both of you, is soon to be in full swing." She nodded and poured herself some more tea. "Anyone else ready?"

Nettie hadn't even had a sip yet. Perhaps that was what powered Mrs. Allsmythe's chatter—caffeine from the tea.

"No, thank you." Nettie took a sip, and then went on. "Might we use your Mudger then? I would like to talk to Gaston. Not really about any invasion though."

Mrs. Allsmythe nodded her head sagely. "Ah, the vampires it is then. You are right. What you think about them, what you want to tell Gaston? You are right. He may not agree, but he will eventually."

"It must be wonderful to know so much." Caden had finished his tea and held his cup out for more.

"Oh, my dear boy, it is a hoot, let me tell you. Of course, not all of it connects in my head at the same time, but it will eventually." She served Caden some more tea, added his requested sugars, and then rose. "Well? Do you wish to contact Gaston? He's not getting any younger. Then, neither am I." She smiled and led the way out of the front room.

"I suppose we follow?" Caden carefully set his untouched tea down.

"I don't see we have a choice." Nettie led the way and was surprised to find that the cottage was far longer than she thought. An entire wing had been added to the back that couldn't be seen from the street. It was in this addition that they finally found their hostess.

"There you are. Come on, the Mudger's about warmed up." Mrs. Allsmythe sat in a room not much bigger than a large closet with her hand on the back of a Mudger. The machine appeared ready to clear its connection. Unlike the one in London, this one had three large glass electrodes in the back. The current danced up and down the ancient tubes.

"Oh, don't you worry, it will work. This is one of the first ones. The Runners designed them. Yes, attached to electrodes they were back then. Just a phase though; they grew out of it." She smiled as a grainy brown image appeared.

"Good morning, Gaston. In fine form today, are we?"

"Elfthrith, I see you are still there." His voice was a dour as his face. "I assume my agents made it in one piece? No problem with airships?"

Nettie shared a look with Caden in confusion, but Mrs. Allsmythe, or Elfthrith as Gaston called her, simply chortled.

"You are in such a state. But then when haven't you been? I believe there was a day in April of 1832...."

"My agents?" Gaston cut in as she drifted into memory.

"So irritable you are. Fine, they are right here, safe and sound." She cocked her head. "And do tell Homer it wasn't his fault. The ballast on the left side was faulty."

"How did you know—?"

Homer's unseen shout of vindication cut Gaston off, but Nettie stepped forward before he could say anything more.

"We have a problem."

"Oh, only one? Let's see... The queen has moved into her northern palace with unknown vampires, we can't get anyone there, Lisselle is still missing, and Homer has now found that crashing into the mansion is a better way to land. Are there any that I've missed?" He folded his arms and glared.

The smallness of the Mudger screen did not make his stance any less foreboding. This would possibly be the worst way to have to tell him that there must be some truth to a vampire myth. Actually, it would be worse if she had to tell him in person, she supposed.

"Actually, yes. Three of the men in brown were waiting for us. They did nothing, but they seemed to want to make sure we saw them. They knew we were coming, Gaston." She held up her hand to cut him off, better to get all of it out at once. "That is not all. Where is Rebecca?" It dawned on her almost too late that it might be best if the master vampire was unaware they knew of him.

"I secured her in her bed chamber. She can't get out and is heavily sedated. Why?"

"I believe Rebecca gave them the information. When she was on the ship, she was bitten by a master vampire. He can receive information through her. Do not let her be privy to any of our plans until we can free her mind."

Gaston peered at the screen for a few minutes as if he was still listening to her, then pinched the bridge of his nose and closed his eyes. "There is no such thing as a master vampire, Nettie. The idea is ridiculous. There have been numerous studies done. Vampires do not behave that way."

Elfthrith pushed her way back in front of the screen. "Oh no, it is not, young man. You have an extremely bright girl here and you continue to doubt her abilities. She is right."

Nettie bit her lip at someone chastising Gaston on that level. Not to mention calling him a young man. How old was Elfthrith? The name was ancient; perhaps the lady was as well.

"I can't address this right now. Let us state, for the sake of expediting things, that you are right. That there is a vampire who controls others of his kind. That said master vampire has been working with the aliens and now is able to spy on us through controlling our newest agent." He finally looked up. "What would you have me do?"

The tone was one of surrender, something she'd never heard before. But Elfthrith again answered for her. "You must keep the young lady away from everyone. She must not be made aware of things. She will cajole others to help her. Nettie can fix her when she returns." She nodded as if she'd solved all of the ills of the world and patted Nettie's knee.

"But I don't know what to do." She felt useless answering in the face on that unwavering smile, but Elfthrith smiled wider.

"You will. You have blood that is stronger than that of both of its sires. It will cleanse away the evil." She turned back to the screen. "Now, shouldn't we let your agents get about their business?"

Gaston opened his mouth, then shut it and took a deep breathe through his nose. Finally, he nodded. "You are correct. I will see you both back here once the job is done. Elfthrith, it was interesting, as always." He shut off the connection so quickly his last words almost didn't make it.

Caden had been silent, but now spoke. "What did you expect? He's got Rebecca under lock and key. Although I would like to know what the issue with the airship was."

"I know, but I suppose I was expecting more ideas on how to save her." She turned toward the tiny lady. "And thank you, Mrs. Allsmythe, for your help with Gaston."

"Think nothing of it, and you'll know what to do. It's all in the blood. And please call me Elfthrith, not many use that name anymore. It is good to hear it." She herded them back toward the parlor and poured more tea.

"As for what our stalwart airship captain has done…Well, let us say there are some forces working against him, as well as you all. His ship was sabotaged. Most likely something the aliens saw through the clairvoyant one." She held up a small china plate. "Biscuits?"

As much as they tried, Elfthrith wouldn't further define any of the events she spoke of. She claimed she didn't see things in whole, but could only provide information about the parts.

Nettie left feeling quite perplexed.

"She's definitely an odd one," Caden said. "Charming and far craftier than even myself, I'd wager. But an odd duck."

Nettie pulled out a paper Elfthrith had forced into her hand as they were leaving. "But a wise one. She gave us a hint as to where we might start our search." After reading it again, she handed the paper to Caden. It wouldn't take them exactly there, not unless the vampires had taken up residence in one of the stately homes on the Royal Crescent. She doubted even immortal vampires could manage to gain housing on what was commonly known as the most majestic street in Britain.

Nevertheless, it was a place to start and Nettie trusted Elfthrith's hunches as if she'd known her for her entire life.

"So we go to this Crescent place and look for a trail? What kind of trail?" Caden flipped the note over, but the back was blank.

"The Royal Crescent isn't simply *any* place. Obviously, the vampires are well-heeled if we start our search there. And it looks like she gave the same information to Lisselle." She tapped the small postscript on the bottom.

"'The flyer followed the path before you'? How is that Lisselle?"

Nettie wasn't sure who was supposed to know Lisselle's secret, but if neither Lisselle nor Gaston had seen fit to share that information with Caden, Nettie wasn't going to do so either. "It's part of a code for her. Don't you American's have codes for agents?"

"Yes, but the flyer? Shouldn't that be Homer?" He almost tripped across a bush that had been knocked sideways. "Well, that's not terribly high-end now is it? They can't even keep their shrubs in place."

Nettie froze as she stepped down the path. Caden had walked off the path while he read the letter, and hit a downed bush, but it wasn't the only one off center. "Look."

Caden glanced around but he couldn't see it from where he stood. "Where?"

Nettie took two steps back to be even with him, then took his arm and marched him the two steps forward and one to the side that he needed to see the line. "There."

His eyes opened wide and he re-did the steps. "That is amazing. You can't see it from anywhere but right here. How did she do it, I wonder?"

"I think she's old, wise, and is from a time not of our own." At Caden's quizzical look, Nettie shook her head. "Never mind, she's just gifted. Come on, it would be best if we found their lair in the day."

The rest of the path wasn't as clear as Nettie had hoped, and led far from the Royal Crescent. A narrow street, seemingly so forgotten that in didn't have a name, lingered at the end of the trail.

"So they're down here somewhere?" Caden looked around but there seemed to be no life in the few houses that lingered.

Nettie shook her head. "No, I'm not sure... Wait. Down there." She pointed toward a small field at the end of the street. It may have held buildings at one time, but now it had reverted to nature.

"I'm not sure about them using houses. It seems too easy to be found out. But something out there? I could see them having a hive, or whatever it is called, out in the unclaimed lands." She adjusted her stash of weapons as they made their way down the empty street. She was grateful she'd worn her toughest shoes. The area before them wasn't raw, untamed forest, but it had an unhealthy air to it.

"I seem to be at the mercy of female intuition on this trip, so lead on." Caden quickly moved some items from a hidden back pouch to his front jacket pockets.

Nettie would venture that the items were explosives; there

was a unique tang to the air. She didn't carry them herself. They seemed to be excessive for most things. But she wasn't going to argue if Caden felt the need for them.

Her intuition, and Elfthrith's hints, had been right. They had only spent a few minutes trudging through the open space when an odd scent drifted past. Nettie froze and held out her arm for Caden to do the same.

"This way." She nodded the direction of the scent, even though she knew Caden couldn't smell it. Not yet anyway. It wasn't the full smell of death, but as if one caught the edges of a grave.

A small cave opening almost escaped her notice, and if it wasn't for the smell, they quite possibly could have walked right by.

"Here. The vampire hive, or whatever it is called, is here."

CHAPTER TWENTY-THREE

NETTIE GAVE THE vampires credit. No one who accidently stumbled upon this small, unassuming cave would think it was anything other than it appeared. Only people with a vampire's keen sense of smell would have an inkling that it was far more than that.

The cave narrowed as it wound its way back into the low hill. The ground also had a slight tilt down. Nettie guessed it would end up being deep underground by the time they got to the end.

"Wait a minute," Caden said. "I have one of Gaston's toys." As he spoke, he struck two pieces of flat metal together. When nothing happened, he struck them again harder. A moment later, both started to glow. "These should give us light for about an hour. After that, we'd better be out of there. I know you can probably see in the dark, but I can't."

"Don't worry, I won't let them have you," Nettie said. "You'd probably give them indigestion." She let a bit of fang slip into her smile and continued walking.

"I am the senior agent. Shouldn't I be the one in the front?"

His tone indicated that, while he was asking about it, his ego wasn't involved. At least that was one thing in his favor. Aside from being hopelessly confused about women being air pilots, he didn't have the wretched male superiority issue she'd come across from time to time. Actually, none of the men involved with the Society seemed to suffer from that affliction, at least any that she'd met so far.

"Since I know you are a far wiser man than you look, I know that you would want to put the agent with keen vision, heightened hearing, and superior strength in the forefront. It is not your fault that you are only human."

She turned back toward a bend in the trail and a large, dark form slammed her to the ground.

"Nettie!" Caden came running behind her but held back when it was clear her attacker wasn't going anywhere. "What did you do?" He used his toe to nudge the now lifeless body.

"I...I don't know. He came at me so fast." She had reacted without thinking. Her hands went out toward his neck... "Oh dear. I may have accidently broken his neck."

His head was twisted completely around with his face buried into the dirt. She rubbed the side of her own and pulled back at a trickle of blood. "And I do believe he was trying to rip open mine."

Caden looked from her to the sad excuse for a vampire in the dirt, then back again. "How can you accidently break someone's neck? Don't get me wrong, it was a good thing in this case, but accidentally? Although he doesn't look like much of a threat."

The vampire before them wouldn't be a threat to an aged grandmother. His arms were little more than sticks, the joints looking abnormally large as they jabbed out of his skin. The skin itself was blotched with a collection of odd gray lesions. Yet, he came at her with a desperate strength. Even so, her automatic reaction, and the strength she exerted without thinking, disturbed her far more than the attack had.

If Caden noticed her unease, he didn't respond. "I'd venture to guess they left him out here as a guard. He was clearly starving." He looked up with a grim smile. "Shall we continue?"

Nettie was extremely grateful he didn't repeat his questions about her actions. He might be as unsettled by them as she herself was, but he helped her by ignoring it. For now. She would, of course, have to put it in her report to Gaston. Most likely, they may have to start watching her for further vampiric developments. Perhaps even lock her up for the safety of others. She shoved that aside. Focusing on the job at hand was the proper thing to do. She would accept anything the Society felt proper afterwards.

"Did you hear me?" Caden whispered at her side and shook her out of her thoughts.

"I'm sorry, I missed it." The path had narrowed a bit, and was going at a steeper decline, but she didn't hear anything out of the ordinary.

"I asked if you noticed anything. The air feels different here."

Nettie quickly muffled her metal lamp as she noticed Caden doing the same. He was correct. The air felt thinner, with an odd smell.

"It is similar to the ship. Not the same, but it reminds me of it."

Caden switched hands with his muted lamp and pulled out a large dissembler. "That reinforces what we thought about them working together. Although I'd like to know how they created the same air as they had on the ship."

"Actually, it wouldn't be that difficult," Nettie said. "The

Society has the ability to, and you were not really asking how." She shook her head. Perhaps staying a Society scientist should be her direction. Being out on an assignment was proving to be mentally difficult for her. She couldn't shut off her scientific brain. It was constantly looking for more things to study and explain. The search for knowledge was her reason for living; she needed to get it through to herself that there wasn't always a time for it.

"No, I wasn't. But it is reassuring to know we could make this awful air if we wanted to as well."

They'd slowed down and Nettie cocked her head. The sound wasn't clear, and at first she had attributed it to her own heartbeat. But there was a low rhythmic thudding coming from somewhere down the passageway.

"I hear a machine of some sort. We're getting closer." She completely muted the metal light, then slipped it into her pocket. Gaston would be most annoyed if she lost it, but right now she could see better without it. "Stay behind me a few feet in case they left a second guard." To be honest, she was afraid of what might happen if Caden got too close to her and she had to fight.

He grunted in agreement and waited before following her.

The passageway looked different in the dark. As her eyes adjusted, she could see things that were beyond her vision with the artificial light. Thin lines crossed and re-crossed the walls of the rocks, indicating faint traces of minerals invisible to the naked eye. Here and there small pockets of a light red appeared. They looked man-made, but were too far into the dirt walls to see what they were. Was this how all vampires saw things? Or was she still unique in that since being the only half-vampire in the known world? She shook off the images and focused on the path ahead.

No further attacks came, but had Caden been alone, he never would have found the room.

Caden gave a muffled cry and tried to grab her when she started to walk through a small portal. "It's a wall."

Nettie turned and took a step back so he could see her face better. His light was still dim. "The entrance is right there," she hissed. "You can't see it because your light isn't strong enough."

"I can't see it because it's not there. You were walking into a wall."

Nettie turned and looked where he held the light up higher. She could still see the portal, but only barely. Mostly she saw a rocky dirt wall.

"You'll have to trust me." Without waiting, she took his metal lamp, muffled it completely, and dragged him toward the portal.

He had enough time to get his feet under him before they were through the doorway.

A low-level light illuminated the room, but somehow hadn't been visible from the outside. The room itself was small and mostly empty. The one thing lying there gave Nettie both hope and concern.

Lisselle's coat lay in a corner.

Nettie picked it up, examining it closely.

"Well, it looks like we found Agent Wilding." Caden kept an eye on the only other door in the room, one that obviously led deeper into the hive.

"Yes, and she was alive when she took this off. Plus, there are no holes or blood so she wasn't physically injured at the time."

Nettie nodded. She admitted to herself that she'd been shaking when she picked up the garment. Death was not a stranger, but not of people she knew. That Lisselle had been alive when she came in was a good sign. And there had been no smell of fear upon it; she'd come in this room on her own volition.

"That's well and good. But I don't think we should stay out here. I don't like places that don't give me room to hide."

Nettie folded the coat into a corner, and then dusted her hands. "Then let us find this hive, cause the aliens to retreat, and regain our missing agent." She marched past Caden, carefully ignoring his mutters.

The next room looked far more like a hive although she wouldn't have thought anything once human could have made such a mess. Even the undead should be neater than the disaster before them. A small work station had been created, but it was mostly piled high with pieces of metal. Twisted, melted pieces of metal that flowed about the room in a great wave of refuse.

"I'd say at least one of the alien ships came down at some point." Caden picked up a piece and held it close to his face. "Although possibly longer ago than we think. This damaged end has rust." He sat it back down, then picked up a larger piece and set it off to the side. "They were doing some excavating. More than simply widening this tunnel." He held up a long-handled shovel and pointed to a pile of mining tools. "These are new. In fact, some of them look decidedly Society-ish."

Nettie looked closely. If they had any remaining doubt that Agent McGrady had been helping the enemy, this was it. "That is one of the newest earth perambulators. No one outside of London has even seen them." She dropped the long telescoping dirt walker to the ground. "Gaston will not be pleased."

"When is he?" Caden walked around toward the far door.

"True. But I fear this shall make him even less pleased than before." She moved aside what appeared like a pile of rubble, then realized they were ancient bricks and artifacts, or what was left of them. Some had been ground to dust, others were in pieces. She wasn't up on her archeology, but they looked suspiciously Roman in make. They'd been taken apart by someone looking for something, and by their condition, she had to assume they hadn't found it.

The next door way had been fortified with a metal frame and the room inside was finished. The lighting was also almost nonexistent.

Once her eyes adjusted, Nettie realized it wasn't a room, but a center hub for a huge warren of chambers. The walls were all smooth and metal, and the low throbbing she'd heard from outside had come from here.

"It's a ship."

Caden took the fabric off his metal lamp and held it up. "But how did they get it here? And underground?"

"Maybe that's what the earth perambulators were for. It didn't come down here; it was dug out." A cold lump grew in her stomach. They thought the aliens were new, but what if they had been here before? And why were they looking for something in Roman ruins? She shook her questions off. She needed to stay on her goal. Get information about the vampires and bring back Lisselle.

"Someone is coming." The fact that Caden heard the steps coming from the outside passage before she did spoke to her distraction.

"This way," she said. They needed to get far enough into the warren of chambers of the ship that they could hide, but not too far that they couldn't get out.

The rooms they ran through were empty for the most part, although many still had mounds of dirt in them, indicating her theory had been right. The sounds from the passage hadn't continued, so while there was obviously someone behind them, and they may even be searching for someone, they were no longer coming this direction.

Caden spotted the man-shaped shadow in their next room a moment after Nettie did and froze. Quietly, both of them moved behind a large, cloth-covered machine. Nettie had to fight the temptation to pull off the covers. The wheels and gears jutting out underneath were sorely tempting.

When the shadow didn't move, Caden inched forward, his hand on his dissembler. "It's a Runner."

He was right—Nettie could see it better now that her eyes adjusted to the dimness. The Runner stood before them, but his head was down and he wasn't moving. Nettie couldn't tell if he was one of the missing ones, or one that had gotten out before they were all quarantined. Some of the Runners hadn't been accounted for and were presumed to be compromised.

"Is that one of the ones the vamp took?" Caden's whisper seemed far too loud. But she knew he wasn't speaking loud; it was so deathly still in that chamber. The finished walls had made the room more foreboding than the cave-like ones before it.

"I have no way of knowing. They all look the same, in case you didn't know. Maybe you'd like to go up and ask it?" They'd been getting along far better than usual since they entered the cave, but she still wasn't sure how she felt about Caden. He was too good-looking, and too well aware of it, for her tastes. He was also damn good at what he did. That perversely annoyed her more.

Still she hadn't intended him to follow her suggestion. He rose from their hidden spot against the wall and began creeping forward.

"What are you doing?" He was almost out of whispering range, but she wouldn't make a bad situation worse by raising her voice.

He heard her. "We can't get back the way we came. We have to go forward, but it is in our way. I'm going to test a hunch."

The grin he flashed no doubt destroyed hearts all over America. But British women were made of sterner stuff. Nettie scowled at him.

"I hate your hunches." She rolled forward onto the balls of her feet, tucking her feet under her in case she had to jump to save him.

"I know you do." His whisper drifted back to her, but he didn't turn.

The Runner still hadn't moved, but its hands were out about half a foot from its sides. Now that she knew what they were, she wondered how she had not noticed it when she first saw them. The stance was too perfect to be human, the proportions off in their perfection.

Caden slowed his steps down to bare shuffles and got within striking range. It was then she noticed he had put away his dissembler and only held a small knife. What was that fool thinking of? A Runner could rip him apart before he had a chance to use that thing. Not to mention the blade was so small it wouldn't do anything.

In a flurry of movement, made even more startling by the comparison to the silent stillness filling the air, Caden leaped in front of the Runner and made faces at him.

Nettie seriously almost took aim at Caden with her own dissembler once she'd recovered.

"What in the hell are you doing?" She couldn't cover that distance with a whisper, but she still didn't want to talk loud. She pitched her voice loud enough for him to hear.

"Ah, the proper British lady does swear," Caden said. "I gathered the true state of the Runner as I got closer. It's been deactivated."

"How could you—"

"They make a faint humming. No louder than the wings of a fly against a glass, but luckily, I'm familiar with that sound."

Nettie put away her dissembler; maybe her throwing knife would be better for him. She hated to admit he kept his calm and managed to turn around an insult she'd given him earlier. It did not change her feelings for him.

"Is there anything useful you can tell about the Runner?" She stepped forward. There was no way she was going to admit to him she'd never noticed the Runners hummed, or that they weren't living. She'd never hear the end of that—a medical doctor who couldn't tell whether something was alive or not.

"They didn't know what he was either." He pulled back the black fabric revealing a smooth white neck, or what looked like a neck. And turning to look at the side Caden pointed to, Nettie saw what he meant. The smooth skin covering had been ravaged. But the vampire hadn't found anything but more metal.

"Could that have been enough to render it inert?" She poked around the torn skin-like substance. Right now, she wanted nothing more than a chance to take the Runner apart in her laboratory.

Her desires had obviously been far too clear.

"Easy there, Dr. Jones. You can't find the answers here. We don't have the time, and I'm not carrying that thing back." Caden patted down the Runner, but didn't find anything.

"We can't leave him here. He is a member of the Society after all. Just because he's not what we would call alive doesn't mean he's not worth our concern."

"First, even a dead human member of the Society is not worth risking the living over. Dead is dead. If you can get them out, fine, but most times they have to be left. This one is dead, or no rather longer functioning. Don't think they count as being alive." He resumed crossing the room, leaving her to sputter behind him.

Again, he made sense, and she herself had been wishing to take the Runner apart, not a humanitarian thought. But still, his coldness told her that if she died on this mission, she wouldn't be finding eternal peace in some green and grassy gravesite. He'd obviously left dead comrades behind before.

"Damn it, wait up." She took on final look at the immobile Runner, then started after him.

"You might want to move faster." Caden was in the next chamber and looking at his watch.

Nettie cleared the room, and then looked backward. "What

did you do?"

"Just because we can't take the time to bring him back doesn't mean we can let him stay in enemy hands." He looked up. "You may wish to duck."

Before she could say anything, he pushed her away from the door, covering her with his own body as a small explosion rocked the room they'd left. The sound hadn't been loud, but mechanical bits and pieces of the Runner would have been hazardous for anyone nearby.

"Get off, damn it. You didn't have to do that." Nettie pushed him off of her.

"Why? They know we're here somewhere. We can't go back that way, nor take the Runner with us. Now it's a bit harder for them to follow us from that direction, and we have one less Runner that can be used against us." Brushing off dust it was too dark to see, he turned and went down the left corridor.

Nettie watched him go. There was simply no dealing with him. He did things his way and that was it. Clearly, she would have to endeavor harder not to be partnered up with him again. Had she been willing to waste time arguing, she would have pointed out that was the only known way out and they now had left a trail for anyone following them.

Finally, her logic got the better of her, and she followed. Regardless of her feelings for him, they had a job to do.

There was no sign of a vampire hive, but the rooms they were entering now were only partially dug out of the mounds of dirt that filled the ship. Whenever this craft had come down, it had been a long time ago. And this ship had been huge.

After seven more rooms, Caden turned to her. "I think there

must be another area we're missing. No one is living in these sections and from Lisselle's notes, Gaston thinks there is a good-sized vampire hive here."

Nettie looked down yet another branching corridor and was about to tell him to pick a direction when the smell of fresh dirt hit her. It was coming from the far left corridor and the echo of the thrumming they'd been hearing was stronger.

"I think that way may lead to the vampires. I can't say how I know, but I don't think they would want to stay in this ship." She really didn't want to figure out how she knew—it was somehow connected to her changing vampiric status. Without waiting for his response, she started down that corridor. He said nothing, but drifted further behind. When she looked back she noticed he was studying some of the side rooms.

The corridor opened into a warehouse of sorts, with giant machinery that had to have come down from one of the alien ships. Massive steam-powered engines produced the heavy thudding noise they'd heard, but what they were connected to wasn't clear.

The machines were a sore temptation as her fingers itched to take them apart. They'd made it past most of them when three aliens appeared in front of them.

CHAPTER TWENTY-FOUR

T HE ALIEN CLOSEST to her jumped in front of her, but had misjudged his leap so he was close enough for her to swing out and get him with her fist. It wasn't pretty, but she managed to knock him flat. Two more appeared in front of Caden, causing him to drop back and take aim with his dissembler.

He quickly shot both, but five more appeared before them.

"They're coming down from one of the ships." Nettie yelled to be heard over the steam engines.

"I noticed. Think we can keep up with this pace, though?" Caden's face was grim as the five were dispatched and eight more appeared in the same place. Nettie check her dissembler and fired it quickly. Caden was an unnaturally good shot, but eventually one of the aliens would get in a shot before he did. There was little cover here, and the aliens could come in wherever they needed to. Luckily, the vampires hadn't appeared. Hopefully, even though one couldn't tell what time of day it was inside here, they would not be able to rise until night fell.

Although there may be a clue. "Caden, watch where the next ones come in. I think they're limited in their entry. Remember that little block we had to stand on to come down? Perhaps it limits the landing area."

Caden hadn't been able to get a good view of the entire room, trapped where he was behind the Roman wall. But she had an excellent view.

The aliens were only coming within a set triangular area.

"I think they must be coming down to a pre-set place. They are limited between the two crates to the left and the three barrels to the right."

"Thanks, that'll help, but it's not going to save us if they keep coming. Even slower, they still can overwhelm us if we can't get out of here."

"There must be something that is pulling them to the same spot. If we can disable it we might have a chance."

The aliens were paying more attention to Caden since he was the one decimating their numbers. This gave Nettie a chance to creep up on the area they were coming in on. Sure enough, the newest group of four landed on a triangular stone wide enough for five, maybe six if they stood close, aliens to fit. As they landed, the stone glowed slightly before fading back into the metal floor. Caden took out this newest group with his dissembler, but Nettie knew he must be running out of power cartridges.

If Nettie gauged their timing cycle of sending new aliens down, it should happen right now.

The stone started to glow, but the aliens hadn't appeared yet. Popping out of her hiding place, Nettie used her dissembler, at its highest setting no less, and fired repeatedly at the stone.

The resulting explosion surprised her almost as much as the two aliens Caden hadn't killed yet. Their wide eyes blinked and they vanished down the corridor.

"You need to warn me when you do things like that!" Caden rose from his hiding place and he wasn't happy. "I could have shot you. I think even a half-vampire might get hurt with an overcharged dissembler shot hitting them."

"I couldn't very well give things away now, could I? Besides, I wasn't sure if it would work or not." She put away her own weapon. She still didn't feel natural carrying it. She supposed it was different for Caden, Americans all had guns from what she'd heard.

"Now, what do you mean by overcharging? Does it increase the weapon's strength?"

"Yes, and no I won't show you now. While you were busying destroying the aliens' landing stone, I saw someone who was definitely not from their planet." He waved his dissembler toward a small door on the opposite side from where they came in. "It's dark down there, but the movement was human."

"Or vampire?" Nettie took the lead since they didn't have time to try for the metal lamps again. The two aliens that escaped were most likely going to be coming back with friends. "I think I see them." She pitched her voice low as the noise from the steam engines in the warehouse faded.

The smell of dirt was stronger here, and the metal walls ended abruptly. Well, that could explain how it ended up in Bath on the ground—half of it had fallen off. Now if they could only figure out when. And of course how to make it happen to all the rest of the ships currently hovering across the globe.

They both crept low to the ground as a shape passed in front of them. There didn't look to be any more corridors down here, but the person had crossed from one room to the other. A moment later, the slight shape darted back out, and a flung tray with what appeared to be food on it almost hit them.

"I told you, you can't fatten me up so your masters can drain me." Lisselle's voice was a welcome thing to hear and she sounded no worse for her trials, that was for certain.

"We found her." Caden waited until the person that Lisselle had been swearing at went into the other room and shut the door. Then he motioned Nettie forward.

Like the rooms in the other dirt portion of the hive, wooden doors had been fitted into both rooms. Lisselle's was open.

Nettie grabbed Caden as he went to move forward. "I wouldn't do that. She may have more things to throw and her aim is even better than yours."

Once Caden stood down, Nettie crept forward. "Lisselle? It's me. Well, us."

"Nettie?" A rattling of chains could be heard, which explained why the person keeping her wasn't worried about the door. "Who is with you?"

Satisfied that Lisselle wasn't going to launch any projectiles at her, Nettie came into the room. It was clear why the door wasn't shut; it looked like it had been blasted open.

"Like my handiwork? Unfortunately, the chains have foxglove on them. They are shorting out my powers."

"Glad to see you're still intact, Agent Wilding," Caden said. He put away his dissembler but only to pull on the chains. "What powers? You're not like our half-vampire here are you?"

Nettie winced. She didn't think most people were supposed to know about Lisselle, but she'd done it to herself.

"Ah, Agent Smith, good to see you. Let's say I have my own unique abilities and that they are currently thwarted, shall we? And speaking of strengths, I believe Nettie has a better chance at breaking these chains than you do." She smiled. "No offense of course, lad."

Caden dropped the chain he had been pulling on with a shrug. "None taken. I'll be the first to admit Dr. Jones here is as strong as a team of horses."

Nettie had picked up the chain and begun pulling. "Thank you for such a flattering comparison." To be honest, a few weeks ago she would have thought that she wouldn't stand a chance at breaking the chains. The changes since she'd been bit were becoming substantial.

The chain snapped and demonstrated that very thing.

"Where are the vampires?" Nettie hugged Lisselle. "I hope you don't mind, but I need to check you for marks."

"Because that worked so well before," Caden muttered under his breath.

Nettie ignored him as she checked all the likely places on Lisselle.

"The vampires vanished two days ago, right after they captured me. At first I thought perhaps they were afraid their location had been compromised, but I think your little alien friends are still roaming around." She held away the collar of her shirt for Nettie. "You can search, but I don't think they bit me. They said they wanted to save me for someone special. A high-ranking vampire of some sort who had already left here."

"Like a master vampire?" Nettie stepped back after not finding any marks. Of course, she hadn't seen any on Rebecca at first check either. But there wasn't much they could do for it.

"Oh great, now we'll never hear the end of it." Caden stayed near the doorway keeping an eye on the shut door across the hall as well as down the corridor.

"Yes, that might be the proper term. The ones who captured me were terrified of him. I wish I knew where they went though."

"Edinburgh," Nettie said. "They took the queen and went to Holyrood. At least three agents were found dead along their path."

Lisselle moved to stand next to Caden, then turned back. "That's not good. I think we can assume, hope really, that the queen's turning didn't go as planned. I'd hate to think Melbourne and his cronies had intended for this."

"Then he was involved?" Nettie thought back to the air crash and the missing bodies. Melbourne's man had signed them out of the morgue.

"Aye. I found out right before I got the lead for the vampire hive here. Her entire inner circle was in agreement about the actions for The Event. Melbourne arranged for the vampires to be brought in the country from the continent. I was afraid they were somehow connected to the current problem. Obviously, the queen's cronies didn't count on retaliatory actions from a master vampire."

"How do we know they weren't working together?" Caden motioned for them to move out into the hall. "What's that way?"

"I think we can get out that way. I smell sunshine," Nettie said. It sounded odd even to her. There was no better word for it; her heightened senses could smell the sun.

Caden tilted his head at that comment, but didn't say what he thought.

Lisselle nodded. "I found no one when I came down into the ship. On my way back to the Royal Crescent, they grabbed me and brought me in this way." Marching past the other two, she led the way.

"Gaston was right; they drained at least seven vampires for the queen's transfusion. I couldn't find any way into the palace, nor find anyone who had seen her since the change though." Lisselle paused and opened the last door at the end of the hall. A pile of what looked like bodies were there.

"Three of the missing Runners. I found them on my one escape attempt. All have been disabled, but I'm not sure where the fourth is."

"We came across it on our way in. It has been destroyed." Caden pulled out a few of his explosive jelly capsules and gently placed them inside the pile. "Does anyone object?" His eyes stayed on Nettie, but she shook her head.

No one said anything else until they saw sunlight a few minutes later.

"I'd say your sense of smell is keeping right up with your increased strength there, girl." Lisselle patted Nettie on the back. "Now, what say we head back to home and find out what Gaston plans to do about getting our queen back?"

CHAPTER TWENTY-FIVE

L EAVING THE GUEST house had been more trouble than it
should have been, as the innkeeper grumbled about people
not staying when they agreed to two rooms. Considering that
Nettie and Caden appeared to be the only two staying there,
Nettie could understand her annoyance.

Lisselle had smoothly stepped in, made profuse apologies,
then told the innkeeper that her employee, Mr. Whittle, would
pay for two full nights for both rooms.

Caden kept quiet until they were on their way to the train
station.

"Why me? You do have another employee." He again had
carried both bags as well as Lisselle's small bag. Much to Lisselle's
amusement.

"You are such a wonderful gentleman, I knew you wouldn't
have it any other way." Lisselle grinned over her shoulder as they
walked. "Besides, Gaston will pay you back in full and that is a
damn convenient guest house. It'd be a shame if we couldn't use
it again because we annoyed the owner."

"So what next? Will Gaston really let us go up to Edinburgh?"
Nettie had never met the queen, and while the current circumstances weren't the most conducive for making a formal royal
acquaintance, it would still be exciting.

Lisselle took pity on Caden and bought the train tickets. She hadn't had a bag when they rescued her, nor did she say where she'd had it stashed. But when Caden and Nettie went to pack their things, she'd vanished, only to reappear with a small navy-type bag.

"I think first you will need to see what can be done about Rebecca." Lisselle sat on a bench in the station. Their timing had been perfect. The last train of the evening was leaving in less than twenty minutes. "Elfthrith is a…unique sort. But she is always right. Somehow, you will be needed to save your friend. And I'd think Agent Zero, Agent Ramsey, and the rest of the large Edinburgh base can probably take care of getting the queen settled."

"But shouldn't you at least go?" Nettie hid her disappointment. It wasn't that she didn't want to save Rebecca; she wasn't sure how. And being involved with bringing back a renegade queen turned vampire would be terribly exciting.

"Don't you worry. They'll find a use for me here, I'm sure." She patted Nettie's arm.

"Our friends are back." Caden hadn't taken a seat, choosing instead to keep the bags on the bench and himself leaning against a nearby wall.

Nettie looked around and saw that two of the aliens had entered the waiting room. Neither of them moved closer, but they both were watching.

"Why are they watching and not acting? They did that before as well." Nettie got up and moved around a bit as if she might walk toward them, but neither alien moved.

"Hmm, that is interesting. I have a theory about their ability to move in sunlight. They seem to be far less perambulatory here in Bath than in London, which is darker and colder." Lisselle nodded. "Might be yet another clue as to how to send them packing." She smiled toward the aliens, but it wasn't friendly.

Nettie and Caden had briefly filled her in on the adventures that had happened while she was gone. A crease had appeared on her forehead at the news of the multiple ships and the aliens' probable intentions that still hadn't left.

"THE TRAIN'S PULLING in, so unless they are planning on buying tickets, I think we'll be leaving your new friends here." Caden picked up all three bags and waited for the ladies to precede him.

"How did they become my friends? They really are more Nettie's friends," Lisselle said.

"They were holding you prisoner; they keep sending Dr. Jones back." Caden smiled and motioned for Nettie to get on the train.

Nettie opened her mouth to retort, then saw he was smiling. It was contagious and she smiled back before boarding the train.

NETTIE RUSHED TO go see her friend the moment she got back, much to the annoyance of Gaston, but Rebecca looked the same as when she'd left.

"She hasn't woken up at all?" She held up her friend's wrist to check her pulse. It was slow but steady.

Gaston bustled into Rebecca's room after her, shutting the door behind them. "You were only gone for a single day. It's not unheard of for vampire victims to collapse. She did lose blood, after all."

Nettie adjusted every pillow and blanket on the bed. "And the report said she was moving fine until this morning. That tells me something has changed more recently than the blood loss issue." She paused and shook her head. "The master vampire, it must be him. Once his embedded command was played out, his absence called her to collapse."

Gaston threw himself into a chair in the bedroom. "Now I don't want to discuss this master vampire situation again."

"Lisselle believes in them. And the aliens who took her were saving her for some special vampire. The regular ones weren't allowed to feed on her. It makes sense, Gaston. I believe in science as much as you do, but you know science doesn't always have an answer."

Gaston fretted for a few moments, then waived her on. "I will agree to let the earlier assumption stand. For now. Now what did Elfthrith mean? Did you get any more clues out of that crazy old lady?"

Nettie leaned against Rebecca's bed. "She seemed nice to me, a bit scattered, but kind. But no, I still don't understand. It's all in the blood? But whose blood? Hers or mine?"

Gaston rocked forward. "Maybe both. Have you ever used a blood transmittal colander?"

Nettie narrowed her eyes. She thought she saw where he was going and didn't like it. "Yes, once in medical school. They tried it on me, but it didn't work because of my condition. Only we didn't know it at the time." She shook her head. "Gaston, those are dangerous machines, little more than tubes and a bucket.

Maybe the vampire influence will work its way out."

"We have one exactly like the one used on the queen." His voice was low and he watched her closely. When she didn't respond immediately, he continued. "I need to tell you that Rebecca does have some of the vampire virus in her bloodstream. It's not much, could have been from the vampire's teeth. But the more worrying thing is that there is a trace of dust in her blood as well. I ran tests when you were off playing in the Roman ruins. Your blood is impervious to the dust. Left in a dish with contaminated blood, your blood will destroy the contamination."

Nettie took a deep breath, then let it out slowly. "I guess that is what Elfthrith meant then. I do hope this works."

Homer and Caden had retreated to the dungeon to work on an idea Caden had to incorporate his agitator into something that might work on vampires. Or aliens. Homer didn't seem to care about the task. He didn't want to be involved in the bloodletting, as he called it.

Lisselle immediately volunteered to help.

They'd pulled in a cot next to Rebecca's bed, but Nettie was fussing over it before she got on it. "But won't my blood make her a vampire? Or half, or quarter, or something?"

Lisselle patted her check and motioned for Nettie to climb on the cot. "It could, except that it's going through an extreme level of pressurization as it circulates. Your blood would be more likely to make her vampiric if you feed it to her. The risk here is minimal." She adjusted the pillow under Nettie's neck and then the one her left arm stretched out on. "I am honestly more concerned that you may develop some of her clairvoyance. The gift is also of the blood, but it's more the interchange of fluids between you. And since you had already experienced some visions, you have already shown a predilection for this, so I'll need you to make sure you report anything you see of the future."

Gaston stayed silent as he connected the various tubes and gears. In theory, Nettie's blood and Rebecca's blood was to be run through the blood transmittal colander. The idea was that Nettie's blood would be able to fight off the infections of both the vampire virus as well as the aliens' green dust. The machine had the ability to keep both patients alive for two hours. After that, the blood would have to go back into the bodies.

Nettie tried not to think of how the machine did what it did. The risk of these contraptions was huge, that the queen had risked an even more deadly procedure spoke volumes as to how frightened she and her advisors had become after the plague scare.

Lisselle looked down at her and smiled. "You'll both be fine. I know what I'm doing."

"You've done this before?"

"No," Lisselle said as she grinned. "But I am very, very, smart. Now take a deep breath." She placed the gas mask over Nettie's face.

YELLING VOICES DRAGGED Nettie to consciousness. Once her mind caught up with what had been going on prior to her being put under, she jumped to her feet.

Or tried to.

Unfortunately, she had been tied to the rails of the cot with heavy leather straps and only managed to lift it and herself up a foot, then crash back down.

"Ah, lass, you need to stay still." Homer's booming voice, not terribly conducive to a recovery room, came from out of her line of sight.

"What's happened? Is Rebecca all right? I heard yelling." She couldn't see anything of Rebecca's bed as her cot was angled the opposite direction.

"I told you we needed to untie her before she woke." Lisselle came around and undid the leather straps. "Rebecca is fine; in fact she's down in the dungeon giving Gaston a full report of what she could recall. Your recuperative powers worked better on her than you."

Nettie rubbed her wrists when Lisselle freed them. "Might I ask why I was tied?"

Homer reached a hand out to help her to her feet. She did feel a bit lightheaded, but it was embarrassing that she fared worse than Rebecca.

"You fought back. Apparently some part of your vampire psyche has an extremely good survival mechanism. Even with two full doses of sleeping gasses put into your system, you still tried to fight."

Nettie looked around, but there was no evidence of damage. "I didn't hurt anyone, did I?"

Homer let a rumbling laugh escape. "Just Caden. He was determined that he could tie you himself. You gave him a nice shiner before Lisselle and I were able to hold you down." He shrugged. "He'll recover."

"The bad blood has been cleansed out of Rebecca then?" It

wasn't that Nettie didn't care that she had struck Caden, but to be honest, he probably deserved it for something.

"Aye, it worked." Homer's smile fell after a moment.

"What else aren't you telling me?" Both of them looked at each other and Lisselle winced.

"Gaston should be the one to tell you. The transfusion got the alien dust out of Rebecca and it appears any in your system is vanishing quickly. But while you were unconscious, I ran more tests on that dust. It's part of the aliens' skin, but it is toxic when it enters human bloodstreams." Lisselle's look was grim as she continued. "Even normal vampires. It will kill every vampire who gets it in them. And we have to assume that all of the Bath vampires were exposed."

Nettie's mind was still foggy from the sleeping elixir, but she caught up quickly.

"The queen. The vampires manipulating the queen were part of the Bath hive."

"Aye, lass."

"I can save her though, can't I?" From the looks on both faces, that was what they were leading to. Of course, the queen was in Edinburgh surrounded by powerful and hostile vampires.

"How long does she have?"

"We don't know. The weaker the vampire, the more likely they are to succumb faster. The queen is a new vampire, not made the normal way, and is by far one of the most stubborn people I know." Lisselle shook her head. "But even given that, I'd say we have a week at the most. But come downstairs. Gaston will be most vexed at me if I tell you of his plans before he can."

"Ladies?" Homer held out both arms to escort them downstairs.

GASTON SPENT THE evening trying to convince Nettie that she didn't have to go through that transfusion with the queen. Nettie, like everyone in that room, including Gaston, knew she didn't have a choice.

Caden spent the evening fighting to get his plan accepted. He wasn't worried about saving the queen. He had faith in the others to come up with a plan for that. He was worried about once they had rescued the queen. He felt that his new Solar Electrode Agitator could bring down the lower flying ships and chase off the higher flying ones. Actually, the weapon was a modification of a long-range elephant gun. It had been turned into a high-powered dissembler that fired the actual Solar Electrode Agitators. Casings about as long as a man's middle finger and five times as wide held a special combination of a powerful sun-mimicking electrode and a mini version of the agitator. The idea was that these chambers would damage the low-flying ships enough to drop them to the Earth. If a few went down, Caden was sure the other ships would leave the planet.

Homer was busy shooting down Caden's weapon as a waste. He was intrigued by the armada of airships that would be required to disperse the weapons, but he thought the dissembler wouldn't work.

Lisselle was quietly preparing the blood transmittal colander for its next run.

And Rebecca was trying hard not to cry.

Although she had claimed to be in fine spirits after her trials with aliens, vampires, and a thorough blood cleaning, it was clear she wasn't herself.

"I'm sorry Nettie," Rebecca said as she dabbed another cloth to her eyes. "I can't seem to stop crying. I feel that presence in my mind again…"

Nettie waited for the tears to settle down. "This was the master vampire? He was in your head?"

"No, that's what I told Gaston." Rebecca's red-rimmed eyes held hers. "It was the aliens. They can control, or somehow manipulate my visions, and the way they can be sent to others. They caused the projection to make you think the fang marks weren't there."

Nettie looked over to the others, but they were still busy arguing the details. She much preferred the mindset of fixing something when it was broken. Not calling a committee to debate the subject.

Lisselle came over, ignoring the arguing men. "How are you holding up?"

Rebecca shook her head and more tears fell.

"She can't get past this." Nettie had a plan, one that she needed training from Rebecca on. But right now her friend wasn't going to be a help to anyone. No new agent should have had to go through what she had in such a short time.

"Is there somewhere else she could stay?" Lisselle held up her hand as Nettie looked ready to defend her friend. "I don't mean for good. But she's under too much pressure right now. She needs to rest and recover." She dropped her voice. "I fear what her gifts might do to others in her current state."

Nettie looked closer at Rebecca. She was exhausted and no one could blame her.

"Her family is from northern Wales, but there are Roman ruins there, so the aliens might have a presence." Something Rebecca had once mentioned came to mind. "Rebecca, don't you have an aunt living in Aberdeen?" Northern Scotland had never been invaded by the Romans, and as far as Nettie knew, there were no vampire hives there.

"Yes, I do. She has a small farm not far outside of town. Why?" Her tears dried up as confusion took over.

This was where it was going to get tricky. Nettie knew Rebecca needed a break, but she also knew her friend was stubborn enough to try to stay.

"I have a special mission for you," Lisselle said. She gave Nettie a quick wink. "We need someone to go to Aberdeen. There's not a case there yet, but we'll need you to relax and blend in. A tired Londoner needing a break will be the cover story. But we'll be in contact once we know what's going on up there and you're securely in place."

Rebecca narrowed her eyes and glanced between both of our faces. "You wouldn't just be trying to move me on, would you?" Her glance fell more on Nettie.

Nettie shook her head, but Lisselle answered. "Not at all, Agent. We don't have time to send people off. This is a real task that will involve some build up. It might seem easy to get into a different lifestyle, one far less fast paced than ours. But it is not. It is crucial that they see you as one of them, however."

Lisselle was so good, Nettie almost believed her.

Rebecca finally nodded. "I can do it. When do I leave?"

"We'll get you on a train first thing in the morning," Lisselle said.

Nettie dried away some of the tear tracks as Rebecca gave a shaky smile. "But before you leave, do you think you could try to teach me how to project thoughts? I think I have a plan."

CHAPTER TWENTY-SIX

T HE NEXT AFTERNOON, Gaston was not pleased to find that Rebecca had left for a few weeks and had cornered both Nettie and Lisselle in the parlor. "We need her here, Lisselle." He paced in his customary tight circle.

Nettie wondered if she put him in a larger space if the pacing would stay the same radius. It seemed extremely consistent.

"Why? Your Scotland Yard agents still have the morgue quarantined, she's unable to talk about anything without crying, and there is still a chance that the master vampire or aliens could get to her." Lisselle hadn't told Rebecca that part, but she had told Nettie after they'd gotten Rebecca sent on her train. She was afraid their blood work would have been for naught if Rebecca stayed too close to either enemy.

"The aliens can't get to her. She'd be with one of us at all times."

Nettie thought out her words before she spoke. "They got inside her head before. They were the ones who created the projection of a bare neck when I examined her. They were Rebecca's skills, but they manipulated them."

"The aliens were talking to her?" Gaston froze mid-stride and his face began to drain.

Nettie shook her head. "Not really. More like through her.

Somehow, they can work through clairvoyants. At least powerful ones like Rebecca. She figured out how they did it, and she taught it to me late last night. Well, what she could teach me, although I don't have her natural abilities."

Lisselle calmly stood and held his stare. "I know you are the team leader, but I couldn't put her through that risk. And it was too much danger to the rest of us. If you had argued in front of her, she never would have left."

Gaston shook his head, and then stepped to the side of her. "I think we need the dungeon for this kind of talk. But you can fill me in as we go down. I may need to inform Edinburgh."

Nettie and Lisselle gave him as many details as they could. Then Lisselle was called away, and Nettie repeated them all again for good measure. Once he got over his annoyance at his junior agent being sent away, Gaston was most concerned about the aliens being able to project thoughts through Rebecca. That the vampires were obviously working through the aliens as to what thoughts to project was another annoyance.

"I'm not going to contact Edinburgh yet. They have enough on their hands. But I need to reach Cardiff. They have a team of clairvoyants and need this information."

Unfortunately, the Mudger was having difficulties again, and he barely got out a request for the team leader when the screen went static-filled.

With a heavy sigh, Gaston sat in front of the tea tray and poured a cup. He loaded his tea with far more sugar and milk than usual, then sat back down in front of the Mudger. It spoke volumes as to how distracted he was that it took him a full minute to look embarrassed. "I say, that was rude of me, wasn't it? Would you like some tea?" He actually almost held out his own too sweet and pale tea, but then shook himself. "I mean I should make you some tea."

Nettie peered closer at her supervisor. It wasn't often she saw him that shaken. "Gaston, as you have been reminding me these last few days, this is my home as well. I am fully capable of getting myself some tea." She patted him kindly on his shoulder. "You are a bit thrown off at the moment."

"Master Gaston?" Damon took advantage of the silence, or perhaps he carried it with him, to enter the dungeon. "Master Homer would like your attendance."

"What? Oh, what does he want now? Drat that man, always poking around where he shouldn't be." He waited, then coughed when Damon stood silent. "Out with it, man, what does Homer need?"

Damon tipped his head. He was clearly getting used to the oddities of his new master and he barely flinched anymore.

"He needs your attendance. Outside. Actually, on the roof outside."

Unfortunately, Gaston had been sipping his tea and sputtered most of a mouthful into the air. Luckily, he was not facing the still-blank Mudger. "What? Get him off of there. What is he doing on my roof? I've told him we need to keep a low profile. Won't do to have the neighbors reporting odd behavior to the constables, after all. *Sacre bleu*, that man is a heathen."

"He's not on the roof, sir. He's above it." Damon winced as Gaston's face started to turn red.

"He's in his airship, is he? *The Drunken Harlot*. Over my house. While it's still light enough for the neighbors to see. *Ca me fait chier!*" Gaston ran for the dungeon door.

Nettie went to follow, but he slowed long enough to stop her. "No, you stay here. Cardiff may call back and they need to be warned." He grabbed an old bluster gun from a display case near the door. "I have warned him before and I will take care of that airship! Damn Homer, he's probably three sheets to the wind up there." Grabbing some shells for the large gun, he ran down the hall.

Nettie watched him go and toyed with the idea of following. After all, Homer did have a fearsome reputation as an airship pirate. Or privateer, as he preferred to be called. But at that moment, the Mudger sprang back to life.

"Is that you, Agent Jones? Where is Gaston? He claimed to have something urgent to pass along." The woman on the other end of the Mudger was thin and had her hair tightly bound. Nettie hadn't enjoyed training with her in Edinburgh, but Agent Maeve Clouster was one of the best clairvoyants they had.

Nettie opened her mouth to explain when she heard shots. Far bigger shots than would have been made by Gaston's gun. They had to be from Homer's airship. But even in the dungeon she would have felt it if the house had been hit.

"I'm sorry, ma'am. We appear to be under attack. I will make sure Gaston reports in once we have fought this off." She knew cutting a superior agent off like this wasn't good form, but the shots were getting louder. "But you have to keep all the clairvoyants protected. There is a way for them to be used against others and themselves. They must be shielded from outside interference."

"Who is attacking you, Jones?" Agent Maeve's scowl deepened.

"I don't know, ma'am, but there's an airship involved." Before she could respond, Nettie grabbed two of the small dissemblers and ran out of the room.

The shots echoed far louder outside of the dungeon than they had within its protective doors. She hadn't realized how well that room was protected until now. Wishing she had time to change into some of her new pants, she raced as fast as was safe up the back stairs.

Why would Homer attack the mansion? Granted, he was a curious man, but he seemed loyal to Gaston and the Society. With a calming breath, she slowly opened the roof door. Her instincts were to charge forth, but that didn't seem prudent if a set of airship canons were firing down at one.

Another shot rocked the air. But while it came from the low flying airship before her, it wasn't aimed down, but across at a small field behind Gaston's home.

Gaston and Damon aimed their weapons into the sky, but they weren't aiming at the airship. Nor did either of them fire.

"Gaston? What's happened?" Nettie stayed close to the high wall that followed the line of the doorway onto the roof, but kept both her dissemblers in her hands.

"Damn it, girl! I told you to stay in the dungeon." Gaston didn't turn as he spoke, but kept his eyes and gun focused on something near the empty field. "The clairvoyants are in danger."

"Agent Clouster came on, but I didn't have time to brief her fully. I warned her to protect the clairvoyants. I feared the airship was trying to fire upon the mansion."

Gaston did take his eyes away from the empty space he was

watching long enough to take in her two small dissemblers. "Your dedication is honorable, even if you don't follow instructions. However, what did you think you would be able to do with those?"

Nettie took up position next to Gaston and mimicked his stance. "They're better than nothing. You and Damon have the only two big guns down there, and I didn't have time to go to the armory. Now, what exactly are we looking at?"

Homer had been quiet for a few moments, but held position over the same section of field.

"Homer believes that the aliens are finally attempting to bring one of their etherships down to land."

Nettie looked harder, but she couldn't see anything beyond the airship. Maybe Gaston was right on his earlier assessment and Homer was simply drunk.

"I don't see anything." Nettie kept her voice low and leaned closer to Gaston. Perhaps it was an angle problem, but to be honest, there wasn't anything for a ship to be hiding behind.

"It's invisible, lass." Homer's voice boomed out from the airship. The man truly had terrifying hearing. "I hit them as they drifted down to London proper. They don't move fast, and they were visible when I first saw them. They have slowed down to almost a crawl, but are almost completely invisible now."

Nettie strained to see anything, but it was only when Gaston turned her head that she saw anything. It wasn't really that she could see a ship; rather, she saw a slight blur to the air that had distinct edges.

"I've been pounding on them to get them to leave, but so far they haven't fought back, nor moved to leave."

Nettie studied what she could see of the blur, but it gave no clues. The wind shifted and a strange smoky burnt odor drifted their way.

It smelled exactly like when the morgue had blown up in Rebecca's vision.

"We need to get off the roof. Homer, you need to move your ship. Now." Nettie tried to grab both Gaston and Damon, but both men held fast. "We need to back away immediately."

"Whatever are you talking about? That ship hasn't even fired back with Homer's great wallowing carcass firing down at it." Gaston shook his arm out of his grasp and held fast to his gun.

"I don't have time to explain." She didn't like to use her superior strength, especially on her superior, but they needed to get off that roof immediately. "Suffice it to say that I have smelled that chemical. Right before the morgue blew up in Rebecca's vision."

Homer and Damon didn't respond and looked at her blankly.

Gaston understood. He turned and yelled as loud as he could.

"Homer, back off now. Get as much airspace between you and that field as possible. Throw things over if you have to." Gaston turned to Damon, but the manservant was already holding the door back into the mansion open.

Homer looked ready to argue, then shook his head and bellowed orders to his crew. With a speed completely at war with its size, the airship rose into the twilight sky.

"But will the mansion be able to withstand the explosion?" Nettie shook off the cold sweat that came over her when she made the connection with the smell. She'd all but decided that Rebecca's foreshadowing vision had been a mistake. The confirmation that there was a connection between the vision and the invading aliens did not sit well with her.

"It will have to, but get as far into the mansion as you can."

Gaston was right behind them and slammed the roof door behind them. An instant later, an explosion shook the foundation of the mansion.

CHAPTER TWENTY-SEVEN

"**W**HAT WAS THAT?" Damon had been fairly unflappable to this point, but this got to him. He was looking a bit ragged about the eyes.

"Easy, Damon." Gaston pried the elephant gun out of his shaking fingers. "Why don't you go downstairs and see if Agent Wilding has returned yet? And see what can be viewed from the street in terms of our pirate friend?"

At his suggestion, Damon's demeanor changed. He wasn't smiling, but he looked far less likely to run off screaming.

Once he'd left, Gaston turned back up the stairs and shoved open the door. Deciding that his earlier order to go deep into the mansion was rescinded after the explosion, Nettie followed him.

The roof was surprisingly unscathed. Burn marks radiated out from the side the ship had been on, but little in the way of debris.

There was also no sign of an airship, either intact and flying or destroyed and crumbled to the ground. Wherever he was, it looked like Homer had gotten the ship in the clear.

Gaston went to the roof ledge and looked down. Nettie joined him.

She wasn't sure what she'd expected, maybe a pile of mysterious twisted metal, but the black crater that ran the length of the field surprised her.

"Shouldn't we see something?" She wasn't disappointed per se. After all, an alien craft entering London airspace wasn't something to be taken lightly. But she had to admit, if even only to herself, that examining an alien body would have been fascinating.

"I'd say they managed to design an effective destruct system." Gaston frowned as he looked over the darkening sky and the surrounding houses.

One advantage of being in a more affluent area of London was the lack of noisy neighbors. But even they should have sent someone out to see what the ruckus had been. Yet not a single servant came out of any of the surrounding houses.

"Where is everyone?" The silence was eerie. And decidedly unnatural for this part of town.

"Ah, it looks like Lisselle is back in the neighborhood. Most likely, she followed Homer in." Gaston pointed to a slim, dark figure hovering in the air about the field. Her arms were outstretched and the feeling of silence and calm seemed to come from her.

"What is she doing?" Even with the demonstration of the other day, it was still a bit shocking to see her friend hovering a good two hundred meters up in the air.

"I'd say the neighborhood and surrounding environs have been spelled. Come on now, let's get you inside. The others will join us when they finish."

Nettie wanted to stay and watch Lisselle, or at least go down to the field and look for any remains. Judging by the way Gaston was herding her, she was only going downstairs.

"Now, young lady, how did you know that ship was going to blow?" Gaston carefully took her weapons as well, before guiding her through the parlor doors.

"Shouldn't we check that Homer got out safely?" They couldn't assume that his ship survived. And she could check that field.

"Damon will do that. He needed to get away from the initial explosion, then he'll do his job."

He carefully sat her down in one of the large wingback chairs. "Tea?" Gaston went over and prepared the tea service with an ease that surprised Nettie.

Until she saw his hand was shaking ever so slightly.

"It scared you too, didn't it?"

"Saw right through me, didn't you?" Gaston gave an awkward laugh. "I have to admit that terrified me. Not so much the explosion, but the ethership itself being able to enter our atmosphere." His hand was steady as he handed her a cup of tea. "And that you obviously recognized when it was going to explode."

Nettie took the cup. "I didn't recognize the smell of an exploding ship, but as I said, that smell was what Rebecca and I smelled right before the morgue blew up in her first vision."

Gaston took one sip of his tea, then paced. "That can't be good. It also can't be a coincidence. I understand your reasons for sending Rebecca away, but it would be better in this case that she was here. Do you know if she noticed anything else?"

"Everything was in the reports. But those smells were the same."

"Then we have to assume it was not an accident that the alien ship blew up, but rather a deliberate act." He resumed his seat and frowned. "And we must assume that they were behind these future attacks that Miss Rebecca has twice experienced."

Both were lost in thought when the door almost shattered. Homer appeared an instant later.

"Damn it, Gaston, you almost killed me!" His thick boots rattled the entire contents of the hall, Damon included, as he marched down it. "Give a man more warning next time. Not to mention, I thought you might want the aliens alive for work in your laboratory. Or even dead and intact. There's nothing left out there but dust." He stopped and bowed to Nettie. "Hello, Dr. Jones." He then marched the rest of the way in and poured himself a large glass of whisky.

Nettie had to admit that did seem to be the more appropriate drink.

"Damn you old, daft bear, I didn't fire at that ship. It came from within. They used something to blow themselves up." Gaston scowled but continued to sip his tea.

Homer flung himself into a wingback chair and downed his glass. His other hand held the bottle, so refilling was easy. "If they had the power to do that," the liquid in his glass sloshed as he pointed to the roof, "why in the bloody hell didn't they fire back at me?"

Giving up on his tepid tea, Gaston took a glass and pried the whisky bottle out of Homer's hands. He was obviously far more rattled that he let on. "I've no idea. How long were you following them?"

Homer studied his glass for a few moments then shook himself out of it. "About two hours. I hate to say it, but that Caden fellow was right. They appeared in the air over Bath. If he hadn't suggested it, I never would have been patrolling that far. But they never moved quickly, almost as if they couldn't."

Nettie looked up from her own musings. "That can't be true, Gaston. If they came here from another world, they'd need to move a lot faster than an airship." She smiled at Homer. "No offense to your ship."

"None taken. But if that's the case, then why didn't it manage to lose me? I was going at full steam, but I never lost sight of it." He frowned. "Until the dratted thing went invisible on me, at any rate."

Gaston resumed his seat by the fire. "I'd venture to say it has something to do with their difficulty in our air. Most likely, the large ship Nettie and Caden went to can't come down here, but can move at great speed in ether."

"Judging by the problems the smaller vessel was having in our air, I'd say they still can't come down here." Lisselle's voice proceeded the diminutive magic user by a few seconds as she stripped off her heavy coat in the hall. "I was following Homer and the ethership for the last half hour. It was having serious problems." She claimed a glass of whisky for herself. "Even without Homer's rather uneven bombing techniques."

"Uneven? I hit that thing more times than naught. I'd like to see you hit something that went invisible."

"Actually, I could see it." The joviality left Lisselle's voice as she curled by the fire. "It was disturbing. As if there was another sense that allowed me to see it as it faded from normal eyes." She gave a shudder and a long drink of her whisky. "Quite unsettling."

"Are you saying they're magical?" Nettie had trouble choking out the word.

"No, not that. It was something else. I've a feeling that Rebecca could have seen them as well." She was clearly disturbed, but obviously wasn't going to say more until she'd sorted things out in her head.

"Damn it." Gaston stomped back to his seat. "It's bad enough we've got people from another planet coming down, now they're somehow talking to you clairvoyants? I don't like this."

"Don't like what?" Caden said as he entered the room. He was dusty and a bit disheveled, but he looked in good spirits. Nettie had no idea where'd he'd gone, but he must have left the house before Nettie and Rebecca left for the train station that morning. "What did I miss?"

Homer rose and handed Caden a shot of whisky and poured himself another. "There's the man we should all be thanking. He suggested that we try out his toys in Bath. We flew up before sunrise and found us a low flying ethership hovering above the town. It was still too high for us to have any effect on it. Or so I thought. He fired off his giant toy gun, and that electrode exploded far below it." He raised one finger in accent, sloshing his drink a bit. Lisselle took the bottle back from him. "But, that's when the ship starting losing altitude. Like an aeronaut that had been drinking on the job, they started lowering. I'd wager that explosion would have been bigger if we'd had two of them electrode dissemblers." He smiled and pounded Caden on the back. "We did light up the early morning sky a bit though, didn't we, lad?"

From the looks shared by both men, Caden and Homer were

now best friends and boon companions. Forget that Homer had called Caden's Solar Electrode Agitator a farce, a joke, and a waste of good gear parts. They had fought together and brought down an enemy together. And now they were drinking together.

"That was a brilliantly idiotic thing to do, and I can't think of two better men to have done it." Gaston took one more swig of whisky, and rose. "I believe that I'll need to be seeing if the Mudger's working now. There are people in Cardiff that need warning, and most likely a few in Cardiff who will want explanations about a certain bright light over their city."

With a studied glare that managed to encompass both Homer and Caden, Gaston left the room.

"It wasn't our fault we didn't warn them. How could we?" Homer didn't sound contrite in the least.

And Caden certainly didn't look it. "I'm sure the fine folks up in Cardiff have dealt with more weirdness than a bright light. The important thing is that it worked."

"Well, to some extent." Lisselle stayed curled near the fire. "We know they are having problems with our atmosphere or they would have been on us long ago. There is no way to be sure how much of their decline was due to your weapon and how much to their own difficulties. We can't let this success, such as it is, make us cocky." Both men dropped their eyes to the floor when she looked to them. "We know little about these aliens, and even less about their physiology. So if you really want to help, find us a nice dead one we can examine."

When it looked like there would be no more Caden bashing, Nettie excused herself and went downstairs to the dungeon. To be honest, she would have liked to speak to Lisselle about some of the recent events, but the tiny witch left for her room.

Fortunately, Nettie had extremely fast reflexes even before the added contribution from the master vampire. The dungeon door slamming open would have surely flattened a slower person.

"Ah! There you are, *ma chère*. So sorry I startled you." Gaston pulled her along with him as he led the way back up to the parlor. "I was able to get through to Cardiff, and they are warned. But I have excellent news."

Nettie let herself be carried along since clearly he wasn't going to tell her this great news unless he found the others.

Caden and Homer were sharing the bottle of whisky and a collection of embellished war stories when Nettie and Gaston came into the parlor.

"I have excellent news, gentlemen," Gaston said. "Edinburgh says that with the intelligence on the status of the destruction of the missing Runners, and new safe guards in place, they will be reactivating the rest of them within the hour. Their first job will be a nice visit to Holyrood."

Nettie put her hands on her hips. "That's all well and good, but shouldn't you have waited until we brought Lisselle in?" After all, he held off telling her until they found Homer and Caden. And Caden's grin at the outcome of his deciding to blow up the captured Runners was this side of insufferable.

"Ah, *chere*, Lisselle keeps by her own ways. If she's left this room, there's a reason. And I'll not to be the one to dig her out." Gaston turned back to the other two. "I'd say we'd best ready another expedition to Bath, a much bigger one this time. I have a feeling our missing vampires will try to take our queen back where the aliens can protect her once things become difficult up north."

CHAPTER TWENTY-EIGHT

A WEEK LATER, the news came down that the hive had relocated to Bath. Luckily, no agents had been slaughtered this time, as it appeared they were trying to move without notice.

That week had been instructive for Nettie, as she mostly tried to stay out of Gaston's way while she worked on trying to strengthen her projection abilities. He took to the dungeon, kicking everyone else out the morning after the downed ethership, and refused to come out for fourteen hours. He spent the rest of the week scurrying out of the dungeon to grab food and supplies, then bolting himself back inside.

Lisselle had stayed out of sight as well, and finally came out of her room three days ago, grabbed her coat and gloves, then left before Nettie could ask her where she was going. Nettie thought about chasing her down, but Gaston's words still lingered in her head. Lisselle was her friend, and giving her space when she needed it was a good idea.

Caden and Homer had been off and about in London, doing Lord only knew what. Today, the crash site had finally cooled enough for investigation and they had gone down to look for any clues. Unfortunately, they returned a few hours later filthy and empty-handed. Not completely empty-handed; Caden had the foresight to bring along some sample containers to scoop up what was left of the ethership. Sadly, he only needed two.

"I'll take those, thank you." Nettie snapped the two vials out of his grimy hands before he could lose them. Not that she really thought he would be so careless, but Homer wasn't a good influence on Caden. Who knew when they'd wander off drinking again? "And don't either of you think of sitting down covered in that filth." Nettie did her best Mrs. Cruddle glare.

"You know, 'tis amazing that one so fair could be so shrewish," Caden said to Homer in a fake brogue. He'd been baiting Nettie far too much this past week, practically even flirting with her on a few occasions.

Unsure of how to best deal with him, she narrowed her eyes even further and stomped back to her private lab. Gaston had taken over the dungeon, but her small lab was outside of it, so she still had access to her research.

Sadly, she didn't have much to research. All of the interesting samples were in with Gaston, and he wasn't sharing. Her work on her projection abilities wasn't really that exciting, and was limited by who she could get to assist her. Considering that her fellow agents all seemed to be pursuing their own angles, she was stuck with Damon. Sadly, even his patience at trying to see through whatever she projected was wearing thin. Nettie still wasn't sure how she could use the projections the aliens processed to her team's advantage, but she knew there must be a way.

She could only speculate on what the master plan would be. To be honest, as long as she was involved, she didn't care. For the first time in her two years with the Society, Nettie felt like a real agent. Gaston had come running out right after breakfast this morning, saying he'd had confirmation of the move to Bath, and that plans would be discussed at dinner. He also sent out a Runner to get word to Lisselle.

It was nice to have the mysterious alien mechanical men back, and once their leader had been activated, he recognized the aliens as something they had seen before. Unfortunately, the Runners' encounters with the aliens were long before their crash to Earth, and most knowledge was lost. However, the lead Runner recalled enough to realize his fellows couldn't go into any of the etherships, even the long crashed one in Bath. It was believed that the four missing Runners actually shut down due to being brought into the ship. But without one of them to study, they couldn't be sure how or why.

Nettie had allowed herself a small smirk of satisfaction at that outcome. She wasn't sure how they could have gotten any of the disabled Runners out of the cave in Bath, but she was vindicated in wanting to do so.

With a sigh at having to wait another few hours before Gaston and the others would gather and make plans, Nettie prepared some slides of the grime that Caden had brought back.

She'd settled in to write up some notes when a knock came to her door.

"I know you're in there, Nettie. Can I use some of your equipment?" Caden asked with far more politeness than he had the entire week. Since she had the only lab outside of the dungeon, she had originally opened it to the other agents. However, Lisselle had access to her own secrets and didn't need it. Homer didn't go for that book learning, per his own speech. Which left Caden.

She'd let him in the first day, but found that he was constantly in her way. And his smile was far too charming, his brown eyes too endearing, and his physique…Well, she tried not to think about that. But he did seem to find a few too many reasons to stand near her.

She was by no means a prude, but she was a serious scientist, and an agent of the Society. She couldn't afford to be distracted by his bold charms. Besides, she had a sneaky feeling he knew his effect on her and was trying to bait her more.

"As I have told you before, Agent Smith, there is simply not enough room in here. If you have some analysis that needs to be run, you may leave the samples with me." She popped open the door a sliver to meet his eye. "I think we both agree that I'm the more thorough scientist of the two of us."

"I wanted to see what was in the dust I brought back from the crash site." There was no forced charm or artifice to him now. Nettie found that even more disturbing.

"Unfortunately, there wasn't anything there. I have the Aligning Constricting Profabulator doing a long-term analysis. It should be done in a few more hours. But there was nothing else but cinder. Not even any dust." She bit her lip as the words slipped out. That was the one thing of interest, and she hoped he wouldn't jump on it.

His brown eyes lit up and he leaned into the doorway enough to block her closing the door. "None? When the little buggers seem to be coated in it? Now that I'd call interesting." He looked like he wanted to come in.

Nettie was wondering how rude it would be to shove him out of the way and slam the door when Gaston happened to pop out of the dungeon.

"What is interesting? Whatever are you doing cluttering up the hallway, Smith?" What little hair Gaston had was sticking up in weird little clumps and he had one pair of spectacles on the top of his head and one on his face.

"Nettie was telling me that there was none of the aliens' dust at the crash site." At Gaston's confused look, Caden elaborated. "Homer and I finally deemed the field cool enough for examination. We didn't find much."

"And no dust." Nettie took advantage of Gaston's appearance to regain control of the doorway.

"Hmmm, I agree. Interesting." But Gaston's face said he had far larger things floating about his head. "Yes, yes, extremely interesting. Actually, I was wondering if I could steal you, Caden. Could use your help on my project before our meeting at dinner tonight." He nodded to Nettie. "You don't mind?"

"Not at all. Good afternoon, gentlemen." She hoped she wasn't too rude as she all but slammed the door.

This was ridiculous. Even being around Caden was starting to get to her. After this crisis, she would have to work on Gaston to see that he got sent back home. Or to Edinburgh. Or some distant remote outpost. The man was far too distracting for a serious agent like herself.

Unfortunately, the only thing she had to study was the grime from the crash, and she'd done everything she could for now. With a sigh, she pulled out some paper and began another letter to Rebecca.

NETTIE WAS WAITING in the dining room by the time the others finally came in. There was only so much she could safely tell Rebecca in her letter so, unfortunately, that project left her with a lot of time on her hands. She thought that perhaps she had something of interest when the Aligning Constricting Profabulator dinged repeatedly, but unfortunately, it was indicating a lack of anything of interest.

"You could have gone into the kitchen if you were that hungry," Homer said as he sat down next to her with a grin.

"I wasn't hungry, I was bored." She glared at Gaston as he entered. He could have included her in some of his plotting this last week. Nettie could handle many things, however, ennui was not one of them.

"Ah, *ma chère*, I was wondering when that might become an issue for you. But never fear. We will have more excitement and adventure than even you could want." He remained standing as Caden held the chair out for Lisselle. "We will begin liberating queen Victoria tomorrow. And if my plans work—and they always do—we will secure a way to get rid of this alien menace as well."

The meeting went far into the evening and the arguments began before the first course was served.

THE NEXT MORNING, Nettie tried to sort everything in her head as she bustled about gathering things she might need for the raid. But to be honest, she was more interested in the doing as opposed to the planning at this point. Perhaps it was the week of inactivity, or perhaps it was yet another sign of her slow change due to the bite of the master vampire, but she had become far more enamored of physical activity than she previously had been.

The idea behind this raid would be speed and numbers. Although they couldn't use the Runners, agents from the nearby towns had been trickling into London for the last week. To keep any watchers unaware, they'd not come to the mansion. Lisselle had gone to them.

That had been a bit of a shock to Nettie. She would have loved to have met some of the other agents in a more relaxed setting than what they were going into. Alas, Gaston explained that since she was one of the more visible agents on this case, they needed to keep her in the mansion.

Nettie muttered to herself as she made sure her daggers were loaded into her arm sheaths, her carved wooden stakes were carefully loaded into a sheath on her left arm, and her dissembler was placed in a matching one on her right hip. She felt quite American with the modified holsters on her, but she needed to be prepared for anything. A heavy feeling of wrongness hit her when she first got up, and she'd been unable to chase it away, or secure the cause.

A light rapping on her door came as she was making her final adjustments. Nettie let Lisselle in to inspect her weaponry.

"Are you sure you're up for this?" Lisselle's face was etched in concern. "I am still not sure this is the best plan."

Nettie impulsively hugged her friend. She had misgivings too, but it was for her friends' participation in this, not her own. This was her part of the plan, and even though no one had liked it aside from her, they finally agreed to it. "I will be fine. You were held by them for days and they never did anything to you."

"We think they know what you are, Nettie. That vampire you brought into the morgue, the one that attacked you—"

"The master vampire," Nettie injected out of habit. Gaston still refused to call him that.

"Yes, yes. The master vampire. He went after you for a reason. Even if he didn't, he would have known you were different once he had your blood."

Nettie led them down the hall and toward the others. This was the same argument that had been causing so many problems the previous night.

"We can't be sure of that, and we simply don't have the manpower to overwhelm them. That ship is far too big and has too many rooms. My going in first as a helpless victim will keep them off guard. Then the rest of you swoop in, rescue Queen Victoria, destroying, of course, the master vampire and using Gaston's secret weapon to free us from the alien menace, and we all leave." Nettie flashed her best bit of fang smile at Lisselle. "It really will work."

Lisselle shook her head. "Ah, the optimism of youth. I've seen far too many better laid plans go horribly awry in my time. But this is what we have; let's make the best of it." She pulled Nettie close a few feet from the end of the hallway. "But be careful. Everyone seems to think you're invincible now, even you." She held Nettie's eyes fiercely. "You're not; none of us are. Things can go wrong. Expect it."

Nettie fought the foreboding that hit her at Lisselle's words and forced out a smile. "I won't forget, but shall we now join the rest of our mad crew?" She didn't have time to worry about what was or wasn't wrong right now. If she couldn't figure out what it was, all she could do was prepare for the worst.

The plan was that they would take the train up to Oxford now, the rest of the agents having already trickled out during the night before. From there, Homer and two more airship pilots would be waiting to bring them into Bath under the cover of darkness.

Nettie had originally planned that she would travel alone on the regular train to Bath, allowing herself to be seen. Her plan had been soundly outvoted by Gaston and the others who feared the aliens may make a grab for her before she could be captured by the vampires. An odd situation to be sure, but one she finally agreed with. Although it certainly appeared the two were working together in some degree, Gaston wasn't sure that they shared everything.

As it was, they were still traveling in small numbers. Lisselle, Nettie, and Damon would be on the first train travelling as proper ladies along with their manservant. Caden and Gaston would go separately on later trains, and Homer had already left for *The Drunken Harlot*.

Considering what they were about to attempt, Nettie found the trip to Oxford frustrating and far too long. They rejoined the new agents and awaited Caden and Gaston in the manor house occupied by the Oxford Society team. Nettie was excited at meeting new agents, but her excitement dimmed when they all appeared to be in various states of last-minute planning or preparing for their raid.

"Not as exciting as you expected, eh, lass?" Homer pulled up a heavy chair next to where Nettie sat by the window.

"Does it show?" Nettie gave an awkward laugh. She didn't want to offend anyone, especially when she didn't know them yet.

Homer patted her knee. "Only to folks who know you. And being honest, I have to say I feel the same. This part of a caper is always dreary. The plans have been made, and now comes the waiting." He pointed to one of the outside agents who had taken apart his supply bag for the fourth time. "And the incessant checking and rechecking. Me, I prep once and be done with it."

Nettie's laughter died as the head of the Oxford Society branch came running out of his study. "Has Gaston arrived yet? I must speak with him."

Homer and Nettie shook their heads, but Nettie's stomach churned as she forced the words out. Something had gone extremely wrong. "He won't be here for another hour at the least. What's happened?"

The Oxford man swore under his breath, but his blue eyes were kind. "I received notice from Northern Scotland. Your friend, Rebecca, has vanished."

CHAPTER TWENTY-NINE

"OH DEAR," NETTIE said as she started to slump to the side. Homer caught her before she fell off the chair. A moment later, she pushed him away. "I'm fine. It's just...I think there is a connection between her and me, up here." She tapped the side of her head. "I knew something was wrong this morning, but I didn't know what. Do we know when she was taken?"

The Oxford man shook his head. "She was last seen after dinner last eve. But then the watchers lost her. A visit to her aunt's home revealed she'd been missing at least since morning." His frown grew deeper. "You knew she'd been taken? Who took her?"

"No, I misspoke. I didn't know she had been taken. I had an awful feeling this morning before we left London."

Homer nodded. "And I think we all know who would have taken her—the aliens. They did it before. There's no reason to doubt they could do it again."

"But I didn't know they were that far north. They would have no reason to be scouting up there." The Oxford team leader marched over to the giant map in the main room.

"Who is that far north? And can I get some help here? I do have all of the backup supplies for the ship. The ones someone forgot to load on his barge before he left." Gaston came in hauling a large fabric bag.

Homer rose and easily took the bag and set it aside. "I told you we didn't need these, Gaston. You're being an old maid."

"The aliens took Rebecca." Nettie bit her lip after she spoke. Certainly, there was protocol for news being given, but she couldn't wait. Gaston needed to know.

"What? *Merde*, that is grievous news." Gaston turned to the Oxford man. "Thomas, what information do you have?"

Thomas studied his map a bit more, shaking his head as he finally turned back. He clearly was not happy that the aliens had done something unexpected. "Not much more. For some reason, there was a miscommunication and the information ended up being routed through Edinburgh."

"But how could they have found her?" Nettie said. "We've established that, except for that time I was taken by accident, they have only appeared around our technology or Roman ruins. Since there are none up there, she should have been safe. There aren't any Society branches in Llandudno are there?"

"No, there's nothing nearby. She was being watched by some Runners who have set up a small base outside of Aberdeen. But she herself could have drawn them there." Gaston took a drink offered by Thomas and eased himself into a chair. "The connection between her and them may be too strong for distance to lessen it." He tapped the glass in thought. "You didn't happen to notice if they had any of their etherships stationed up that way when you saw their maps?"

Nettie searched her memory. She was able to retain large amounts of information without difficulty. Normally. As of late, her retention hadn't been as good as it once was. "I don't think so. No, I'm sure of it."

A door chime rang to announce their last attendee. Caden entered, looking for all the world as if he stepped out of a fancy salon. Nettie had to admit the upscale look did do him justice. Unfortunately, she was beginning to think every look did him justice. With suppression of that thought, and a shake of her head, she focused on her missing friend.

"What did I do now that you're already scowling at me?" Caden asked as he removed his coat, hat, and gloves.

"She's upset. We've found out Rebecca is missing," Gaston said, but he did give Nettie a searching glance.

Forcing her face into a more pleasant demeanor, Nettie ignored the question. "Do you happen to recall if the aliens had any etherships on their map stationed near the north of Scotland?" She was certain they wouldn't. It would have been out of keeping with their Roman ruins theory—the Romans never made it far into northern Scotland.

Caden bit back whatever comment he was going to make. "No, I don't think I saw one up there. But it couldn't be that hard for them to move a ship up there. They seem to have gotten here well enough; they just have trouble coming into our air."

Gaston nodded, then rose to his feet. "Then, most likely, it was the vampires who took her." He didn't remind people that the alien had referred to Rebecca as bait when she had been in their ship. Nettie mentally vowed her friend would be no one's bait, or further victim.

The rest of the agents to be involved in the raid moved in closer as final arrangements were made. "I want it understood that, while we are all to be on the lookout for Agent Rhys, getting the queen back has to be the highest priority." He softened his look as he glanced at Nettie. "We may have to worry about getting Rebecca back after this raid."

Nettie gave a small nod, but she would do whatever she needed to do if there was any sign of Rebecca in the vampires' cave.

It was a sober crew that loaded onto the waiting airships. Right before they left, more word had come down from Edinburgh. The morgue that Nettie and Rebecca had worked at had blown up. Luckily, due to the Scotland Yard quarantine, no one was inside, but the building was destroyed.

Concerned that one of Rebecca's visions had come true—granted, without Nettie or Rebecca actually being there—Nettie boarded the airship. She was heartsick that she might have sent her friend into danger. She found herself sitting between Caden and Lisselle out of luck. Or judging by the comforting smiles Lisselle sent her way, luck may have had nothing to do with it.

"I'm sure she's fine." Caden was the one who first spoke. All of his charm was gone now, and what Nettie had to assume was the real Caden remained. This one was actually more of a danger than the charming version. His eyes held hers as he briefly squeezed her hand. "There's no way we're going to let anything happen to her. I support your monarchy, but Rebecca is a friend. She comes first."

He'd kept his voice low; obviously he wasn't trying to cause dissention in the group. But his support meant more to her than she could say.

"Thank you." She took a deep breath and was surprised at how good it felt. Having Caden on her side made a difference. It wasn't that she thought Gaston and the others would abandon

Rebecca, but an agent of the Society always came second to the benefit of the nation.

This was one time Nettie didn't agree with that sentiment.

"Me as well," Lisselle whispered from the other side. "I won't let her, or you, down."

Nettie felt her eyes start to tear. "Thank you both. I can't say—" she cut herself off as she wiped away the tears and saw her glove. The tears were of blood.

"Child? What's wrong?" Lisselle leaned forward and tilted Nettie's face toward the lamp that hung in the middle of the airship cabin.

"That can't be good." Nettie fought to keep her voice low.

"No, it's not. I'm not going to lie to you, Nettie. You know what that means."

Nettie nodded, but Caden had to say it out loud anyway. "She's becoming a full vampire."

Nettie spun in her seat, ready to defend herself if need be. She didn't feel any different. He must be wrong. She was surprised to see nothing had changed on Caden's handsome face. Except it held a twinge of sadness.

"But I don't want to drink anyone's blood."

Lisselle took her hand, and Caden reclaimed the one near him.

"You're going to be fine."

"Now what are you two hovering over Nettie for?" Gaston refused to sit on the airship, preferring to wander about in a wide-ranging form of pacing.

Nettie started to make up something when Caden smoothly stepped in. "Just the usual. I was trying to charm said lovely lady, and Lisselle was defending her," he added with a leer.

Nettie could have hugged him at that moment, but didn't want to ruin the image. She didn't like hiding things from anyone, least of all Gaston. The fact was, she wasn't sure if he would allow her continued participation in the raid if he felt she was compromised. Blood tears or not, she knew she was still in control of herself. She wasn't a vampire. She couldn't be.

"Eh, you've got to tone down that American charm. It won't work with proper English girls, eh, Nettie?" Gaston patted Nettie's head, then continued on his route.

"Thank you both. I truly appreciate it."

"Not a worry, my dear. That one lies well enough for all of us." Lisselle smiled.

The rest of the trip down to Bath was decidedly dull. Most of the agents were lost in their own worlds, preparing for a fight from which some might not come back. But to die in the service of the queen was a goal for most agents.

Nettie was actually starting to doze off when a cracking sound popped overhead.

"It's time." Homer's voice sounded tinny coming through the cabin speakers. "I'm going to have all of us disembark a few miles from the nest. We don't need to warn them we're coming." *The Drunken Harlot* drifted lower as he spoke and Nettie knew he was switching positions with the agent who would pilot the ship back up.

All of the agents disembarked silently, joining with the groups from the other ships. All total, there were sixty-five men and women up against an unknown number of aliens and vampires. Nettie wouldn't like the odds if she didn't know how well agents of the Society were trained.

"Now remember, whatever you do, don't let them knock you unconscious. You need to stay aware at all times. And make sure to use that trick I taught you when they tie you up. Don't fight back too much or it won't work." Gaston looked ready to continue when Nettie cut him off with a hug.

"I'll be fine. You've taught me extremely well, including your little finger trick." She waggled her fingers at him. Gaston had a way of turning one's fingers and wrists when being tied up that left the ropes loose enough for escape. He'd made her practice it for hours.

"I'll see you all back at the rendezvous after this is over." She hugged Lisselle and had turned to go when Caden caught her up.

"Be careful," he whispered with a quick kiss before abruptly letting her go.

Nettie had been kissed before, not often, granted. But some young men had tried upon occasion. But it was nothing like this. The kiss had been little more than a touch, but her lips felt like they'd been touched by fire. Not sure how to react, and certain her face was quite red, Nettie nodded and turned away.

One would really think that when wandering around a downed alien ship that now functioned as a vampire hive, it wouldn't be difficult to become captured.

One would be wrong.

It took Nettie almost a half hour of loudly tromping about, stumbling in the dark, and making as much noise as possible before two vampires finally grabbed her from behind. After a discussion about draining her or bringing her in, it was finally decided they should take her in.

Nettie held back a sigh of relief at finally being caught. One she was sure was echoed by Thomas. The Oxford gentleman was on special lookout in a small single-man dirigible hanging low enough to look like an extension of the tree line—at least in the dark when all one could see was a mass of darkness. He would signal the rest of the team to move forward now.

"I don't see why we can't have a taste. Dragoi asks too much." The tall blond vampire to Nettie's left complained as he pulled her closer. His accent was faint, but still carried vestiges of an Eastern European heritage.

The smaller, darker vampire behind her snorted. "And you are going to go against him how?" His accent was far deeper than the first, and it too came from the same area. "You did not see him in the old country. He could destroy you between one blink of an eye and the next."

"You old ones exaggerate. He is like us. Older, yes, but like us."

But Nettie saw that he didn't believe his own words. There was a fear in his eyes and he watched the corridors carefully. This Dragoi must be the master vampire. Clearly, the other vampires feared him, even the ones who said they didn't. She wiggled her fingers as a test. It would take a while, but she should be able to free herself when the time came.

They were bringing her in from yet another entrance, meaning there were at least three. She had hoped to be brought in by either the one they'd come in previously or the one they left through. The fact there was a third one, and that they were traveling through it for some time before she saw an area she thought she recognized, was disheartening. So was the sheer size of this downed ship. If the ships hovering over the major cities of the globe were of similar size...She shook that thought off. First, find Rebecca and distract the vampires. Then deal with the alien menace in the sky.

Finally, Nettie heard the steam engines that she and Caden had found the first trip. They weren't that close, but at least it gave her a sense of direction.

Used to the sparseness of most of the downed ship she'd been in so far, Nettie was unprepared for the room she was led into.

Ornate wall carvings ripped from some distant palace lay up against the walls like silent tribute to fallen worlds. Thick swaths of heavy embroidered fabric, some possibly hundreds of years old, lay draped and forgotten over heavy wood furniture. The chamber itself was huge, half part of the ancient alien ship and half dug from the earth. A dozen or more vampires lounged around, none of them showing much interest as she was brought forward toward a dais.

The raised section held a blood red throne with a seemingly asleep occupant. Next to it was a medical table and chair completely at odds with the rest of the décor. A medical screen kept the upper portions of the table and chair hidden.

"Oh, this is a lovely selection." The vampire Nettie had thought was sleeping was actually watching her from barely open eyes. His voice indicated far more interest than his posture did. "Moldovan and Radu, you may go now. This is the one I was looking for. You may feed on any others you find."

The vampire rose and Nettie finally got a good look at him. Although she'd suspected that the vampire who'd bitten her had been the master vampire, the confirmation of the fact was still distressing. His face showed he was the vampire she'd found with a stake stuck in him. But where he had looked old and deformed then, he was young and powerful now. He smiled and tipped his head toward the medical table and screen.

"Hello, Nettie." The voice came from behind the screen, but Nettie didn't need to see the speaker. She knew that voice far too well. Rebecca.

CHAPTER THIRTY

"IF YOU HAVE me, why do you need her?" Nettie surveyed the room as she spoke. She had wanted to find Rebecca, but if she'd already been turned, then it was even more vital they get out quickly.

"Why should I only limit myself to one treat?" He motioned behind the screen and Rebecca stumbled forward. Her jerky movements and blank stare made Nettie relax a bit. Judging by her awkward movements, the master vampire, or Dragoi, as the other vampire had named him, obviously hadn't brought her over yet.

"No, not yet. She's a delicacy. Not the same as you, or your flying friend who's off lurking about somewhere, but special just the same." His laugh was a cloying sound. At first strangely enticing, but it quickly turned her stomach. "Don't worry, I didn't read your mind. It will take a few more sessions before I can do that. But your face gives your thoughts away almost as if you shouted it. We shall have to work on that."

Two vampires dragged her to a chair in the center of the room. The smaller one pushed her into it with enough force to rock her backward. However, he got too close and nicked her wrist with a small ring shaped like a claw. Before she could gasp, he'd grabbed her wrist and began drawing from the slight wound.

Nettie reacted instinctively. She ripped the rope off her hands and backhanded the vampire across the room. Part of her was fascinated that she'd been able to do that with such ease and speed against a full-blooded vampire. The other part of her saw red, literally. A red haze filled her vision as she fought with five other vampires. She'd almost fought her way free—two of the vampires that tried to hold her wouldn't be rising again—when the remaining three slammed her to the ground.

"Don't damage her." Dragoi stepped down from his stage and slowly walked toward her as she struggled on the ground. Rebecca trailed along mindlessly behind him. "I intend to enjoy your blood for a long time. There is something exotic about you. Not the half-vampire status. I already knew that." He gave a shrug as he kneeled down next to her. "It happens sometimes, half-vampire bastards. Usually, they go insane before their first ten years of life. No, you have something else floating in your blood. Exotic, dangerous, and powerful." He licked the side of her neck, then pulled back to see her eyes. "Oh yes. I'll be feeding on you for years."

Nettie fought to free herself as he leaned down to her neck again. His fangs punctured her skin. A moment later, she lost consciousness.

THE YELLING CAME first.

Nettie couldn't force her eyelids to obey her commands, but her ears were working fine. Shots being fired, voices yelling, screams of burning vampires filed the air.

Had she been able to move, she would have smiled. So much for Dragoi's claim he would be feeding on her for years. Although the plan hadn't been for the rest of the team to come this far into the nest, obviously they had.

But she couldn't let them do it all without her. Drawing in a deep breath, she forced the heavy feeling from her body, opened her eyes, and rolled to her feet.

Or tried to.

She got her eyes open, but there was a weight on her she hadn't felt until the blood started moving again. Thomas from Oxford, his eyes starring lifelessly at her from his location draped across her lower body. A long, jagged tear in his throat told her how he died. She closed her eyes as hot tears fell, but there was no time for grieving.

This battle wasn't going as planned at all. With as much care as she dared, Nettie rolled the dead agent off of her. More dead agents lay scattered around, but none of her friends were in sight. They were losing the fight, and it appeared the aliens hadn't even joined in the battle yet.

A small group of ten agents, battered and bloody but still upright, were edging toward the door.

"Oh no. Why would I let you leave after I worked so hard to invite you here?" Dragoi sprawled across the throne-like chair. The look on his face was one of a well-fed cat, not ready to give up the game even though he was too full to enjoy the rewards. "Your companions here all died far too quickly. And unfortunately, my people haven't captured the rest of you."

He waved a hand and a tall, slender vampire appeared at his side. "Do secure them without any more waste. I grow tired of this."

Nettie was close enough to the stage and Dragoi's chair that she knew he would hear her without letting the rest of the agents hear. "They won't let you take them."

"Ah, my repast speaks. Did you have a pleasant nap?" He didn't look toward her, but Nettie felt a horrible shiver as if he had. His power almost struck her down as it flowed over her. There was no way to get away from him.

"The agents won't let you take them alive." She crept forward, but her slowness was due more to the lead in her veins than to trying to be cautious. She reached up to her throat and was surprised that there was the faintest of puncture marks. It felt like half of her blood had been drained.

"Hungry yet?" This time, he did turn, his eyes the red that marked a feeding vampire. But he seemed in full control of himself. His words had an unsettling impact on her, however.

A terrible pulling started in her gut, as if she'd never eaten in her life. She suddenly knew the only thing that could cure her exhaustion and hunger.

And she knew why Dragoi was trying to bring in the remaining agents alive.

"No!" She turned toward the agents. Almost a fatal mistake, as the gnawing at her gut turned her vision back to red. She grabbed onto the edge of the stage to keep herself from charging the agents. "You have to leave. NOW."

The agents were clearly terrified of the vampires around them, but not her. With a few choice swear words that Homer would have been proud of, she noticed that only the youngest agents remained. The more experienced ones had been slaughtered first. Clearly, the vampires knew who to take out of the equation. She still couldn't see her friends, but if they had been in here during the fight, they were hidden among the dead.

If she didn't get those agents to leave they'd be kept as food. Most likely for her.

Tears filled her eyes as she gripped the stage tighter to keep from running into the cluster of agents and attacking them herself. Slowly, she forced her eyes to look away from the agents and fought to slow her heart rate. There had to be something she could do that wouldn't involve her letting go of the stage.

Visions.

As far as she knew, it was the aliens or their technology that allowed them to be shared. But she was in a nest made out of one of their old ships, and their machines were still in place in more than a few areas.

And Dragoi had fed on her slightly clairvoyant blood.

She really hoped that the stories she read about master vampires and their minions were true.

Nettie closed her eyes and focused all of her remaining energy on an image, one that would terrify vampires. A long-ago destroyed window on the side of the ethership wall gave her the idea. A moment later, a blaze of pure sunlight seemed to fill the room.

The vampires reacted immediately, all of them screaming and fleeing deeper into the chamber. Even Dragoi's shouts couldn't bring them back.

"Go!" Nettie moved slowly toward the enraged Dragoi as she shouted to the agents. It wouldn't take long for the vampires to realize that wasn't the real sun.

"But, Agent Jones—"

"I will kill you myself if you don't leave now." Her voice didn't even sound right, high and needy, almost pleading for them to stay even as her words told them to leave.

The agent who spoke nodded once, then pushed the rest of them out the door. Nettie could only hope they made it out before the vampires returned.

"Well done," Dragoi said as he slowly clapped his hands. The fury he'd shown when his people reacted to her vision vanished. "But you aren't strong enough to try that again. I did so hope to wait in my turning of you. You really do have lovely blood." He rose and lightly walked to where she was. His eyes held hers as he rolled up the sleeve of his shirt.

"I will never drink from you." Nettie would have liked to spit in his face but she didn't think she had any spit left. It was as if all the fluid had left her body.

"My dear, you already have. Oh, you don't remember it, but that night in your morgue? You drank well. This time, I won't let you forget. You will remember everything. How it feels. How you needed it. How you needed me." With a quick slice, he cut open a vein and held it to her mouth.

Nettie whimpered, but she couldn't help herself. She was dying and only this could save her. Although a small part of her screamed that it would be better to die, she grabbed his arm nonetheless.

What felt like seconds later, she was lying on the ground in a heap. At first, she forgot what had happened, but then it all came rushing back as Dragoi said. The horrific joy she'd taken as she drank his blood.

He stood with his back to her, no longer concerned about her actions.

"Oh, don't worry, little one. You are mine now." He spoke without turning, his focus on something spread on the medical table before him. Nettie noticed Rebecca slumped in a chair behind him, but she was too far away to tell if she was dead or unconscious.

"She's only unconscious. I am saving her for your next meal. But not now. Now we have something new to play with."

With a jerk, Nettie found herself being drawn forward and up the stairs by her own feet, but not by her own will.

Spread before her was one of the aliens. Or rather, what was left of one of the aliens. Its body was crudely hacked open and as much as she wanted them gone from her planet, she didn't think it deserved whatever fate had brought it here.

Then she noticed the marks.

"You...drank him?" Had she had room to be ill without it getting on herself, she would have.

Dragoi leaned forward, his eyes flashed red. "Its blood gives quite a kick."

"But you're working for them." She didn't really think so. That they were working together was probable, but she had a feeling the aliens weren't in charge. Hopefully, if she got Dragoi mad enough he'd lessen the hold on her.

"So they think. I work for no one. I have finally taken advantage of their presence to take what is ours. With their blood in our veins, we will be unstoppable."

"You do realize that the aliens have a disease. It's not one that affects them. Although it would if they tried to stay here too long.

But it doesn't mix well with human blood." The sense of control of her limbs was starting to return, as if blood was flowing back into them after a long time of no movement. "Doesn't mix well with vampire blood either."

The original plan had called for her to distract the master vampire long enough for the rest to free the queen. That some of them had obviously been lured into this chamber didn't bode well. That she had been turned completely boded even worse. But the fact was, she was an agent of the Society. She would continue her mission.

"Ah, science has let you down on this, my mouse. Their blood invigorates us. I am so much faster now." Before she could even draw a breath, Dragoi vanished out the main door and returned with an unconscious form. He dropped it at her feet. "I was good before, but without their blood I never could have brought him down so quickly."

With a nudge he rolled the injured man over.

Caden.

CHAPTER THIRTY-ONE

EVEN THOUGH NETTIE knew she was now an undead thing, and therefore had no heartbeat, she felt it stop as she saw Caden. The shallow rise and fall of his chest cheered her, but his nose was bloody and his face bruised. Along with Rebecca, Dragoi could have only one reason for keeping Caden alive. He would control her through those she cared about. He would destroy her by making her take their lives. She forced her hand to stay away from him, and steadied her breathing and voice.

"He is no different than any of the agents you slaughtered here." She tapped him with a toe, and then turned away. "I don't know why he wasn't with the others—"

Dragoi laughed, and this time there was no false sweetness. It was pure acid. "He was lurking out there trying to come in and save you. His heartbeat has been pounding in my head for the last five minutes. I'm surprised you didn't hear it."

Nettie pulled herself up and refused to look at Caden. "He is another one of them. I don't want to see them killed, but he means nothing to me." She held her breath and willed a fierceness she didn't feel into her eyes as she looked up to face Dragoi. "You removed that."

Dragoi came back down the stairs smiling. "Really? Then why could I hear your heart stop when I brought him in? Oh, you are mine, but something about that deliciously mystical component in your blood is keeping you more human than you should be." He walked slowly around both of them. "I do believe that perhaps giving him to the queen to take might be the best turn. She can come over to our side completely by draining and turning another. He can be lover and pet to her."

Nettie clenched her hands and fought to keep her eyes from looking at the unconscious form before her. Dragoi meant what he said. He would make her feed on both Caden and Rebecca, turning them into what she was fighting not to become.

Her weakness from before was starting to flee.

She fought to hang on to every fear or terror she'd ever felt and funnel it into anger. Anger was her weapon against what he'd made her into. More strength returned. Dragoi yelled something to his people, probably chastising them for running away.

Nettie didn't pay attention. Blood was pounding in her ears and her sensitive hearing picked up the whine of the aliens' machines. They hadn't shown themselves yet, at least not living ones. But they were still here.

Anger filled her and her eyes were covered by the red film, but this time, she was in control. She slowly walked over to Rebecca as if she was in a hunger trance.

Still no interest in her from Dragoi.

Nettie bent Rebecca's head to expose her neck. But instead of feeding, Nettie focused on sending another image—this time to the aliens. The amount of effort was harder this time, but touching Rebecca seemed to help.

She flooded the alien minds with what had been done to their companion on the table behind her. Then she added what Dragoi had said about them. Sweat was trickling down her back and her hand was shaking, but she felt the aliens receive her message.

Weapons fire could be heard in the chambers outside of this one. That got Dragoi's attention.

His eyes were huge as whatever was happening to his people out there slammed into him. The vampires who had returned ran for the doorway.

"What have you done?" Dragoi snarled and smacked her hard enough to cause her to fly off the dais.

She hit with a heavy thud, but was back on her feet immediately.

"Leveled the field," Nettie said and licked her lips. She tasted blood, her own, from where he'd split her lip when he hit her.

Gun and dissembler fire came down the hall as well. And Nettie smiled.

"How are you doing this?" There was a tiny bit of fear in Dragoi's voice, which was enough for Nettie. She couldn't bring back Thomas and the others who were murdered. But she could take Dragoi down with her.

She'd landed near Thomas' body and gently freed the unused stake from his hand. Then she ran to the dais and attacked Dragoi.

Dragoi was older, larger, and a master vampire. Her first attempt brought another backhand that tumbled her to the floor. But it was weaker than the first time.

He moved to the back of the dais, but the only exit was to the front, through her. His eyes were wild; the theory of master vampires drawing strength from the ones they created had merit. Most of the vampires Dragoi had created were dead. Nettie wasn't completely turned, and had already held her own against his will. He was strong, but his resources were vanishing.

Another charge. This time Dragoi managed to pin the arm that held the stake backwards. Nettie twisted out of his grip, but he'd backed away again before she could get a strike in. The arm he'd twisted hurt, but wasn't broken. She switched hands and charged him again.

This time, she hit him with enough force to knock him off his feet. Her heart sang with joy as she stabbed him in the heart, the force of her action almost bringing her to her knees.

His screams shattered every non-living thing in the room regardless of what it was made of. She jumped off of him as his lifeless body turned to a sickly gray-green goo.

Rebecca stirred in her chair, looking around weakly.

Nettie ran to her. "Can you stand?" She breathed a sigh of relief as Rebecca looked groggy, but herself.

"I think I can," Rebecca said, then frowned and squinted. "What's wrong with your eyes? There's a red film draining from them."

Nettie quickly looked away. "Nothing, maybe I damaged them in the fight. That's Dragoi. I killed him. How do you feel about that?" She wasn't sure how Dragoi's minions, any that survived anyway, would react.

Rebecca shook her head, then stiffly walked over and spat on the remains. "That's how I feel. Can we leave now?"

Nettie laughed and hugged her friend. "Yes, but we—"

"Agent Jones?" The owner of the voice was a younger agent, and not one who Nettie knew. "We've retrieved her Majesty and are coming to rescue you." His face paled as he took in the bodies in the room, but he motioned the rest of his people forward.

"Thank you," Nettie said as she helped Rebecca off the dais. "The remaining vampires will be in disarray. Their master is dead, and the aliens are after them. But we need to leave before the aliens finish their job."

Caden groaned and Nettie rushed over.

Two agents beat her to him. "We have him, ma'am. Do you and your friend need help?"

Nettie looked to Rebecca. "She does. I will be fine." She was barely standing, but needed her friends to get out of here.

Once Rebecca and Caden were being escorted by agents, she led them out of the cavern and into the cool night air.

Three dirigibles hung low in the dark sky, their lights muted and only their lines showing where they were. It only took a short time to get all of the remaining agents onboard and leave Bath behind.

The agent who had found them sat next to her. "Agent Jones, we have our queen back. Now let's see if you can save her."

CHAPTER THIRTY-TWO

H OURS LATER, NETTIE wiped down her hands for what had to have been the seventh or eighth time. With all she'd been through in the last day, it was almost embarrassing how concerned she was about the next step. She knew one would be nervous meeting the Queen of England, but this was abject terror. Part of it, of course, was that the queen was little more than a vicious animal at this point. The transference to try and change her into a full vampire performed by the vampires hadn't gone well at all.

The other part involved the blood transmittal colander itself. She had been concerned when they'd done it with Rebecca. She was terrified they were going to do such a procedure with a crazed royal. Again, it wasn't fear for herself; it was fear for what both she and Queen Victoria might become.

The queen wasn't a normal vampire. She'd been created using the blood of seven full vampires and aided by alien technology. Nettie was a unique, born half-vampire who'd seen her own abilities grow and change thanks to the bite of the master vampire.

What if combining the blood didn't help things but made them worse?

"You're doing it again, aren't you?" Lisselle spoke softly as she sat next to Nettie outside the large room they were using for the transference. "Gaston warned me you have self-doubt issues."

"It's not doubt, Lisselle. It's fear. How do we know this won't make things worse? My blood could combine with that of the queen and make—"

"A horrific monster?" Lisselle took Nettie's chin and pulled her face up. "That won't happen. Simple. I won't let it. You won't let it. And that woman in there, who is ranting and raving right now, won't let it. Queen Victoria is a strong, powerful woman. Honestly, given enough time, she'd probably beat this on her own. This wasn't what she had intended to happen at all. But we don't have the time."

"I'm acting foolish." Nettie rubbed the side of her head.

"No, you're acting sane. No one can blame you for having worries. Now, let's see about turning this situation around." Lisselle held out her hands and helped Nettie to her feet.

Nettie had never met Queen Victoria before, so she had nothing to compare with. But she had to assume that the wild-eyed harridan before her was not what she normally looked like.

"We think it's the dust and the way she was transformed. She's completely mad, but there are times of lucidness." Lisselle's eyes were grim as she led Nettie to the table next to the chained queen. "We hope that the transfusion with your blood will nullify the dust, and weaken the vampire hold." She smiled. "She might even end up only half-vampire like you."

Nettie didn't trust herself to say anything. She knew it wouldn't be her fault if this didn't work, but she couldn't help the fear that grabbed her that it might not.

As before, she was slowly anesthetized. She held on to Lisselle's hand until she faded away.

SHE AWOKE IN her room with a pounding headache. Stirring around, she tried to find her lamp, but a shape in the corner got up and lit it for her.

"Easy. Lisselle said you might have a pounding head. They had to go through the transference many times." Caden's voice was full of concern and when the low light came on, she saw his face was as well.

"You stayed with me?" Her voice was raspy and Caden gently held a glass to her lips. "Are you sure you're supposed to be up and about?"

"Lisselle said it was all right for me to get up. They didn't drain me. Apparently, the vampire bastard had other plans for me. As for being here, of course I did. You're my partner and I believe you saved my life." He kept the glass there until she had finished it all. Too late she realized there was something more than water in it.

"Why did you…" A yawn cut her off even as she tried to fight it.

"Lisselle also said you needed to spend at least the next day sleeping." He turned down the light again. "Don't worry, I'll be here when you awake."

Nettie tried to come up with a retort, but her eyes closed instead.

BY THE TIME Nettie was allowed to stay awake, the queen had been returned to Buckingham Palace, and the plans had been moved forward on removing the alien menace.

The Society had been able to commandeer or command airships from all parts of Great Britain. Getting the Solar Electrode Agitators and dissemblers to them had been a bit more difficult. However, the return of the Runners to active duty had seen to that. Everything had been completed within twenty-four hours of the return of the queen to Buckingham Palace.

Homer's beloved war bird was the first in the air as he would be the flagship. Modified with special enhancements courtesy of the Society, his airship could go far higher than the norm. Gaston and Lisselle stayed on the ground to monitor the results there. Lisselle and her fellow witches were already lying forth calm and be-well spells in case the Agitators affected the human population.

"Are all of the ships in place?" Homer called down to where Nettie was watching for the signals. Each ship was hovering as high as they could go within eyesight of the next closest ship. As each ship fell into place, they lit a lamp. So far, the lines were true and clear from all of the sections except from the west. Bath and Cardiff's line had not signaled in yet. Since those two cities were believed to be the most at risk, Nettie was nervous at their absence.

"They'll be there. Just give them time." Caden gave a supportive grasp of her shoulder. The dissembler next to him was as long as his leg and made Nettie nervous just to look at. If fired wrong, those weapons could bring thousands of airships crashing down all over Great Britain.

A few tense minutes later and the lights from the two most western lines flared to life. Nettie closed her eyes, trying to concentrate on the ships they knew were right above London. In theory, she hopefully would be able to tell when they left. The connection between Rebecca and the aliens had been based on her clairvoyant abilities. Nettie had developed some of those when she and Rebecca shared blood. She'd reinforced those when she and Queen Victoria had done the same. She still didn't recall much of the entire transference, but she recalled the voice in her head, pleading with her not to let her secret be known. The queen's secret would be safe.

It took a few moments, but a vague pressure in her head told her she was feeling the aliens.

Then, a few thousand elephant-gun-sized dissemblers flared to life, firing their small cargo into the heavens. And the low-flying alien vessels.

At first, there was nothing but silence after the ammunition had all been spent. Nettie knew one way they would find out if they failed in their job—the almost immediate destruction of the airship armada.

But it worked. The smaller ships were slowly drifting earth-ward, exploding as they got into the lower atmosphere. Although she couldn't see them, Nettie fought hard to keep a mental grasp of the closest ethership. The pressure in her head faded quickly as the etherships left orbit.

"It worked!" She opened her eyes and waved to the gunner to change the color of the light to tell the ships to disperse.

Caden threw down his giant dissembler and grabbed Nettie around the waist. "We saved the world, Dr. Jones."

Before she could respond, he kissed her. Lightly at first, then with more intensity. Both of them were unbalanced when he broke the embrace.

"I'm sorry. I shouldn't have done that." Then he gave a crooked smile and shook his head. "Who am I kidding? I'm glad I did that." With a peck on her cheek he ran toward the cockpit. "It's a good day to be alive, Dr. Jones."

Nettie scowled as he left, then smiled. "So it is, Agent Smith."

THE END

Dear Reader,

Thank you for joining in on the first adventure for Nettie, Caden, and their fellow members of the Society.

This series will continue with THE MAYHEM OF MER-MAIDS in 2019.

If you're also interested in a little bit of space opera, please check out the first book in The Asarlaí Wars trilogy – WARRIOR WENCH.

Magic, mayhem, and drunken faeries run loose in THE GLASS GARGOYLE, the first book in The Lost Ancients fantasy series.

I really appreciate each and every one of you so please keep in touch. You can find me at www.marieandreas.com.

And please feel free to email me directly at Marie@marieandreas.com as well, I love to hear from readers!

If you enjoyed this book (or any book for that matter ;)) please spread the word! Positive reviews on Amazon, Goodreads, and blogs are like emotional gold to any writer and mean more than you know.

Marie

ACKNOWLEDGEMENTS

Books are the dreams that a writer gets down on paper—and it takes a lot of people to help make them come true.

I'd like to thank Jessa Slade for editing magic—her ability to keep me from running off a cliff with my stories continues to amaze me. Thank you also to editors Brenda Salamone of Ibis Literary and E.A. Copen for cleaning things up. For my most awesome beta reader/typo hunter who plowed through the entire book—Sharon Rivest. Any remaining errors are mine alone.

Thank you to Deranged Doctor Designs for the awesome cover.

ABOUT THE AUTHOR

Marie is a fantasy and science fiction reader with a serious writing addiction. If she wasn't writing about all of the people in her head, she'd be lurking about coffee shops annoying innocent passer-by with her stories. So really, writing is a way of saving the masses. She lives in Southern California and is currently owned by two very faery-minded cats. And yes, sometimes they race.

When not saving the general populace from coffee shop shenanigans, Marie likes to visit the UK and keeps hoping someone will give her a nice summer home in the Forest of Dean.

More information can be found on her website
marieandreas.com

Made in the USA
San Bernardino, CA
13 August 2018